THE GOBLIN TWINS

KIT BARRIE

The Goblin Twins

First edition (revised March 2023)

Copyright © 2022 by Kit Barrie

All rights reserved.

This is a work of fiction. Names, characters, places, and incidents are either the product of the author's imagination or are used fictitiously. Any resemblance to actual persons living or dead, business establishments, events, or locales is entirely coincidental. Revisions made in March 2023 are typographical only and do not contain changes to the plot.

Cover Art by Elyon

Edited by Sierra McLean (EditingBySierra.com)

ISBN Ebook: 979-8-9868670-0-7

ISBN Paperback: 979-8-9868670-1-4

ISBN Hardcover: 979-8-9868670-2-1

For my husband, the Joel to my Sheila, who supported
me every step of the way and whose musings shaped
this story more than he knows.

CONTENTS

Author's Note

This story deals with the effects of post-traumatic stress disorder (PTSD) as a result of an incident of sexual assault, as well as physical and psychological torture. These acts are graphically and non-erotically described on-page early in the book, and the characters refer to them throughout. While it is ultimately a book about processing and healing, if you are sensitive to these topics, this book may not be for you. It also contains strong language, graphic violence, and explicit consensual sex scenes, and it is not intended for children. It does not contain twincest. For more details on the content, please visit www.kitbarrie.com.

A Guide to the Goblin Dialects and Pronunciations

<u>Hanen – The language of the goblins</u>

There are 3 dialects of Hanen spoken in the goblin continent of Hanenea'a. All 3 dialects can be mixed together in any variation, and it is normal for most goblins to speak a mix of at least Hanen-shii and Hanen-sha. Some words/phrases have alternatives in multiple dialects.

- <u>Hanen-shii (hah-nen-SHEE)</u>: The common dialect used by all levels of society.

- <u>Hanen-sha (hah-nen-SHAH)</u>: The elevated dialect often used by nobles and the more well-educated.

- <u>Hanen-vir (hah-nen-VEER)</u>: The most affected and formal dialect, primarily used by high-ranking nobles, officials, and royals. This includes the use of the "royal we". Not everyone will know this dialect. Exclusive use of this dialect could be considered very austere but also very pretentious.

The goblin language of Hanen is very sibilant and does not contain the letters/sounds 'o' or 'u'.

- The letter 'a' by itself is always an 'ah' sound (adorable, auto), not a short 'a' sound (ambulance, apple).

- An 'ea' makes an 'ay' sound (they, play).

- An 'ae' makes two separate vowel sounds that run into each other 'ah-eh'.

- An 'ai' makes an 'i' sound (eye).

- The letter 'e' is pronounced with a short 'e' sound (get, hen).

- The letter 'i' is pronounced with a long 'e' sound (pizza, thief).

- The letter 'g' is always a hard sound (gift, gone), not a soft sound (giraffe, giant).

- A double vowel indicates the sound is extended.

- A double consonant indicates the sound is specifically pronounced.

A hyphen in the name/word indicates that the sound slides into the next one instead of having a hard stop.

- i-sha (EE-shah)

An apostrophe in the name/word indicates that the emphasis is on the syllable preceding it, with a hard stop in between.

- Shi'chen (SHEE.chen)

- A'bbni (AH.Bnee)

- Er-Ha'sen (Air-HAH.sen)

- Ahea'a (ah-HEY.ah)

- En'shea (ENN.shay)

- Hi'jan (HEE.jahn)

- Ra'shii (RAH.shee)

- Er'hadin (AIR.hah-deen)

- Sha'kri (SHAH.kree)

- Kandrea'a (kahn-DRAY.ah)

- Hanenea'a (hah-nen-NAY.ah)

- Hila'ra (hee-LAH.rah)

- Zea'dda (ZAY.dah)

- Sher'vaat (SHER.vaht)

A lack of apostrophe indicates that there is no hard stop, and the emphasis is on the final syllable.

- Heshar (heh-SHAR)

The Goblin Naming System

Prefixes on last names are a hold-over from the days of slavery when a caste system was more strictly adhered to. A person's individual prefix could change if their status in life changed. Family members share the same "base" name, but individual prefixes can vary. The highest "rank" of prefix dominates. (Example: A soldier with the family name Jea would be Har-Jea, but if his family was descended from nobility, even if he was a soldier, his name would be An-Jea.) The emphasis is not on the prefix for any last name; it follows the rules of apostrophe or no apostrophe.

- Er- Descended from the emperor's line, not by marriage; a noble would retain An- (pronounced air)

- An- Descended from nobility, addressed as "Your Eminence" (pronounced ahn or on)

- Ii- Risen to a higher status, addressed as "Your Prominence" (pronounced ee)

- Hin- A palace guard, regardless of rank (pronounced heen)

- Har- A soldier, regardless of rank (pronounced hahr)

- Chea- A commoner (pronounced chay)

- Ge- A slave, regardless of station (pronounced ge, like 'get')

- Var – A title for noble women (rhymes with car)

- Vr – A title for noble men (rhymes with burr)

- Ven – A title for noble them or if gender is unknown (rhymes with hen)

- Ma'iir – A gender-neutral title of respect (MAH.eer)

A Guide to the Elves

<u>Cserethian (k-ser-RETH-ee-an)</u>

Both the C and the S are pronounced separately. Cserethian is an entirely separate language from Hanen and does not follow the same rules or exclude the same letters. Cserethian does not use apostrophes to indicate emphasis or vocal separation.

Many goblins, especially those closer to port cities, speak Cserethian, as it is the primary elven language spoken in Kendarin (kehn-DAHR-in). The city of Csereth (k-SER-eth) was named after this language.

Elves do not use Hanen prefixes for family names, though some goblins will add them when speaking in Hanen.

<u>Kendarin</u>

Kendarin is the continent across the sea from Hanenea'a, primarily inhabited by elves. Hanenea'a and Kendarin are connected by an isthmus, though it is not used as frequently by travelers due to the danger presented by bandits. It is only a few days' ride via ship across the Coral Sea from Csereth, the northernmost port city in Hanenea'a, to Roshan, the southernmost port city in Kendarin.

CHAPTER ONE

SHI'CHEN

The sands on the training ground were burning hot under sandaled feet. Dust swirled up in clouds, stinging the exposed skin of the palace guards as spears met shields in a cacophony of wood against metal. The sound reflected off the walls of the palace courtyard as the guards sparred, the glare from the sunlight on the sands and stone walls nearly blinding.

On the edge of the courtyard, a young goblin man watched, his own shield resting at his feet, spear in hand. Like his troops, Shi'chen had on a helmet with a black layer of sand silk over it to protect his eyes and face from the stinging sand and blinding sun overhead as he observed his Honor Garrison spar with Allegiance Garrison. He could see where the weak points were on some of the newer guards, where they dropped their hands too low, where they left a leg vulnerable, where they got in too close. To get into one of the three branches of the palace guards, not just the usual soldier grunt work, was no easy feat, but there was always room for improvement.

He leaned on his spear, watching a younger Allegiance guard take a much-too-wide swing at one of his Honor guards, who ducked low and drove her shoulder into the young goblin's gut, knocking him to the ground with a grunt. The Honor member held out her hand to help the younger Allegiance guard up; he brushed sand from his armor with an embarrassed smile before the two continued sparring.

A taller goblin passed by Shi'chen and gave a small smirk that curled his thin lip up with disdain. "Good day, Captain Er-Ha'sen."

"Good day," Shi'chen said, barely giving him a glance out of the corner of his eye.

The older man came to a stop on his other side, silently watching the sparring for a moment. "And how is your brother today?" he asked, his voice light and full of innocence.

Shi'chen gritted his teeth, his fingers clenching around the shaft of his spear. "Did you need something, Captain Hin-Ve'ssa?"

"Just making conversation," the older Captain said.

Shi'chen pulled his helmet and sand silk veil off so he could glare into the man's hawk-yellow eyes with his own ember-orange ones. "Do not play me for a fool, Hi'jan."

"Of course not, Your Highness," Hi'jan said with a small, mock bow. "I know I could never play you." He was silent for a long moment before he leaned in a bit closer so only the shorter Captain could hear him. "Of course, your brother is much easier." Shi'chen's eyes flashed, and Hi'jan laughed softly. "Ah, come now, Your Highness, surely you don't think the whole palace doesn't know that your brother will spread his legs for any pretty face. Even yours."

Shi'chen hissed through his teeth and pushed his shield out of the way with his foot before leveling his spear toward Hi'jan. "You will watch your mouth, *Captain*." The title came out as a growl.

Apparently Hi'jan had been expecting this reaction, because he immediately dropped into a fighting stance, pulling his short sword from his belt. "I'd like to see you make me, Captain." He shifted, and Shi'chen only had a moment to realize that Hi'jan was moving so the sunlight hit him in the eyes before charging at him to try to close the distance. He dodged back, using his spear to keep Hi'jan at bay. The taller man moved quickly, avoiding the tip of the spear as his own blade whistled closer and closer to the smaller goblin with little regard for the places his armor protected. Shi'chen used his spear to block a strike from the short sword, thrusting it at Hi'jan, being careful not to do more than just drive him back with it. Hi'jan seemed to be showing no such caution, circling Shi'chen and darting in with his blade before moving back again when Shi'chen knocked it aside.

Shi'chen registered in the back of his mind that the sounds of others fighting had faded away except for the clash of his own weapon with Hi'jan's, and the guards had all turned to watch them. Jeers and shouts of encouragement rang out from the assembly as they watched the two Captains dodge and thrust. Damn it all to the gods, why had he let Hi'jan taunt him into attacking him in front of their companies? But it was too late to stop it now.

He knocked Hi'jan's blade away with his spear again, deftly changing his grip to strike toward his chest, forcing the taller man back a step. Hi'jan suddenly lunged in, grabbing the shaft of the spear with his free hand and yanking. Shi'chen let the momentum carry him, ducking under Hi'jan's swing at his face to kick his foot out from under him. Hi'jan stumbled and righted himself as Shi'chen regained the spear and leveled it again, to the hoots of laughter from the watching troops.

"What is the meaning of this?" The bark came from a tall goblin woman dressed in the same armor as the Captains but with a scarlet cape over her shoulders. The guards scattered out of her way like sand against the wind. Shi'chen turned his eyes toward Commander Ahea'a, dropping his spear tip in response to her words. That was enough of a distraction for Hi'jan to duck in and swipe his blade's edge across Shi'chen's unprotected left forearm, parting the charcoal gray skin under it, followed by a streak of crimson. Shi'chen hissed and dropped his spear, clasping his right hand to the spot as Hi'jan assumed an innocent look, straightening up and holding his gleaming blade out from his side as if he had only just heard their Commander. Several of the guards muttered amongst themselves, having seen what Hi'jan had done, but they immediately went silent when the Commander's eyes landed on them. "This is training, not a street brawl. Honor Garrison and Allegiance Garrison, laps, now! Captain An-Hila'ra, keep them running until I tell them to stop."

The guards of Shi'chen's unit, and the others who had stopped to watch, along with the Captain of Allegiance Garrison, who had been following behind the Commander, scrambled to obey, hurrying across the courtyard to a nearby running path.

Commander Ahea'a turned to the two Captains with fire in her violet eyes. "Captain Hin-Ve'ssa, quarry duty for you and Courage Garrison. Go."

Hi'jan bowed his head. "Yes, Commander," he said before turning sharply on his heel and walking away, his back saying everything his mouth would not, his troops who had stopped to watch the fight following after him. Commander Ahea'a's eyes turned back to Shi'chen. "And you, Captain. Are you injured?"

"It is just a scratch, Commander," Shi'chen said, moving his hand so she could see the cut that was no longer bleeding.

"You are suspended for the rest of the day, Captain Er-Ha'sen. If I catch you fighting with Captain Hin-Ve'ssa again, it will be a week."

Shi'chen's ears flattened shamefully. "Yes, Commander."

"Go get that cleaned up," Ahea'a said, pointing away from the barracks and instead toward the stone wall of the palace beyond the gate. "Report to me tomorrow morning."

Shi'chen bowed his head at her again, then turned and headed for the palace gate with as much dignity as he could muster, his pride stinging more than his arm. At least "the rest of the day" was not very long, as the sun had already started its slow downward descent. When he reached the door, the guard who had been waiting there snapped to attention, then followed him as he stepped inside the cool doorway into one of the many hallways of the Emperor's palace. "Please tell me you did not hear any of that," he said to her.

"I heard nothing, Captain," she said in a voice that told him she had heard every word loud and clear.

"Thanks," Shi'chen grumbled, heading up one of the wooden staircases toward the wing he shared with his father and brother. "Lieutenant Hin-Re'nna, would you be so good as to find my brother for me?" Though he phrased it as a question, it was not. Anything he asked, as the Regent's son, was a command, not a request.

"Yes, Captain." The guard bowed and broke off to head down the hall.

Shi'chen continued up the stairs. His adrenaline was wearing off now, and his arm throbbed painfully. He gritted his teeth as he reached the North Wing of the palace, the area that was specifically designated for the royal family. He turned down a hall that led to his family's apartments, bypassing his brother's rooms to the double doors that led to the main living area that the twins shared. He pushed open the doors and strode inside, keeping his ears and head high until the door closed behind him.

Two servants were waiting nearby, a girl and a boy not much younger than himself. They both bowed their head at him, waiting for instructions. Shi'chen sighed and rubbed at the bridge of his nose. He did not spend every night in the palace; he was usually out in the barracks with the other guards, and he always felt awkward when dealing with the servants that seemed only to stand around until they thought he needed assistance. "Water, and then leave me."

The girl hurried to take one of the two glasses from a nearby table and pour water from a pitcher into it before presenting it to him with a small bow. Shi'chen took the glass with a mumbled "thank you," and the two servants moved over to his personal rooms further down the length of the hall, closed off from the main room by another set of double doors. The doors closed behind them, leaving him alone.

Shi'chen sat down on a pile of cushions, taking a long sip of the water before setting it aside and lying back against a pillow. He closed his eyes, draping his non-bleeding arm over his eyes to rest. He didn't know how long he laid there, pretending he was not angry at himself for rising to Hi'jan's bait, before the doors opened, and his twin brother, A'bbni, hurried into the room with a swish of black scholar robes. "What did you do?" A'bbni asked, hurrying over to him and dropping to his knees next to the cushion.

"Hello to you, too," Shi'chen said, not moving his arm from his eyes.

A'bbni suddenly grabbed his arm and pulled it toward him to examine the cut. Shi'chen winced. "Ouch," he said pointedly.

A'bbni rolled his eyes, getting to his feet. "I will be right back. Do not move." And then he was gone into his rooms with the same haste as he had entered.

Shi'chen sighed and stood up, moving over to the low table to refill his water glass. A'bbni was going to fuss over him, and he was not going to hear the end of it for the rest of the evening. At least his brother didn't seem upset about him pulling him away from whatever he had been doing. A'bbni often became lost in a book, or researching something he had just discovered, or trying his hand at some new scientific venture. Or sometimes, he found one of the pretty library guardians, and they disappeared deep into the archives, to emerge later a bit more ruffled and bright-eyed. Shi'chen very much decided to leave all that nonsense to his brother.

A'bbni came back into the main room, carrying a black bag. He gave Shi'chen a slight glower. "I told you not to move."

"I am not going to bleed out on the floor, i-sha," Shi'chen said, moving back to the cushion to sit down.

A'bbni tossed his ponytail over his shoulder, but his posture softened at the affectionate address. He knelt down next to him, pulling out a cloth and some sort of oil from the bag before taking Shi'chen's arm. "At least it is a clean cut. What happened?"

Shi'chen shrugged, taking another sip of water with his free hand. "Hi'jan," he said by way of explanation.

A'bbni sighed, starting to swab the oil-covered cloth over his twin's arm. "You know he tries to provoke you to get you in trouble."

"I know," Shi'chen said.

"Then why do you let him?" A'bbni asked pointedly.

"Because I don't like the way he talks about you," Shi'chen said darkly.

"I do not need you to defend my honor, i-sha." A'bbni's touch on his wounded skin was gentle.

"I know you don't," Shi'chen said, his ears dropping shamefully. "But that does not mean he should be able to say such things."

A'bbni was silent a moment, his eyes on his work as he wiped away the drying blood from Shi'chen's arm. Hi'jan was and always had been after as much power as he could get. When he had joined the palace guards a year ago after being transferred from a northern company, already almost ten years Shi'chen's senior, he had immediately tried to seduce the elder twin. His efforts had proven more than a little futile, as nearly everyone in the palace knew that Shi'chen had no interest in bedding anyone and found the whole notion entirely unappealing. That was when Hi'jan's attention had turned to the Captain's twin brother, who had more of a reputation for trysts. But A'bbni had seen through the attempts as easily as through a pane of glass. He was kind and compassionate, almost to a fault sometimes, but he was not stupid. Even without Shi'chen's warnings of what Hi'jan was trying to do, he knew the older Captain was only trying to use him to gain more power within the court. With his advances to both of the Regent's sons rebuffed, Hi'jan's flattery and romancing had turned to spite.

"I understand. But they are just words."

"For now," Shi'chen mumbled into his glass as he took another swallow of the water.

"We are princes of the realm, i-sha," A'bbni said, giving Shi'chen's arm a last pat with the oiled cloth. "He would not be able to act against us without repercussions."

Shi'chen gave a pointed look at his arm. "Perhaps not against you."

A'bbni frowned, giving his twin's hand a squeeze. "Do not let him goad you. He is not worth it."

Shi'chen slumped back against the cushions and swirled the water around in the bottom of his glass to avoid answering.

A'bbni sighed again, then suddenly brightened as he dug in his bag. "This is actually perfect. Hold still."

Shi'chen sat up sharply. "What sort of test are you going to try to run on me?" he asked. It was not uncommon for A'bbni to develop new treatment ideas, and patching up his twin brother was often the easiest way for him to try them out.

"It is just a powder to prevent infection," A'bbni said, finding a small vial in his bag and pulling the stopper out. "But I think it may also help with coagulation."

Shi'chen groaned. "I-sha, do you have to?" he asked with a dramatic whine.

A'bbni ignored him, and Shi'chen didn't protest further. He would cut off his own leg if his brother asked him to, and seeing the excitement in his twin's ember-orange eyes, so much like his own, was his favorite thing in the world. He held still as A'bbni sprinkled the slightly pinkish powder over the shallow cut, then reached for a bandage to wrap around it. "I will check that later. Try not to scratch it."

"Yes, Your Reverence," Shi'chen said teasingly, addressing A'bbni by the formal title his scholarship merited, then winced as the spot began to sting. "Ke'sa's balls, what the fuck did you use?"

A'bbni closed the bag and set it aside, then turned to Shi'chen with a much less compassionate look as he started to wrap the bandage. "It is your own fault for getting into a fight."

Shi'chen sighed angrily, trying hard not to rub at the bandaged spot that was itching like crazy now. As usual, his brother was right. "Is Father joining us for dinner after the Senate meeting?"

"I notice you trying to change the subject, i-sha," A'bbni replied, rolling his flame-colored eyes.

Shi'chen sighed, giving his brother an overly-innocent smile. "You know me too well."

"I should. I've known you since before you were born."

"I'm still older than you, baby brother."

"By eight minutes," A'bbni said, giving him a poke in the ribs that resulted in Shi'chen giving him a playful nudge in return. "You're not going to be promoted to Commander if you let others get under your skin."

"Commander Ahea'a isn't going to die for like three hundred years," Shi'chen said, rolling his eyes dramatically. "She will return from her grave to lead the guards before letting any of us take over."

A'bbni let out a soft snort. "Depends on if she follows Cousin's orders once he takes over the throne. It's very obvious she disagrees with almost everything he says."

Shi'chen winced a bit, waving a hand lightly as if to brush A'bbni's words out of the air. "Yes, but he is the Emperor. Or will be. She will not have a choice if she wants to retain her position." A'bbni smiled sardonically and stood up, brushing a few strands of auburn-black hair out of his eyes. "And where have you been this afternoon?" Shi'chen asked, eyeing a smudge of ash now visible on his twin's cheek and the way his hair was pulling free of its ties.

"With Reverence Sa'ben," A'bbni said as he picked up his bag. "We did an autopsy and then took the body to the crematorium. It was fascinating!"

Shi'chen wrinkled his nose. "Will you please go wash the remains of whomever you were studying off your face?"

A'bbni laughed and exited back through the doors that led to his private rooms with his bag. Shi'chen sighed and glared at the bandage on his arm that prevented him from scratching at the cut. It was already feeling much better. Even at a young age, his brother had shown an aptitude for science. When both their Mother and then their Uncle, the reigning Emperor, died during the plague that had swept through the goblin continent of Hanenea'a a few years ago, it had solidified A'bbni's desire to become a physician. "I have no reason to be afraid of death," he had told Shi'chen and their Father. "It is only a byproduct of life. My fear is not being able to alleviate suffering."

It was not unusual for a prince of the realms to devote their life to study. Knowledge was valued more than anything in the goblin empire, and those who dedicated their lives to gaining knowledge were revered. And it suited his bookish brother much more than military life would have. A'bbni was smart. Much smarter than him, Shi'chen freely admitted. A'bbni had a head for languages and facts. Shi'chen did not. Luckily, their Father had recognized this early on in their lives. He had originally pushed Shi'chen, as the older twin, into a life of study befitting an elder prince, and A'bbni into military service. But it became clear in very short order that the twins had no interest in their Father's chosen paths for them, as they would often switch places with one another when it came time for specialized lessons.

Shi'chen headed back to his own rooms to change out of his dusty guard outfit and splash water over his face. The two young servants had disappeared, but he was used to taking care of himself in the barracks, so he changed into a light tunic and loose pants before heading back out to wait for his brother.

CHAPTER TWO

A'BBNI

Though his evening clothing had been laid out earlier, and water and oils had been left for him to wash up, there were no servants around in his private rooms. That was unusual, but A'bbni wasn't about to complain.

He hung up his black physician's robes to be cleaned, then washed himself and his hair, wringing it out before tying it back into a loose ponytail at the base of his neck with a silk cord. While both of the twins had auburn-black curls on the top of their heads, Shi'chen kept his hair short in the back, and A'bbni grew his out, a standard fashion for scholars. It fell down past his shoulder blades in soft waves, but he always tied it back. It was much more difficult to read or lean over someone with his hair in his face, and A'bbni was nothing if not practical when it came to such things.

He pulled on a sleeveless green tunic, embroidered with a delicate pattern of red and blue along the neck and hem, and a pair of loose tan pants tied with a gold silk cord. Nearly all of the fabrics in the imperial city of Er'hadin were light and flowy. The sun blazed every day in the center of Hanenea'a. Rain was scarce in the area of the palace, only falling a few times a year. It grew colder further north, closer to the sea and the elven continent of Kendarin, but the area near the palace and its surrounding cities were quite dry. Even at night, it could be sweltering, depending on the season. He slid on a comfortable pair of silky slippers before heading back out to the main room.

Shi'chen was already sitting by the low dark rosewood dining table, having changed into an almost identical outfit to his brother, except his tunic was a dusty red color and covered with an embroidery of gold leaves. He smiled when A'bbni entered, the soft smile that he rarely allowed anyone else to see, that was meant only for his twin. A'bbni knew Shi'chen had to be tough outside of the privacy of their rooms, but most of his bravado and swagger was just for show around the guards he commanded. Being named a Captain of a branch of the palace guards at seventeen was an amazing accomplishment, but his age, combined with the fact that the whole Er-Ha'sen family were not the tallest goblins to begin with, made others see him as inexperienced and young. A'bbni knew that bothered his brother.

A'bbni sat down on a cushion at the other end of the table. "Have you seen any of the servants? There were none in my room."

Shi'chen blinked. "Not since right after I returned," he said.

"Mm." A'bbni flipped his hair over his shoulder. Shi'chen only stayed in their rooms once every few nights, but A'bbni stayed in this wing with their Father, the Regent, every day, and there were almost always servants bustling around, cleaning or preparing meals or drawing baths or laying out clothing. And normally, by now, the table would be filled with dishes, with servants laying place settings for himself, his twin, and their Father. But the table was bare except for a tray with a pitcher of water, a wine decanter, and two glasses.

"Come to think of it, there were no guards stationed by our doors," Shi'chen said as he picked up the wine decanter and held it out in offering. "Did Father say anything to you when he returned from the Senate meeting?"

He had been so focused on checking on his brother when Lieutenant Hin-Re'nna had come to fetch him from the library, A'bbni realized he hadn't noticed if there had been guards or not. He leaned over so Shi'chen could pour the wine in his glass. "No. I have not seen Father since he left for the meeting."

"Shouldn't he have returned by now?" Shi'chen asked.

The shadows in the room through the stained glass were lengthening. A'bbni would have sent a servant across the hall to check their Father's private rooms, but there were no servants to be seen. He lifted his glass to his mouth, frowning thoughtfully, then paused as a familiar but unexpected scent met his nose. "Was this here when you came in?" he asked, motioning with his filled wine cup at the decanter in his brother's hand. Shi'chen nodded, halfway through pouring his own drink, but A'bbni held up a hand. "Wait."

"What is it, i-sha?"

A'bbni took another cautious sniff of his glass, then reached over to take the decanter from Shi'chen, tipping it to examine the contents under the light from the gas flame lamps and the sunlight through the stained-glass window behind them. Shi'chen watched him curiously as A'bbni took another sniff from the decanter, then set it down. "There is hargren root in this."

Shi'chen frowned. "Are you sure?" A'bbni nodded.

The root of the desert flower was crushed, and its dark juice was used to ease pain and cause drowsiness, especially during painful medical procedures. He worked with it quite frequently while training with the physicians. The root itself was not poisonous, but the bright yellow flower that bloomed from it could kill a goblin with only two drops of its petal's extract in water. A'bbni felt his stomach drop, like the floor had suddenly vanished from under him. "It is much too earthy to be the poison extract, so it's meant to incapacitate, not to kill. And..." The thought suddenly occurred to him as he looked at the table. "There are only two glasses."

Even though Shi'chen was not in their rooms very often, any tray in the common living areas they shared always had four glasses: three for the twins and their Father, and an extra in case of a visitor. This had been deliberately left here for them, and someone was expecting only the twins to be here, without the Regent.

Shi'chen's ember-orange eyes quickly scanned the room as A'bbni set down the decanter. "Something is not right. Do you hear that?" Shi'chen asked, suddenly turning his eyes toward the double doors across the room that led to the hallway.

"What is it?" A'bbni asked.

Shi'chen was already on his feet, frowning. The sound of hurrying feet, a dozen or more, was approaching fast, the jangle of armor creating a commotion. A'bbni rose and moved to his side, just as the double-doors to their chamber burst open like a thunderclap. Inside surged palace guards, in full helmet and chest plate armor, spears at the ready, short swords stuck in the belts at their hips. At least ten guards entered in a cacophony of footfalls, creating a half circle around the twins, blocking the doorway, spear tips pointed inwards. "What is the meaning of this?" A'bbni demanded, feeling Shi'chen stiffen by his side and giving the hand closer to his brother the barest of flicks to keep him from moving.

"Reverence A'bbni Er-Ha'sen, Captain Shi'chen Er-Ha'sen, you are under arrest for conspiracy to commit high treason against the crown," said the lead guard, his yellow eyes glittering under his burnished helmet. Both of them immediately recognized Captain Hi'jan, and a quick glance at the insignias on the armor showed that the guards were all members of Hi'jan's Courage Garrison.

"What are you talking about?" Shi'chen demanded.

"On whose authority?" A'bbni asked at the same time.

"Ours," came a familiar voice from the doorway. The guards by the doors parted, and, flanked by two more guards, Crown Prince En'shea entered. "Good evening, Cousins."

En'shea was not much taller than the twins, his skin the same dark charcoal color, his eyes a bright gold. His long, black hair was plaited into a braid and pinned to his head in an elaborate twist. The yellow and gold of his silk robe swirled around him, his hands tucked into his long sleeves as he calmly crossed the room, a cold smile playing across his gold-painted lips.

"What is the meaning of this, Cousin?" Shi'chen asked, his flamelight eyes narrowing at the younger goblin.

En'shea laughed, a high, harsh sound that reverberated off the beamed ceiling. "As if you did not know the Regent's plan."

"What are you talking about?" Shi'chen demanded.

"Our Father will not let this stand," A'bbni said, his ears flattening in anger.

"Ah, yes, about that," En'shea said, waving his hand as if batting away a particularly irritating fly. "We are afraid Uncle will not be able to help you. You see, he is dead."

The silence in the room was absolute for a long moment as the twins stared at the crown prince before a strangled sound escaped A'bbni's throat, and Shi'chen forced out, "What did you do?" through clenched teeth.

"Ah, do not worry, you will see him again. Though it might have gone easier on you if you had drank the wine," En'shea said, giving them a calculated smile that made his gold eyes glitter. "But no matter. Arrest them."

The guards took a step forward, and the twins backstepped as one. "Come now, Cousins," En'shea said. "Do not make us have to spill more blood tonight."

A'bbni's eyes darted around the room as his mind frantically calculated their escape options while also still trying to understand exactly what En'shea was saying. The guards had purposely surrounded them in a two-tiered crescent, preventing them from running to the right or left toward their private chambers without breaking through the line, which he was sure they could not do.

Shi'chen was an excellent fighter and could have taken three of the guards down unarmed, probably half a dozen or more if he got his hands on any sort of blade, but there was no way he would be able to dispatch a dozen armed and armored guards on his own before they overwhelmed him, and especially not if he was trying to protect A'bbni at the same time. The only other accessible exit he could think of would be over the table and out the large arched windows behind them, and that was if they could avoid tripping on the table or cushions and break both the colored glass and the crossbars. Even then, it was still a two-story drop to the ground into a stone courtyard, so that also did not seem like a wise choice.

Several of the guards had drawn their short swords in addition to the spears they held up to engage if necessary. A'bbni's breath hitched in his throat, feeling his eyes and throat burning with the threat of tears. He could not see through the crush of guards to the crown prince now. He swallowed hard, his ears flattening, realizing there was only one reasonable response. Slowly, he held his hands out from his side, palms up, and slowly lowered himself to his knees. Slightly behind him, he heard a soft growl of anger in his twin's throat, but then Shi'chen did the same, following him to his knees on the ground, palms out and up.

The points of two swords touched the base of their throats to keep them still as several guards came forward to pull their arms behind them and tie them roughly. A'bbni winced as one of the guards holding him wrenched his arm as if he had been resisting, though he remained pliant and limp. Shi'chen sucked in a breath as he was jerked around, the guards making sure they grabbed his bandaged arm where Hi'jan had cut him earlier that day. Hi'jan smiled coldly down at him, the tip of his sword on Shi'chen's throat biting into his skin and scraping across his collarbone, drawing a thin line of harmless but painful blood. Shi'chen glared murder at the rival Captain.

With the guards working to tie them, they could see En'shea in front of them now, a dark smirk playing across his gold-painted lips. A'bbni gazed up at him from the floor. "What have you done to our Father?" he asked, his voice thick in his throat.

"Only what he intended to do to us," En'shea said, gazing down at A'bbni with glittering eyes. "We are sure you know."

"We don't," Shi'chen hissed, giving a little jerk against the arms that held him.

"Mm, we very much doubt that," En'shea purred, narrowing his eyes under delicate, dark brows at the older twin. "But no matter. We will soon pry the truth out of both of you, and you will be punished."

"Cousin, you know that we had no-" A'bbni's protest was cut off sharply as one of the guards behind him grabbed him by the ponytail at the base of his neck and yanked his head back, the point of the sword pressing harder against the charcoal expanse of his throat. Shi'chen jerked toward him, but the guards held him firmly in place on his knees.

"You will address us properly," En'shea said, his voice low and soft. "We are your Emperor now, and you are nothing but traitors to our house."

"We are not traitors!" Shi'chen snapped, giving a little surge under the hands that held him but unable to move off his knees. "Cousin, what-"

The sound of Hi'jan's backhand echoed off the walls, and Shi'chen slumped to the side, his eyes unfocused. A'bbni let out a yelp and tried to move to him, but the hands holding his hair and shoulders did not give at all. He turned to En'shea again, feeling bile surge into his throat. "Cous... Your Sovereignty," he corrected himself quickly. En'shea's eyes flickered with amusement at the address. "We do not know what you have been told, but my brother and I are loyal to the crown. You have to believe us."

"No, we do not," En'shea said coldly as Shi'chen struggled to get up from the floor with his hands still trapped behind him. Hi'jan planted his foot on Shi'chen's shoulder and pushed him back down to the floor again.

"What happened to our Father?" A'bbni asked, painfully aware that his voice cracked on the question.

"He found out too late that he should not have drunk the wine at the Imperial Senate meeting," En'shea said through that cold smile. "They all did."

"The... the entire Senate?" A'bbni gasped, feeling his heart sink in his chest, and several tears that he could not hold back wet his dark lashes. Their Father and the six specially-chosen members of the Imperial Senate, representing the various areas of economy in Hanenea'a, made up the governing body of the goblin continent, with the Emperor, or in this case, the Regent, being the final say in all decisions. At least, until En'shea reached the majority age of 20, when he would assume the role of Emperor.

"We are sure you will tell us all about it." En'shea said before motioning his hand in a dismissive wave. "Take them to The Keep."

The guards pulled A'bbni up from his knees while another pair of guards wrested Shi'chen from the floor. The guards gave them a shove, and A'bbni almost tripped as they started walking, glancing behind him to ensure that Shi'chen was also there, though he could barely see through the tears that started to spill down his face. The guards marched them down the hallway of their private wing to the main stairs, barely preventing them from falling down them.

Servants and other guards turned as they were walked past, eyes clouded. A few gasped and put their hands to their mouths, but no one moved to help them. A'bbni could not blame them for it. He noticed with a sinking feeling in his stomach that none of the servants were ones that directly attended the twins or the Regent. "Sovereignty," he said, trying to turn in his cousin's direction. "What have you done with our servants?" En'shea ignored the question, and A'bbni was rewarded for his inquiry with a shove that tripped him and sent him heavily to his knees on the stone floor, feeling his teeth clack together at the impact.

Shi'chen reflexively tried to move to help his twin, but the guards had their hands on him and jerked him back sharply. "Get your hands off of him!" he snarled, giving another surge under their grip, and one of the guards grabbed him by the top of his hair to still him.

"You will remain silent unless you wish to confess your guilt," Hi'jan said from where he followed behind them, walking protectively in front of En'shea like something might happen to the young Emperor.

"I have nothing to say to you, Hin-Ve'ssa," Shi'chen snapped. Hi'jan just laughed.

"I'm all right, Shi'chen," A'bbni said softly over his shoulder as he got to his feet, the guards at least levering him up a little so he could get his balance again.

They exited the palace through one of the arched doorways, the low sunlight casting long shadows over the stone courtyard. The Keep was a circular tower in the far back corner of the outer edge of the wall that surrounded the palace grounds. The only visible door leading into it was in the courtyard of the palace. It was five stories tall, the tallest building in Er'hadin. It towered above the palace, often casting its long shadow over the entire area. But the most stunning part of it was its location. The Keep was built at the very edge of a stone cliff that fell a thousand feet into a desert canyon – referred to as the Red Canyon – that stretched for several miles in both directions. This made The Keep almost impossible to breach from that side, so it often was used as a stronghold for the Emperor and royal family in the event of conflict. It also could serve as a prison for important political prisoners or prisoners of war, as they would not easily be rescued, with any attack having to go through the palace grounds to reach it. Small windows offered options for archers to fortify it, but otherwise, it was an imposing structure of solid stones.

The only other opening on The Keep was at the back, looking out over the canyon. A large space had been cleared from the stone wall, almost at the top, so that looking out from it, one only saw the sky. Approaching the edge, the stone underfoot was worn smooth at a sharp angle, pointed toward the open wall. When it had been built, this room had been used as a courtroom for those accused of the most heinous crimes. Upon conviction, the condemned would be taken to the edge, referred to as Traitor's Ledge, and thrown off it, to drop the thousand feet into the canyon below, which was often sardonically referred to by the guards as Traitor's

Landing. As such, rather than being cremated in the traditional goblin funerary practice, the body was left in the canyon to decay and crumble to dust.

Traitor's Ledge had not been used in the twins' lifetime; the last they knew, it had been under the reign of their Uncle before En'shea was born, for a convicted murderer brought to the imperial city for sentencing. After the abolishment of slavery, anyone condemned to death had to be condemned by the Emperor. Since then, death sentences had fallen out of fashion, and prisoners convicted of violent crimes were instead condemned to hard labor in the mines or quarries.

The guards shoved them through the single heavy door that led inside The Keep, then up a flight of stone stairs that circled through the tower. A'bbni had no idea how high up they were, as there were very few windows in the stone stairwells, but he estimated it was only the second or third story when the guards went through another heavy, wooden door into a longer corridor lined with several other doors. One of the guards at the front of the group moved to one and pushed it open into a small room. There was a single slitted window on one wall, with a wooden table in the middle of the room and torches flickering in sconces for light, but it was otherwise bare.

Three sets of metal stocks were attached to the wall opposite the window, and the guards pushed them roughly towards them. Shi'chen jerked, trying to get the hands off him, but Hi'jan jabbed his sword into Shi'chen's side, and Shi'chen stilled, fire in his eyes. If looks could kill, A'bbni did not doubt that Hi'jan would have been nothing but a smoldering pile of ash on the floor.

The guards untied their hands, then pushed their arms up over their heads to cuff them to the wall. A'bbni was oddly grateful the stocks were not any higher, or they would be on their toes. He winced as the metal cuff caught his wrist and locked tight. Shi'chen let out a growl and gave a cursory struggle against the guards as two of them wrestled his arms above his head and locked them in place. Then, satisfied that the twins were not going anywhere, the guards stepped back.

En'shea leaned back against the edge of the wooden table, his hands still tucked into the long sleeves of his imperial robe. Hi'jan stood next to him, looking much too comfortable at the Emperor's side as he gave Shi'chen a smug grin.

"Now," En'shea said, as if they were all settled in for a pleasant dinner conversation. "We have questions for you. Are you ready to tell us what you know? Or do we have to work on loosening your tongues?"

A'bbni flinched and tugged at his restraints. "We know nothing of what happened, Your Sovereignty," he said, trying to keep his voice from wavering.

"Your Father was the head of the rebellion," En'shea said coolly. "Of course you know."

"We do not!" Shi'chen insisted, glancing over at A'bbni then back to the crown prince.

"Mm. Well, we will tell you what we know, and then you can fill in the gaps for us," En'shea said. "Your Father convinced several Senators, and some members of the merchant-nobility, to depose us and install one of you two on the throne instead."

A'bbni felt his ears droop backward as he realized the gravity of what the Emperor was describing. "We knew nothing of this, Sovereignty," he said, and Shi'chen's denial echoed his own.

En'shea laughed and shook his head. "You expect us to believe that you had no idea your Father, the Regent, was planning to overthrow our succession? What sort of fool do you take us for?"

Several choice words came to his mind, but A'bbni kept his mouth closed, and he was thankful that

Shi'chen did the same. "You poisoned the entire Senate, even those not opposed to you?" he asked instead.

En'shea ignored the question. "We shall eventually discover all your traitorous associates. You may be able to avoid unnecessary bloodshed if you tell us who they are and what they were planning."

"We told you. We know nothing about this," Shi'chen hissed.

En'shea glanced between them, then turned toward the door. "Perhaps we are not making ourselves clear. Bring it in."

A guard entered with a canvas bag held gingerly in his hands. The bottom of the bag was soaked with blood, and A'bbni felt a sick feeling in the pit of his stomach, sure he already knew what it was. "No…"

The guard moved over to the table and turned the bag upside-down. With a dull, wet thud, the weight in the bottom hit the wooden table, and the guard pulled the bag away. A'bbni could not hold back a scream, jerking in his restraints and burying his face in his arm as his legs almost gave out under him. Shi'chen turned his head away, clenching his jaw so hard A'bbni could hear his teeth grind.

En'shea reached out and picked up the severed head of the Regent, arranging it on its bloody stump of a neck to face the twins, adjusting it carefully, as if it were a precious vase of flowers. "We think you do not understand how serious we are," he said, brushing back a tuft of blood-crusted dark hair from the head's glazed, wide-open eyes.

A'bbni moaned, his fingers clenched so tight into his palms that he could feel his nails cutting into his skin. His stomach threatened to turn on him, but he forced it back with a thick swallow. He might have hoped earlier that En'shea had been lying about their Father and the Senate being dead, but that hope was gone.

"You monster. I will fucking kill you for this!" Shi'chen snarled.

En'shea laughed, wiggling the tips of the head's long ears, making the whole thing rock a little on the table, the torchlight glinting off the jeweled earrings and gold hoops that still lined them. "You are hardly in a position to be making threats to us, Cousin."

"That is not a threat. That is a promise," Shi'chen growled.

"We shall add that to the list of charges against you," En'shea said. "Would you like a few minutes to say goodbye to your Father, or are you ready to talk?"

A'bbni felt a shudder wrack his whole body, wishing more than anything he could hold his brother, take time to grieve, to think, but he knew that was only fanciful thinking on his part. "Please," he said, the word sour on his tongue. "Please do not do this, Sovereignty."

"We have always wondered if you actually could feel the other's pain," En'shea said, glancing between them. "We were never able to figure that out as a child. We suppose we will find out shortly. Unless you want to tell us what you know, Cousin." He turned to Shi'chen.

"We do not know anything," Shi'chen protested. The next moment, he doubled over as one of the guards strode over and punched him squarely in the stomach. His legs buckled under him, and the stocks were the only thing that kept him from falling over altogether as he coughed, struggling to draw in a breath. A'bbni gave a sharp jerk that strained all the muscles in his back, but the iron bar held tight.

"Tell us who else was involved in the insurgency." En'shea might have been inquiring about the weather, leaning back on the edge of the table again.

"I do not know," Shi'chen growled, trying to regain his footing on the slick stone. The next punch hit his jaw, and A'bbni could hear the snap of his head to the side.

"Tell us." En'shea's voice was as cold as ice.

"I don't know," Shi'chen said, a trickle of blood coming from where his lip had split, reverting to Hanen-shii, as if En'shea might understand the informal goblin dialect better.

"Stop this, please!" A'bbni protested. "Sovereignty, we do not know anything about what our Father may have done."

En'shea's golden eyes turned to him, and despite the fact that he had known En'shea his whole life and was used to the unsettling coldness of his cousin, A'bbni felt his stomach clench as their eyes met and he saw the malice in them. "Dear Cousin, do you have anything you wish to admit to us?"

A'bbni shook his head, trying hard to calm his breathing that was starting to speed up. "No, Sovereignty. We swear to you, if we did, we would tell you."

En'shea gave him a sticky sweet smile. "You would, Dear Cousin. Because you know if you do not, we will start executing your servants, one by one."

A'bbni jerked, his fingers clenching again as he realized the potentially dozens of lives that balanced on knowledge he did not have. "Please, Sovereignty, do not hurt anyone else for whatever crimes our Father may have committed."

En'shea laughed, a harsh sound that reverberated dully off the room's stone walls. "You will have plenty of time to reconsider, Dear Cousin," he said. "If you confess, we may be merciful." Hi'jan, who had been quietly observing this whole time as he stood behind the wooden table, laughed at that.

A'bbni very much doubted there was any truthfulness in that statement. He swallowed hard, his mouth completely dry.

"Do not fucking confess to anything," Shi'chen said, his voice harsh but obviously not directed at A'bbni. He glowered at En'shea. "You know our Cousin has never told the truth in his life."

En'shea's eyes sparked maliciously as he looked back over at Shi'chen, unblinking. "Would you like to hear a truth, Cousin? This is nothing. We could have you tortured for days. We would not ever get tired of hearing your screams."

"I am not going to beg you for my life," Shi'chen hissed through gritted teeth, his ears straight back like a snake about to strike.

"We do not expect you to," En'shea said in his light, dismissive way. "But, you would beg us for his." He turned his eyes toward A'bbni and motioned to the guards. "Take him down."

A'bbni felt more than heard everything go strangely silent, as if he had suddenly been dunked under water, shrinking back against the cold stone wall like he could disappear into it.

"No!" Shi'chen protested, and A'bbni was painfully aware how much desperation was suddenly in his twin's voice. He knew En'shea was aware of it, too. His tolerance for pain, whether someone else's or his own, had always been low, even when he was a child. Shi'chen knew it, En'shea knew it, and En'shea knew the easiest way to hurt the strong-willed Captain was through the one person he cared about more than himself. The guards moved forward, one pulling a key from his belt to undo the lock that held A'bbni's hands in place. Shi'chen gave another yank on his bindings. "What are you doing? Sovereignty, please!"

En'shea ignored him as the guards pulled A'bbni away from the wall and over to the shadow-lit table. He tried to struggle and drag his feet, but the guards were impossibly stronger than him. One held his arms behind his back while another picked up a thick strap of leather from the table. A'bbni found the strap suddenly shoved into his mouth, almost choking him.

He struggled, trying to throw his head away from it, but the guards held him in place and tied the strap securely behind his head. His teeth sank uncomfortably into the thick leather, the taste and smell of it filling his senses and stopping his breath for a moment as he forced down the panic. He realized somewhere in the back of his mind that he would not be able to answer anything En'shea might ask him with the gag in his mouth. He did not know if that was because En'shea knew he did not know anything about it, or because he knew that Shi'chen was a terrible liar and would be the most likely to say what En'shea wanted to hear; he suspected it was both.

"Let him go," Shi'chen said, giving yet another yank, but the iron bars were as solid as ever.

En'shea motioned again, and the guards suddenly shoved A'bbni down, bent over the table, hands forcing his head down so his cheek rested mere inches away from their Father's decapitated head. A'bbni screamed around the gag in his mouth, trying to push back against their hands, but they held him firmly. En'shea reached down and turned the head so the dead eyes and gaping, bloody mouth were facing A'bbni on the table. A'bbni let out a sob, squeezing his eyes closed.

"Stop this. Let him go," Shi'chen said, his voice rough.

"Maybe we will start with the whip," En'shea mused. "Or perhaps we will remove the skin from his fingers, one by one. What do you think, Cousin?"

A'bbni moaned, jerking under the hands that held him as he struggled to turn his head away from the ghastly sight next to him and toward his brother instead. His mind raced with something, anything that they could do or say to make this end, but there was nothing, which was more frightening than any of En'shea's threats. His mind so rarely was blank; the fact that there was absolutely nothing he could do was terrifying. All that was there was the smell of blood and leather, the flicker of the torches against the walls, and the racing of his own heart in his chest, so painful it felt like it would choke him more than the gag.

Shi'chen jerked violently at his cuffs, straining so hard against the stock that the metal creaked, though it still did not budge. "Do not touch him! I will kill you!"

"Your Father already tried. And look where he ended up," En'shea said bemusedly, patting the top of the severed head. "Come now, Captain. This refrain is beginning to bore us."

"We told you we do not know anything," Shi'chen said, his voice rising in panic, his eyes meeting A'bbni's. "If we knew anything, we would tell you, I swear it!"

En'shea turned toward Hi'jan who was standing off to the side watching his guards. "We believe our Cousin needs some motivation, Captain."

A'bbni let out a gasp that was audible around the gag, giving another jerk, feeling his ears flatten with fear. En'shea smiled at him.

"Yes, Sovereignty," Hi'jan said. He stepped forward, and Shi'chen let out a strangled-sounding moan. Hi'jan moved to stand behind A'bbni, gazing across the room at Shi'chen. "I suggest you answer the questions, *Captain*, or things will get very unpleasant for your brother very fast."

"No!" Shi'chen protested, and A'bbni could see he was trembling. "Please, Your Sovereignty. I swear to you that we know nothing of this plot. I swear it on my life."

"Your life is worthless to me," En'shea replied dismissively.

"What do you want?" Shi'chen pleaded. "What can we do to prove our loyalty to you?"

En'shea laughed, the sound hitting their ears like the rasp of a thousand bees. A'bbni felt his heart sink. The crown prince had no intention of letting them out of here alive, regardless of what they might say or do. The best they could hope for was a swift execution instead of days or weeks of torture. He gave another twist against the two guards that held his arms behind him, but it made no difference. They only pressed him down harder into the wooden table, so hard his ribs ached.

En'shea waved his hand toward Hi'jan. "If you will not tell us anything, Cousin, your brother becomes Captain Hin-Ve'ssa's personal property until he tires of him."

A'bbni's blood turned to ice in his veins. Even though he couldn't see behind him, he could feel Hi'jan's cruel smirk, and he was suddenly much too aware of how close Hi'jan was standing behind him, almost pressed up against the back of his legs. He instinctively tried to shift away, but the guards at his sides only dug their fingers more firmly into his arms to hold him still.

"S... Slavery is illegal," Shi'chen said, though his voice shook, and A'bbni saw his ears flatten in fear.

"Do you think we are stupid?" En'shea asked, raising a brow. "We are Emperor, we are changing the law. And you, Dear Cousin," En'shea turned to give A'bbni a honeyed smile, "will be the first punished under it for your family's treason."

The world swam before his eyes for a moment, and A'bbni struggled to take in a breath around the leather gag in his mouth and the pressure on his ribs. Hi'jan suddenly pulled a knife from his belt and slid it down the back of A'bbni's tunic, being none too careful. The fabric parted under his blade, and beads of bright red blood welled in several places where the knife grazed his charcoal skin. A'bbni let out a cry around the gag, jerking against the hands that held him, but the guards held him firmly in place.

"Dammit, stop this! I don't know what I can tell you!" Shi'chen yelled, turning desperate eyes from Hi'jan to En'shea and back. "We were not involved in Imperial Senate meetings. We have heard nothing about a rebellion or any attempt on Your Sovereignty's life, I swear it! Please! Don't do this!"

The tip of Hi'jan's blade bit into the skin under A'bbni's shoulder blade and stayed there, not pushing deeper, just breaking the skin and letting the blood pool around the tip of the blade. A'bbni jerked under the touch, a keening noise escaping around the gag in his mouth, but the guards held him still.

"Cousin, please," Shi'chen said, focusing his eyes only on En'shea. "Stop this. If I knew anything at all, I would tell you. You know I would!"

Hi'jan's knife tip dragged over the skin on A'bbni's back, following the curve of one of his ribs. Light flickered in his vision as he tried again to pull away, but there was no chance of him breaking the hold of any of the guards that held him. His ears drooped in pain and fear, his eyes squeezing closed so he did not have to look into the filmy eyes of their Father's head next to him.

"We grow bored of your denials, Cousin," En'shea said, studying his gold-lacquered fingernails as if no one else were in the room.

"What do you want me to say?" Shi'chen asked, and A'bbni opened his eyes to look at his brother in desperation.

Please don't, he thought, trying to send the thought to his twin with his eyes. Admitting anything right now would not make the situation any better for anyone.

En'shea waved a hand at Hi'jan, as if he had not heard Shi'chen, and A'bbni froze as Hi'jan's knife slid down his back, grazing a cut in his skin that welled with blood. Then, the knife sliced through the gold silk drawstring that held his pants. The fabric slid off him, pooling by his ankles, and he flinched as the flat of Hi'jan's blade caressed over the small of his back and down over the curve of one bare hip. He could barely hear Shi'chen's words over the sound of his own heartbeat pounding in his ears as he struggled to take a breath, each one a little harder to bring into his lungs. The leather dug tighter into his jaw as he tried to draw breath around it, another spot of bright light flashing in front of his eyes.

"Damn you to the gods, En'shea, what do you want from me?" Shi'chen demanded, his voice higher and more desperate than A'bbni had ever heard it. "We have not done anything, I swear it! But let him go, and I will admit to whatever you say! You can execute me for treason, I will not deny it! Please!"

En'shea smirked, suddenly crossing over to him with deliberate steps, not taking his golden eyes from Shi'chen's. A'bbni froze, too, praying that Shi'chen would not do anything stupid, though right now none of their options were good ones.

En'shea was only an inch taller than the twins, but he still managed to tower over Shi'chen as he reached up with his gold nails to trace them lightly down Shi'chen's jaw with an almost lover-like sweetness. "You will, Cousin. You will admit to everything."

"Yes," Shi'chen said, gazing back into En'shea's eyes. "Anything you want me to say, Sovereignty, I will."

"You will admit that you were part of the Regent's plan to overthrow our reign."

"Yes." Shi'chen's eyes didn't leave En'shea's, like he was watching a cobra waiting to strike.

A'bbni let out a soft whimper, then froze as Hi'jan's fingers trailed down over his ass, feeling them sticky with his blood from the knife cuts.

"You will admit that you are a traitor to our empire."

"Yes," Shi'chen said again. The back of En'shea's fingers stroked over Shi'chen's cheek, and A'bbni shuddered to feel Hi'jan's fingers do the same on the back of his thigh. He saw En'shea take the smallest step back so he was just out of Shi'chen's range, his fingertips the last thing to leave the space from where they had been on his brother's face, before he said, "But you would do that even if we stopped now. And we do not want to." He turned away from Shi'chen, and his brother's voice was drowned out in A'bbni's head as Hi'jan suddenly grabbed his hips, and he felt Hi'jan thrust forward into him.

The unexpected pain jolted through him like he had been struck, and he couldn't stop the scream that tore out of his throat, muffled as it was by the leather in his mouth. His teeth clenched around it as Hi'jan began to move, suddenly unable to catch his breath. He could hear his brother and En'shea somewhere beyond his vision, but he could not hear what they were saying. He felt a rivulet of blood from the cut under his shoulder blade slide down his ribs to land on the wooden table beneath him, his skin itching along the path the droplet had traced.

His eyes didn't know where to focus as he struggled to find each breath in his lungs in between each thrust of Hi'jan's hips against his. Finally, they roamed over their Father's ear that was closest to him, his left, where, up in the tip of his ear's helix, two tiny gemstones glittered side by side. Unlike the rest of the Regent's jewelry that was yellow or rose gold, the barely-visible stud settings were silver and caught the flicker from the wall torches. One stone was a bright red ruby, the other a vivid green peridot. Red for Shi'chen, green for him, their favorite colors, and silver, because it was so rare in Hanenea'a. He remembered when their Father had commissioned those earrings, a set for himself and a set for his wife, when the twins had turned 12. Their Mother's set had been removed before her body was cremated after she passed from the fevers, and they were stored in the vault with the other precious jewelry of the royal family, though he had not seen them in years. He vaguely wondered what would happen to those two shining stones in his Father's ear. There was a drop of blood on the edge of the ruby, and he wondered if it was his or his Father's. He thought it might be his Father's, since it had already dried into rusty brown. Fresh blood was so much brighter. The smell of it was different, too, and he could smell fresh blood around his own skin, and the coppery tang of blood that had dried along where the Regent's head sat, as well as the slightly sweet scent of the beginnings of decomposition.

His vision was starting to go black, and then white. He vaguely realized that somewhere he had stopped breathing, and when he tried to take a breath now, it was like trying to breathe through a pillow over his face, unable to get more than the tiniest bit of air into his lungs. Panic set in before he could stop it, feeling more than hearing Hi'jan grunt as he thrust against him, his pants rough against A'bbni's skin, the fabric scratchy and stiff, probably from blood. Somewhere, as if from down a deep well, he could hear Shi'chen's voice again, unintelligible no matter how hard he tried to listen, but everything had suddenly grown very hot, and all he could see was the flicker of white light in front of his eyes before everything went blessedly dark.

CHAPTER THREE

SHI'CHEN

Shi'chen watched his brother slump against the wall, streaks of crimson blood gliding down and drying on his sides and legs. He felt sick, even more sick than he had seeing his Father's head on the table. He hoped that being unconscious was helping his brother, but it worried him with how shallow A'bbni was breathing. He stretched out a leg, trying to reach him, but even straining against the cuffs, he could not get close enough to even brush his twin's leg with his foot. "I-sha," he said softly, trying to rouse his brother without getting the attention of the guard outside the door.

A'bbni did not stir. Shi'chen tried again, but still no reaction. "A'bbni!" he said, louder. A'bbni's ears flicked, and his eyes fluttered open. Shi'chen let out a sigh of relief. "Hey. Look at me."

A'bbni shifted against the wall, hissing softly as he got his feet back under him, several fresh rivulets of blood starting to flow down his dark skin, visible even in the torchlight. He coughed softly, his jaw moving stiffly as he drew in a deeper breath.

"I-sha. I am so, so sorry," Shi'chen whispered, feeling hot tears run down his cheeks and drop off to hit the stone floor by his feet. A'bbni's head drooped, his ears low, shaking all over. Shi'chen stifled a soft sob. He would have taken all that pain and hurt and humiliation, a hundred times over, if it would have kept A'bbni safe. "I understand if you cannot forgive me for not protecting you."

A'bbni sniffled softly, turning his eyes toward Shi'chen in the dimness, and the look in A'bbni's eyes hurt him more than an arrow to his heart. "You do not have to be sorry. You did what you could."

"I should have told them something. I should have made something up to make them stop." Shi'chen's voice rose higher and louder, making A'bbni flinch.

"You know you're terrible at lying, i-sha."

"I know, but I am supposed to protect you."

"They would not have stopped, no matter what you said," A'bbni said softly, dropping his head again. "You would only have gotten others killed."

He knew his brother was right, but that did not stop the guilt from surging in his chest like something was trying to get out. He could hardly hear anything over the blood racing in his ears as he watched A'bbni slump against the wall, the cuff bar the only thing keeping him on his feet. "I-sha," he said softly. A'bbni grunted softly without opening his eyes. Shi'chen frowned. "I-sha," he said more firmly. "You need to keep your eyes open."

"Easy for you to say," A'bbni mumbled, his head lolling downwards again, causing the restraints to dig further into his raw wrists.

"I know it hurts, but you have to stay awake." It was the same advice he knew A'bbni would have given him if their positions had been reversed. He wished they had been. His twin forced open his eyes, and even that looked like more effort than he had in him. "Talk to me," he prompted, trying to keep A'bbni's attention.

"Wh... where did they go?" A'bbni asked.

Shi'chen swallowed hard. "En'shea said something about returning after you woke up."

A'bbni shuddered, his fingers clenching, and Shi'chen felt his heart shatter in his chest. When they came back, they would torture A'bbni again, and Shi'chen was sure it would be worse. Much worse. "What can I tell them to make this stop?"

A'bbni shook his head slowly, a few of his curls falling over his face in limp tendrils. "I do not think you can."

"I will not let them continue to hurt you," Shi'chen replied, aware that his voice was much too high to sound convincing.

A'bbni's flame-orange eyes met his own in the flickering darkness, wet and red-rimmed and heartbroken. "Do not make promises you cannot keep, i-sha," he said softly. "I know you would if you could."

Shi'chen gritted his teeth. "I would take all of it for them to leave you alone."

"Which is exactly why they will not," A'bbni said. "We are dead no matter what either of us says. Do not implicate others just to try to save me when it will do no good."

Shi'chen knew his brother was right. At this point, En'shea was only toying with them because he could, not because he expected answers that they did not have. Maybe he had never expected answers at all.

His eyes flicked over to their Father's head on the table, vacant eyes still staring dully at nothing, mouth lolling in a silent scream that mirrored the one in his own throat that he refused to let out. That was going to be him soon, and Hi'jan would continue to torture his brother until he grew tired of him and executed him, too. He hated feeling so helpless. Maybe he could convince Hi'jan to keep him alive, too, to enslave them both. At least if he was alive, he could try to get A'bbni free. The thought of being on his knees for that pig of a Captain made bile rise in his throat, but it was better than it being his kind-hearted brother.

He gave another yank against the manacles, more out of frustration than an actual attempt to get loose from them. A'bbni gave him a weak smile that didn't reach his eyes. "No guard training on how to escape those?"

"Shut up," Shi'chen said, though his tone was affectionate. "I will bring it up with Commander Ahea'a once we get out of here."

A'bbni was silent for another moment before softly saying, "En'shea planned our arrest for tonight."

"Why do you think that?" Shi'chen asked.

"Because not only was there a Senate meeting today, but you were planned to be in our rooms, not in the barracks with your guards. He knows that if he had tried to arrest you in front of your Garrison, they would have fought back, as most of them are loyal to you, not to him."

He had a point, Shi'chen conceded. He had been promoted to Captain of Honor Garrison at seventeen, and while he was not an easy Captain, he was fair, and his troops respected him. Even being the crown prince's cousin did not keep them from talking with Shi'chen about what the future of Hanenea'a might be like under the young, cruel crown prince's reign. He felt sick to his stomach as he wondered how much of those discussions had gotten back to En'shea. Not in his wildest dreams had he even considered overthrowing his cousin since En'shea's older sister Prii'sha had died almost three years ago. Evidently their Father had, but his concerns for the country had never been more than words. Or so he had thought.

A'bbni was shivering badly, and Shi'chen wished he could fold his arms around him. He couldn't feel his hands anymore; he couldn't have moved his fingers if his life depended on it. A'bbni let out a soft moan, just as the sound of footsteps approaching down the stone hallway reached them. He let out a whine and curled against the wall, as if trying to make himself small enough to not be seen, and Shi'chen fought back a sob at the terror in his brother's face. He couldn't let them take A'bbni again; his brother would not survive. He would come up with something, any lie that could get them to take him instead.

Just outside the door, there were a few muffled words exchanged, followed by a sudden ring of steel, and then the heavy thump of a body hitting the ground. A key creaked in the lock, and the wooden door swung inwards, but instead of the Emperor or Hi'jan or even one of the guards from Courage, Commander Ahea'a hurried in, closing the door behind her. "Commander?" Shi'chen asked in surprise.

"Shh," she hushed him as she moved over to the cuffs, reaching up with a ring of keys to undo the lock holding his wrists up. "We do not have much time, Captain. I need you to do exactly what I say."

"Yes, of course," Shi'chen said as his arms dropped. He tried to shake the blood back into them, wincing at the stinging sensation as they dangled at his sides like lead weights.

Commander Ahea'a moved over to A'bbni, frowning darkly. "Your Reverence, can you walk?"

A'bbni forced his head up to meet her eyes. "Not well," he croaked.

Ahea'a unlocked A'bbni's arms and gently leaned him against the wall as he trembled. She reached up and quickly pulled her scarlet cape off her shoulders, wrapping it around A'bbni like a makeshift tunic. She then took the Commander pin from her chest and used it to secure the fabric in place before jerking her head at Shi'chen. "Take one arm, I will take the other."

Shi'chen slipped himself under A'bbni's arm, trying to force his own arms to work despite the pins and needles of blood coming back into the limbs. Ahea'a slid A'bbni's other arm around her neck and her arm around his waist. "Come with me." She led them over to the door of the room, taking most of A'bbni's weight on her so his feet would not drag. She opened it and glanced out, then motioned for them to follow her. Shi'chen cast a last glance behind them at their Father's head, still sitting on the table, seeming to watch them go. He shuddered and followed after the Commander. She closed and locked the cell door again.

The guard who had been watching the door was slumped on the floor, a pool of dark blood forming around his head from where his throat had been slit. Commander Ahea'a led them quickly down the hall into one of the stone corridors. Shi'chen hurried next to her, glancing at A'bbni who was biting his lip to keep from crying out. Ahea'a took a sudden left turn into a short hallway that ended in a dead end. Shi'chen frowned. "Commander—"

"Shh," she hissed again, shifting so Shi'chen was supporting his brother before moving over to the wall. She placed her shoulder against one of the large stones and pushed, digging her feet into the rough stone floor. The stone suddenly swung slowly inward, showing a flight of stairs leading down into darkness. Shi'chen blinked. Why had he never known there was a passage there?

Ahea'a tossed her head for them to get inside. "Follow the stairs all the way down. At the bottom through the door, there will be a cart. Get into it. The soldier will take you to the port. You will learn more once you arrive there."

A'bbni looked like he had a thousand questions, and he probably did. "Will they know it was you who helped us?" he asked, his voice trembling.

"Most likely," Ahea'a said, giving him a small but determined smile. "But the rebellion against the Emperor is more important. Go, now, and push the wall closed behind you."

Shi'chen ducked into the space, A'bbni following after him. In front of them was a set of stone steps carved into almost solid rock on either side, with no lights along the way, just the light from the hallway. They disappeared downwards into darkness. Shi'chen turned back to her. "Come with us."

Ahea'a shook her head. "I cannot. Go now, quickly. May the gods grant you wisdom and safety." She touched her fingers to her forehead, to her heart, and then to his shoulder in the traditional travel blessing.

Shi'chen returned the motion to her before planting his shoulder against the stone door and digging in. The door slid a little. A'bbni reached out and put the last of his strength into helping, and the door swung shut, plunging them into complete darkness. Shi'chen wrapped his arm around A'bbni's waist to pull him close as A'bbni's legs gave out, looping his twin's arm over his shoulder to take the sudden weight. "I can carry you if you can't do it, i-sha," he said softly.

"I can," A'bbni said firmly, his fingers giving Shi'chen's arm a trembling but reassuring squeeze.

Shi'chen moved tentatively forward in the dark until he found the first stair, then carefully started to descend, feeling for each step in the darkness. The stairs were narrow, and the air around them was thick and stale, as if it had not moved in many years. Perhaps it hadn't. "Did you know about this passage?" Shi'chen whispered. His voice sounded hollow in the small space between the two rock walls on either side of them.

"Not this one," A'bbni said softly. After a moment he added, "En'shea will have her executed when he finds out." *When*, not *if*. Shi'chen didn't respond, just set his jaw more firmly as they took each step, one by one. He had no desire to fall down them in the dark, especially not knowing how far down they went.

The stairs seemed to go on for miles, though he suspected it was not quite that much. Both of their legs were aching when they suddenly hit a flat landing that seemed to be a long, straight tunnel. Shi'chen tested each step going forward, but it seemed like there were no more stairs. "How are you doing, i-sha?" he asked his brother softly, barely able to make out his twin's outline in the dark but feeling the warm, reassuring presence against him.

"All right," A'bbni said, though it sounded like he said it through clenched teeth.

"Do you need me to carry you?"

"No," A'bbni said, giving him a gentle squeeze. "I just want to find our way out of here."

Shi'chen gave him the barest of squeezes back, not wanting to hurt him, then placed one hand on the wall, keeping it there as they moved in the darkness. The wall was rough and unfinished, not like the smoothed stones of the palace, and the ground under their feet felt similar. He had a vague idea of where they might be, but he would not be able to tell until they reached the end of the tunnel.

By the time he saw a faint light up ahead, he could feel A'bbni swaying next to him. The pinprick of light was just visible in the distance, like a single star in an otherwise empty sky. Shi'chen slid his arms under A'bbni and lifted him into his arms. "I can walk," A'bbni protested, but his voice was exhausted.

"It's just a little further," Shi'chen reassured him, and A'bbni relented, curling against his chest. The bit of light grew larger with each step until Shi'chen could finally make out the outline of a door. A few more echoing steps, and he could see the door in the dim light. There was an iron ring handle on it, the rest of the door seeming to be made out of wood. Shi'chen carefully set A'bbni on his feet, then grabbed the ring and pulled. Sunlight flooded into the passage, blinding them both and making them throw their hands up to shade their eyes.

"Captain, Your Reverence," came a quick, sharp voice. Shi'chen squinted, making out the cloaked and hooded shape of a goblin woman standing nearby. "Quickly, get into the cart."

They stepped out into the light, which was blinding after their time in the dimness of The Keep and the crushing darkness of the stone stairwell, even though the sun was only barely rising. He vaguely realized that the whole night had passed, and exhaustion was starting to settle into his body. In front of them was a wooden cart with two horses attached to the front, and a cloaked older man holding the reins.

The woman in the hood offered a hand down to Shi'chen, giving him a strong pull up into the wagon bed, then did the same for A'bbni, who stifled a cry of pain through gritted teeth. She then reached down and pulled open a trap door in the bed of the wagon that he had not noticed.

"Lie down in here," the woman instructed. The space was narrow and not very deep, but it would fit the two of them. Shi'chen helped A'bbni step down into it as he cast a quick glance around, trying to figure out where they were. The stairs had gone down further than the tower was tall, of that, he was sure. And the long tunnel would have taken them out of the borders of the palace walls, just based on the length of it. He could see the Red Canyon not far on the horizon, and when he turned, the walls of the palace were quite near. The door they had exited was an innocuous wooden door built into a wall of finished stone alongside several shops in a dark, seemingly deserted alley. The air around them was heavy and damp with the scent of trash and horse sweat.

He wanted to look around further, but A'bbni had settled on his side in the compartment, and the woman was watching him closely, so Shi'chen stepped down into it and curled up next to his brother. The next moment, the woman had closed the heavy, wooden lid over them, plunging them once again into darkness except for a few cracks of light that showed between the boards. And then, something else was placed on top of it, probably a blanket, that smelled heavily of hay and horse. It smothered all light and made the small space impossibly more oppressive.

A'bbni curled close to Shi'chen in the dark. Their foreheads pressed together, the way they sometimes used to sleep when they were younger. They heard the woman step up onto the cart, then the snap of reigns, and the horses began to trot briskly. Every bump of the wagon over the cobblestone ground seemed to send a jolt of pain through A'bbni. Shi'chen let him cling to his arm, not protesting a bit at A'bbni's nails digging in his own arm, holding him close like he would never let go. He was shivering, and Shi'chen carefully tucked Commander Ahea'a's cape around him as best he could, feeling places where A'bbni's blood had soaked the material.

The cart rumbled to a stop after a short bit, probably at one of the gated checkpoints, he figured. The palace housed the royal family, secretaries, couriers, guards, and servants needed to run the palace on a daily basis, but just outside the palace walls was where the nobility and the richer merchants lived. Many of them came to the palace and its surrounding markets on a daily or weekly basis for business. He could hear muffled words being exchanged, but there were no sounds of violence or protest, and the cart began to move again.

Next to him, A'bbni shifted painfully and tucked his head under Shi'chen's chin. He hugged him closer, trying to be mindful of his injuries, stroking his twin's hair gently as the wagon continued to bounce and roll down the streets. The quieter, more refined sounds eventually gave way to the outer city sounds and smells, though overpowered by whatever covered the cart's hidden door. This was where those not of noble birth or wealth lived. He had not been to this area more than once or twice in his life, and usually only while traveling through it.

They hit a large bump, and A'bbni let out a muffled whimper against Shi'chen's shoulder. "Shh," Shi'chen tried to soothe him, stroking his hair again and cursing Hi'jan and their cousin with every horrid thing he could think of.

It felt like hours – though his sense of time was obscured – before the cart suddenly stopped, with more words being exchanged. Then, the cart started up again, but the bump and clatter of cobblestones was now replaced with what felt like dirt. The horses picked up speed, and he could feel them racing down one of the roads that led out of Er'hadin, toward the gods only knew where. The dirt road seemed less rough than the stones, and he eventually felt A'bbni relax in his arms and heard the rhythmic breathing of sleep, which soothed his own tension a little, too. But despite how tired he was, Shi'chen could not sleep.

It was a very long time before the cart suddenly seemed to dip a little, and the texture of the ground changed to less packed earth. This continued for a short time before the cart came to a stop. Shi'chen tensed as he heard someone approaching the back of the cart, but the hidden door was pulled up by the same hooded woman. She gave him a sympathetic smile. "My apologies for the cramped quarters, Captain. We are only stopping for a short break, but we have some food, and you can stretch your legs."

Shi'chen nodded and sat up, giving his brother a light shake to wake him. The woman helped them out of the cart, which had pulled off the road into a copse of trees, hiding them from the traffic on the road, of which Shi'chen knew there would be much. The older man unhitched the horses and led them a short distance away to a stream for them to drink while the woman steered the twins over to a group of large rocks to sit.

Shi'chen saw as she handed them a bag of food that she had a short sword strapped to her hip under her cloak. "You are a soldier," he commented.

She nodded slowly. "Was," she said. "I retired several years ago."

If he had to guess, she seemed to be around their Father's age, late forties or early fifties, which lined up with the age of retirement for soldiers and guards, who were given a pension to live on after their years of service ended. She looked vaguely familiar, but Shi'chen was fairly sure he had not served with her, and he could not place her.

"What is your name?" A'bbni asked curiously.

The woman smiled again. "I am afraid I cannot give you my real name, Your Reverence, for all our sakes. But you may call me Rell, and him Nen."

"Do we have you to thank for our rescue?" Shi'chen asked, breaking a hunk of cheese from the bag in half and passing it to his brother.

Rell shook her head. "We are only one of many involved in the rebellion against the crown pr—pardon me, the Emperor. We do as we are commanded."

"What is the rebellion?" A'bbni asked, being polite enough to wait to ask his question until his mouth was not full of food.

"I cannot give you much detail, but I can tell you that we have been anticipating the young Emperor's idea of reinstituting slavery for several years. More shall be revealed to you in time."

"Where are we going?" Shi'chen asked, pulling out a pouch of water and passing it to his brother first.

"The port at Kandrea'a," Rell said. "We will give you further information upon arrival."

Shi'chen had a hundred questions, and he knew A'bbni had at least twice as many as he did, but Rell pulled out food for herself and Nen, who also looked vaguely familiar to Shi'chen. Possibly one of the many servants around the palace?

The twins ate eagerly, but Rell stopped them after a bit, warning them to not make themselves sick, as they had not eaten in some time. "Go stretch your legs," she offered. "Just stay in sight. We have a long ride ahead of us."

Shi'chen helped A'bbni to his feet, leading him toward the stream with careful steps. "I should look at your wounds, i-sha," he said softly, noticing several patches of blood that had dried dark brown on the bright red cape wrapped around him.

A'bbni nodded, sitting down next to the water, holding the fabric over his lap as Shi'chen undid the Commander pin that held it and lowered the back. A'bbni hissed softly as the fabric pulled away from where it had stuck to his injuries. Shi'chen flinched, feeling hot tears sting his eyes, but he pushed them back, surveying the damage the knife had done to his twin's soft, charcoal skin. "Gods, i-sha, I am so sorry."

A'bbni shook his head. "You need to stop saying that. You could not have done anything, and continuing to berate yourself is not helping either of us."

Shi'chen grabbed the hem of his own tunic, tearing off a few strips to dip in the cool stream before moving to gently clean the dried blood off A'bbni's back. A'bbni held still, his fingers clenched in his lap, his eyes closed, which Shi'chen knew he did when he was concentrating very hard. A few spots made A'bbni jump when he touched them, but he made no sound until the last of the blood had been carefully wiped away. Shi'chen pressed a soft kiss to the top of A'bbni's head as he pulled the cape up over his shoulders again and fastened it in place. "The next time I see Hi'jan, I swear to you, I am going to kill him."

"I would not stop you," A'bbni said softly, which was about as much vengeance as he would probably ever condone, making Shi'chen smile softly as he helped him back to his feet.

Rell approached them with an apologetic smile. "We must go, Your Highnesses."

Shi'chen nodded and helped A'bbni back to the cart, where they settled again into the small space under the wagon bed. Kandrea'a was a few days' journey, maybe a full day by fast horse without a wagon, passing through several cities and smaller towns on the way. It was not how he would have ever chosen to travel to Kandrea'a, but at this point, he was just grateful to be alive and to have A'bbni next to him, curled up in his arms and holding onto him like he would never let go.

CHAPTER FOUR

A'BBNI

They stopped several more times to eat and rest the horses, always outside of any cities or towns they passed through. Rell and Nen switched places driving as well so the wagon was almost always moving except for a few hours here and there to let the horses sleep. It was impossible to guess how much time had passed since they had climbed into the hidden compartment in the wagon, and A'bbni was grateful that he was able to sleep for much of the journey. Shi'chen made him a pillow out of his own tunic and held him close to keep him warm, stroking his hair until he fell asleep. The pain was not gone, but it at least faded into the background of his subconscious, like the drone of flies, making itself known once in a while with a sudden sharp stab of fire that made him grip his brother's fingers so tightly, he might have crushed them without knowing it. If he did hurt him, Shi'chen never said a word about it.

During their last break, Rell informed them they were approaching Kandrea'a and needed to stay quiet until they were safely to their destination, though they were sure she knew the warning was unnecessary, as they had been silent the entire way.

They began to hear more carts and people passing along the dirt roads the closer they got to the city gates. Eventually the cart stopped in what was likely the line to get into the city. A'bbni wondered if news of the

Regent's death, their cousin assuming the throne, and their disappearance had reached the city yet. The only way would be via courier on horseback, but there were shorter ways to get to the various cities for a single rider. It had only been a day or two since their disappearance from the prison, as far as he could tell, but so much could change in such a short time.

The wheels hit what sounded like paved roads again, making A'bbni bite his lip to keep from crying out as the sudden change sent a jolt of pain up his spine. Shi'chen's fingers traced gently through his hair reassuringly, and he leaned into the touch. Despite the circumstances that necessitated it, he was extremely grateful that Shi'chen was by his side, as their time together in the palace had often been limited as they grew older and took on various responsibilities.

The sounds of people talking and doing business was getting louder, and the smells of the city once more reached them through the horse and hay smell. There was also something in the air that was not quite familiar, and his heartbeat quickened when he realized it was the smell of the sea.

They had gone a rather long way through the city, he estimated, before the sounds became muffled, and the cart came to a stop. A few minutes later, the wooden lid creaked open, and Nen reached a hand down to help them up. Shi'chen got out first, jumping down, then supported A'bbni down off the cart, being mindful of his injuries. They seemed to be in a closed and covered stable of some kind, the smell of fresh hay and manure and horses reaching their noses. The light outside the windows of the stable was fading to create long, dim shadows, and A'bbni assumed that the sun was setting.

Rell held out a bundle with some food and a water pouch, and Shi'chen gladly took it, steering A'bbni over to a pile of hay nearby. Nen moved over to unhitch the horses from the wagon and take care of them, their bodies damp with sweat. One was a piebald, the other entirely chestnut except for a white star on its forehead, and Nen crooned softly to them in Hanen-shii as he got them settled.

Rell gave the twins an appraising look in the dim light as they sat and ate. "Are you well enough, Captain, Your Reverence?"

They both nodded slowly. "You have our eternal gratitude," A'bbni told her softly.

She gave them a gentle smile that reminded him so much of his Mother that his heart gave a little hop in his chest. "I am sure you both are exhausted. I am afraid you will not have long to rest, but please try to sleep now."

A'bbni had so many questions he wanted to ask, but Shi'chen was already making a sort of nest for them in the hay with some blankets from the stall nearby. He pulled Shi'chen down next to him, wrapping an arm over his brother to keep him as warm as he could, and closed his eyes, thinking it would be difficult to fall asleep with so much on his mind. That was his last thought before sleep claimed him.

The sky was showing no hint of the coming dawn when Rell woke them. A'bbni struggled to his feet, his body stiff and aching from the last few days catching up to him. Next to him, Shi'chen looked like he hadn't slept a bit, looking groggy and more than a little grumpy. Rell motioned to a trough of cold but clean water nearby, then moved away to give them some privacy. A'bbni stripped off the makeshift tunic that was crusted with blood and dirt, finding the least dirty area of it to clean himself. It felt more than a little disrespectful to Commander Ahea'a to use her cape for such a base task, but he sent up a silent prayer to the gods to bless her for the comfort it had brought.

Rell suddenly returned, carrying two wrapped bundles, handing one to each of them. "Your Reverence, Captain, you need to change into these, quickly please."

A'bbni finished cleaning off and threw on the sea green silk tunic and white pants in his bundle with no concern for modesty, only for not further aggravating the wounds on his back and legs. They at least had stopped bleeding and were scabbed over now, though every movement of his muscles made them feel like they might tear open again. Shi'chen flushed and turned aside a bit to pull on the casual jacket and pants that he had been given.

"Your jewelry," Rell said softly but firmly, holding out her hands to Shi'chen. Shi'chen quickly slid off all his earrings and rings as Rell turned to A'bbni and handed him a pouch with different jewelry in it, motioning for him to swap them out. She then took Shi'chen's jewelry and stuffed them into her cloak pocket, except for Shi'chen's rose gold signet ring, which she motioned for him to tuck into the pocket of his jacket. A'bbni handed her his old jewelry, minus his signet ring, which she also had him pocket. "Braid your hair, quickly," she commanded, and A'bbni complied as she continued speaking. "We have arranged travel to Csereth for you both separately."

"Separately?" Shi'chen asked.

"Yes. I am sorry," Rell said, sounding genuinely apologetic. "You will be reunited in Csereth."

Csereth was the northern-most port city of Hanenea'a, and the closest goblin port to the elven continent of Kendarin, just across the Coral Sea. That made it one of the largest centers of trade in the entire nation, with ships coming and going dozens, if not hundreds, of times a day. It also had a large elven population, many of whom had dual citizenship on both continents, to facilitate trade and distribution of goods.

A'bbni also remembered, with a hint of envy, that there was a large university there that catered to both the elves and the goblins in a variety of areas of study, from agriculture to philosophy. Several of his private tutors at the palace had come from the university at Csereth, and he had even considered going there himself in a few years to continue his studies. It was accessible by land, but the trip took almost two weeks by horse, and bandit attacks were common due to all the trade and exchange that went on between Csereth and the rest of the continent. By sea, the journey was just over a week.

Rell handed A'bbni a missive, and he held out the end of his braid to Shi'chen to tie off while he took the envelope that was sealed with a plain smudge of black wax and no signet. "These are instructions for Lord Kella, only after you have set sail. For his eyes only," she said firmly, and A'bbni nodded. "Your ship will be departing shortly; we must leave soon. Nen will escort you there." She turned to Shi'chen, holding out a folded square of plain paper. "This is where to go after your ship docks in Csereth."

"Ship?" Shi'chen asked, his ears flattening a little.

"Yes. There are two ships headed for Csereth today, one leaving this morning, and the other on the evening tide. We have detained one of the sailors for you to take his place, Captain."

"I... I cannot do that." Shi'chen's voice suddenly sounded thick, like he was trying to swallow around something in his throat, and A'bbni looked over at his twin with a puzzled frown.

"Do what?" Rell asked.

"Get... get on a ship."

"We need to get you away from the central lands," Nen said, crossing over to them from where he had obviously been listening to everything they were saying. "Csereth is a safe harbor where we have contacts, and it is much faster and safer than going by land."

His brother had broken out in a cold sweat and had gone about as white as a goblin could. A'bbni reached up to press a hand to Shi'chen's forehead. "What is it, i-sha?" Shi'chen just shook his head mutely, both of his hands now tangled in A'bbni's free one.

A mostly-forgotten memory surfaced in A'bbni's mind. One of the few times they had been apart in their childhood. Their Father and Mother had taken them to the sea when they were young, no more than five or six, and they were going to go out on a boat with some of the other nobles for an afternoon of sailing. Shi'chen had screamed and cried and refused to move until their Mother had stayed with him on shore, and Father and A'bbni had gone on the boat alone that afternoon. That had been the only time they had ever gone to the sea, and one of the only times in their whole life A'bbni had seen Shi'chen in a visible panic. A'bbni felt a hard pit starting to form in his stomach. "Shi'chen. Are... are you afraid of water?"

The desperate look his twin gave him was all the answer A'bbni needed, but Shi'chen choked out, "Not... not water. Just... large amounts of it."

A'bbni wondered to himself how Shi'chen had managed to avoid anyone knowing about this when he was a guard. The only way to get to elven lands with any sort of expediency was by boat. If they had been alone, he might have scolded his twin, but this was not the time or place.

"Come with me," Shi'chen pleaded, grasping A'bbni's hand tighter with both of his. "I will be all right if you are there."

"I am sorry, Captain, but this is the only way that—"

"No." Shi'chen's voice was stronger now as he cut Rell off. "We go together, or not at all."

"I do not believe we have any choice in this matter," A'bbni said softly.

"Why... why can't we go together?" Shi'chen asked, his voice barely escaping his throat.

A'bbni could feel his brother's hands shaking in his, and he gave them a gentle squeeze. "Because the guards will be looking for twins, i-sha," he chided gently. Twins were rare enough in their country that together they would stand out like a white horse in a field of black. As two young men with palace accents, the same age as the princes who vanished from the Emperor's prison, it would be extremely obvious who they were if they were together.

Shi'chen shook his head vehemently. "No. I can't."

A'bbni grasped Shi'chen's shoulders and turned him to face him, gazing back into the eyes so identical to his own, it was like looking in a mirror. "Shi'chen," he said, using his brother's name instead of their usual term of endearment, which seemed to bring Shi'chen's focus back to him. "This is the way it has to be. If we do not go, En'shea will kill us, and everyone who helped us. Commander Ahea'a is likely already dead. You cannot let her sacrifice be in vain."

Shi'chen still looked like he might vomit at any moment. A'bbni leaned in, pressing his forehead to Shi'chen's in the familiar gesture from their childhood. "Please."

Shi'chen's eyes closed, and A'bbni could feel him trembling in his arms, which was more than a little disturbing. It was so rare that his brother was scared of anything; even when Shi'chen was afraid, he had too much bravado to let it show. "We might not ever see each other again, i-sha."

While he knew the words were true, they still hit A'bbni in the face like a slap. Ships were lost all the time at sea, to storms, pirates, or sometimes, they just simply vanished. "We will be together again," he said firmly.

"Your Reverence, we do need to go," Nen said, sounding more than a little apologetic.

A'bbni nodded to him, then held up his right arm, hand fisted closed, bent at the elbow. "I swear to you we will be together again." Shi'chen swallowed and slowly held up his arm in return, touching the inside of his wrist to A'bbni's. A'bbni gazed back at him. "Swear to me you will get on your ship, no matter how afraid you are."

"I swear it," Shi'chen said, his words firm, though his voice was barely above a whisper. A'bbni nodded and uncurled his fingers from their fist with his wrist still pressed to Shi'chen's. Shi'chen uncurled his fingers, too, and they both drew their open palms back to touch their own hearts, binding the promise.

Shi'chen suddenly wrapped his arms tightly around A'bbni's shoulders, still conscious of his brother's wounds, clinging to him like he would never let go. A'bbni slid his arms around his twin's waist, holding him tightly, burying his face in his shoulder. There were so many things to say, but he could get none of them out. He and Shi'chen had been together from the day they were conceived, and even if they were not side by side every moment of every day, they still saw each other and knew where the other was. The idea that he might never see the other half of his heart again terrified him more than A'bbni ever wanted to admit.

They stood like that, silent, for a long moment before Rell spoke gently. "I am sorry, Your Reverence, but you really must go."

A'bbni forced himself to pull back and placed his forehead against Shi'chen's again for a moment. "We will see each other again soon, i-sha."

Shi'chen gave him another squeeze, and then A'bbni pulled away and moved to the stable door where Nen had the horses saddled. He swung up onto the horse with the star forehead and forced himself to not look back, or he knew he would not go. Tears burned in his eyes, and he squeezed them shut to keep them in, but they fell down his cheeks, hot and stinging, anyway. His horse began to trot after Nen's into the dawning light. He straightened his shoulders, swiping quickly at the tears on his face, forcing his eyes toward the path in front of him so he didn't focus on every beat of hooves taking him further away from his family, his life, and his heart.

CHAPTER FIVE

SHI'CHEN

Shi'chen watched the horses disappear down the street until they were lost to view. He wanted to cry; the lump in his throat was there, but the tears seemed stuck behind them. He was not a strong believer that the gods did anything to help, but he cast a silent prayer up to anyone who might be listening that this was not the last time he would see his brother. His Mother and Father were dead, his cousin had betrayed him, his Commander had committed treason for him, and now his brother was gone, in a flash of green silk and chestnut horse.

He slid his hand into his pocket, clenching his fingers around his signet ring until it hurt too much. Rell looked like she wanted to say something, but he knew if he opened his mouth he would start screaming, so he just turned and stumbled back to the pile of hay they had slept on, and Rell moved away to fiddle with something in the cart.

Shi'chen scooped up the cape that had belonged to his Commander, now stained with his brother's dried blood. His fingers found the gold Commander pin that Ahea'a had pulled off her chest to keep the cape around A'bbni. He pulled it free from the fabric, running his fingers over the signet there, a trio of crossed spears, tied together by a flowing vine that encircled the circular edge of the pin. Three spears, for the three branches of the palace guards, and for the three virtues they encompassed: Courage, Honor, and Allegiance.

He felt a sardonic smile cross his face. Commander Ahea'a An-Sher'vaat had all three, but not to the Emperor. In exchange for a guard's loyalty, an Emperor was expected to be merciful, wise, and to act honorably. En'shea was none of those things, never had been. Their older cousin, Prii'sha, would have been a fine empress, and Shi'chen would have served her without compunction. The thought that he had only days ago been willing to serve in the guards under En'shea's rule now turned his stomach. He squeezed the pin lightly between his fingers, wondering if his noble Commander was still alive. He hoped she was, but then, he guiltily remembered what had been done to A'bbni, and he changed his mind, hoping she was now at peace. He sent up a prayer to the gods to bless Ahea'a for her sacrifice, pressing the pin lightly to his forehead respectfully before tucking it into his pocket next to his signet ring.

He sat down on a pile of hay to examine the paper Rell had given him with the location he was to go to once he arrived in Csereth. *Vayalla Oren.* He wished he knew what that translated into. His Cserethian was terrible. A'bbni had the head and ear for languages, while Shi'chen did not, no matter how hard he tried. He wondered if that was going to make things more difficult for him on the ship. He had never been on a boat, minus the few he had toured being built during his guard training, and those were on land, not yet on the water. The thought of a couple planks of wood being the only thing between him and the black, crushing depths of endless ocean made him dizzy, and he lay down in the pile of hay, closing his eyes, hoping for sleep that never came.

CHAPTER SIX

A'BBNI

"Re'len An-Bersha," A'bbni repeated the name Nen told him several times. "Son of Lord Mech'jer An-Bersha, the duke of Har'lesh, traveling to Csereth to study at the university."

Nen nodded as they dismounted from their horses a short distance from one of the docks, A'bbni having to bite his lower lip to stifle a whimper of pain as he slid down from his horse. The silk of his tunic rubbed on the wounds that he prayed had not split open during their ride through the city. Every step hurt, but he gritted his teeth and forced himself to straighten and lift his chin, as a well-bred nobleman's son would be expected to do. He could collapse in pain later on the ship, not on Kandrea'a's streets.

The cries of seabirds rattled the air as they dove toward the water and, occasionally, a basket to snatch bits to eat. The port was bustling with movement, even this early in the morning. A'bbni could see goblins and elves, and many individuals who had blood of both in them, loading and unloading crates, tossing ropes and rigging around ships, yelling in a number of languages, most of which he recognized, a few of which he did not. That thought made his stomach flip-flop. Shi'chen only spoke the three dialects of Hanen, as A'bbni's and their tutors' attempts to teach him other languages over the years had failed miserably. Would he be able to function on a ship if they did not speak a language he understood?

"Once the ship has departed, find Lord Kella. He is our contact on board and will be expecting you. He will help you find your brother when you arrive in Csereth and will direct you further." He forced himself to pay attention to Nen's words as they approached the docks. Nen had put on a tunic and cloak more in line with what the servant of a prominent nobleman would wear to complete the ruse that A'bbni was the son of nobility traveling to study. A'bbni still had so many questions. He was a planner; he didn't like surprises when it came to what was happening. But he knew he would not get answers, and that thought made his stomach roil.

They approached the dock where the ship A'bbni was to sail on was moored. It was a long, elegant elven ship, designed for comfort. Nen had told him it was primarily a passenger vessel, that also often carried luxury goods that its wealthy patrons brought with to sell or trade. The name on the side read *Hiyallen Wordan.* The Eastern Star in Cserethian, the primary language that most elves and goblins shared in common. He turned to Nen. "When will my brother's ship depart?"

"This afternoon, on the tide," Nen replied. "He will be on a cargo ship, *Dianol Elledun.* With fair winds and steady seas, you should only arrive in Csereth a few days before him."

"Thank you," A'bbni said, bowing his head gratefully. "Will you please let him know that my ship has departed safely?"

"Of course, Your Reverence." He reached out and placed a hand on the prince's shoulder. "May the gods grant you wisdom and safety."

A'bbni placed his hand over Nen's, repeating the traditional travel blessing back to him before turning toward the ship. In another lifetime, with Shi'chen by his side, this would seem like a fun adventure, traveling to a new city on the sea. But now, standing alone on the pier without his brother's familiar warmth next to him, he felt lost. The screeching cry of seabirds and the plunk of waves lapping against the wooden hull, the voices around him, and the briny salt smell of the water felt like it might consume him entirely.

He glanced back over his shoulder at Nen, who stood at the edge of the dock, the faithful servant waiting on his master, before he turned and began to climb up the elegantly crafted gangplank. The water churned below him, which was disconcerting when he had hardly ever been around such a large body of water. He checked his pocket one last time for his signet ring and the missive for Lord Kella before he took a deep breath and stepped onto the deck of the ship.

"Good morning, my lord," came a voice in Hanen-sha, and it took A'bbni a moment to realize the unfamiliar address was meant for him. He turned to see a young elf with sandy blond hair and a sprinkling of cinnamon freckles across his nose and cheeks, probably a few years older than him, dressed in a handsome porter's uniform. The young man bowed his head respectfully and gave him a bright smile.

"Good morning," A'bbni greeted back in Hanen-sha. Of course, it made sense that a passenger vessel that carried merchants and other nobles would speak the more formal dialect, but not Hanen-vir, the most formal of dialects used primarily by members of the royal family.

"May I help you find your cabin?" the porter asked.

"Yes, thank you," A'bbni said. The porter waited for a moment, and A'bbni realized he was waiting for his name. It took him a moment to recall it, and he covered it by adjusting his clothing, as if walking from the dock might have mussed them. "Re'len An-Bersha, of Har'lesh."

"Welcome, Vr An-Bersha," the porter said, easily pronouncing the goblin name with its honorific prefix. "Please follow me."

A'bbni followed after him, trying to not stare too openly at the ship around them. The sails were beautifully white and trimmed with an embroidered gold swirling star. The wood was all burnished so bright it shone in the sunlight. "Have you traveled with us before?" the porter asked as they descended a staircase with a gleaming, gold banister, into a long hallway lit by torches carefully covered with decorative glass. The wood under their feet had been covered with a soft, blue carpet.

"No," A'bbni said. He wanted to examine everything. Perhaps there would be time for it on the journey.

The porter smiled and began pointing out the various decorations on the walls. They passed several doors, all of which were closed, before they descended another flight of stairs into an almost identical hallway, except this carpet was a jewel-tone purple. A'bbni heard something about meals being served in the dining hall and where that was located, unless he wanted them in his room, in which case he only had to ring the bell for assistance, any time of the day or night. He felt a stab of guilt in his stomach. It seemed like he would be well cared for; he doubted Shi'chen's ship would be anything like this.

The porter stopped before a door with a copper plate with *Gellenium* inscribed on it, a Cserethian word. A'bbni smiled a bit. "The highest star in the constellation *Imedras*, the lovers."

"You know your stars, my lord," the porter replied, seeming pleasantly surprised. He opened the door for A'bbni, who stepped inside. The main room was a sitting room, designed more in elven style with higher tables and furniture than the ones closer to the floor that goblins favored. There was a large window across from them, where he could see the nearby ships and docks, and where much of the light came from. The porter gestured to the left. "Your sleeping accommodations are in there, my lord, as is the freshening room." He gestured right. "Over there is your office."

He could get used to this. "Thank you," he said to the young man before turning to him again, feeling the envelope in his pocket. "I am supposed to meet with Lord Kella. I believe he is expecting me."

"Of course, my lord. He is meeting with the captain, as we are about to set sail, but after we have left port, I shall inform him of your presence. Do you require anything else at the moment before the ship departs?"

Nothing that this eager young man could give him. "No, thank you," A'bbni said politely.

"Then I shall bid you good morning," the porter said, giving him another respectful bow before he exited the room, shutting the door behind him.

A'bbni heard him walk down the long hallway and up the stairs. He turned back to the luxurious room. If Shi'chen had been with him, it would have been perfect. He moved over to look out the window, which was some of the purest goblin-made clear glass he had ever seen. The ropes were being untied from the dock, and a sudden rumbling made him jump. He realized the anchor was likely being raised. There was so much to learn on this ship while he was here, and he hoped he could take advantage of it.

The ship began to move, and A'bbni put his hand up on the window frame to catch himself at the slight vibration under him. He sucked in a deep breath, watching the world glide past outside of his window. It was really happening; he was leaving Kandrea'a, leaving his brother behind. The world blurred, and A'bbni realized hot tears had filled his eyes. He leaned his forehead against the cool glass of the window as the tears fell silently onto the carpet beneath his feet.

A'bbni had settled into one of the soft chairs in the office with a book from off the shelf when a knock sounded at his door. He carefully got up to answer, finding the young porter there. "My lord, apologies for interrupting you, but Lord Kella is available to see you now."

"Of course, thank you," A'bbni said, following after the young man. He checked that the envelope was still in his pocket as he followed after him. "What is your name?"

The porter turned to look at him in surprise, then smiled a bit. Obviously, the question was not one he was often asked. "Johrenn, my lord."

"Thank you, Johrenn," A'bbni said, giving him a smile in return. It was nice to know someone on this ship. Hopefully no one would recognize him, he realized with a momentary panic, but that wasn't exactly something he could do anything about right now. "Your Hanen-sha is excellent."

The elf blushed, his ears dipping in modest pleasure. "Thank you, my lord." After a moment's hesitation, he added, "My father was the assistant to a translator. I learned several languages from him."

"His work is commendable," A'bbni said, and the young man flushed again, his step picking up just a little. He led A'bbni up the stairwell and out into the sunshine. There were crew members moving around controlling the sails and other things A'bbni was not familiar with, and there were several finely-dressed people on deck, both goblins and elves, who were obviously passengers. A'bbni quickly scanned their faces, trying to keep his own turned away, but he did not recognize any of them. They crossed the deck, the sun higher in the sky now and warming the air around them quickly. It would be quite hot by midday. The waves splashed against the boat as it moved smoothly through the water, little sprays of mist flying into the air and gently cooling the skin of the people it touched.

Johrenn led him all the way across the deck to another set of stairs. He motioned to one door. "That is the captain's quarters. Captain Nehema has been captain of the *Hiyallen Wordan* for almost seven years now."

A'bbni wondered how many times Captain Nehema had made the trip between Csereth and Kandrea'a. They went down another hallway and stopped in front of an elaborately carved door made of a stunning white wood that A'bbni had never seen before. Most of the wood in Hanenea'a was very dark, but this was almost pure white, with a few swirls through it that almost looked like marble. The depiction on the door was as if they were looking underwater at sea creatures swimming; A'bbni had no idea what all the creatures were. His knowledge of the sea was quite limited, beyond the occasional seafood on their dinner table. Perhaps there would be a book about it in his office library.

Johrenn knocked lightly on the door. "Come in," came a pleasant voice in Cserethian from inside.

Johrenn opened the door and stepped aside for A'bbni to enter, bowing his head. A'bbni stepped inside the lavish room, trying very hard not to stare. He was used to elegance and finery at the palace, but where the goblins favored warm, earthy colors, this room was bright with jewel tones on the walls, furniture, and carpet. The furniture seemed to be made from the same white wood as the door. "Vr Re'len An-Bersha of Har'lesh to see you, my lord."

"Thank you, Johrenn, that will be all for now," came the warm voice again, and A'bbni saw the speaker seated across the room at a large desk. Johrenn bowed and exited, closing the door behind him, and A'bbni found himself alone except for the man across the room. He took a deep breath and slowly approached the desk.

Lord Kella sat behind the white wood desk that was strewn with all manner of papers, ledgers, and a few tools A'bbni did not recognize. His head was bowed, his long hair black and loose around his shoulders. When he looked up, A'bbni found himself staring into the bluest eyes he had ever seen. Lord Kella's eyes were even more blue than the water they sailed upon, and his doublet was the same jeweled blue as his eyes, with tiny silver swirls embroidered into it, so fine they only could be seen when he moved and they caught the sunlight from the wide windows behind him. He was younger than A'bbni had expected, perhaps early thirties. A'bbni bowed his head and bent a knee in the goblin bow between two higher ranked members of society. "Lord Kella, thank you for meeting with me," he said in Cserethian.

Kella's dark brow lifted along with the corner of his mouth. "You speak Cserethian?"

"I do, my lord," A'bbni replied. "I am quite fluent in it, but I know several other languages as well."

"No, please, Cserethian will do. I am afraid my Hanen-vir is a little rusty," Kella said.

So, Kella knew he had come from the palace if he knew A'bbni spoke a mix of Hanen-vir, the elevated dialogue of the palace, along with Hanen-sha, spoken by nobility. He wondered how much Kella actually knew; he guessed it was more than he himself.

A'bbni reached into his pocket and drew out the envelope, holding it out to Kella with another bow of his head. "I was instructed to give this to you, my lord."

Kella took it, motioning for A'bbni to sit in a chair in front of the desk. A'bbni sat as Kella examined the seal, then picked up a silver letter opener to break it. "You did not read it?"

"No, my lord."

Kella gave him a small smile. "I suppose I should commend your honesty, if not your wisdom."

A'bbni tried not to feel offended, glancing down at his hands as Kella opened the letter and scanned it. It took him a few minutes, and A'bbni found himself alternating between watching Kella and looking around the room at all the beautiful details. The shelves built into the walls were all hand-carved, with swirls that looked like ocean waves. On the shelves were a variety of books and knickknacks, a few model sculptures, and a few sea creatures that seemed to be frozen in lifelike suspension.

Kella set down the letter and turned to him. "I am sorry to hear of the death of your Father, Your Reverence."

"Thank you," A'bbni said softly, trying very, very hard to not picture his Father's decapitated head on the table next to him.

"I am sure you have many questions." Kella stood up and crossed over to a little table nearby that held a decanter and several beautifully cut crystal glasses. "Umberian wine, may I tempt you?"

"Yes, thank you."

Kella poured the dark wine into a glass and carried it over to A'bbni, then sat down on the edge of his desk. "Please forgive me for not indulging myself," he said, resting a hand lightly on the underside of his stomach, and A'bbni could see the slight swell of Kella's belly against the soft, supple leather of his breeches.

"Congratulations, my lord," A'bbni said, lifting his glass in a toasting gesture.

"Thank you. How much do you know, Your Reverence?"

"Assume I know nothing," A'bbni said, taking a sip from the glass. Umberian wine was sweet and also expensive. Probably like everything in this room.

"Fair enough. To start, my Father is Lord Ashtor Arvay. He is one of the most prominent ferriers on the continent."

"I have heard the name," A'bbni replied. This did not surprise him at all with the lavishness of his surroundings. Lord Arvay's ferrying business was the main source of transportation for any of the nobles or merchants who needed to travel across the sea to the elven continent and back, and the more common people as well. Based on that alone, A'bbni could deduce that the Arvay family was extremely wealthy, even without Kella's luxurious suite saying so.

"I am the third son of Lord Arvay. I have two older brothers, and three sisters. Only my second brother is aware of my association with the goblin resistance." Kella crossed one ankle over the other as he leaned against the desk.

"May I ask you why?" A'bbni asked curiously.

"Why I am a member of a goblin revolutionary group?" Kella asked with a small smile. When A'bbni nodded, he said, "I do not have to be a goblin to know that both slavery and the crown prince, excuse me, the Emperor, are repellent." His smile turned a bit sad. "My family was involved in the slave trade, years ago, before I was born. I cannot make up for the mistakes of my ancestors, but I can do my best to make things right in my time."

A'bbni gave Kella a small smile. "You are wise beyond your years, Lord Kella."

Kella gave a soft chuckle at that. "I hope to remain so. Do you know of the rebellion?"

A'bbni shook his head. "I only heard about it when we were rescued from the prison."

Kella frowned, not seeming happy that the information had been withheld from him. "The idea, from my understanding, has been that your Father would continue as Regent, your Cousin would be forced to renounce his claim to the throne's succession, and the Regent would then name one of you to the throne, as your age of majority is coming up."

"One... one of us? You mean, Shi'chen or myself?" Kella nodded again. "Why did neither of us know about this?"

"I do not pretend to know your Father's mind," Kella said. "I only listen and report back. But if I had to venture, I would say you were not informed because of a situation like this. If you or your brother were captured and interrogated, knowing nothing would keep those involved in the rebellion safe."

A'bbni frowned down at the dark liquid in his glass. "That certainly seems to be something that we should have been able to decide for ourselves, seeing as it is our lives that were the most endangered by it."

"I do not disagree with you on that," Kella said. "I can only speak for myself when I say that I am truly sorry for what happened to you and your brother, and your Father."

A'bbni was silent for another long moment. He looked up into Kella's ocean-deep eyes, then flushed as his stomach gave a loud growl of protest.

"Oh, forgive me, I have been a truly ungracious host," Kella said, pushing himself off the desk and moving over to a nearby pull rope. "I am sure you have not had much to eat in the last few days."

"I am sorry for any imposition," A'bbni replied.

"None at all," Kella said, waving his hand as a door on the side of the room opened, emitting another porter, with his almost white-blond hair piled on top of his head. "Please have lunch for two brought here. Whatever is ready now, we do not wish to wait."

"Yes, my lord." The blond elf gave him a quick bow and disappeared again.

Kella turned back to A'bbni. "My apologies, Your Reverence."

A'bbni shook his head. "No, please, there is no need to apologize. And, if you wish, please call me A'bbni. Reverence is only a title, and I certainly am in no position to maintain it."

Kella gave him a small smile. "But you are royalty, and still a scholar, whether you are in your home or not."

A'bbni tried not to laugh. "Please. While I am in your grace and away from my home, I would enjoy not being royalty for a time."

"As you wish, my lord," Kella said, changing to the less formal address.

"If... if I may impose upon your goodness further," A'bbni said, bowing his head, his fingers toying with the wine glass uneasily.

"Yes, my lord," Kella said, giving him a kind smile that almost brought tears to his eyes, but he forced them back.

"Do you have a physician on board?"

"I do."

A'bbni felt his face go scarlet, his ears dipping a little as he replied, "While we were imprisoned, I..." He wished more than anything Shi'chen was with him right now, holding his hand for support, having the courage to say the things that he did not. "That is..."

Kella's eyes softened. "Someone hurt you," he said, in the same tone that A'bbni used when at the bedside of a patient.

His ears drooped more, and A'bbni nodded slowly, raising his eyes to meet Kella's own, feeling like he at least owed him that much. Kella moved over to him, suddenly kneeling next to his chair to look up into his face. "I am so sorry, my lord," he said, laying his pale hand on A'bbni's arm lightly, which surprised him. Elves were much less physical than goblins tended to be, especially when it came to strangers. But the kindness of the touch sent a small spark of warmth through him, and he looked into Kella's eyes that appeared just a little bit wet. "My physician is at your disposal, for as long as you need. Let us get some food into you, and then I will send them to your rooms."

"I am grateful," A'bbni said, giving Kella a weak smile. "I apologize for the imposition all of this must be causing you."

Kella shook his head, his raven-dark hair swishing a bit. "No imposition, my lord. I would hope if my own kin were in need and sought help, it would be freely given."

There was a light tap at the door, which opened again to admit the porter, bearing a large, covered silver tray, which he set down upon a table nearby. Kella thanked him, then motioned for A'bbni to sit at the table. A'bbni moved over while Kella took the porter aside and asked for him to send the physician to attend to the young lord in his room upon his return. Then he poured A'bbni another glass of wine and sat down with him at the table to eat.

CHAPTER SEVEN

SHI'CHEN

Shi'chen's attempts at sleep were not rewarded, and he ended up spending the time pacing around the stable, trying to find a use for all his nervous energy. He cleaned up their clothing, shredding it into unrecognizable rags. At one point, the tears had finally come, and he sat on the hay pile and cried. Before their interrogation, he couldn't remember the last time he cried. He suspected it was when his Mother had died.

Later in the morning, Nen had returned, and A'bbni was not with him. Shi'chen helped him care for the horses, no words exchanged between them. Rell went out for a bit and then returned with several bags of supplies, including a loaf of warm, fresh bread and a bag with nuts and figs that he eagerly devoured. As the sun reached the top of the sky, Rell gave him basic information about his new identity, and he listened and tried to ignore the ache in his chest as he thought about getting on a ship without his brother.

Later that afternoon, he and Rell rode the horses down to the docks, dismounting a few streets away. This was as far as she would go; while it made sense for someone to escort a young nobleman to a ship, it did not make sense for a common sailor. She would watch from nearby to ensure he got on the ship safely and that the ship left port. She handed him a bag of belongings like those the other trade-sailors carried, and then Shi'chen left her, heading down the streets, a cap pulled over his auburn-black curls, keeping his head down as he blended into the crowd of people.

The smell of the docks, of rotting trash and salt and something slimy, filled his nose, and he sighed silently to himself. While he figured at some point in his military career he'd have to be on a ship, he had hoped it would be much later in his future. He wove his way through the various goblins and elves on the planks, finding the ship, *Dianol Ellendun*, that Rell had pointed him to. He had no idea what that was in Cserethian either.

He stopped at the edge of the dock, the water lapping at the wooden walkway only a few feet in front of him. His heart started to thunder in his chest, so fast he worried it would fly away, his ears flattening with a show of fear that he rarely displayed. There was still time to turn and run, to find another way to be reunited with A'bbni. He would rather fight all Hi'jan's Courage Garrison unarmed than take another step onto the dock. He knew he was being foolish; ships sailed back and forth every day, had for hundreds of years. But yet, some still sank, or were attacked, or caught fire, or...

He was not helping himself with his thoughts swirling like a whirlpool in his brain. If he didn't move soon, he would start to draw attention to himself, and that would only make his anxiety worse. He remembered his wrist pressed to A'bbni's as he swore he would get on the ship. He had never broken a promise to his brother, except the promise to keep him safe from En'shea, and that thought compelled his feet to start moving again, onto the dock and up the cargo ship gangplank.

The angle was steep, the wood slick from the spray of water. It took Shi'chen, normally sure-footed, a moment to find his balance as the water sloshed at the dock below him. He glanced down into it, seeing his dark silhouette reflected at him in the churning surface.

How easy it would be to just fall into the water, to sink into the inky blackness. He swallowed hard, feeling like the whole plank was swaying with the water, and he almost bolted. Only A'bbni's words in his head kept him moving, and he was grateful there was a rope along the edges to help pull himself up the last few paces.

It was a relief to step onto the deck, which was much more solid and sturdy than the gangplank. Around him was a mix of sailors, tying ropes, hauling crates, getting the ship ready to sail. Some were full elf, some full goblin, others a mix of both, with skin colors varying from creamy white, to storm gray, to almost black. All were dressed in plain but well-tended clothes, except for one woman toward the helm of the ship, who was wearing a fine silk shirt and breeches with a warm-looking coat of bright green draped over her shoulders. She was full elf, with red hair, though it was cropped short, unusual to see on an elf of any sort of means. Shi'chen assumed her to be the captain. But he didn't have much time to look around, as a heavy-eyed goblin woman approached him. "Name?" she grunted.

"Cha'she Chea-Bakk," he said, giving the name Rell had supplied him with.

The woman grunted again and pointed to a set of stairs that led down into the darkness that was the underbelly of the ship. "Crew down there," she said in Hanen-shii, in a similar cadence to what his guards would use when they were not on the training fields. "Find an empty bunk, and then get back up here."

Shi'chen nodded, deciding not to say anything until he had a chance to listen to the sailors around him talk more. While the guards in his Honor Garrison often spoke Hanen-shii or a version of Hanen-shii mixed with Hanen-sha, he was still used to the mix of Hanen-sha and Hanen-vir that the nobles and royal family used, and his troops often teased him – good-naturedly, of course – that his palace accent was very distinct. Which made sense, as he had lived there his entire life, but was not good when he was trying to pass for a commoner. He headed across the deck and down the stairs. The ship didn't feel like it was moving too much, which was good, but of course, they were anchored in place right now.

The crew area was not overly crowded, but he assumed that was because most of them were on the deck or the hold, preparing to set sail as soon as the tide came in. There were hammocks strung up, as well as berths built into the walls, like crypts in a mausoleum. He suppressed a shudder and was glad that A'bbni was not there with him to sleep in something like that. While he had his rooms in their shared apartments in the palace, Shi'chen often slept in the barracks with his Garrison, on similar style bunks, but A'bbni was used to the finer things, like soft pillows and cool sheets. His brother having to lie on a rough bunk with his injured back was a distressing thought. He hoped A'bbni was being taken care of better than this.

Finding a row of berths that seemed to not have been claimed with any personal items, Shi'chen shoved the bag of his few clothing pieces into one of them. He decided against the top bunk, instead opting for the lower one. If he was going to fall out of bed if the seas got rough, he would rather it be a shorter distance. The thought of rocky seas made his gorge rise in his throat, and he swallowed it back so as not to bring up the meal he had eaten.

A quick assessment of the area gave him the idea that there were about forty-five sailors on the ship, based on the number of spots taken. He sent up a silent prayer that none of the sailors would be people who had been to the palace and could potentially recognize him. He readjusted the cap on his head, then turned and headed back up the stairs.

The light was blinding, going from the dimness of the cabin lit only by lanterns to the deck and the reflection of the sun off the water; he had not thought to check his pack for dark glasses or a sand silk veil. The sun was past being overhead, and it was slightly cooler than it had been earlier. He spotted the woman that had directed him down the stairs and moved over to her, where she was giving instructions to a few other crew members. They scurried to obey her when she finished speaking. She turned to Shi'chen, giving him a once-over look like she was appraising a goat for slaughter. She was a full head and shoulders taller than him, and wider as well, and when he looked closer at her, he realized that one of her eyes was red and the other was purple.

"I'm the bosun, Deana'nen. Have you been on a ship before?"

"No, ma'iir," Shi'chen said, bowing his head at the bosun as he addressed her with the gender-neutral title of respect.

Deana'nen blinked and smiled just a bit at the address. "You're a polite one," she said. "Bosun or ma'am is good."

"Yes, ma'am," Shi'chen replied. She studied him for a moment longer, and Shi'chen realized he was standing at his military attention stance, with both hands behind his back. He flushed just a bit, loosening his stance under her gaze. He was going to have to be more careful.

Deana'nen glanced around. "Once we're at sea, I'll have you work with some of the seasoned sailors to learn the ropes. But for now, head down to the cargo hold," she pointed to another set of stairs toward the front of the ship, "and help make sure everything is secure."

"Yes, ma'am." Shi'chen turned and headed to the stairs, glad he could get off the deck so he couldn't watch the water move out of the corner of his eye.

He spent most of the afternoon helping several sailors stack and tie boxes and crates in the cargo hold. At some point, he felt the rumble of the anchor being weighed, and the ship began to move. He did his best to ignore it. Throwing up would not help the situation in any way. At least securing boxes helped him keep his mind off the unsteady movements beneath his sandaled feet.

At some point, the cargo crew was called for dinner, and Shi'chen followed them to the galley. He barely noticed what they were given, too tired and hungry to care, swallowing his meal without conversation, before heading back to work. His thoughts kept drifting to A'bbni and wishing he knew that his brother was at least safe and being taken care of. As much as people often joked that the twins shared a special connection, he could not sense when A'bbni was hurt or in danger, any more than he could sense it about anyone else who was not around him.

He tried to remember what Rell had told him about the ship A'bbni was on, but after A'bbni had left, she had not spoken much to him, obviously not wanting to upset him further. A'bbni had at least been dressed in the clothing and jewelry of a noble, so he doubted that his twin would be working on a ship the same way he was. If that was the case, he was profoundly grateful.

Once all the cargo had been secured and double-checked against the manifest, most of the crew moved up on deck to converse and probably act a lot like soldiers did when they were off duty, but Shi'chen did not care. He just made his way to his bunk and crawled into the darkness there, pulling a blanket over himself. His fingers found the Commander pin in his pocket, and he clutched it tightly, running his thumb across it, over and over, until exhaustion caught up to him, and he finally fell asleep for the first time in days.

He spent the night more unconscious than sleeping, but even the blackness was better than his racing thoughts as Shi'chen awoke early the next morning. It took him a moment to remember where he was and why the world did not feel entirely steady. When it suddenly came back to him, it hit him like a thunderclap to the head, and his stomach turned upside-down. He dove off the bunk and hurried to the latrines where he threw up everything that was in his stomach, and then some. This was going to be a long voyage.

He picked at the breakfast for the crew, drinking more water than actually eating anything. He had a pounding headache, and all he wanted was to be at their home in the palace, A'bbni safely by his side. He reported with the rest of the crew on deck, and Deana'nen gave them their assignments.

Shi'chen would have given everything he owned in the world to have A'bbni next to him, holding his hand, as he forced himself over by the railing to grab a coil of rope the riggers had asked him for. The splash of water against the wooden planks that were the only thing keeping them from plunging leagues into the dark water made his skin crawl, and he swallowed back another wave of nausea. Trying not to look over the side, he grabbed the coil of rope the riggers had indicated, staring instead at his feet, where they were planted on solid ground, or as close to solid ground as they would be for a while. Dizziness made him stumble, and he turned without looking, his shoulder crashing into a firm chest. His eyes moved upward to see a bulky goblin man with a very square jaw glowering at him.

"Watch where you're going, bitch," the goblin snapped in Hanen-shii, giving him a sharp shove that sent him staggering several steps back. Distracted from dizziness, Shi'chen narrowed his eyes at the man.

"Don't touch me."

The man laughed loudly, throwing his head back. "Who do you think you are, giving orders, kid?"

If this man had been one of his guards, Shi'chen would have taken him to the ground immediately. But he was new on this ship and trying to not draw attention to himself. "I apologize," he said stiffly.

"You don't sound too sorry," the man said, giving him a small, cold smile. "Where I come from, we expect children to respect their betters."

"Where I'm from, we only respect those who deserve it," Shi'chen said before he could stop himself.

A few whistles and jeers came from some of the nearby sailors, and Shi'chen realized with a sudden pit in his stomach that their exchange was gathering the attention of a small crowd. Damn it to the gods, why did that keep happening to him when he got into an argument?

The goblin raised one heavy eyebrow at him. "You need some lessons in manners, pup. Get down on your knees and kiss my boot, and I'll forget this whole thing happened."

"Not a fucking chance," Shi'chen snapped, narrowing his eyes.

"Hah, puppy has some teeth," the large man snickered. "Come on then, show me what you got."

Shi'chen was sorely tempted to rearrange the goblin's teeth, but he could hear A'bbni in his ear, warning him to not get into trouble. He hiked up the coil of rope over his shoulder, giving the man a look down his nose, despite the big goblin being at least a foot taller than him. "You're not worth my time."

The sailors nearby let out another hoot of laughter. The man glowered. "Why you sonofa—"

He hadn't even finished his threat before he sprang forward, trying to land a punch on Shi'chen's face. Shi'chen saw it coming and ducked away. What he did not see coming was another goblin moving up behind him, the second man's fist blindsiding him across the temple. He saw white, stumbling forward, which gave the first goblin a chance to connect his fist to Shi'chen's jaw, sending him sprawling. The next moment, a foot connected with his chest, causing him to double up, before another kick landed on his back, and suddenly there were fists and boots raining down on him from all directions as more sailors joined in the skirmish. His arms went up to protect his face, several blows finding his ribs and legs.

A shout from nearby drew the sailors' attention, one of the senior crew members yelling something in Cserethian that Shi'chen did not understand or even pay attention to. The group around him backed off and dispersed back to their duties. The first goblin spat a gobby mouthful of spit at Shi'chen's feet and gave him a final kick with his boot before strolling away. Shi'chen debated not moving ever again, just staying curled up in a ball on the deck of this ship for the rest of his life. He coughed softly as he struggled to pull in a breath, uncurling his arms from his face. He knew he had to get up. He couldn't lie here and look weak, even though that was all he wanted to do.

A pair of worn leather boots hit the planks in front of him with a soft *thump*. Shi'chen lifted his eyes up a pair of slender legs in light breeches, past a clean but faded blue jerkin and white shirtsleeves, into a tanned face that peered down at him. It took him a moment to focus on the face against the brilliant blue of the sky. Eyes the color of springtime grass peered down at him from a delicately-curved face, strands of brilliant blond hair escaping from a high ponytail.

"You all right?"

The accent was strange to Shi'chen's ears, and it took a moment for him to process the Cserethian words. He blinked, trying to get his arms under him to push himself up. The elf bent and extended a calloused hand to him. After a moment of hesitation, Shi'chen took it, and the stranger helped pull him to his feet. The world swam a moment as the blood rushed back to his head, and he felt some of it dripping from his split lip.

The elf let go of his hand and dug in his pocket, pulling out a handkerchief and holding it out to him. He said something that Shi'chen did not understand. Shi'chen blinked. "What?" he asked in Hanen-shii. The stranger repeated what he had said, a little slower, and Shi'chen shook his head. "I'm sorry, I don't understand you."

A wrinkle furrowed the stranger's brow. "You don't speak Cserethian?" he asked in slightly accented Hanen-shii.

Shi'chen shook his head. "No," he said back in Cserethian. One of the few words he knew.

The elf held up the fabric again for him, motioning to his lip. Shi'chen took it, and the elf smiled, the look lighting up his face. Shi'chen pressed the cloth to his lip, feeling the sting of salt on the torn flesh.

The elf watched him a moment before pointing to himself. "Lai."

"Cha'she," Shi'chen replied after a moment to remember his alias, motioning to himself with his free hand.

"Cha'she," the elf repeated, the name a little odd-sounding in his accented voice.

Shi'chen held out the cloth back to the elf, but Lai shook his head, motioning for him to keep it. "Are you all right?" he asked in Hanen-shii.

Shi'chen nodded slowly. "Yes," he replied. "Thank you."

The blond motioned for him to follow him, and Shi'chen moved to obey, not wanting to be left alone on the deck where the other sailors had just kicked the shit out of him. Lai scooped up the coil of rope Shi'chen had been carrying, tossing it over his shoulder with practiced ease as he moved down the deck toward the bow of the ship. Shi'chen kept his eyes on the back of Lai's blond ponytail that whipped around the young man's face as they walked. He quickly assessed his throbbing chest and back, determining nothing was broken. He sent up a quick prayer to whomever might be listening that A'bbni was not on a ship where the same thing could happen to him. Shi'chen had been hit numerous times in guard training; A'bbni had not, and even the thought of it happening made his blood boil.

Lai moved over to one of the masts, yelling something up to another sailor above them who answered back, and Lai tossed the coil of rope up to him before he turned to Shi'chen again, gesturing for the goblin to keep following. He moved over to a large, covered barrel that was secured to the wall, pulling off the lid and picking up one of the tin cups hooked to the wall next to it. He dipped it in the barrel and handed it to Shi'chen. It was filled with water, and he took it gratefully, taking a few large swallows, and then using a bit to wipe the blood off his chin where it had started to dry from his lip.

Lai gestured to the stairs nearby that led up to the forecastle. "Sit." He did gratefully while Lai leaned against the stair railing. The wind whipped past them, smelling of briny salt and some sort of ocean plant smell he didn't know.

"Thank you," Shi'chen said, motioning with the cup.

Lai nodded to him. "First time on a ship?" he asked in his slightly accented Hanen-shii.

Shi'chen nodded slowly. "Yes," he said softly. "I'm still trying not to get dizzy."

When Lai looked uncertain, Shi'chen spun his hand in a circle in front of his eyes. "Dizzy."

Lai nodded in understanding. "It will go away soon," he said as the wind whipped past again.

Shi'chen suddenly spotted Lai's ears from where they poked out under his blond hair as the wind tossed it. Where his own goblin ears and the ears of elves were long, extending almost past the back of their head in slightly rounded points, Lai's ears were only about half that long, ending in a more severe point, lying against the side of his head, unmoving. He had never seen such short ears before. He also noticed that the young man's hair was plaited into a braid on the sides of his head in such a way that, at a quick glance, or under a cap or scarf, his hair would look like he had longer ears like other elves did.

"You're... you're not an elf," Shi'chen said softly.

Lai turned to study Shi'chen's face a moment, as if trying to read what emotion might be there, his body tensing against the railing he leaned on, as if he were preparing to run. Shi'chen swallowed hard, then slowly held out his arms from his sides, palms up. "No, please. I won't hurt you. I've just never seen ears like yours before." He motioned to his own longer ears, hoping that Lai would be able to understand his tone, if not his words. Lai seemed to understand what he said, and his tension eased a little, though he still seemed like a cat prepared to dash at the slightest movement. Shi'chen felt his stomach clench. It was the body language of someone who was used to running.

Lai's green eyes searched Shi'chen's face another moment before he let out a breath. "My father was an elf," he said slowly in careful Hanen-shii. "My mother was human."

Shi'chen blinked. He might have been less surprised if Lai had said he was part sea dragon. "Human?" he repeated. He suddenly had so many questions. He had heard of "human," though he had never met one himself. The lands inhabited by their race were on the other side of the world, in places that very few elves, let alone goblins, had traveled to, and returned from. There had been rare stories of "humans" in elven lands, and the few goblin stories of humans were from generations before his time. They were no more real to Shi'chen than the mythical beasts of legends. But yet, here stood Lai, with the strangest ears he had ever seen, saying that his mother was of the race of humans. He opened his mouth to ask a question, but Lai suddenly spoke first, in his accented but clear Hanen-shii, seeming to have made some sort of decision.

"Look, you're on a ship. There's only so many places you can go. Just be careful. Not everyone will be your friend."

The words sounded like a warning, but not a threat. Shi'chen nodded slowly. "Thank you."

Lai gave Shi'chen a small smile. "If you get dizzy again, go stand at the bow and watch the horizon." He pointed up the stairs to the forecastle. "It helps."

Shi'chen nodded again, but before he could say anything more, Lai had moved past him and over to the main mast, climbing up the rope ladder with a speed and grace Shi'chen had never seen before. He watched him until the sun caught his eyes and Lai was no longer visible amongst the blue sky and white sail.

CHAPTER EIGHT

A'BBNI

A'bbni had never been more grateful for a physician than he was for Thelara, the ship's physician Kella had sent to him. Thelara had gone to work with a gentle compassion that A'bbni admired, cleaning and bandaging his wounds, being very sensitive and kind about the injuries in more personal places. They used several special blends of healing medicines that A'bbni had to ask about. By the time Thelara had finished their ministrations, A'bbni felt better than he had in days, and he sat eagerly talking with Thelara for most of the afternoon until the physician was called away by a seasick passenger.

A'bbni went to work, scribbling notes on a piece of paper in the office. He was not about to squander the opportunity to continue learning, especially from an elven physician with years of experience working with both goblins and elves. He really needed to compliment Lord Kella on his staff, as they had all been nothing but professional and kind.

A few days went by, and he was at least able to occupy his time with helping Thelara, reading books in the library, and having meals with Lord Kella on occasion when Kella was available. He learned that Kella was married and had two children at home already, which he was quite curious about. Goblin families often were small, usually no more than two children, but

Kella had five siblings, most of whom had at least two children already. He was learning so much about elven culture that he had not known before. If the reason for his travels had been different, it would have been a welcomed lesson.

A'bbni had lost track of time since they had been taken from The Keep, but the weather growing colder the further north they sailed prompted him to look at the date. There were three seasons, and today was the second day of the third season. His heart jolted at that harsh realization. Tomorrow was his birthday, and the day he would turn 20, the age of majority in goblin society. Their Father had been planning a celebration for them for months now. A'bbni wondered to himself if that would have been the day that their Father would have tried to force En'shea to surrender his claim to the throne. He also wondered which of them their Father would have named as his successor. By all rights, Shi'chen would have been the next in line, being the elder of the two twins, but he already had a successful military career before even reaching adulthood.

He forced himself to not think about it anymore. Their Father was dead; anything he might have wanted died with him. He thought again of those two earring studs in their Father's ear, and that sent him racing to throw up as he felt the sting of Hi'jan's knife against his skin, the heat of him pressed against the back of his legs, the smell of blood and leather trapped inside his lungs. A'bbni did not sleep at all that night, just lay awake in the darkness of his room, staring out the window at the seemingly unchanging ocean.

The morning of his birthday dawned cloudy, mirroring his feelings as he tried to drag himself into some semblance of presentable. Never in his wildest dreams had he imagined he would reach his majority day without his twin by his side and not even in the only home he had ever known.

Kella summoned him to his office after breakfast. A'bbni tapped lightly on the door, and Kella answered it himself, giving him a warm smile. "Welcome, my lord," he said, gesturing for A'bbni to enter and sit on the comfortable couch. A'bbni sat, his fingers twisting nervously into the hem of his tunic. Kella sat down in a chair nearby, pouring A'bbni a cup of tea from the pot on the table without asking, then picking up his own that he had been drinking before A'bbni arrived. "I wanted to ask you, what are your plans when we arrive in port?"

A'bbni blinked, his fingers curling around the warm cup. "I... What do you mean, my lord?"

"I know you were thrown into this situation quite unexpectedly," Kella said, his blue eyes somber above his cup. "Do you have a place to stay?"

A'bbni shook his head slowly, turning his eyes down into the teacup. "No. All I know is that I am supposed to meet my brother at *Vayalla Oren.*"

"That's what I thought," Kella said with a soft sigh, lowering the cup again. "I am sure things would have been more prepared had the crown prince not initiated the strike against the Regent, but as such. When we arrive in Csereth, would you like to stay with my family?"

His cup paused halfway to his mouth. "Really?"

"Of course," Kella said. "Part of my duty to the rebels is to ensure your safety, and I can hardly do so if you are left to fend for yourself in a strange city."

A'bbni flushed a bit at that. "I would be eternally grateful to you, my lord. But I do not wish to put you out."

Kella waved his hand. "Not at all. We have a large house. Obviously, your identity will have to remain a secret to all but my husband, but it is no trouble."

A'bbni knew the Arvay family had dual citizenship with Hanenea'a and Kendarin, which meant that they were subject to law under both countries' rules and regulations. Harboring a fugitive member of the goblin royal family could be considered not only an act of treason against the Emperor, but could be considered a break of the treaty between their two nations without the elven High King's permission. He wondered if the High King and Queen knew about the death of the Regent and the disappearance of his sons yet. It would take a messenger many days, if not weeks, to travel across Hanenea'a, over the isthmus, and into Kendarin, and from there, arriving at the elven royal court.

A'bbni took a sip of tea, letting the warmth soothe the tension in his chest, before replying, "I do not know if that is a good idea, my lord. I do not wish to cause an international incident."

Kella's mouth quirked a bit at that. "I am pretty sure I have already violated a dozen laws in both countries just by having you on my ship and being a member of a potential goblin rebellion. I would not have offered if I was not willing to accept the risk."

The thought of trying to find his way in Csereth with nothing but the clothing on his back was nerve-wracking. A'bbni took another swallow of his tea before replying, "I will accept your gracious offer, my lord, if you will promise me one thing."

"What is that?" Kella asked.

"Should someone discover me and come to arrest me, you will say it was my idea that I stay with you. I do not wish to put you or your family in any more danger than necessary."

Kella laughed softly, shaking his head. "You are much too altruistic, my lord."

A'bbni gave him a small smile. "My Father used to say that about me, too."

Kella nodded. "As you wish. Hopefully it will work in our favor that neither the goblins nor the elves are all that eager to try to enforce anything with our family."

"What do you mean?" A'bbni asked curiously.

Kella gave a small smile with just a hint of a smirk in it. "Of course, you know the Arvay family is very rich. But we are also rich elves in a goblin nation. The goblin enforcers would rather not create, as you said earlier, an international incident, and the elvish enforcers would rather not be on our family's bad side. And there are fewer of them on this side of the Coral Sea than in Kendarin. So, unless we murder someone in the street, it is likely that we will just be left alone. At least," Kella's eyes dropped down into his teacup, "that is how it was under your Uncle and your Father."

A'bbni could hear the uncertainty in Kella's voice. "My Cousin is unfortunately not like my Father, or even my Uncle. I... I am very worried about the future of Hanenea'a under his rule." He had not said those words out loud in a very long time, and never not in a whisper.

"As am I," Kella said, setting the cup aside and settling his hand under the swell of his baby bump. "I do not wish to see slavery return to these lands."

A'bbni nodded slowly, feeling a shiver go through his own body at the memory of En'shea telling him that he would become a slave to Hi'jan. The thought that anyone might experience that fear again made him feel sick. "I do not know what the future holds for us," he said softly, setting down his own cup and digging his fingers into the knees of his pants to stop the shaking. "But I will do everything I can to ensure that does not happen."

"I am certain that you will," Kella said with a small smile. "And I think you will find that others support you in that."

"I hope so. I'm terrible at fighting," A'bbni said, returning the smile.

Kella laughed softly, then tipped his head to the side. "I could be mistaken, but isn't today your majority day, my lord?"

A'bbni blinked, then nodded slowly. "Yes," he said softly.

"I'm sure this whole situation has been a shock to you, not the least of which is not getting to celebrate such a special occasion with your brother," Kella said softly, pouring himself another cup of tea. "I hope you will excuse my forwardness, my lord, but as a parent myself, I hope it is not inappropriate of me to say that I believe your Father would be very proud of you."

Heat burned in A'bbni's face, then his eyes. He gave Kella a grateful nod. "Thank you, my lord. That is very kind of you. I... I feel the need for some air."

"Of course," Kella replied, standing to give him a bow, which A'bbni returned before leaving the office as calmly as he could. He made his way back to his room, managing to shut the door before the tears began to fall.

CHAPTER NINE

SHI'CHEN

The morning dawned cloudy, and Shi'chen prayed that it would not rain. The last thing he wanted was rough seas. *How ironic,* he thought. At the palace, any time it rained in the central part of Hanenea'a was exciting. Here on the ocean, it was something to dread. Deana'nen had assigned him to mop the upper decks. It was not difficult, and it kept him mostly away from the railing, so he was able to pretend that he was on solid land. His stomach still dipped every time the ship rolled beneath his feet, but at least he had not thrown up this morning.

"Well, well, if it isn't the little puppy." Shi'chen felt the skin on the back of his neck crawl as he turned around to see the large goblin that he had smacked into the other day. He felt a cold pit in his stomach but forced it down. He moved back to swiping the mop across the planks, though he kept the corner of his eye on the man and heard the creak of wood as he stepped closer to him. "What's the matter, pretty boy? You had a mouth on you before."

Shi'chen bit his tongue to stop the retort forming in his throat, continuing to ignore him.

The goblin's meaty hand reached out and grabbed the top of the mop, jerking it to a stop. Shi'chen turned to face him but said nothing. The man pulled the mop from Shi'chen's hand, and he let it go, waiting for the other man to make a move. The man dropped it to the deck with a clatter, giving Shi'chen a smirk. "Better pick up your stick, puppy."

"Hey now," came a voice behind him, and Shi'chen heard Lai jump lightly down from the rigging nearby and cross over to them. "He's not worth your time, Jaa'jen," Lai said in his accented Hanen-shii, giving the large goblin a small smile.

"This has nothing to do with you, half-breed," said Jaa'jen, the insult coming out as a snarl.

Lai did not react, barely even moved except to smile a little wider. "Such an original insult. I hear it from your mother at least six times a day."

Jaa'jen let out roar, and Shi'chen could see him telegraph his punch before he threw it. Lai did too, leaning back just enough so that Jaa'jen swung past him, throwing himself off balance. Lai held out both his hands from his sides. "Come on, let's not do this."

Jaa'jen turned to Lai with fire in his yellow eyes. "I'm going to toss you off this ship myself, Ablewood."

"You're welcome to try," Lai replied, dodging back another step as Jaa'jen grabbed for him.

Shi'chen slipped his foot under the mop handle where it lay on the deck and easily kicked it up into his hand. A mop was hardly different than a spear, and he had been handling spears since he had been old enough to stand. He spun it around his back and stuck it out in Jaa'jen's path. The large goblin tripped over the end and went sprawling with a hollow thud that reverberated off the sails. Laughter met their ears from all around. Lai glanced over at Shi'chen. "I got this."

"I know you do," Shi'chen replied as Jaa'jen pushed himself to his feet, turning his murderous stare on Shi'chen.

"You think you're cute, pretty boy? Won't be so tough when I shove that stick up your ass."

Shi'chen gave the mop a spin around his hand. "You're welcome to try," he said in the same flippant tone that Lai had used moments ago.

The big goblin looked torn, suddenly realizing that there were two asses he wanted to kick but only one of him. With a growl, he made his decision and lunged at Shi'chen. Shi'chen thrust out with the handle end of the mop to catch the goblin sharply in the chest, right in the soft place between his ribs, sending him back with a grunt of air and a spot that would bruise. Jaa'jen glowered at the smaller goblin. "You think you're cute with your little stick, puppy? Too scared to face me like a man?"

"I'm not the one who attacked first," Shi'chen replied, not taking the bait. He wanted so badly to thrash this man within an inch of his pathetic life, but he was already taking a risk of revealing himself with this basic amount of defense already, and while he was not sure of the rules of the sea, fighting amongst his guards was severely punished, especially if there was a serious injury involved.

Jaa'jen feinted right, then lunged left, trying to throw Shi'chen off, but Shi'chen easily pivoted the mop and caught the goblin in the face with the wet rag end. Jaa'jen stumbled backward again, his hands fighting off the dripping pieces that clung to his face. Snarling with rage, he surged forward, lowering his body to try to get under the mop and tackle him, but Shi'chen spun and whacked him across the back with the mop handle, only hard enough to not do more than smart. He caught Lai's eye a few paces away, where the blond half-elf stood watching the exchange with a curious smile on his face, his hand on his hip cocked to one side. Jaa'jen saw it, too, and lunged at Lai instead. Shi'chen felt a moment of concern for the young man before he saw what Jaa'jen had not.

The hand not on Lai's hip came up, the gleam of a silver dagger catching the light as Jaa'jen nearly ran his throat into it. The big goblin pulled up short, but not short enough that the tip of the thin blade didn't sink slightly into the soft area under his chin, drawing an immediate stream of bright red blood that ran down his throat. His hands went up in surrender, and he backed up, yellow eyes wide, as Lai's stance had suddenly gone from casual to prepped to lunge. He seemed to realize that, while the two young men were both smaller than he, both were now armed. He backed up another step, a few drops of blood falling off his chin to land on the deck. He turned his eyes to Shi'chen, who still stood with the mop handle aimed toward his face. "You can't run forever, pup. Both you and your half-breed boyfriend better watch your back."

"Thank you for the warning," Shi'chen replied, meeting the man's steely gaze with his own. With a last glance between the two, Jaa'jen backed up another step and then turned and strode away at a pace barely slower than a run.

Only after the big goblin had disappeared inside the stairwell did Shi'chen lower the mop again and turn to Lai. Lai pulled a rag out of his sleeve and wiped the drops of Jaa'jen's blood off his dagger. "Thank you," Shi'chen said, watching Lai curiously.

Lai nodded his head, giving him a gracious smile. "I should have guessed that you could handle yourself."

"I beat men twice his size daily," Shi'chen replied, rather happy to have the chance to brag to someone that wasn't his brother about his skills.

"I may have to have you teach me," Lai replied before kneeling down to slide the dagger into his right boot.

"I can," Shi'chen said with a bright grin. "Hidden dagger, huh?"

Lai returned an equally bright smile. "That's just the one you know about. Must be prepared for anything on the ocean."

Ah, yes, they were still on water. He had forgotten, but now he felt the roll of the waves against the side of the ship, and he leaned on the mop quickly, closing his eyes to push back the wave of dizziness that hit him. "Sorry," Lai said, quickly reaching into his pocket and extracting the small flask, holding it out to him. "Here. I meant to give you this anyway. It will help with the dizziness."

Shi'chen took it and swigged a mouthful. The bitter spice burned all the way down, but his stomach almost immediately calmed. "What is it?"

"Just a special blend of herbs," Lai said. Shi'chen tried to hand him the flask back, but Lai shook his head. "It's for you."

"I can't take it from you," Shi'chen argued.

Lai held up a hand. "It's for you, to help. Please keep it."

Shi'chen gave him a grateful smile and slipped it into the pocket of his pants. "Thank you."

Lai watched Shi'chen curiously. "Where did you learn fighting? Military?"

Shi'chen quickly shook his head. "No," he said, the lie thick on his tongue.

Lai raised a brow, and Shi'chen was positive the half-elf did not believe him, but the blond just smiled and shrugged. "If you say so."

Shi'chen didn't respond. He was a terrible liar; A'bbni told him that all the time, and he was horrible at coming up with stories on the fly. He was sure his face and ear tips were bright red, giving away his guilt at the denial, so he quickly turned away and ducked his head as he went back to mopping. When he finally looked up again, Lai was gone.

The air around him felt thick, and Shi'chen gave the blanket over him an annoyed shove off. He was feeling the rocking of the ship more so in his bunk at the center of the ship, and combined with the overly warm and malodorous air from the crew all being in the berth area, he was starting to feel nauseous again. Picking his way gingerly through the swaying hammocks by the light of the few lanterns hung nearby, he moved over to the stairs and up onto the deck.

The cool night air hit his face as a welcome relief, and he took a deep breath. The salty, slimy smell of the water was still not something he was used to. He hoped that when he returned to Er'hadin – *if,* he corrected himself bitterly – he would not have to get on another ship again for a long, long time.

Only a few crew members moved about on deck, keeping the ship on course in the darkness. The sky above him was almost pitch black, each star a tiny but clear pinprick of light. He moved over to one of the crates nearby, sitting down on it to look up at them. He wondered if A'bbni was doing the same thing, and he felt a stab of homesickness in his stomach. He wished that he could sense if his brother was in trouble, but he couldn't. All he could do was hope that they would be reunited in Csereth. And then perhaps one day they would get to go home. He had no idea if that would happen. Really though, he didn't care. His Father was dead, his cousin was after their heads. What sort of life would be left for them if they returned to the imperial city?

He tugged lightly at the bandage that had been wrapped around his left forearm since the day the Emperor had arrested them. It came loose in his fingers, and he unwound it carefully. The spot where

Hi'jan had cut him had healed, better than he might have expected, with only a thin, silver scar barely gleaming under the light from the moon as proof of their fight. He smiled softly. He would have to show A'bbni when he saw him. His brother would be excited, and that would make this whole wait worth it.

He shivered as the breeze picked up again. Without the sun, it was much colder on the water, and nothing broke the wind's path as it gusted over the railing, ruffling his hair and causing his skin to prickle. Shi'chen hated being cold; he was much more at home in the warmth of the central lands of Hanenea'a.

Something moved at the corner of his vision, and he quickly turned, ready to defend himself, but his eyes caught blond hair, and the figure's hands came up in defense. "Sorry," Lai said, giving him a sheepish smile.

Shi'chen relaxed a little, settling back down on the box. "It's all right. I thought you were Jaa'jen."

"Thanks," Lai said with a good-natured roll of his eyes that made Shi'chen chuckle as the half-elf settled on a nearby crate.

"Thank you again for helping me today," Shi'chen said softly. "Where did you learn to fight?"

Lai shrugged. "All over," he said, in a tone that made Shi'chen figure he was not going to tell him much more. "How about you? You said no military."

Lai's green eyes met Shi'chen's, and he flushed, ducking his head and flattening his ears. "Uh…"

Lai gave him a small grin. "It's all right. Keep your secrets, we all have them."

Shi'chen doubted that any of Lai's secrets were even slightly similar to his own, but he was not about to keep beleaguering the point. "Why are you out here?"

Lai raised one shoulder. "Just felt like it."

And then they lapsed into silence again, the only sound the snap and creak of the sails and the continuous muted roar of the water around them. The wind ruffled Lai's hair, pulling a few of the blond strands out of his ponytail as the half-elf closed his eyes and tipped his face upward.

Shi'chen tried to keep his teeth from chattering, but he knew he was doing a terrible job of it, his arms wrapping tightly around his torso. Lai opened his eyes and glanced over at him, then frowned and grabbed a piece of canvas off a nearby pile of boxes, handing it to him. "Here. New sailors never seem to have clothing warm enough."

Shi'chen gratefully wrapped the canvas around himself, pulling it over his head and ears like a hood. If he made it to the end of this journey without frostbitten ear tips, it would be a miracle. "Thanks. I don't understand why anyone likes the cold."

Lai laughed at that, nodding in agreement. "I don't like it either."

Shi'chen smiled, curling his hands inside the canvas. "Most of Hanenea'a is very warm."

"I'll have to spend more time in it then," Lai said, leaning back on his hands. "I've barely been off ship in goblin territory."

"Why not?" Shi'chen asked curiously.

Lai shrugged one shoulder. "I don't know. I guess..." His green eyes turned thoughtfully upward toward the starry sky. "I already get treated like shit by elves and humans for being a half-breed. I don't really need goblins doing it, too."

Shi'chen frowned. "I don't think many goblins would do that. If anything, you'd interest them greatly, as most of us have never seen a human before."

"Well, you still haven't," Lai said with a grin. "I'm just some filthy," he said a word in a language that Shi'chen did not know, "that isn't elf or human."

"I don't know what you just called yourself, but it's not true," Shi'chen replied firmly. "You've treated me better than anyone else on this ship, including other goblins."

"No reason to treat anyone like shit," Lai said. "When others do it, you either do it back or be nice to everyone."

"I wouldn't blame you if you treated others like they treated you."

Lai shrugged, shifting to tuck his legs underneath him. "It's not going to change how they feel about me."

Shi'chen supposed he had a point. He readjusted the canvas around him. "How long have you been a sailor?"

"Most of my life," Lai said, brushing a bit of dirt off his pants. "Since my mother died."

Shi'chen's ears fell back sympathetically at that. "I'm sorry."

Lai shrugged. "One of many."

Shi'chen felt sure Lai was trying to say something deeper, but the words were not there. He was having trouble reading Lai's emotions and wondered if it had to do with the fact that Lai's ears did not move, the way goblin or elf ears did; he was having to rely much more on the half-elf's eyes and tone, which Lai seemed to be very aware of at all times. "What about your Father?"

Lai let out a short, bitter laugh, and Shi'chen thought back to En'shea's sharp laughter when they had asked what happened to their Father. He waited for Lai to say anything, but when he didn't, he ventured, "My parents are dead, too." He realized he had not yet said that out loud, and he forced back the sudden heat behind his eyes.

"I'm sorry," Lai said, turning to him with genuine sympathy in his eyes.

Shi'chen shook his head, taking in a sharp breath that he was sure sounded like trying to stop tears. He cleared his throat, quickly asking, "Where are you from?"

Lai gave him a look that clearly said he knew Shi'chen was changing the subject but was going with it anyway. "Yuntillo."

"Yuntillo," Shi'chen repeated, tripping over the syllables, the word feeling strange in his mouth with its odd open sounds. He was vaguely aware that was completely on the other side of the map from the lands he knew, where it was almost impossible for ships to go. He knew A'bbni would know more about it. A'bbni would find Lai fascinating, he was sure. "I'll have to introduce you to my brother. He would love to talk to you about it." *If we actually are reunited,* his mind added glumly.

"Your brother?" Lai asked, and Shi'chen realized he hadn't yet mentioned A'bbni to anyone on the ship. "Is he like you?"

"We're twins," Shi'chen said. When Lai didn't seem to understand the Hanen-shii word, Shi'chen circled his face with his finger and then held up two fingers. "Brothers, who look the same."

Lai laughed softly, shaking his blond ponytail back. "If he's like you, I like him already."

Shi'chen flushed just a bit at that, looking down at the wooden planks of the floor. "I miss him so much."

"Where is he?" Lai asked, as if he expected to hear something terrible.

"I don't know," Shi'chen said softly. "We were separated leaving Kandrea'a. He is supposed to be on another ship headed for Csereth, and I'm supposed to meet him." He took a deep breath, looking up to meet Lai's leaf-green eyes with his own glowing ember ones. "But I'm worried he's dead or captured."

"Captured? By who?" Lai asked, tipping his head curiously.

"The Emperor."

The words came out before Shi'chen had time to think about them, and he bit his tongue sharply. Fuck, he had just revealed his secret to someone who was barely more than a stranger to him because he didn't think quickly enough to come up with a half-decent lie. Though he suspected anything he had said would not be believed either; A'bbni told him several times a month he was terrible at lying. He sent a quick prayer to whichever gods might be listening that Lai would not understand his words, and for a moment it seemed like his wish might have been granted as the half-elf gazed back at him in confusion.

Shi'chen was trying to come up with a way to rephrase his words into something that sounded similar when Lai's eyes narrowed, and he repeated the words back, enunciating them as if to confirm that was what Shi'chen had said. "The Emperor is trying to capture you."

Dammit. Shi'chen let out a breath and nodded, feeling his ears flatten in a mix of fear and shame.

"Why?"

Of course, he would want to know why. And Shi'chen had no good answer he could come up with as the silence stretched between them. "Because we are next in line for the throne," he finally replied, watching Lai's face carefully.

Lai blinked. "I... I don't understand..."

"The Emperor is our Cousin," Shi'chen said, his voice soft, his ears still flat. What would the half-elf do? Certainly, he wouldn't run yelling to the captain that he had found the Regent's missing son, right? Would anyone on board even know about the situation in the palace yet?

There was a long moment of silence where Shi'chen wondered if Lai understood what he had said before the half-elf slowly ventured, "So... you are a... a prince?" He said the title in Cserethian, and Shi'chen at least understood that word from their lessons at court.

"I... suppose that's the official way of putting it," he said with a weak laugh. When Lai didn't seem to understand what he meant, Shi'chen responded simply with, "Yes."

Lai stared at him for another moment before solemnly replying, "You're not joking."

"No," Shi'chen said, shaking his head. If he had been a better actor, he might have been able to pretend it was just a jest, but Lai was watching him too closely.

Lai's eyes narrowed slightly. "Who else on this ship knows?"

"Just you," Shi'chen said softly.

Lai exhaled something that sounded like a curse in a language Shi'chen didn't understand before returning to Hanen-shii. "I guess you have to kill me now." His words sounded like a statement, not a question.

"What? Why?" Shi'chen asked in surprise.

"For learning your secret. You can't have anyone finding out, right?"

"Are you going to tell anyone?" Shi'chen asked. Damn it all to the gods, he didn't want to have to hurt the only person who had been kind to him on this ship; plus, if Lai disappeared, everyone was sure to notice his absence.

Lai shook his head slowly. "It's your secret, not mine, Cha'she."

"Shi'chen," the goblin admitted softly. "My real name is Shi'chen." It felt good to say it out loud.

"Shi'chen," Lai said thoughtfully, trying the name in his accented voice.

"But you won't tell anyone?" Shi'chen asked softly, aware that his voice had a pleading to it that made him sound much more desperate than he wanted to.

Lai shook his head. "I won't tell anyone," he replied. He gave Shi'chen a small smile and a shrug of his shoulders. "Who would I tell anyway?"

"I'm sure there would be some benefit for you if you *did* tell someone," Shi'chen said carefully, watching Lai's face in the light from the lanterns nearby.

Lai shook his head again. "I know what it's like to have a secret you're trying to hide," he said, gesturing to his short ears. "I'm not going to tell yours. It's not my secret to tell."

Shi'chen held up his right arm, elbow bent, fingers closed into a fist. Lai looked at it in confusion. "This is how goblins make a promise." Lai extended his right arm in a similar fashion, and Shi'chen touched the inside of his right wrist to the inside of Lai's, realizing this was only the second time they had actually touched skin-to-skin. Goblins were much more physical than elves, and it had been strange to not touch anyone, other than a few punches, the last few days. Lai's pale skin was warm against his own.

Lai blinked at their conjoined wrists. "Now what?"

Shi'chen opened his fingers from their fist, and Lai repeated the motion. "This shows the other that they're not hiding anything or keeping anything back. And then," he almost didn't want to break the contact, but he drew his hand back to put his own open palm over his heart. "This seals the promise."

Lai watched him, then slowly moved his own hand to his chest, smiling softly. "I promise." He reached his hand up to brush a bit of blond hair off his face. "What happens if I break the promise?"

"I suppose the gods could do something to you," Shi'chen said with a shrug. "But they probably wouldn't, so you would just lose my trust. And in this case, probably get me killed."

Lai placed his hand on his heart again. "I am very... what's the word..." He frowned, seemingly searching for the word in Hanen-shii. "Trust for my friends?"

"Loyal?" Shi'chen offered, and Lai broke into a brilliant smile.

"Yes. I'm very loyal to my friends."

Shi'chen blinked at that. "Are we friends?"

"Aren't we?" Lai asked.

Shi'chen gave him a small smile. "I guess we are. I certainly could use a friend around here."

"So, you *do* have military training," Lai replied suddenly, his eyes lighting up as he seemed to realize he had been right.

"Ah, uh…" Shi'chen flushed a little. "I'm the Captain of Honor Garrison of the imperial guard."

"A Captain," Lai said, followed by an exclamation in a language Shi'chen didn't know. "So, am I supposed to salute or bow to you?"

"Neither!" Shi'chen said quickly, eyes wide.

Lai laughed. "I'm just teasing you. Relax, Your Majesty."

"I'm not a majesty," Shi'chen said, rolling his eyes.

"So, what do they call you?"

"Captain."

"Is your brother a Captain, too?"

Shi'chen shook his head, a pang in his chest. "No. He's not a fighter. Terrible at it, in fact. But he's smart. Much smarter than me. He could speak Cserethian with you, and probably a couple other languages. He's a scholar, and he wants to be a physician."

Lai looked thoughtful. "I don't know much about goblin jobs, but aren't scholars important?"

Shi'chen nodded. "Scholars and physicians are revered because knowledge is precious. They're referred to as Your Reverence."

Lai blinked at the words, and Shi'chen tried to clarify the language. "Study is important, so those who spend time learning are…" Shi'chen wished right now he spoke Cserethian like A'bbni did so he could make Lai understand the significance of academics for goblins. "They are important," he finished awkwardly, unable to come up with a better word in Hanen-shii that Lai might know.

Lai seemed to at least understand the point behind his lack of eloquence. "I'd like to study more."

"What sort of things?" Shi'chen asked curiously.

Lai shrugged. "Anything. I can't write well. But I love history and culture."

Yes, A'bbni would definitely like Lai. "If... if we ever go home again, you could come with us."

"Home? You mean, to the imperial city?" Lai asked in surprise.

Shi'chen nodded. "Yes."

"Only if the Emperor wouldn't try to kill me, too," Lai said with a bright grin.

Shi'chen couldn't stop a bitter laugh. "We may never go back." His eyes dropped to the plank floor. "And I may never see my brother again."

"You will," Lai said in a soft but firm tone that Shi'chen had not heard from him before.

"My heart hurts without him," Shi'chen admitted, looking up into Lai's eyes.

The half-elf gazed back at him before looking away. "I understand."

Shi'chen watched Lai for a moment as the half-elf stared out over the deck to the open water. He had seen that look before. The same look that A'bbni and his Father had worn when their Mother had died during the fevers. "You lost someone."

Lai was silent for a long moment, still staring out at the water before replying without turning his head. "My husband."

Shi'chen blinked in surprise. "You were married?" Lai nodded, reaching up to brush his hand over his forehead as if pushing away strands of hair, but Shi'chen could see that it was to cover his eyes for a moment while he regained his composure. "I'm sorry. I shouldn't have said anything."

Lai quickly shook his head. "No," he said, giving Shi'chen a weak smile that didn't reach his eyes. "It's all right."

Goblin instinct kicked in, and Shi'chen reached out and took Lai's hand in his. Lai jumped, but he didn't pull back, glancing down at their joined hands. Shi'chen held him, loose enough to let him pull away if he wanted. "What was his name?"

Lai's eyes met his. "Talen. Talen Ablewood."

Lai's last name. Shi'chen felt a sharp pang in his heart at that. "How long were you together?"

"Three years," Lai said, looking back out to the water. "He died almost a year ago."

Shi'chen gave Lai's hand a gentle squeeze. "I'm so sorry."

Lai shook his head, dropping his eyes to his feet, his free hand clenching into a fist, but he didn't say anything more. Shi'chen felt a hollowness in his chest. If A'bbni died, he didn't know what he would do. He had to imagine, for Lai who had lost his mother and father, being half human in a land full of elves who did not look kindly on him, and then losing his husband, the world probably seemed like a very large and lonely place. "What... what did you do? After he... was gone?"

Lai shrugged, finally pulling his hand away from Shi'chen's, and the goblin immediately missed the warmth and connection. "Survived, I suppose."

That hurt his heart even more. Shi'chen stared down at his feet for a moment. The world already felt vast and cold without A'bbni there, and he imagined that surviving was all he would really be able to do as well. "What do you live for now?"

"I don't know," Lai admitted after a long silence. "Sometimes I think being dead would hurt less."

Shi'chen followed the line of Lai's eyes out to the water on the horizon. "But you are alive. That has to mean something." How had this turned into him trying to give Lai advice about loss?

Lai shrugged, then suddenly put on a bright smile that Shi'chen could see didn't quite reach his eyes. "I'm alive, and I've met a goblin prince. I guess that's something."

Shi'chen laughed softly. "I really hope that is not the most exciting thing that will ever happen to you."

"I would be fine if it was," Lai said with a shrug. "Sometimes surviving is enough."

"I understand that," Shi'chen replied. He tried to fight back a sudden yawn but was unsuccessful.

Lai glanced over at him. "Think you'll be able to sleep, now that someone else knows your secret?"

Shi'chen rolled his eyes. "Secrets be damned, I just want to get off the water."

"Did that medicine help you?"

"It did. Thank you," Shi'chen said, giving the half-elf a grateful nod.

Lai smiled back. "I'll have the physician make more for you if you want."

"Thank you," Shi'chen said. "Are you going to sleep, too?"

"In a bit," Lai said with a shrug. "Going to sit out here a while longer."

"Do you want me to stay with you?"

"No. Go get some sleep, Your Majesty."

Shi'chen rolled his eyes as he folded up the canvas that had kept him surprisingly warm. "You're a pain in the ass, Lai."

"I've been told that many times," Lai said with a smile that reached his eyes this time. "Good night."

"Good night," Shi'chen replied before turning and heading back toward the stairs to go below. Before he descended, he glanced back to see Lai had moved to lean against the railing, gazing out at the dark horizon line that was barely distinguishable sea from sky in the blackness, the way he had looked at the stars in the hopes he would feel his twin doing the same. He headed back down to his bunk, hoping he would never have to feel the pain that Lai did from losing the person he loved most.

CHAPTER TEN

A'BBNI

The *Hiyallen Wordan* docked in Csereth just shortly after lunch. A'bbni stood by the window in his cabin, watching people bustle around on the docks, disembarking from ships, unloading baggage and freight, greeting each other. He watched a goblin woman with a little girl run across a dock and hug a tall brunette elf that must have been her father. He scooped her up and gave her a kiss, then put his arm around the woman and kissed her, too. A'bbni felt a pang in his heart as he watched, and several unexpected tears suddenly landed on his cheeks. He swiped them away, continuing to scan the docks.

He did not expect to see his brother. They had left before Shi'chen's ship had by almost a full day, and passenger ships tended to be faster than merchant ships, as they were not as heavily loaded with cargo. They had seen a few ships at a distance on the sea, but ocean travel was so common, it was impossible to say if any of them had been Shi'chen's ship. A'bbni was just thankful they had not run into any pirates, though he suspected those were less likely to hit passenger ships than trade ships anyway.

It was very late in the afternoon before Kella was ready to disembark, as he had paperwork and other things to go over with the captain and the dock crew, but eventually he summoned A'bbni to meet him on the deck, and together they walked down to meet a black carriage pulled by two all-black horses. The driver was a middle-aged man in some sort of livery, half-goblin and half-elf from the looks of his coloring, and if he found anything odd about Lord Kella escorting a young goblin nobleman into the carriage, he didn't show it.

Kella sorted through several files as they drove, and A'bbni took the time to look out the carriage windows. He had never been to Csereth, or even more than a few days' horse ride outside of the imperial city. Due to its heavy elven influence, Csereth was much different than the goblin cities he was used to. This close to the water, everything was brighter and more built up, no sand dunes or canyons in sight except for the sandy beaches at the edge of the water. He found himself enthralled watching several street performers doing flips as they passed by. If his brother had been by his side right now, this would have been an exciting adventure.

Lord Kella's house was not far from the docks, but the street it was on was surprisingly quiet for being in the midst of the city. There was a white stone wall with a wrought iron gate around it, which A'bbni suspected also had to do with the privacy afforded them by the authorities. Goblins, at least, very rarely had fences or walls around their homes. Except, of course, for the palace, he reminded himself. Closed off from the world.

The carriage pulled to a halt, and the driver helped Kella down from the carriage seat, then did the same for A'bbni, nodding his head in deference to the young noble. Kella's house was only two stories tall, like the palace, but it was long and deep, with beautiful glass windows, some stained, others clear, that glinted in the late afternoon sun, the white of its walls not quite blinding. The area between the wall and the house was manicured green grass, and A'bbni tried very hard not to stare at it. The palace had very little grass around it, and what was there grew wild and natural, not even and cared for. Cserethians definitely lived much differently with better access to water and port trade.

Kella led him inside, and A'bbni was not surprised to find that the inside was decorated in a style very similar to Kella's office on the ship. Despite being from a different culture, its lavishness likely rivaled the palace, and A'bbni could not help but wonder just how rich the Arvay family actually was. He had heard stories, but seeing it for himself was entirely different.

The sound of pattering feet came across the dark wood floors, and two little elven children came sprinting down the hallway. The older one was almost an exact replica of Kella, with black hair and brilliant blue eyes, while the younger one had light brown hair and hazel eyes. The older one clutched a white and orange kitten in his arms, its fat tummy and hind legs dangling awkwardly. "Papa!" they both cheered in almost unison.

Kella laughed and dropped to a knee to embrace them, first the younger girl, then the boy, using one hand to support the struggling kitten. "Cressus, use both hands, please."

"Sorry," the boy said, shifting to hold the kitten like he was balancing a full glass of water in his hands.

The little girl gazed at A'bbni with wide eyes, sucking on a finger in her mouth as she stared at him over Kella's shoulder. He gave her a soft smile, and she giggled shyly and buried her face in Kella's chest. Kella turned to A'bbni with a proud smile. "These are my children. This is Cressus," he motioned to the boy with the kitten, "and Nadria. Children, this is Lord An-Bersha. He is going to be staying with us for a while."

"A pleasure to meet you, my lord," Cressus said, giving a perfunctory bow and almost losing the wiggling kitten.

"The pleasure is mine," A'bbni replied, giving him a bow in return.

The little girl tipped her head curiously. "Are you a whole goblin?"

"Nadria!" Kella chastised.

A'bbni laughed softly, shaking his head at Kella. "It is all right. Yes, I am," he said to the little girl, who blushed and giggled again.

Kella stood, giving A'bbni an apologetic smile before turning to the children. "Go wash up for dinner, and make sure that kitten gets back to its mother."

"Yes, Papa," Cressus said, letting go of the kitten's bottom half again to take Nadria's hand and lead her away down the hall. She stared back at A'bbni, not watching where she was going until her brother nearly ran her into a table, at which point she removed her finger from her mouth and followed after him.

"They're adorable," A'bbni said, giving Kella a smile. He had been around some children in the palace, but most of them were older, in training to be servants. A few of the nobles had young children, but he didn't interact with them on a regular basis, usually only in the process of performing his physician duties. Now that he thought about it, it seemed rather odd that he had spent most of his childhood surrounded by adults, other than his cousins. Perhaps that was just the nature of palace life.

"Thank you," Kella said as the tap of heeled boots came down the stairs from the upper floor. A'bbni glanced up to see a handsome elven man with light brown hair and gray eyes coming down the stairs and guessed that was Lord Quenn, Kella's husband. He was proven right when Kella moved to him to give him a soft embrace, and he kissed Kella's dark hair. "My husband, Lord Quenn de Kove. Love, this is Re'len An-Bersha. He'll be staying with us." A'bbni saw Kella's eyes meet Quenn's in a look that clearly said he would answer questions later but needed Quenn to accept the current explanation.

Quenn gave a bow to A'bbni, who returned it with a bow of his own. "A pleasure, my lord." Quenn's voice was lower than he expected, but his face was kind. A'bbni wondered if he was not the first person Kella had come home with after a voyage.

"I am grateful to you and your husband for allowing me to stay in your home," A'bbni said, and Quenn seemed to brighten at his flawless Cserethian.

"I'm sure you would like to refresh yourself, my lord," Kella said as an elven servant approached. "Garina will show you to a room so you may rest, and then will summon you for dinner."

"Thank you," A'bbni replied, giving another grateful bow to the dark-haired noble before following after the woman to a guest room up on the second floor. Surprisingly, or maybe not surprisingly, considering how organized Kella was, the small trunk of clothing from the ship that Kella had furnished him with was already in his room. It was unpacked, some of the clothing hung up in the wardrobe, some of it seeming to be gone for washing.

"May I bring you anything, my lord?" Garina asked with a polite curtsy.

"No, thank you," A'bbni said, giving her a gracious smile, which she returned before turning to head back down the stairs, once again leaving him alone in a strange, new place, far away from home.

Dinner with Kella and his family was enjoyable enough, but his mind was miles away, wondering how Shi'chen was doing, wondering what was happening back in Er'hadin, wondering what their next steps would be.

A'bbni wasn't even sure how much he ate or what it tasted like, feeling a queasiness in his stomach that would not abate.

After dinner, Kella offered to take a walk with A'bbni in the gardens at the rear of the house to discuss future plans, and A'bbni gratefully accepted. Kella gave him a cloak to pull on, as the night had become quite cool now that they were further north. They walked together through the manicured gardens with its stone benches, carefully groomed topiaries, and beds of flowers, most of which were starting to lose their luster with the cold weather. Kella was silent, letting A'bbni compose his thoughts as they walked.

"I must confess, I feel very lost," A'bbni said, pausing by a stone figure of a cat perched on the edge of a low wall, reaching up his hand to lightly touch the cat's cold ear.

"That is understandable, my lord," Kella said, moving to sit on a nearby bench. "Your whole world was turned upside-down in a matter of moments."

A'bbni nodded slowly, stroking the cat's stone muzzle. "I usually have a plan, but at this time, I am entirely at the mercy of yourself and the members of the rebellion."

"It will take time for things to come together," Kella said softly. "But I promised you, Your Reverence, I would not abandon you, and I will not."

A'bbni turned to look at Kella, smiling gratefully, though he could feel that the smile didn't reach his eyes. "Thank you."

"Tomorrow I will send word of your arrival to our contacts here. I will also send a letter to *Vayalla Oren* with information for your brother when he arrives, and I will go to the port master to find out when his ship is expected."

"I do not know how I can ever repay you for all you have done for me," A'bbni said, moving to sit on the bench next to the dark-haired elf.

Kella smiled gently at him. "I do not expect any sort of payment, Your Reverence. I believe in maintaining peace in Hanenea'a, and by extension, Kendarin. I had to put blind faith in your Father, and his sons whom I had never met, based on nothing more than principle. But now that I have met you, I see that my trust was not misplaced. If your brother is even half as kind and compassionate as you, either of you would make a fine Emperor."

A'bbni gave Kella another smile that did not make it past his lips, his ears drooping a bit. "I will do my best not to let you down."

Kella slowly reached out and laid a hand on top of A'bbni's. A'bbni glanced up in surprise at the touch, but Kella's hand was warm and gentle as he curled his fingers around the goblin's hand and gave it a reassuring squeeze. "It is not I that you should aim to please, Your Reverence. I am no one of importance when it comes to the affairs of Hanenea'a. I would hope your focus would be on those less fortunate than I." He gave A'bbni a slightly ironic smile that indicated he knew that was pretty much the entire population.

A'bbni gave Kella's hand a grateful squeeze in return. "As always, I appreciate your wisdom."

Kella laughed, patting A'bbni's hand with his other free one before standing up. "I must go say goodnight to my children. Do you wish to come in?"

"I think I'll stay out here a little longer," A'bbni said softly. "Thank you, Lord Kella."

"Of course. Good night, Your Reverence."

"Good night." A'bbni watched Kella return to the house, pulling the cloak tighter around his shoulders, glad that the sting from the wounds there seemed to be almost gone. He gazed up at the stars that blinked overhead, so many he couldn't even count them, wondering if Shi'chen was looking at the stars, too.

CHAPTER ELEVEN

SHI'CHEN

The next few days passed without incident, but Shi'chen still felt himself jump whenever someone approached him too quickly. The weather was calm, and Shi'chen did not think he had ever been so grateful for it not to rain. Captain Harrana, the red-haired elf Shi'chen had seen the first day, was a very competent leader and directed the crew on catching the wind that gusted over the water. "If she gets her ship into port early, everyone gets a bonus," Lai explained one afternoon as he and Shi'chen sat side by side mending a ripped sail. Lai had a pair of dark glasses on over his eyes, which Shi'chen had seen some crew members, mainly elves, wear when it was extremely bright out. "Since the continents rely so heavily on trade, the faster the better."

That much he understood. There had been stories floating around the scholars about new inventions that were starting to show up that sailed in the sky using some sort of gas combined with the wind to move, but almost all of it was still experimental. Even A'bbni had never actually seen one in person. Shi'chen realized with a start that that was the first time today he had thought about his brother, and a pang of homesickness and longing made his chest tighten. "Would you sail back to the human lands?" he asked to take his mind off thoughts of his twin.

Lai shook his head. "There's nothing for me there. Maybe if trade happened more there, I would, but just as a job, not to stay."

"Is it hard to not have a place to call home?" Shi'chen asked.

Lai shook his head. "Not really. When you're always moving, it's easier to not get attached to places or people."

"I think that would be hard for me," Shi'chen mused, then winced as he accidentally jabbed the heavy needle into his thumb. "I like having familiar things around me."

Lai blinked at that. "I don't understand."

"I like… knowing where I am."

Lai nodded thoughtfully. "Your world must be much smaller than mine."

"What do you mean?" Shi'chen asked, examining his thumb and glad to not find any blood.

"You live in a palace," Lai said, dropping his voice so only Shi'chen could hear him. "Do you leave it very often?"

Shi'chen blinked. He had never really thought about it that way. "No…"

Lai gave him a pointed look. "So, your world is small. I have no home, but I've seen much more of the world."

Shi'chen mused on that for several moments. "You're right," he said at last.

"I know," Lai said with his usual bright grin. "It's not a bad thing. You like having a home. I like seeing the world."

"Would you ever stay in one place?"

Lai shrugged his shoulders. "Maybe one day. If I had a reason to stay."

"You and Talen didn't stay in one place?" Lai jerked slightly at the sudden name, and Shi'chen flinched. "I'm sorry! I shouldn't have brought him up."

Lai shook his head, his blond ponytail swinging. "It's all right. I just wasn't ready for that question."

"You don't have to answer it," Shi'chen replied, feeling guilty he had caused his friend any sort of distress.

Lai shook his head again. "I can. Talen was a sailor, too. After we met, we worked on ships together. If I had wanted to stay some place, I think he would have been fine with that. We talked about giving up sailing."

"May I ask how he died?" Shi'chen asked softly.

"There was a bad storm," Lai said, his eyes on the horizon behind his dark glasses, his hands gone still. "He was swept overboard."

Shi'chen felt his stomach drop. He couldn't imagine anything more terrifying than hitting the black water of the roiling ocean, especially as he did not know how to swim. "Fuck," he murmured softly. "I'm sorry."

Lai shrugged, turning his eyes down to the sail in his hands. "Hazard of a life at sea."

"That's terrifying. I never wanted to be on a ship," Shi'chen admitted.

Lai let out a soft chuckle. "I could tell. First time I saw you, I knew you were not meant to be a sailor."

"Yeah? What did you think I was meant to be?" Shi'chen asked, raising a brow.

"An emperor," Lai said with a playful mock bow that no one would mistake for seriousness.

Shi'chen rolled his eyes, glancing around, but no one was paying attention to them. "What will you do when we get to Csereth?" he asked.

Lai shrugged. "Find another ship to work on, most likely. What will you do?"

"I'm supposed to meet my brother when I get there. At *Vayalla Oren*." He had made sure to memorize the name, staring at the paper every evening, as if he could see his brother inside of it.

"Have you ever been to Csereth?" Lai asked. Shi'chen shook his head slowly. "Do you want some help when you get there?"

Shi'chen blinked. "Do... do you mean you?"

"I mean, I can ask Jaa'jen, but I'm pretty sure he wouldn't be interested," Lai replied with a perfectly innocent smile.

Shi'chen rolled his eyes. "Your sarcasm reminds me of my brother sometimes."

"And I want to meet your brother," Lai added with another bright grin. "I have never met twins before."

Shi'chen smiled at that. "You'd like him. And he'd like you. But be prepared, he will ask you a thousand questions about the human lands."

Lai shrugged. "As long as he doesn't chase me off, I'll answer any questions he has."

"He would never," Shi'chen said. "He's a much nicer person than I am."

Lai laughed brightly at that, pulling his knife from his belt to cut the end of the thread he was sewing. "You have to be tough, Captain, otherwise your troops will eat you alive."

"Definitely true," Shi'chen said. He stilled his hands to look into Lai's shaded eyes. "I would like it if you came with me to find my brother when we get to Csereth."

"Then I will," Lai replied.

Shi'chen felt his heart give a little hop in his chest. He knew A'bbni would find Lai fascinating for a number of reasons, and it would be nice to not be completely alone as he tried to reunite with his brother in a strange city. "Thank you."

Lai nodded and got to his feet, brushing off his pants and his hands. "Want to try the rigging with me?"

Shi'chen blinked. "You mean, climb up there?" he asked, turning his eyes toward the mass of canvas and rope that stretched across the sky.

Lai nodded, leaning a shoulder against a crate. "Scared of heights?"

"No," Shi'chen said quickly. "I just have never climbed rigging before."

"Your soldier training is so incomplete," Lai lamented, gazing at Shi'chen over the rim of his darkened glasses. "Come on, I won't let you fall."

"I am a guard, not a soldier," Shi'chen said with a slight huff that made Lai laugh. He stood and moved over next to Lai, who handed him a pair of leather gloves before he grabbed the netted rope ladder that led up one of the masts. Quick as flash, Lai was up the rope and balanced on the first platform, gazing down at him. Shi'chen pulled on Lai's gloves and grabbed the rope ladder to follow him, surprised at how tough it was to pull himself up. By the time he reached the top, his hands and shoulders were protesting. "How do you do this all day?" he asked as Lai took his hand and pulled him up next to him.

"A lot of practice," Lai replied.

Shi'chen wrapped his hand around the railing of the platform. He was feeling the sway of the ship even more up here, with nothing but air and rope around him. "Have you ever fallen?" he asked, gazing at the deck below them that suddenly seemed much further away than it had when he had been looking up at the rigging from below.

"Yeah, lots of times," Lai replied with a shrug.

"You're awfully nonchalant about that."

"I'm what?"

"You act like falling is not important," Shi'chen clarified, his hand wrapping around the rope that ran up the main mast.

"It is, but it's what happens when you're a sailor. You learn to catch yourself," Lai replied, grabbing one of the rigging ropes, and before Shi'chen could do anything, Lai had stepped off the platform and swung himself around the rope, letting go to suddenly drop several feet, and caught himself on the rope ladder with both hands.

"Stop that!" Shi'chen said, eyes wide. "You're going to give me a heart attack!"

Lai laughed and climbed back up next to him, sitting down on the platform, rubbing his hands on his jerkin. "It's better to have gloves on so you don't tear up your hands."

"Sorry," Shi'chen said, glancing down at the gloves Lai had loaned him as he sat down next to him.

Lai shook his head. "I've been doing this so long, I hardly feel it anymore."

Shi'chen was starting to appreciate how much work went into sailing a ship and bringing its cargo and crew safely into port. "When we get back to the palace, I'll get to brag a little more."

"About what?" Lai asked, brushing a few strands of blond hair out of his eyes.

Shi'chen gave him a grin. "Your skills may be on rope, but mine are on the ground. I've been fighting with a spear since I was a kid. What I did to Jaa'jen was nothing."

Lai smirked. "Nothing, huh?"

"I'm not exactly trying to show off my training," Shi'chen replied, rolling his eyes. "You already guessed I was military from a few strikes. But I'm one of the youngest Captains to ever be recruited to the palace guards."

"How old were you?" Lai asked curiously.

"Seventeen," Shi'chen said, trying hard not to preen but not quite succeeding.

Lai let out a soft whistle. "And you're how old now?"

"Nineteen. Wait..." Shi'chen frowned. His sense of time had left him since he had been on the ship, each day running into the next. "What day is it?"

"Fifth day of the third season."

Shi'chen sighed and rubbed at his eyes. "The third day was my birthday. So, I'm twenty." The age at which he would be considered a full adult in goblin society. The age that En'shea would be to take the throne from the Regent if he had not killed him. If Shi'chen had been at the palace with his brother, there would have been a massive celebration held for them. He took a deep breath that shuddered more than he meant it to. He hadn't even remembered the date for the sake of his brother.

Lai rested a hand on his shoulder, giving it a light squeeze. "You're pretty mature, even though you're barely an adult. And you've had to deal with a whole lot of shit in a short time. Just because you're young doesn't mean you haven't worked your ass off to get where you are."

Shi'chen lifted his eyes to give Lai a small smile. "I know my brother and I have had more opportunities than most. My Father always reminded us that we have to use that to benefit our people. Unfortunately, that lesson got lost on our Cousin."

"Some people are just bad people," Lai said with a shrug. "No matter what you do, they will never be good."

Shi'chen opened his mouth to respond, but a sudden huge crash from somewhere below deck shook the ship all the way up to where they sat. "Shit," Lai said, leaping up. "Come on." He hurried down the rope ladder and was almost to the bottom before Shi'chen was on his feet. There was chaos on the deck below him as people rushed toward the entrance of the cargo hold from all directions. Shi'chen followed Lai down, being careful not to go faster than his experience would allow. He jumped the last few feet onto the deck and took off after Lai.

The assembled crew was murmuring, and Shi'chen caught words in Hanen and Cserethian that several large crates had fallen, trapping crew members underneath them. He couldn't see Lai and nudged his way through the crowd to the darkened stairwell. Suddenly, Deana'nen came sprinting up the stairs, her mismatched eyes casting around the assembled crew before pointing to Shi'chen and a female elf standing nearby. "You two, come with me."

Shi'chen quickly followed on her heels down the dark stairs. Deana'nen talked as she went, almost tripping over her words from speaking so quickly. "Crates fell, there's three crew members trapped behind them. I need you two to get under them to help from the inside."

"Yes, ma'am," Shi'chen and the elf said as they hit the bottom of the stairs and entered the cargo hold. The massive crates had snapped the ropes securing them to the wall, and two of them had fallen into another stack, sending multiple pallets toppling. Several of the boxes were split open, the scent of tea and spices making the air thick. The fallen boxes leaned precariously against one another, taller than any of the crew members by a good two feet, but he quickly realized that the crew could not go up and over because of how unbalanced the boxes were, which could cause the entire stack to collapse. Behind the wall of wood and iron, he could hear someone moaning in pain. He glanced around and spotted Lai with a group of sailors nearby, working to secure the crates that were in danger of falling into the space behind the pile-up, where the trapped crew members were.

Deana'nen grabbed a lantern and held it up so they could see better. There were a few gaps between boxes where corners jutted and balanced against other boxes, looking more than a little unsteady. "Someone is trapped, but we don't know how bad," she said, turning to Shi'chen and the elf. "They need help getting him loose and getting all of them out of the way of these boxes in case they fall."

"Yes, ma'am," the elf said. She was maybe an inch shorter than Shi'chen, with chestnut hair in a coiled braid across her head. She turned to Shi'chen and pointed to one of the openings. "This looks like the best way to get in."

"Agreed," Shi'chen said. His heart was racing in his chest, so loud it almost overpowered the shouts of the crew around them. He pulled off Lai's gloves and set them aside.

The elf got down on her stomach and began to inch her way under the box corner. She barely fit, pushing herself along with her booted toes and her arms until the light from Deana'nen's lantern no longer hit her. Then, Shi'chen heard her call, "I'm in, watch that corner at the end!"

He got down and pushed himself into the small space, sending up a prayer to any gods who might be watching to not let the boxes unbalance and crush him. The sounds around him were muffled as he got entirely under the oversize crate, pulling himself along with his forearms, more than a little glad they did this in training on the sand. At least the wood beneath him was solid. Deana'nen had definitely chosen him and the elven girl because of how slight they were; anyone bigger than him would not be able to get through the small spaces created by the fallen cargo.

Something creaked, and he braced himself for the box to fall, but it didn't. He let out a breath and dragged himself forward. As he reached under the other side, the girl grabbed his hand and gave him a tug to assist him, helping him to narrowly miss the broken board with nails that was hanging right over the edge, one of the nails snagging his shirt and ripping it just a little. He got to his feet and surveyed the area.

There were three crew members penned in by fallen boxes. The two standing were a half-goblin woman with locs and an elven man with dark hair. The woman had blood running from a cut on her forehead over her eye, and the man had a few cuts and rips in his shirt, but they seemed to be all right. Shi'chen turned to check the person on the ground and found himself face to face with Jaa'jen. The big goblin was lying on his back, and Shi'chen quickly realized why the man had been moaning. One of the crates had landed on his left leg and crushed it beneath its weight. One of the boxes that made up the tunnel they had used was propped against it at a precarious angle.

"Shit," he muttered softly, looking around. The other crates seemed relatively stable for now.

The elf girl turned to him. "Should we get the other two out of here first?"

Shi'chen shook his head. "No," he said. "We need to get him out from under the crate." He vaguely remembered a conversation with A'bbni, maybe a year ago, when his brother had learned that an extremity being crushed could result in organ failure if the person was not promptly un-trapped. He couldn't remember how long it was, but he already knew they were losing precious minutes.

His eyes roamed over the boxes that were supporting each other. "If we can lever that up just enough, we should be able to pull him out without that whole pile coming down." He pointed to the half-goblin woman. "Grab his arms. As soon as I tell you, pull as hard as you can, and drag him as far back as you can, got it?" She nodded numbly. Shi'chen turned to the two elves. "Don't push it," he warned, "or that is coming down. Just lift straight up. Once Jaa'jen is free, go that way." He pointed toward the back of the tumble of boxes where the woman would drag Jaa'jen.

The two elves nodded, and Shi'chen moved over by the box that pinned Jaa'jen, digging his fingers under it. The elves squatted next to him, sliding their fingers in, too. Shi'chen glanced over his shoulder at the half-goblin woman to make sure she was ready, then turned to the elves. "On three," he said, taking a deep breath. With a quick count, he put all his strength into lifting the crate up. He felt Jaa'jen jerk, and then the goblin's mangled leg slid past him. "Drop and back up on three," he said. On three, the crate hit the deck with a crunch, and all of them back-pedaled quickly. One of the other boxes being supported by the angled one suddenly slid, and Shi'chen tackled the dark-haired man out of the way as the box hit the floor with a crash and the sound of glass shattering. He threw up his hand to block the dust that went flying, momentarily blinding him, the reverberation of the box hitting the floor going through him like a wave hitting him in the chest.

After a moment, he looked around. The five of them were against the pile of boxes at the back of the space, but none of them were trapped under any of them, at least. Jaa'jen was pale, his leg a mess of blood and tattered fabric. Shi'chen wished A'bbni was there; his brother would know what to do to help him. "Stay here," he said to the group, moving over to carefully pull himself up onto one of the box piles that seemed fairly sturdy. He could see the crew where the boxes had initially fallen, still working to try to secure cargo, and he caught Lai's eye to give him a nod before turning to survey the rest of the area. If they could get over the boxes he balanced on, the rest of the cargo hold was intact, with walkways and another stairwell at the other end.

He leaned over the boxes to the four sailors below. "Come on," he said, holding out his hand to the half-goblin woman. She took his hand, and he pulled her up. She scrambled up over the box edge. "Can you two hand him up to us?" he asked, holding out his hands toward Jaa'jen. The two elves pulled Jaa'jen to his feet – well, foot, Shi'chen realized dryly – and he reached up trembling arms to them. Shi'chen grabbed his wrist and locked his hands around it, and he and the woman pulled Jaa'jen up onto the box. The woman jumped down on the other side, and Shi'chen shifted to slide Jaa'jen down by his arms into hers, Jaa'jen's massive bulk straining his muscles as he carefully lowered him down. The goblin grunted as the woman caught him and laid him heavily on the wood floor.

Shi'chen turned as the elven man gave the girl a foot lift with his hands, and Shi'chen grabbed her and pulled her up, and then they pulled the man up with them. The boxes wobbled, and Shi'chen held his breath, but they settled again, and the three carefully made their way down the pile to the path. Without prompting, they all slid their hands under Jaa'jen and lifted him up, carrying him across the hold and up the stairs.

The sunlight blinded him when they hit the deck, and Shi'chen had never been so glad to inhale sea air. Once Jaa'jen had been set down, he doubled over, breathing hard, leaning on the stair railing. Several people ran over, but Shi'chen barely noticed them. Jaa'jen and the two others were whisked away toward the physician's quarters, and the female elf stumbled over to a half-goblin man who might have been her boyfriend. Shi'chen lowered himself to sit on the top step, burying his face in his grimy hands and trying to calm his racing heart.

He didn't know how long he sat like that before someone sat down next to him and put a hand lightly on his shoulder. It was Lai. "Hey. You all right?"

"Yeah," Shi'chen mumbled into his hands. "You?"

"I'm fine," Lai said. "You sure you're all right? Do you need to see the physician?"

"No. No, I'm fine," Shi'chen insisted, pulling his hands away from his face to look into Lai's eyes. The half-elf wore the same concerned look that A'bbni wore when

Shi'chen injured himself. "I'm fine," he repeated again. "Just... a little shaken, is all."

Lai nodded, giving his shoulder a gentle squeeze. "That was pretty impressive, Captain."

"Is he going to be all right?" Shi'chen asked, taking the handkerchief that Lai pulled out of his pocket and offered him, wiping at his face with slightly trembling hands.

Lai shrugged a bit, looking more melancholy than Shi'chen had ever seen him look. "Hard to say. That kind of injury can do a lot of damage. He at least has a chance because you got him out so fast." He sighed and tossed his hair back. "But this is going to delay us. When the ship has an accident like this, the captain heads to the nearest port for medical attention and to do an evaluation of the inventory."

Shi'chen felt his stomach sink. "How long will that take?"

"A couple days at least, maybe more," Lai said sympathetically.

Shi'chen groaned and swiped at his face with the handkerchief again. "Dammit..."

"We have a couple options," Lai said. "Once we land, we can leave if you want, and travel to Csereth on our own. Otherwise, we can wait."

"How far are we from Csereth?"

"Nearest port is Genhin'saa, so four days or so by horse."

Shi'chen swore under his breath and swiped a couple strands of hair out of his eyes. He knew sailing was dangerous, and he could hardly be mad at the crew for the accident, but it was one more step that was going to keep him away from his brother longer. "I don't know," he groaned.

"We'll figure it out," Lai said, and Shi'chen found himself oddly grateful that Lai had said 'we' and not 'you.' Lai was not planning to abandon him.

Deana'nen suddenly strode up to them. "Cha'she," she said, and Shi'chen jumped at the unexpected name, turning to her.

"Yes, ma'am."

"Good work," she said, holding out her hand. He took it, and she gave it a firm squeeze. "Jaa'jen is asking for you."

"For me?" Shi'chen asked in surprise. Deana'nen nodded, and Shi'chen followed after her, Lai trailing him, to the physician's quarters.

The elven man and the half-goblin woman were sitting on benches and talking softly with several of the senior crew, their wounds having been bandaged. Deana'nen moved further into the room, gesturing them over to where Jaa'jen lay on the long examination table. His pants leg had been torn away, but the physician had draped a white sheet over him so no one could see his injuries. His goblin-gray skin was oddly pale, sweat beaded on his face and neck. The rise and fall of his chest was uneven. When Shi'chen approached, his yellow eyes opened, a little unfocused, and Shi'chen realized he probably had been given something for the pain.

"Hey, pup," Jaa'jen said, his voice rough as Shi'chen and Lai stopped by his side.

Shi'chen had no idea what to say, so he simply asked, "How are you doing?"

"Hurts like a motherfucker," Jaa'jen grunted, but then he gave a small smile, and Shi'chen found himself smiling back. "Look, kid, I'm not good at apologies. But I wanted to say thank you."

Shi'chen shook his head. "No need. I wasn't going to leave you there."

"Yeah, but you could have," Jaa'jen replied, every word sounding like a strain. "So, thanks. And I'm sorry. You're a good kid."

Shi'chen felt a little surge of pride. "Save your strength," he said, reaching out to place his hand on Jaa'jen's shoulder.

Jaa'jen nodded slowly, glancing over at Lai. "I'm sorry to you, too, Ablewood."

Lai shrugged, giving him his usual sunny smile. "No hard feelings."

Jaa'jen grimaced in what was probably as close as he could get to a smile before the physician appeared and ushered them away. Once back in the sunlight, Lai moved over to lean heavily against the railing. "Fuck... He's not going to make it."

Shi'chen felt his stomach drop as he stood next to Lai. While he didn't like Jaa'jen, he would never have wanted actual harm to come to him. "What will happen if he dies?"

"If he has family, the owners of the ship will pay out a sum to them for compensation," Lai said, digging his thumbnail into the wood of the railing, not meeting Shi'chen's eyes. "That's about it."

"How often does that happen?" Shi'chen asked.

Lai shrugged. "It's not every voyage. But it's not uncommon."

Shi'chen was suddenly profoundly grateful for Lai's experience. He would have had no idea how to handle any of this without him, especially if the ship had gone to a different port. He laid a hand on Lai's shoulder reassuringly. "Thank you for being there for me."

Lai glanced over at him in surprise, then smiled softly. "You're welcome."

Jaa'jen died that evening, just as the ship pulled into the harbor at Genhin'saa.

CHAPTER TWELVE

A'BBNI

The first few days at Lord Kella's house had A'bbni's anxiety through the roof. He did his best to control it, but with no word from the port master of the planned arrival of the cargo ship, his mind spun to every possible worst-case scenario. The ship had gone down in a storm. The ship had been attacked by pirates. The ship had been stopped by imperial guards. The ship had caught fire. Every scenario was worse than the last, and he spent his days restlessly pacing from his room to the library to the dining room to the parlor, back to his room again. He tried to find solace in reading, as Lord Kella had an amazing assortment of books, but he couldn't focus, and he found himself reading the same page for almost an hour before he gave up.

Cressus and Nadria were usually with their tutors during the day, but in the evenings, they often came to find him, and A'bbni was at least temporarily distracted from his thoughts by letting them show him their rooms, their toys, their books, the mama cat and her four fat kittens that slept in the kitchen. He had offered to Kella and Quenn to stay in his room if they didn't want him wandering, but both had reassured him that his presence was welcome. Cressus and Nadria at least gave him something to do besides fret.

After the second day of pacing the halls like a lost spirit, Kella let A'bbni know that he had heard from the port master that the *Dianol Elledun* had been delayed due to an accident on board. He had no more information than that, and A'bbni had to go take a walk in the garden to clear his head as his thoughts spiraled into the abyss of his mind. All he could do was wait, and worry, and pray to the gods that his brother was all right. He wished he and Shi'chen could feel each other's pain in the literal sense that En'shea had mentioned, so he would at least know if his brother was all right.

The news out of Er'hadin was not great as other ships arrived in port and messengers reached Csereth by traveling over land. The story being spread was that the Regent and the entire Imperial Senate had been killed by a rebel group and that Captain Shi'chen Er-Ha'sen and Reverence A'bbni Er-Ha'sen, sons of the Regent and Cousins to the Emperor, had planned and led the rebellion, then disappeared when they failed to kill the crown prince, too. A substantial reward had been offered by the Emperor for anyone with information that would lead to their arrest.

A'bbni wondered how many people might actually believe that he and Shi'chen had murdered their own Father in a bid for the throne. Anyone who knew them would know that the entire concocted plot was completely ridiculous, but he realized, how many people in Hanenea'a did not know him or his brother, or even the Emperor? The royals were not part of the day-to-day lives of most goblins. He suspected that many people would also be inclined to believe the worst things they heard about the imperial families, assuming their lives to be nothing but endless parties, drunken orgies, and literal backstabbing to gain power. Unfortunately, that last one was not entirely untruthful, at least not since their Uncle had died and left Prii'sha and En'shea as the successors. And when En'shea began reinstating some of the barbaric laws of the past, A'bbni had no doubt that the common people would have very few reasons to trust the imperial families again, and every reason to gain favor with the Emperor by turning them in. That sent him down another anxiety-filled vortex that he was only able to break free of when Lord Kella had one of the apothecaries make a sleeping draught for him.

The fourth day brought a letter, addressed to A'bbni's merchant son alias, bearing a seal that he vaguely recognized as one of the Cserethian noble families. He took the letter curiously from Lord Kella, breaking the seal to pull out a single sheet of parchment.

Greetings to your excellency. The Council is glad to hear of your safe arrival in Csereth. We know his grace has been delayed, but we wish to speak with you as soon as possible. Please come to the address below tomorrow at mid-day, that we may formulate a plan.

A'bbni handed the letter to Kella with a frown. "That is not a lot of information."

Kella nodded. "That address is an old bookkeepers' building. I have been there once and met with one of the Council members. A Lord An-Gea'la, I believe."

"What is the Council?" A'bbni asked curiously.

"I do not know how many of them there are, but my understanding is that it is the heads of some prominent families in Hanenea'a, who have their hands in palace affairs," Kella said.

That sounded more ominous to A'bbni than Kella probably meant it to be. "So, you trust this?"

Kella nodded. "I do. Do you wish for me to accompany you, my lord?"

"No," A'bbni said, shaking his head. "Please, do not trouble yourself." He didn't add that if this ended up being a trap of some kind, he did not want to put Kella or his family in more danger than they already were.

"You can use our carriage," Kella said. "I will instruct the driver to wait for you."

A'bbni nodded at that. "That would be most appreciated, Lord Kella. I continue to be eternally grateful for your assistance."

Kella gave him a warm smile. "Of course, Your Highness. It is my pleasure to help. As I said before, I cannot make up for the deeds of my ancestors, but I will do what I can now."

"I understand," A'bbni replied. "Please do not concern yourself with me. You have been a very gracious friend."

Kella nodded and gave A'bbni's hand a squeeze. "It will come together soon, Your Reverence. You'll see."

A'bbni felt his heart race as he walked down the windowless hallway. He wondered if he had made a foolish decision to meet with the Council without his brother, but what choice did he have? Until he knew where Shi'chen was, his only options were to continue to hide at Lord Kella's house or find out more about the rebellion and the plan to overthrow En'shea.

The young goblin man that met him at the building's entrance led him around a corner and over to a pair of elaborate carved rosewood doors, emblazoned with a scene depicting one of the goblin legends of Tai-mith'en, who rode into battle on a horse gifted to him by the gods that caused himself and the horse to grow until they crushed the invaders underfoot with every gallop. The image had once been accented with gilt leaf, but most of it was worn away now.

Two goblin soldiers stood on either side of the exterior of the double-doors, not in full armor, but wearing leather chest plates and holding spears. They pushed open the doors as the young man and A'bbni stopped in front of it. He ducked his head as he walked past them, his heart rate speeding up a little. The young goblin led him into a large interior room that was brightly lit from many gas lamps on the walls and a large chandelier of colored glass overhead that strategically illuminated the room, but this room also had no windows. It did have a very large fireplace on one side that crackled softly with a roaring fire that warmed the space. There was a large, rectangular table in the center of the room, with three chairs on one side and one on the other.

Occupying the three chairs that faced him now were three goblins. There was an elderly man with long, white whisps of hair, an enormously fat middle-aged man with a long, braided black beard and thick moustache, and a woman who looked to be about Kella's age, her skin goblin-dark but her hair dyed a sunny blond. All three rose from their seats as he entered.

His guide gave them all a hasty bow and backed out of the room. The double doors closed firmly behind him, leaving A'bbni alone in the room with the three elders. "Your Reverence," the oldest goblin said, bowing his head at him, but noticeably, not his waist or his knee.

A'bbni took a deep breath and squared his shoulders as he lowered his hood and pushed his cloak back from his shoulders. The man gestured to the vacant chair. "Please, sit."

"We would have your names first," A'bbni said in Hanen-vir, keeping his voice pleasant. Until he knew more about the situation, he was going to maintain his noble bearing and exude a confidence he did not feel.

The older man gave him a smile that did not reach his yellow eyes. "I am Ba'shea Ii-Heshar."

A'bbni felt his stomach clench as he immediately recognized the name. The suffix, Ii-, indicated he was not nobility, but that he or his family had risen to a place of importance, whether through study, trade, or other success. He remembered from his studies that the Ii-Heshar family had been the largest slave traders on the continent when slavery had been abolished almost sixty years ago by their grandmother, the Empress Chiia'jen. If his memory was correct, Ba'shea had been the youngest son of the Ii-Heshar household at the time, probably in his early teens when their slaves had been compensated and freed, judging by his age now. "Your Prominence," he greeted, forcing his voice to remain neutral.

Ba'shea motioned to the bearded goblin next to him. "Jin'fen An-Gea'la." The large man nodded his head. "And Mii'ra An-Sha'kri." The blond woman bowed, a little deeper than the other two had. Both Jin'fen and Mii'ra had the suffix An-, indicating they were descended from nobility. The An-Gea'las were well known at court; the position of Minister of Trade was held by Gia'den An-Gea'la, Jin'fen being his nephew. And the An-Sha'kri family had married into the Er-Ha'sen line more than ten generations ago.

"Your Eminences," A'bbni greeted Jin'fen and Mii'ra. These were not insubstantial members of goblin aristocracy, he realized, the nervousness in his stomach intensifying. It also explained how the Council knew about the inner workings of the palace; they had close family members high in the court.

"Now, please be seated," Ba'shea said.

A'bbni took his time removing his cloak and draping it over the back of his chair before sitting down. Once he was seated, and the three Council members as well, Mii'ra said, in a voice that was sticky sweet, "We are honored to have you with us, Your Highness."

"Do we have you to thank for our escape?" A'bbni asked.

Jin'fen's mouth curved into a smile beneath his thick moustache. "Indeed, Your Highness. It had been planned for some time, you see, but the need had not arisen until the sudden death of your Father, may he rest in the tranquility of the gods."

A'bbni bowed his head automatically at the blessing. "We would not be alive today if it were not for your help. We are most grateful."

"We thank the gods you arrived safely, and we hope that your brother will also reach us soon," Mii'ra said with a warm smile, using the plural 'we' in Hanen-sha, not Hanen-vir. A'bbni noticed that they were almost exclusively using Hanen-sha. He wondered if that was deliberate on their part, to make it seem like he was the one in control.

"We would wish to hear your plans and how we may help," A'bbni replied.

The three Council members looked uneasily at each other. Ba'shea broke the silence with a soft cough. "Unfortunately, our plans have had to change with the assassination of the Regent and other prominent leaders. The details are yet to be fully worked out."

"Then we shall be happy to assist in working those details out with you," A'bbni said pleasantly.

"No, Your Highness," Jin'fen said, shaking his head. "You do not need to concern yourself with such matters."

"If it concerns us or our people, we do," A'bbni replied, his voice just a little firmer.

"Your Highness, while we appreciate your willingness to help, this is a matter of state," Mii'ra said.

"Yes. And we are the heirs apparent to the throne," A'bbni said, the pleasant smile still on his face. "Therefore, it concerns us."

Ba'shea gave him a tight smile that did not reach his glittering, yellow eyes. Something about them made A'bbni's stomach turn sour, and he had to take a long breath in and out for the feeling to dissipate. "Your

Reverence, the best thing you can do right now is let us make arrangements on your behalf."

"Perhaps you did not understand us," A'bbni said, determined to keep his tone pleasant. "We wish to know what is expected of us, or we will not be a part of it."

Jin'fen gave him a look that was probably an attempt at fatherliness. "Your Highness, you did not know of the plan earlier, which ensured that we were able to rescue you without the rebellion being revealed."

"Yes, and we were tortured for information we knew nothing about," A'bbni replied, unable to keep a slight hiss out of his voice. He was not about to go into detail of what happened to him with these strangers, but he was sure they at least knew how En'shea would have treated them.

"And if you had known, would you have revealed what you knew to the Emperor?" Mii'ra asked.

"We do not know, but that would have been our decision to make," A'bbni said firmly.

"Your Highness, if you had informed the Emperor of the plan to depose him, you would have been executed, along with many others," Jin'fen said.

"We were going to be executed anyway," A'bbni retorted. "And due to our rescue, many more will have been executed now. Their lives are no less important than those of any who would see our Cousin overthrown."

Ba'shea waved his hand in the air as if swatting away an irritating insect. "Necessary sacrifices, I am afraid."

A'bbni's eyes narrowed. "If their lives were worth the saving of ours, we deserve to honor their memory by making sure their sacrifices were not in vain."

Jin'fen cleared his throat. "Your Highness, please understand, we are shielding you for your own good."

"We fail to see how this is for our own good in any way, nor have we asked you to shield us, Vr An-Gea'la," A'bbni replied, feeling his normally mild temper flare hot in his chest. "We have requested pertinent information from you, and if you do not feel that we should have such information, we have no reason to trust you."

Ba'shea glowered at A'bbni in a way that made the back of his neck prickle. Mii'ra held up her hands placatingly. "Please forgive the tension, Your Highness," she said, giving A'bbni an apologetic smile. "We are all feeling the strain of the suddenness of the Regent's death, and I am sure emotions are running high."

"Indeed." A'bbni swallowed back the angry words he wanted to say, instead forcing a diplomatic smile to his face. He would catch more flies with honey than vinegar in this situation, and if Shi'chen had been by his side, his brother would have been an entire basin of vinegar. He took a deep breath, then allowed his ears to flatten a little to make him seem more apologetic. He was not unfamiliar with the manipulations that every noble played at, and he had no qualms about using his youth to his advantage. He could play dumb when he needed to, and that was starting to seem like the best course of action. "We do apologize for our harsh words. We are afraid the unexpected death of our Father has affected us greatly, perhaps more so than we realized." That was not a lie, at least, and it pained him to know that he was letting the Council see this point of weakness to manipulate him, but there was often much to be gained from giving.

"Of course," Mii'ra said in a motherly tone, her expression kind. "I am sure it was a great shock to you and your brother."

"It was," A'bbni said, giving her a feigned attempt at a brave smile. "But again, we wish to express our gratitude to you, to all of you," he added, nodding to Ba'shea and Jin'fen, "for saving our lives."

Jin'fen waved his hand in the air. "We are glad you are safe, Your Highness."

A'bbni nodded, starting to doubt very much that anything the Council said was genuine. "We are sure you understand our reluctance to agree to any sort of plan without knowing what may be expected. Obviously, we do not wish to put ourselves into further danger after you have risked so much to gain our freedom, nor do we wish to endanger the lives of those who make up the rebellion of which you speak."

"We understand your compunction, Your Highness," Jin'fen said. "Your compassion is admirable."

A'bbni was sure they were looking at his compassion as a way they could manipulate him, but he just gave the man a bob of his head. "Thank you, Vr An-Gea'la."

Mii'ra tossed her golden hair off her shoulder. "We will certainly inform you with what you need to know, Your Highness, once details have been finalized." She gave him another maternal smile, like a mother trying to wheedle her child into bed with promises of treats.

"Thank you, Var An-Sha'kri," A'bbni said, giving them all a gracious smile that he knew at least looked genuine, even if all he wanted to do was scream.

Ba'shea cleared his throat. "But, Your Reverence, there is the concern of the line of succession."

"What is your concern, Vr Ii-Heshar?" A'bbni asked, keeping his smile in place even as he felt the subtle shift in the air.

"Your brother is the elder and would be granted first rights to the throne after the Emperor is unseated."

"Yes," A'bbni agreed, waiting for the older goblin to come around to his point.

"If Captain Er-Ha'sen is not interested in assuming the throne, we would need him to formally abdicate to you," Ba'shea said, his gnarled fingers tapping absently on the tabletop. "To permanently give up his right to succession."

A'bbni felt a prickle of ice in the pit of his stomach. While he knew that to technically be true, the fact that the Council was bringing it up felt suspicious. He wanted to dig further, but the three sets of eyes on him were watching his reaction closely.

"We cannot speak on behalf of our brother," he said, choosing his words carefully. "But we shall discuss the matter with him when he arrives. Is our brother's right to the throne a concern?"

"No, Your Highness," Jin'fen said warmly, giving him another of those fatherly smiles. "We simply wish to know which of you will take the throne so the transition will be a smooth one."

The words made sense, but A'bbni was still feeling the unease in his gut. He dropped his ears a little to appear meek and asked in a slightly softer tone, "Do you feel that he may be more suited to the throne than us?"

"We cannot say, Your Reverence," Ba'shea said diplomatically. "We only wish to ensure proper protocol is followed."

The Imperial Senate and the Regent were dead; who exactly was going to enforce anything that did not follow the protocols of succession? The Council could not be so entrenched in tradition that it could not see the dilemma being presented. A'bbni decided to try one more exploratory question. "Would it behoove us to do our best to convince him that a peaceful secession of power would be a wise course of action?" He purposefully made the end of his words sound meek, hoping the Council would think he had not seen through their manipulations and was trying to do what they asked of him.

Jin'fen smiled, Mii'ra nodded, and Ba'shea's eyes glittered. "We believe that would be prudent, yes," Mii'ra said, her tone light.

So, they wanted him to take the throne, and for Shi'chen to permanently sign away his claim. A'bbni could think of several reasons why, none of which were good. He gave them what he hoped was an unwitting smile. "We shall speak to him regarding this matter."

The Council all nodded this time. "Please do," Jin'fen said. "He will listen to you."

Yes, he will, A'bbni thought. That was exactly what they wanted. "Does this conclude your business with us?"

"Yes, Your Reverence," Ba'shea said, with his cold smile. "Thank you for your time. We shall plan to speak with you again when your brother arrives." A'bbni stood up, collecting his cloak with as much poise as he could muster before giving them all a last small nod and heading out of the room, feeling the three sets of eyes burning holes in his back until the doors to the den of vipers had at last closed behind him.

He headed down the hall, his heart still racing in his chest. All he wanted to do was talk to his brother and find out what Shi'chen's thoughts on the situation were, but that was not an option right now. He was entirely alone in this venture, and while he logically knew that dealing with this on his own was not unexpected, it still made his heart ache. He was nineteen – *no, twenty,* he corrected himself – barely considered an adult, shoved violently into this world of political machinations that he had never intended to be a part of, and certainly not without at least his brother, if not his Father, by his side.

As he stepped out into the bright sunlight and the crisp, cool air, A'bbni felt his stomach settle just a bit. Something was nagging at his mind, but he couldn't figure out what it was. Not that that was unusual, his mind was usually full of thoughts, like now, but something about the Council besides just their manipulative tactics was burrowing into his brain. The black carriage the Arvay family had provided appeared in front of him, and A'bbni gratefully stepped up into it, pressing his fingers to his temples as a headache caught up to him. Perhaps when he arrived back at Lord Kella's estate, there would be news of his brother. That was the only positive thought in his head as stared glumly at the empty spot on the seat next to him.

The troubled feeling in his stomach was still there as he replayed the Council's words over and over in his head, trying to figure out what they were trying to accomplish and why they had made him feel so uneasy. By the time the carriage pulled to a stop at the Arvay estate, A'bbni had a pounding headache. He made his way up to his room and laid down, trying to rest, but sleep would not come. It did not that night, either.

CHAPTER THIRTEEN

SHI'CHEN

Shi'chen could barely stand still during the unloading of the ship but forced himself to focus so no one got hurt. There were way too many boxes for his patience, but he realized he didn't have much of a choice yet. The hard work distracted him from the cold that caused his fingers, toes, and ears to tingle unpleasantly. He already hated how cold it was, and he knew it would only get colder. A'bbni had told him about "snow" that fell the closer one went north toward the elven continent, and he was not at all excited to see such a thing for himself if it only came when it was this cold outside.

After the ship had docked in Genhin'saa, the ship had been waylaid for three days while the injured crew members were examined, damaged inventory removed, new inventory taken, and the ship's stores restocked. Shi'chen was at least glad he was kept busy helping, or he might have tried to run all the way to Csereth with how impatient he was. He was oddly grateful that Lai knew his secret, so he did not have to try to come up with some reason why it was so important for him to get to Csereth without being stopped.

After discussing it further with Lai, they decided that staying on the ship was best, as they could not be certain that the roads were not being watched; enough time had passed for a message to get to both Genhin'saa and Csereth. A waylaid cargo ship was also less likely to draw extra attention, as the captain and ship owner would be anxious to continue their journey after the delay, and the city soldiers would not originally have the ship on their docking list.

Eventually all the crates were unloaded, the ship scrubbed, and the crew were given their compensation from the captain and the merchants whose cargo they had carried. Shi'chen almost sprinted down the gangplank as the crew members were released, Lai following him at a leisurely pace, a rapier that Shi'chen had never seen him wear before securely buckled to his side under his cloak.

"Come on," Shi'chen insisted, trying very hard not to bounce up and down on the balls of his feet as Lai finally stepped onto the dock next to him.

Lai rolled his eyes. "You can't go dashing through the street, you know."

Shi'chen looked like he was going to disprove that point, but he sighed and shouldered his bag. "I know. But let's go!"

Lai shook his head. "No. First we need to get you some warmer clothing. Your brother would not forgive me if I delivered you," he said a word in Cserethian that Shi'chen assumed was 'frozen.'

One more obstacle between him and A'bbni, but Lai had a point. His tunics, pants, and sandals were not designed for the colder weather of the northern city, and now that he was aware of it, he was starting to shiver, and it was only going to get colder. "All right," he relented.

Lai smiled. "Come on." He led him down the street, seeming to know where he was headed. Shi'chen followed after him, trying very hard not to stare. He had never been to Csereth, and while it was not entirely dissimilar from Er'hadin, there were noticeable differences. The buildings were taller, many of them more than the usual one to three stories of the buildings in the imperial city. He knew that the elves tended to build taller rather than wider, and there was definitely much more elven influence on this city, likely due to how close it was to Kendarin, just a few days' trip further north across the isthmus, or the Coral Sea. There was quite a bit of glass used in the windows, though more of it was clear rather than colored like the stained windows that decorated most of the palace and the surrounding imperial city.

The colors seemed cooler here, as well. Where most goblins in the center of Hanenea'a favored earthy tones, warm reds, oranges, yellows, and pinks, the colors here were brighter. Vivid jeweled tones of green, blue, and purple were everywhere, on buildings, signs, clothing.

Once they had moved a few blocks from the sea, the salty, tangy smell of the water that he had grown used to faded into other, more familiar, street smells. Cooking meat and baking pastries, sweaty horses and their droppings, the occasional sweet waft of perfumes, oil from streetlamps that were not currently lit in the middle of the day. He felt a painful twinge of homesickness in his chest. It felt strange to be back on land again, and once in a while, his step faltered. He saw Lai notice it and give him a grin. "That will pass soon."

"Good. I want to not be on a boat again for a long time," Shi'chen replied.

"No promises," Lai said with a shrug as he paused by a stall to buy two warm pastries wrapped in brown paper. He handed one to Shi'chen, who took it gratefully. Almost two weeks of food on the ship had left much to be desired, and his stomach growled eagerly as he took a bite, finding the inside filled with a spiced mix of ground meat and vegetables. He was sure he had not ever tasted anything so good as he followed a step behind Lai.

The mix of languages around him was distracting. Most of it was Cserethian, but he caught bits of Hanen-shii and Hanen-sha, as well as a few other languages he recognized as primarily elven, though he did not understand most of it. A'bbni would have been excited to try to decipher all of them, but he just felt lost in the sea of unfamiliar faces. This close to the docks, there were many full-blooded elves, as well as a larger than usual amount of people who obviously had both elf and goblin in their blood. He found himself scanning to see if any had ears like Lai, but none did.

Lai stopped at a corner where a small group of people had gathered and seemed to be waiting. "We'll take a carriage there, and then to the inn," he explained to Shi'chen.

Shi'chen nodded, finishing the pastry in his hand and trying very hard not to lick his fingers in public. "You know Csereth well?"

Lai nodded. "It is the main port for this side of Hanenea'a, so I go through here often."

"How far is it to *Vayalla Oren*?" Shi'chen asked, hugging his pack a little closer for warmth now that he was standing still.

"It's across the city," Lai said as a covered multi-passenger carriage drew near, pulled by two horses, both black with white boots. "Half a day's carriage ride or a full day's walk."

Shi'chen sighed. "So, we won't get there today."

"No," Lai said, giving him an apologetic look. "But I promise we can leave first thing tomorrow morning."

That would have to do, he supposed. He was not about to go rushing through the city on his own, in the dark, with no guide and no idea where he was going. He followed Lai aboard the carriage, taking in everything he could as it started through the streets. He had never had much chance to travel outside Er'hadin, and if he ever did again, it would likely not be as an unknown citizen who could come and go as he pleased.

The carriage eventually pulled to a stop, and several passengers got off. Lai hopped down as well, and Shi'chen followed. Lai led him down several streets and more than a few turns before stopping in front of a modest-looking shop. He headed inside, and Shi'chen followed. The shopkeeper seemed eager and friendly, helping them find a few longer shirts and trousers for Shi'chen, as well as a warm cloak, gloves, and a hat. Lai moved to pay, but Shi'chen held out his hand and shook his head. "I can pay for my own things," he said. What other use were his sailor's wages going to be good for?

Lai shrugged. "Up to you."

Shi'chen did not bother to try to explain to Lai that he had never paid for anything in his life; if he ever went somewhere that required money, there were servants or secretaries who took care of it. The act of handing over money he had earned on his own was entirely new to him. He realized as he did so how quickly money was depleted. It made no sense that he would not be able to get things he needed because he did not have enough coins in his purse. He was going to have to talk to A'bbni about this in more detail.

After that, Lai led him down a few streets to a nearby inn. "Do you want your own room?" he asked as they made their way inside.

Shi'chen tried hard not to roll his eyes, knowing that Lai was trying to be respectful of his space. "No, I'm used to sharing."

"I suppose so," Lai said with a laugh, moving over to talk to the woman behind the bar. After a few moments, he handed her some coins, and she pointed up the stairs. Lai tipped his head for Shi'chen to follow him, and they made their way down to the empty room.

The room only had one bed, which, while spacious, was still not going to be large enough for them to both spread out. "You take it," Lai said, closing the door behind them and turning the key securely in the lock. The fire in the hearth crackled brightly, casting dancing shadows over the wall. "I'll sleep on the floor."

"Absolutely not," Shi'chen said with a frown.

"No arguments, Your Highness," Lai said, already moving over to grab some of the blankets off the nearby chair. "I'm sure you miss sleeping in a proper bed."

He did, but he was not about to tell Lai that. "You've been at sea longer than I have."

Lai shrugged. "Yes, so I'm used to it." He was already undoing the belt that held his rapier at his side and nudging off his boots.

Shi'chen set his things aside. "May I ask you a question?"

"You just did, but yes."

"Would you be doing this if I wasn't royalty?"

Lai blinked and turned to him in confusion. "What?"

"If I was just a sailor looking for my brother, would you be helping me?"

Lai gave him a small smile. "I'm not doing this for a reward, if that's what you're asking."

Shi'chen felt himself flush at that, realizing how he must sound. "I... Why? Why are you helping me?"

Lai gazed at him for a long moment, so long that Shi'chen wasn't sure he was going to answer him, before Lai exhaled softly. "Do you remember on the ship when you asked me what I live for now, with Talen gone?"

Shi'chen nodded slowly. "You said you didn't know."

Lai shrugged, sitting down on the floor and leaning back on his hands. "I have no one waiting on me. Nowhere I have to be. You have someone who loves you that you need to find. If I can help you get to your brother, I have something to live for."

"Lai..." Shi'chen moved over to kneel next to him by the fire, taking Lai's hand in his own. Lai glanced down at it, then back up at him.

"I still forget how much goblins touch each other," he said with a small smile.

Shi'chen laughed, giving his hand a squeeze. "If you're going to come with us to the palace, you better get used to it."

Lai raised a brow at that. "Am I coming to the palace?"

"Aren't you?" Shi'chen asked in surprise.

Lai shrugged. "Guess I hadn't thought that far."

"I'm getting ahead of myself anyway," Shi'chen admitted. "But... you've been a good friend to me. Thank you."

Lai grinned and gave his hand another squeeze before pulling back. "All right, get to bed, Your Majesty. Can't have your brother seeing you with bags under your eyes."

Shi'chen gave him a smile back, then got up to move over to the bed. He toed off his boots and slid under the sheets, which felt absolutely amazing after the wooden berth on the ship. "Good night," he said softly.

"Sleep well, Shi'chen," Lai said in return.

The next morning, Shi'chen woke up even before Lai did, which was unusual for him. He took advantage of the time to wash and try to clean his clothes as best he could, and by the time he had dressed and returned to the main room, Lai was awake and had ordered breakfast for them. Shi'chen barely paid attention to the food, too eager to get on their way.

"You know he may not be there," Lai said as he slid his boots on.

Shi'chen let out a frustrated breath. "I know... But I think he's safe. I can feel it."

Lai raised a brow. "Really?"

Shi'chen laughed and shook his head. "Well, not literally. I can't hear his thoughts or anything," he clarified when Lai didn't seem to understand him.

"If you could, that would make this whole trip a lot easier," Lai said as he secured his belt with his rapier to his waist and tossed a cloak over it. "But we will find him."

Shi'chen nodded, pulling on his new warmer clothes, extremely grateful for them when they stepped out of the warmth of the inn into the coldest air he had ever felt in his life. His breath came out of his mouth in a puff of white, and it took him a moment to realize that it was because of the temperature. Lai watched him with a slight smirk on his face. "You really are not used to the cold, are you?"

"Not at all," Shi'chen replied, waving his fingers through his next breath to watch it swirl.

"You can do that while we walk," Lai pointed out with a chuckle, and Shi'chen quickly moved to follow him, his cheeks and the tips of his ears reddening in embarrassment under his warm coverings.

Without asking, Lai got them onto a carriage that took off through the streets, the bells on the horses' harnessing tinkling merrily. Shi'chen watched the city go by for a few minutes before turning to Lai again. "I've never seen you use it. Where did you get that sword?"

"From Talen," Lai said, giving him a slight grin. "He taught me to fight with it."

"Was he a good swordsman?"

Lai nodded. "He was. I think you kind of have to be when people hate you."

"I don't understand that," Shi'chen said. "I've never met a half-elf besides you, but you don't seem any different from the other elves I've known. Except your ears are shorter."

Lai shrugged. "Some people can't see past that."

"Well, that's ridiculous," Shi'chen said, rolling his eyes.

Lai gave him his usual bright grin. "Agreed. If I'm going to be hated, I'd rather it be for my sparkling wit, not my ears."

Shi'chen laughed at that. "How could anybody hate your wit?"

"You'd be surprised," Lai said, giving his hair a little toss.

The horses clip-clopped down the stone road, and Lai did his best to distract Shi'chen from his tension by pointing out various places they passed and recounting a few stories from his time there. Shi'chen wondered to himself what it would be like if he was not a prince, if he was just some unknown sailor, with no ties to anyone or anything. Finding a friend like Lai would probably be exciting.

He wondered how Talen and Lai had ended up together and debated asking, but the last thing he wanted to do right now was cause his friend any pain. He suspected that once A'bbni met Lai, Lai would spend a lot more time with them and the opportunity would come up later to find out. That train of thought took him down a whole new path. He knew A'bbni would like Lai, but would Lai like A'bbni? And if he did, was he all right with that? He loved seeing his brother happy more than anything, and especially now, after everything that had happened to them, he wanted A'bbni to experience happiness again.

He wondered how his compassionate brother was doing without him, if his injuries had healed, if his mental state was all right. He felt like he had left his twin at the worst possible time, so soon after the abuse and shock of what Hi'jan had done to him and what En'shea had done to their Father. He had grappled with it as best he could while on the ship, but he was sure that it had affected his brother infinitely more than it did him. That thought alone brought a sour taste to his mouth.

"And that was how I fucked a dragon," he heard Lai say next to him, and his mind snapped back to reality.

"What?"

"Ah, there you are," Lai said with a grin. "You went away there for a bit."

Shi'chen flushed. "Sorry," he said softly.

Lai shook his head. "Don't apologize. You obviously have something on your mind."

Shi'chen shook his head. "Just... nervous."

"I know, you haven't seen him in almost two weeks, he might have forgotten you by now," Lai teased as the carriage stopped in front of a block of shops, one of which seemed to be a tavern. The sign over the door read *Vayalla Oren*. Lai jumped down, and Shi'chen followed close after him. He suddenly found himself more than a little anxious. What if A'bbni truly was not here? What if something had happened to his ship, or he had been discovered by the guards? He felt Lai's eyes on him, and then the half-elf's hand landed lightly on his shoulder, making him unexpectedly jump at the contact. "It will be okay," Lai said reassuringly. Shi'chen nodded slowly. "Come on." Lai adjusted the warm hat he had on that covered his short ears, and then pushed open the door.

The warmth and scent of some sort of beer met his nose, and Shi'chen pushed his hood back so he could see better. The tavern was crowded, with a mix of goblins and elves, most of whom seemed to be middle-class from what he could tell, maybe merchants and tradesmen. Most paid them no mind when they entered, and he swept his eyes around the crowd. Lai let him lead as he moved amongst the patrons, looking for the familiar shape of his twin. But he did not see him, and his heart began to pound a little harder in his chest. He turned to Lai with a worried frown. "I don't see him here." Not that he expected A'bbni to just be sitting out in the open in a place like this for days on end, but he had no idea what else to look for.

Lai glanced around, then took Shi'chen's arm to steer him toward the bar where a goblin with a large moustache was pouring drinks into glasses. Lai said something to the man in Cserethian that Shi'chen knew was a greeting, and then the half-elf was speaking at a fast clip to the man, of which Shi'chen only caught the word "goblin" and "friend." The bartender glanced at him and then turned back to Lai, asking a question.

Lai turned back to Shi'chen, switching back to Hanen-shii. "He says a Lord Kella left a note for a sailor who was supposed to be arriving and wants to know if that might be you?"

Shi'chen remembered Rell giving A'bbni a note, telling him it was for Lord Kella only. "Yes!" he said in Cserethian.

The bartender grabbed a piece of paper from under the bar and held it up but did not give it to him. Lai pulled a coin from his pocket and handed it to him. The bartender took the coin, then glanced at the envelope with its black wax seal and crest and said something else to Lai in Cserethian. Lai rolled his eyes, pulling two more coins from his pocket, which he tossed on the counter instead of offering them, and the bartender handed the letter over.

"Come on," Lai said, grabbing Shi'chen's shoulder to pull him along. "Let's get out of this crowd so you can read it."

"Would he not have given us the letter if you had not given him the money?" Shi'chen asked curiously as they threaded through the crowd toward the door.

"Probably not," Lai said with a shrug.

"Even though the letter was not for him?"

Lai laughed as he stepped out into the cool air again and moved over to a stone bench nearby. "You really have never had to rely on money, have you?"

"No," Shi'chen admitted, sitting down next to Lai. He resisted the urge to snatch the letter when Lai held it out. Even though the envelope was blank, it was a good quality parchment, and the black wax seal was that of the Arvay family crest, the rich elven family whose business for ferrying people between Hanenea'a and Kendarin was well-known. He broke the seal and pulled out a single sheet of paper, written in elegant Hanen-sha.

Greetings, we hope you experienced safe travels. I have a guest at my home who is eager to meet you. Please come at your earliest convenience, where you will be most welcome.

There was an address at the bottom, and Lai glanced around when Shi'chen showed it to him. "That's not far from here. Close to the passenger docks. We can walk there within an hour."

Shi'chen was on his feet before Lai even finished speaking, already heading down the street in the direction Lai had indicated. The half-elf had to jog to catch up with him, and Shi'chen reluctantly slowed a little to let Lai take the lead again. "You trust this?" Lai asked, gesturing to the letter.

Shi'chen shrugged. "What choice do I have?"

"I guess that's true," Lai replied.

"If it turns out to be a trap, I have a very talented swordsman to defend me," Shi'chen pointed out with a grin.

"You haven't even seen me fight," Lai replied, rolling his eyes.

"No," Shi'chen admitted. "But I can tell from the way you handled that dagger against Jaa'jen that you knew how to use it."

Lai shrugged. "Any idiot can hold a dagger."

"Sure, but not every idiot stands in defense like you did," Shi'chen replied with a grin.

Lai laughed softly at that. "I should have guessed you'd see that, Captain."

Shi'chen rolled his eyes. "You figured out I was a guard just from me wielding a mop."

"Which you still need to teach me, by the way," Lai reminded him.

"I'm pretty sure you know how to mop a deck," Shi'chen replied with a grin.

Lai gave him a playful shove. "Asshole."

Shi'chen laughed. "Come back with my brother and I to Er'hadin, and I'll teach you spear fighting if you help me with my Cserethian."

"Deal," Lai said with a bright grin. "I'm sure you're a great teacher."

Shi'chen shrugged. "I've been training with a spear since I was ten, and I would practice with staffs before then, since my Father didn't want me using a blade until I was old enough to control it."

"Your Father was a wise man," Lai said sagely.

Shi'chen smiled softly and chuckled. The fact that he laughed at that instead of experiencing sadness felt good. "He was. I think he would have liked you."

"I'm sure he would have, I'm amazing," Lai said with a toss of his hair over his shoulder, and Shi'chen couldn't hold back a snort of laughter. Lai gave him a grin, then sobered again. "Was your Father more like you or more like your brother?"

"My brother," Shi'chen replied immediately. "He was an accomplished soldier, but he was smart. More about policies and history. I'm more like my Mother."

"How old were you when she died?" Lai asked softly.

"Fourteen," Shi'chen said. "You?"

"Almost eleven," Lai said. "Old enough to remember her, but not clearly."

"I'm sorry," Shi'chen said.

Lai shrugged a little. "At least I know where she is. She didn't just disappear or get snatched up by the slave traders."

"By the what?" Shi'chen asked in surprise.

"The slave traders," Lai repeated, saying it slower and clearer as if that was why Shi'chen had not understood him.

"You mean, in the human lands?"

Lai shrugged. "It happens in the human lands, too, but I've seen it happen here and in Kendarin."

"You've seen it in Hanenea'a?" Shi'chen stopped walking, and Lai turned to face him. "But slavery has been illegal for over fifty years."

Lai let out a cold laugh. "Since when has that stopped anyone when they could make a fortune?"

"How do you know this?"

"About six years ago, I ended up on the crew of a slave vessel," Lai said, fiddling with the edge of his cloak uncomfortably. "As soon as I found out, I jumped ship. But I knew that's what it was."

Six years ago. That would have been when their Father was still Regent. That twisted Shi'chen's stomach into a painful knot. Had their Father known? Unfortunately, he would never be able to ask him. "Is... is it still going on?"

"I would guess so," Lai replied. "I've heard rumors, at least."

"Why didn't you tell anyone?" Shi'chen asked.

Lai gave him a pointed look. "Who in the name of the gods would I tell? I was already trying to keep myself safe. Who would listen to a half-breed sailor from nowhere?"

Shi'chen let out a frustrated sigh, realizing Lai had a point and not wanting to harangue his friend over it. "We can't allow that to continue."

"Who is 'we?'" Lai asked, raising a brow, taking a step back, though it seemed to be to get Shi'chen to start moving again, not to get away from him.

"My brother and I," Shi'chen said, following after Lai. "If what you say is true, and slavery is still happening, we have..." He dropped his voice lower again. "We have to depose En'shea and stop this. There really is no other option if slave-trading is still occurring. If he makes it legal again, countless more people could be hurt." Lai nodded solemnly. Shi'chen let out another frustrated sigh and rubbed at his eyes with his gloved hands. There was no way he could simply turn a blind eye to it now or walk away and leave Hanenea'a to En'shea. Even if he could, A'bbni wouldn't, and there was no way Shi'chen would leave his brother to try to fix something like that on his own. He turned his eyes to Lai. "Would you be willing to help us with that, Lai?"

Lai blinked at him. "How?"

"You know the seas probably better than most," Shi'chen replied. "You know the types of ships out there, who the big names in trade are. Your information would be invaluable."

Lai blinked at that last word, and Shi'chen clarified, "important," to which Lai nodded slowly. "I... I would help as much as I can. I don't want to see slavery continue anywhere."

Shi'chen suspected Lai's thoughts were not completely altruistic. A half-elf, already looked down upon by society, seen as a novelty, with no home and no family, could easily disappear, and no one would ever think to look for him. The thought made him sick to his stomach that something like that had probably happened. Someone had been taken from their life and forced to do something, whether in the mines or on a ship or in someone's bed, and no one was looking for them. And knowing his cousin, En'shea would wield that power against anyone that might oppose him without hesitation, the way he had used A'bbni as a bargaining chip with Hi'jan.

"I meant to ask," Lai said, pulling Shi'chen back from the spiral his mind had started to fall down. "Which of you is older?"

"I am," Shi'chen replied, forcing himself to pay more attention to Lai and their surroundings. The buildings around them were starting to become more upscale and more residential. The shops they passed looked to be much more affluent than the ones they had been at earlier in the day as well.

"So would you be the one taking the throne?"

"Keep your voice down!" Shi'chen hissed, but Lai rolled his eyes.

"We're two sailors in a rich neighborhood. No one is listening to us."

Shi'chen glanced around, but Lai seemed to be correct. Most of the people in the streets, which were not that many with the cold pressing in, seemed to be deliberately avoiding the two lower-class individuals walking amongst them. That felt very strange to Shi'chen, who was usually hyper-aware of all eyes being on him whenever he was around. He supposed anonymity brought privacy, and at the moment, he was grateful for it.

"I don't want it," he said after a moment.

Lai blinked. "You don't want the throne?"

Shi'chen shook his head. "I know that probably sounds ridiculous, but I would much rather be a guard. I know how to lead a Garrison. I don't know how to lead a country."

"From what I know of royalty, most people don't know how to lead a country," Lai replied with a shrug.

"But we were raised in the palace."

"So was your Cousin," Lai pointed out.

Shi'chen blinked. "I... guess that's true."

"So, your brother would become Emperor?"

"I suppose so," Shi'chen replied. That thought was strange. While he was sure it had crossed his brother's mind at some point, since A'bbni always seemed to have considered every possible scenario, he was also sure that A'bbni had assumed he would never need to do so.

He had been so far down the list of succession, even in the last few years, following their Father, Prii'sha, En'shea, and his older twin. A'bbni wanted to be a physician, wanted to help people and study. Would he even want to take the throne? If he refused, and Shi'chen refused, the Er-Ha'sen line would be done, and the entire line of succession would be thrown into chaos. But who would enforce any of it since En'shea had murdered the entire Imperial Senate as well? This whole train of thought was starting to give him a headache.

"It should be two blocks that way," Lai said, taking a turn at the end of a street. Shi'chen felt his heart speed up, and he forced himself to keep the same walking speed. Lai turned to him again. "I know you want to see your brother, but will you let me go check it out first? If it is a trap, I don't want anyone to see you."

"I can defend myself, you know," Shi'chen said, though his heart surged at how concerned Lai was for his safety.

"I know you can," Lai replied.

Shi'chen nodded. "All right. Just, please be careful yourself."

Lai gave him a grin. "Of course. I'm always careful."

Shi'chen couldn't stop a snort of laughter at that. "Sure you are."

"I'm hurt," Lai said, placing his hand on his chest in mock outrage, then pointed to a large, white house with a wall and wrought iron gate on the next street. "That should be it."

Shi'chen was sure he looked ridiculous, staring at the large house with undisguised awe, but he didn't care. His heart gave a little jump in his chest, wondering if A'bbni was looking out from one of the many windows.

Lai gave him a nudge. "Give me the letter." Shi'chen handed it over, and Lai motioned to the corner. "Wait here. If it's safe, I'll come back and get you." And with that, he strode off before Shi'chen could ask what the alternative was if it was not safe. Not that he really had many options in the matter.

He leaned against the wall of the building next to him, keeping his hood up as best he could without it blocking his peripheral vision. The street did seem quiet, and nothing seemed out of place. He watched Lai walk up to the black wrought-iron gate and say something to someone standing there he could not see clearly, and then the gate opened, and Lai disappeared inside. Shi'chen's heart thundered in his ears as he watched and waited. He couldn't see the front door from this angle, so he just had to wait and hope that Lai was all right. Every second felt like an eternity as he waited, trying to remain still and not shift from foot to foot.

He was sure the sun would set before Lai came back, even though it really was only a few minutes before his friend appeared at the gate and crossed the street to him, giving him a nod. He pushed himself off the wall, trying very, very hard not to bounce on the balls of his feet as Lai approached. When the half-elf was close enough to not have to shout, he said, "I spoke with Lord Quenn, who is Lord Kella's husband. Your brother is here. Come on."

Shi'chen almost ran, but Lai grabbed him by the back of his cloak. "Slow down, Your Majesty, you're going to get unwanted attention if you run."

Shi'chen let out a frustrated sigh, but he returned to walking at a steady pace, each step making his heart beat faster in his chest. Lai led him through the gate, past an elf in livery who nodded them in. "He said to go to the back garden," Lai replied, motioning his head around the side of the house as he pulled his hat off. The high walls would afford more privacy so the twins would not be seen as easily together. Shi'chen wanted to take in the lavish yard, intricate architecture on the house, and all the other small details that spoke to the Arvay family having money, but he couldn't think about it now. His chest felt too tight, and his breath caught in his throat as he and Lai rounded the corner of the house into a beautifully laid out hedge garden.

And then, there his brother was, coming out of the door of the house next to a tall, dark-haired elf. The relief that flooded Shi'chen was like a splinter suddenly gone from beneath his skin. He hadn't even taken two steps before A'bbni's eyes met his, and they sprinted across the garden, skidding to a stop that almost tumbled them both over, throwing their arms around each other in a tight embrace.

He could feel tears streaming down his face, but he didn't care. All that he cared about was holding A'bbni in his arms, so tight that he never wanted to let go. A'bbni's arms wrapped around him, his face burying itself in Shi'chen's shoulder as he started to shudder with sobs, clinging to his twin.

"I thought I'd lost you forever, i-sha," Shi'chen whispered into his twin's ear, tangling his fingers into the long curls at A'bbni's neck.

"And I, you," A'bbni said, his voice muffled by Shi'chen's shoulder.

Shi'chen pressed his forehead to A'bbni's, the way they had when they were children, the way they had in the cart ride to the docks that separated them. "I swear to you that I will never leave you again."

A'bbni gazed back at Shi'chen, and Shi'chen could see himself reflected in A'bbni's teary eyes, better than any mirror. "Please forgive me for not fighting harder to stay with you."

"You have nothing for me to forgive you for," Shi'chen replied firmly. "I would rather die than put you in harm's way again."

Kella cleared his throat softly, and the twins' faces turned toward where he and Lai stood awkwardly off to the side. It was obvious that neither of them had thoroughly understood the breathy mix of Hanen-sha and Hanen-vir exchanged between the two.

A'bbni flushed, giving Kella an apologetic bow of his head as he quickly swiped a few errant tears from his cheeks. "My apologies, Lord Kella, for our rudeness," he said in Hanen-sha. "This is my brother, Captain Shi'chen Er-Ha'sen."

Shi'chen bent his knee in the bow between equals. "Lord Kella. My eternal gratitude to you and your family for taking care of my brother."

Kella smiled and nodded in return, touching a hand to his chest. "It was our honor, Captain."

Shi'chen gave A'bbni's hand a tug to pull him forward. "I-sha, I want you to meet Lai Ablewood," he said in Hanen-shii, giving the blond half-elf a bright smile. "This is my baby brother, A'bbni."

He waited for the jab that A'bbni usually gave him when he called him his "baby brother," but it didn't come. Shi'chen turned to his twin and found A'bbni staring at Lai with wide eyes, taking in Lai's short ears, his lanky frame, his golden blond hair, his elegantly handsome features. He had known from the start that A'bbni would find Lai exquisite, and not only for the novelty of his ears or the languages he spoke. A'bbni's goblin partners, both male and female, had always been more delicate than most goblins, with more pointed, fine elven features. He could already see his brother's infatuation with the half-elf shining in his ember eyes.

"Your brother told me all about you," Lai said in Cserethian, giving A'bbni a dazzling smile. "I'm pleased to finally meet you."

"The pleasure is mine," A'bbni said in return in Cserethian. "Did you serve on the ship with Shi'chen?"

Lai nodded. "I did. He is quite the competent sailor, once he got used to it."

"I'm so glad to hear that," A'bbni said. "Thank you for bringing him safely back to me."

"I can't really take credit for that," Lai said with a dismissive wave of his hand. "He would not let anything get in his way."

"I know you are talking about me," Shi'chen cut in in Hanen-shii, only understanding the basics of what his brother and Lai were saying to each other. Though he had known that it would happen, now that it suddenly had, he wasn't sure how he felt about it. It was ridiculous to be jealous that his brother had eyes for more than him right now, now that they were safely together again, but he still wished that A'bbni was just a little less enchanted with Lai on sight.

A'bbni laughed and squeezed his brother's hand. "Of course we are, i-sha, because I'm so glad you're safe!"

Shi'chen wrapped his arm around A'bbni's shoulders to pull him closer, relaxing a bit more when A'bbni curled against his side. Kella gave them a small smile. "I am relieved as well, Captain. I have been in contact with several of our partners here in Csereth, and plans are being formulated to meet with you both."

"We are most grateful," Shi'chen replied.

"Is there some place you and your friend are staying?" Kella asked.

Shi'chen shook his head, glancing over at Lai, who seemed to be following the conversation in Hanen-sha relatively well. "No, we stayed at an inn across town last night but have not settled anywhere today."

Kella nodded. "Would you rather stay nearby or with your brother?"

"With my brother," Shi'chen replied emphatically almost before Kella had finished the words.

"Shi'chen!" A'bbni scolded under his breath.

Shi'chen flushed, bowing his head in apology to the dark-haired elf. "My apologies, Lord Kella. I would prefer to stay with my brother to ensure we are not separated again, if that is not an imposition upon you."

Kella's smile was kind. "I understand. I will be happy to have you here as my guest as well, Captain, and your friend if he would like." He inclined his head at Lai. "But if you are to stay with me, I would ask that you please stay within this house, to ensure your identities are known to as few individuals as possible."

Shi'chen nodded. "Of course. We will accept any stipulations you may place upon us."

Kella turned to Lai and spoke in Cserethian, of which Shi'chen caught very little but was sure his brother understood perfectly, and Lai replied with something that sounded positive. Kella motioned for them to follow him, and A'bbni held tightly to Shi'chen's hand. Lai trailed after them, which Shi'chen was grateful for. He had never asked Lai what he would do or where he would go after he had found his brother; he had just assumed that Lai would stay with him, and the thought of Lai suddenly leaving made his heart hurt just a little bit. He caught A'bbni giving Lai a shy smile out of the corner of his eye and forced back the jealous feeling that surged in him. He had never been jealous of A'bbni's other romantic interests, and he knew Lai better than any of the other partners A'bbni had had. He gave his brother's hand a squeeze and was relieved that A'bbni gave him one in return.

Kella led them up the stairs. Shi'chen tried very hard not to stare at the luxurious surroundings. After being on a ship for almost two weeks, seeing all the ornate designs and architecture gave him a strange feeling of homesickness he had not anticipated. He glanced back at Lai to see the half-elf also trying not to stare. While he had grown up in this sort of finery, he was sure most of this was new to Lai and not something the sailor could ever have afforded on his own. It reminded Shi'chen again of the handful of coins in his pocket that constituted the wages he had earned and how quickly they could vanish as he bought things he needed.

He wondered about Jaa'jen's family. Lai had said that they would be compensated by the owner of the vessel, but surely the amount of money they received would not keep them comfortable forever, nor would it replace the man they had loved in their hearts. The whole concept was almost beyond comprehension.

Kella stopped across the hall from A'bbni's room, pushing open a door for Shi'chen. "You may stay here, Captain. And you may stay here, Vr Ablewood," he said, pointing to the room next to it.

"Thank you," Shi'chen said, bowing his head. "We appreciate your hospitality."

Kella nodded. "I will have a meal sent up shortly for all of you. In the meantime, do you need anything?"

"No, thank you," Shi'chen said, and Lai echoed him in his accented Hanen-sha. Kella nodded and departed down the stairs. Shi'chen turned to his brother. "You already know I am staying in your room, right?"

"Of course, I do," A'bbni replied with a laugh, pushing open the door across from Shi'chen's to the room he had been staying in. "Do you want a bath while you wait for food?"

Shi'chen made a face. "Gods, yes. We washed at the inn, but I feel disgusting."

A'bbni gave him a nudge into the attached washroom, then moved to the wardrobe to pull out a long-sleeve tunic and pants for his brother. Shi'chen knew it had been a harrowing time for both of them the last almost two weeks, but A'bbni looked so tired, his eyes a bit sunken, his shoulders a bit more tense than usual, and his heart twinged painfully in his chest. He took the proffered clothing, then glanced over A'bbni's shoulder where Lai was standing, leaning one shoulder against the doorframe and watching them both with an amused smile on his face. He realized there was no way he could talk to Lai without A'bbni understanding every word he said in any language, so he just gave his friend a grin. "Be nice to my brother," he said before disappearing into the washroom and closing the door behind him.

CHAPTER FOURTEEN

A'BBNI

A'bbni was sure his face turned bright red when Shi'chen told Lai to be nice to him. He suddenly became very aware of the handsome young half-elf gazing at him across the room, and he unconsciously brushed a few strands of hair off his face. "Please sit if you'd like," he offered in Cserethian, motioning to the only chair in the room that was at the desk.

Lai set down the bundle of belongings he had been carrying before he crossed into the room and took off his cloak, draping it over the back of the chair. A'bbni saw that he had a rapier in a sheath attached to his hip, as well as a knife in his belt. But Shi'chen obviously trusted him, so he was not going to worry about it. The sword by Lai's side made him rather dashing, he thought. Almost like an elven prince. That thought sent A'bbni's mind tumbling down several memories he did not need to think about right now.

Lai spun the chair so he could face him, sitting down on it cautiously like he might break it. A'bbni wondered if the finely carved chair was better than most furniture Lai was used to. He slowly sat down on the edge of the bed, facing Lai, suddenly very glad he had taken the bed instead of offering that spot to the young man. He gave Lai a small smile as he tucked his legs under him. "I wish to thank you again for taking care of my brother."

Lai gave him a grin that lit up his green eyes, and A'bbni had to swallow as his breath caught in his throat. "No need to thank me, Your Highness. Your brother is a good man."

"He is," A'bbni said. "I'm sure he's told you everything about me."

"Not everything, I'm sure," Lai said with a soft laugh. "But enough to feel like I know you already."

A'bbni felt a blush creep over his cheeks and ears, and he twisted his fingers into the hem of his tunic to distract himself. "I'm glad. What about you? Your Cserethian is excellent."

"Yours is too," Lai replied. "But I'm not from here. I'm from Yuntillo."

A'bbni sat up straighter in surprise. "Really? I mean... I assumed..." He blushed deeper, suddenly at a loss for words, which was not usually like him.

"You assumed I had some human blood because of my ears," Lai said matter-of-factly, turning his head so A'bbni could see the short, sharper-pointed ears against his head. A'bbni nodded wordlessly. "My father was an elf, and my mother was human."

"That had to be a strange childhood," A'bbni said softly, his fingers itching to touch Lai's ears, and, he realized with a start, not just from scientific curiosity.

Lai shrugged a little. "My father was not around. He didn't even know about me until I was almost ten."

"That's awful," A'bbni said softly.

Lai shrugged again. "Not a big loss as far as I'm concerned. He was a first-class asshole."

"What about your mother?"

"She was great," Lai said, his voice softening a bit as he leaned back in the chair. "She worked hard and loved me. But she got sick and died."

"During the fevers?" A'bbni asked softly.

"No, before."

"I'm sorry."

Lai gave him a soft smile. "Don't be. If I hadn't started sailing the world, I wouldn't have met your brother, or you."

"I suppose that is a positive way to look at it," A'bbni said. "I have never known anyone from Yuntillo, or even someone who has visited there. What is it like?"

"Kind of similar to Csereth," Lai said. "Weather-wise, at least. Hot in summer, cold and snowy in winter. Definitely not as built-up as Kendarin and Hanenea'a. More mountains, too."

A'bbni loved the way Lai pronounced the names with his slight accent. "You've been to Kendarin?"

Lai nodded. "Many times."

"Where is your home?"

Lai blinked. "What?"

"Where do you live? When you are not on a ship?"

Lai shrugged. "Wherever I am."

"You... you don't have a... a house or a family?" A'bbni asked, not sure why he felt the need to ask such a personal question.

Lai shook his head. "Nope. Just me, wherever I am."

A'bbni felt the blush creep back up his neck. "Is it hard to not have a place to call home?"

"Your brother asked me the same thing," Lai said with a laugh, which made A'bbni laugh, too. "No, I've been traveling for so long, I've never felt the urge to settle in one place. And I make my living mostly by sailing anyway."

"What do you do on the ships?" A'bbni asked, forcing himself to a new topic, afraid what else he might ask if he inquired too much more about Lai and homes and families.

"Whatever I need to, but usually rigging," Lai said, tossing his hair back a little. "Climbing the masts, adjusting the sails, that sort of thing. I am pretty good with a rope."

A'bbni felt his ears go scarlet, and he cleared his throat, staring down at the pattern on the comforter below him. Was Lai flirting with him? Or was he just reading way too much into a purely innocent comment? He tucked his ears back, hoping Lai would not see the redness that was creeping over his cheeks. He glanced up at Lai through his lashes, and Lai gave him a friendly smile. "Did I say something wrong, Your Highness?"

"N... No..." A'bbni said, ducking his head again. What was wrong with him? He was never this shy around someone he found attractive. And he did. Lai was gorgeous. Everything about him, from his strange ears to his fine elven features to the beautiful cadence of his accent, sent a thrill through A'bbni that he had never felt before.

He lifted his eyes again, only to find himself staring at the curves of Lai's legs in his skin-tight breeches as the half-elf shifted a bit, crossing his ankles in front of him, which stretched those long legs into a line up his slim frame. He felt the blush spread further over his skin, sure he was not hiding it anymore. He had met this man not even an hour ago, at the same time he was reunited with his brother, and yet all he wanted to know right now was how the handsome sailor's arms would feel around him. Which he knew was presumptuous of him. While most goblins did not care about gender, he couldn't just assume that Lai liked him, or even liked men. He realized that he had been quiet for much too long and that Lai was staring at him like he was waiting for an answer. "I... I'm sorry, did you ask something?"

Lai cocked his head to the side, which made his high ponytail swish, catching A'bbni's eye like a feather catching the attention of a cat. "I asked if you had ever been on a ship before?"

"Ah... Once, when I was younger," A'bbni replied, forcing his eyes away from the golden hair. "I didn't realize at the time that Shi'chen was afraid of water. But my parents must have, because we never went on a boat again."

Lai nodded. "He still is, but he worked through it pretty well. And I had the ship physician make up a remedy for dizziness that helped him a lot."

A'bbni could not stop his ears from perking up. "I will have to get that information," he said, probably with a little too much excitement in his voice.

"I know what it is, I'll give it to you," Lai replied, giving him a bright smile.

"That... would be wonderful," A'bbni said, his voice catching in his throat. What in the name of the gods was going on with him? "I'll have you write it down for me later."

Lai suddenly was the one to flush, and A'bbni frowned. "What is it?"

Lai uncrossed his ankles and sat up, suddenly looking a lot less sunny than he had been moments ago. "I, uh..."

"I... I'm sorry. I've offended you in some way," A'bbni ventured softly.

"No!" Lai said quickly, then ducked his head as his own face went red. "No, you didn't. I just... my writing is not very good."

A'bbni let out a breath he didn't realize he'd been holding. "Ah, I see. That's all right," he said quickly, giving Lai what he hoped was a reassuring smile. "You can just tell me then, and I will write it down."

Lai still looked flustered. "I'm sorry."

"You have nothing to be sorry for!" A'bbni replied, his eyes widening. "I should be apologizing to you for making assumptions."

Lai shook his head. "No, Your Highness, you don't have to apologize to me."

"Please," A'bbni said, waving his hand a little. "Just call me A'bbni."

He saw Lai's cheeks grow pink at that. "Are you sure, Your Highness?"

"Yes," A'bbni said firmly.

Lai gave him a small smile. "As you wish."

The thrill was back, making him blush. "I... I assume you don't want me to call you Vr Ii-Ablewood."

"Gods, no," Lai said, jerking up just a little at the address. "First of all, thank you for the compliment, but it would be Chea-Ablewood. And you can just call me Lai." A'bbni blinked in surprise, and Lai laughed. "Yes, I know the goblin class structure, Vr Er-Ha'sen."

A'bbni laughed. "You are full of surprises, Lai."

"I am," Lai agreed with a grin that sent heat through A'bbni's veins again. "I'll tell you a secret not even your brother knows, if you'd like."

A'bbni ducked his head slightly. "Only if you want to," he said, more than a little aware he was shyly gazing up at Lai through his lashes again.

Lai shrugged. "It's not much of a secret, but my name is actually Nikolai."

"Nikolai," A'bbni repeated. "Why don't you go by that?"

Lai shrugged again. "My mother called me by my full name. When she died, I left it with her."

A'bbni felt unexpected tears burn in his eyes at that, and he quickly blinked them away. He was not going to cry in front of Lai. "Thank you for telling me," he said, giving the half-elf a small smile. "Nikolai is a lovely name, but I'm sure I'm mangling it." There were multiple sounds in there that were not found in Hanen.

"No, you have quite a good ear," Lai replied with another bright smile. "I do prefer Lai, though."

"Then I will call you Lai, and you will call me A'bbni."

"All right. A'bbni."

His name on Lai's tongue stole the breath from his lungs, and A'bbni ducked his head again, feeling his heart race in his chest. He jumped when the washroom door opened, and Shi'chen stepped out, dressed in fresh, clean clothes, his hair still damp. A'bbni took the opportunity to distract himself, giving his brother a warm smile. "Feel better, i-sha?"

"Much," Shi'chen said, sliding onto the bed next to him and giving him a hug. A'bbni closed his eyes as the familiar scent of his brother enveloped him, along with the underlying scent of sandalwood and honey from the bath oils. "Almost like home."

"Almost," A'bbni said softly.

Lai stood up from the chair, stretching just enough that A'bbni couldn't help but stare. "I should go, let you two talk," he said in Hanen-shii, giving them both a warm smile. "It was nice to finally meet you, A'bbni."

"You too, Lai," A'bbni said softly, the heat dancing over his face again as Lai said his name. The half-elf grabbed his pack and strode out the door, closing it with a click behind him.

CHAPTER FIFTEEN

SHI'CHEN

"You like him." Shi'chen hadn't meant to make A'bbni jump after the door had closed behind Lai, but he did, and his twin gave him a soft jab in the ribs with his elbow. "I knew you would."

"I just met him."

"Hasn't stopped you before," Shi'chen teased.

A'bbni grabbed a pillow and whacked him lightly in the face with it. "Can we not talk about this right now?"

Shi'chen laughed and pulled A'bbni down next to him on the bed so they were resting forehead to forehead. "How are your injuries, i-sha?" he asked, letting the familiar warmth of his brother wash over him.

"Better," A'bbni replied. "A few scars, but nothing permanent."

"Good." Shi'chen was silent for a moment before he pulled back so he could look into A'bbni's eyes. "I know you don't blame me, but I blame myself, and I am so, so sorry for what happened to you. That was my failing."

"It was not," A'bbni replied, reaching up to catch Shi'chen's hand in his own and giving it a soft squeeze. "There was nothing either of us could have done."

"I did not protect you, i-sha," Shi'chen said, curling his fingers against A'bbni's. "And for that, I can never forgive myself."

"No," A'bbni said firmly. "If anything, I was the impediment to you being able to escape."

"You are not an impediment," Shi'chen replied, sitting up sharply. "You are my heart. I would never leave you behind."

"Then you cannot say you failed," A'bbni said, sitting up to meet his gaze. "In fact, I forbid you from saying that you did."

"Ah, you forbid it, Your Highness?" Shi'chen said, raising a dark brow.

A'bbni rolled his eyes. "I do."

"As my lord commands," Shi'chen said, giving him a playful bow, making A'bbni laugh, a sound that he had missed more than he could have ever imagined. "Have you heard any news from home?"

A'bbni nodded weakly. "En'shea has blamed us for killing Father and the Imperial Senate, and now there's a reward for our capture."

Shi'chen sighed. "Fuck... Well, not much we can do about that right now. How much damage do you think En'shea has done already?"

"A lot," A'bbni said with a flinch.

Shi'chen brushed a stray hair off A'bbni's forehead. "We will set it right again."

"But how many people will suffer and die before then?" A'bbni asked.

Shi'chen's ears drooped at that. Of course, A'bbni was more concerned for their people than he was about their situation. "I know," he soothed, stroking his hand down A'bbni's back gently. "But you can't stop all the suffering in the world, i-sha, no matter how hard you try. And that's not your fault."

A'bbni nodded, his eyes brimming with tears, and Shi'chen reached up to wipe them away. As his thumb brushed A'bbni's face, his brother jumped and pulled back, his hands curling into involuntary fists on his lap, and Shi'chen blinked in surprise. "Are you all right?" he asked.

"Y... Yes," A'bbni said, using the back of his hand to wipe away the tears from his cheeks. "I am sorry."

"You do not have to apologize." Seeing his brother's tears made his heart ache, but he was at least glad he could be there to comfort him now and take his mind away from everything for a little while. "I saw your notes on the desk. Tell me what you learned."

"You don't have to distract me, you know," A'bbni said, giving a last swipe to his eyes with the back of his hand.

"I know. But I've missed hearing about all the autopsies and bedside rounds you used to do," Shi'chen said with a playful smile. "And, I had to let you know that your experiment worked." He held out his left arm so A'bbni could see that the cut from Hi'jan's blade that he treated had healed and was now only a barely-visible white scar against his dark gray skin.

A'bbni's smile warmed him all over as his brother moved to examine the spot, stroking his fingers over Shi'chen's arm. This was all that he wanted, to be here with his brother, safe and happy, away from En'shea and Hi'jan and the dangers of the palace and the court. He would give anything in the world to just be able to run away with him, find a quiet place to live, let A'bbni finish his studies and become an amazing physician, and never have to think about any of it ever again. He knew that was foolish on his part, but just for now, being back with A'bbni was enough.

Lord Kella sent up meals for them, and somehow, all three of them ended up in Lai's room to eat, sitting on the floor goblin-style while they did. Shi'chen tried very hard not to get jealous when Lai would say something to his brother in Cserethian, and A'bbni would laugh and say something back, his cheeks unusually red whenever

Lai looked at him. The flirting was obvious even to him, but hearing his brother laugh again made Shi'chen's heart flutter. A'bbni had been so hurt and frightened the last time he had seen him. His laughter and banter with Lai and the shy way he looked at the half-elf out of the corner of his eye when he thought no one was looking reminded him of the way their lives had been so carefree back at the palace. He knew those days were over. They had been over as soon as En'shea had murdered their Father and the Senate. But knowing that, somewhere inside, A'bbni was still the brother he loved was reassuring.

Eventually the conversation turned to the meeting A'bbni had a few days ago with the Council. Shi'chen felt his blood heat as he listened to the way the three nobles had talked to his brother and tried to manipulate him. "Can we trust any of them?" he asked.

"I wouldn't," A'bbni replied, shaking his head.

"I don't know any of them, and I already don't trust them," Lai added.

Shi'chen sighed heavily. "But we need them for now. We don't know anything about this rebellion or how to find them. And now there's a price on our heads." Just the thought of that made him feel sick. It was a quick and easy way to ensure that the entire country was looking for them and that they couldn't trust anyone. If the Council were members of nobility, as A'bbni had said, they might not be as motivated by money, but who knew for sure? Currying favor with the ruler of a country was certainly not nothing either.

A'bbni sighed and squeezed Shi'chen's hand. "I think for now we need to play their game until we can figure out exactly what it is that they want from us."

Shi'chen couldn't stop a groan. "You know I hate court politics."

"I know," A'bbni soothed.

"You mean you can't just punch everyone in the court you don't like?" Lai asked, tipping his head curiously.

A'bbni choked on a laugh, and Shi'chen gave Lai a shove on the arm. "You think you're funny."

"I know I am," Lai replied, giving him a bright grin that Shi'chen returned. He was more than a little happy that his friend had not run off as soon as he had delivered Shi'chen to his brother, though whether that was because of A'bbni or not, he had no idea.

"I have a feeling the Council will want to talk to us soon," A'bbni said with a sigh, leaning his cheek on Shi'chen's shoulder.

Shi'chen stroked his fingers gently through his brother's curls, glad that A'bbni did not pull away this time. "We'll be ready for them," he reassured. "Until then, I'm just glad to be back with you."

The meeting with the Council came sooner than anticipated. By the time the twins had awakened the next morning – Shi'chen curled up in A'bbni's bed around his brother – there was a message waiting, informing them that the Council wished to meet with them that afternoon.

"I can already tell you this is going to go poorly," Shi'chen grumbled, staring down at his fingernails like they held the answers to the universe. They were sitting in one of the offices in Lord Kella's house. The Council had sent word that they would meet with them at the Arvay estate rather than risk having them travel on the streets where, even separately, they could be recognized. While Shi'chen knew this made sense, it still put him on edge. He already knew he did not like the Council, and he was not eager to meet with them in a place that was supposed to be safe for them.

Sitting next to him, A'bbni looked entirely too calm for the situation. "Agreed. But we're using this as an opportunity to learn more about what the Council wants."

Shi'chen growled softly in his throat. "I would bet anything they want us dead."

A'bbni did not respond to that, just curled his fingers around the cuffs of his tunic, as if to pull the long sleeves further down. Shi'chen caught the movement and placed his hand lightly on A'bbni's wrist. He did not need to be reminded of the scars that still marked A'bbni's back or the humiliation and pain Hi'jan had inflicted on him. "I'm sorry, i-sha. It will be all right. I will not let anything happen to you."

"I know," A'bbni said softly, shifting to lay his head on Shi'chen's shoulder for a moment. They had decided that Shi'chen was going to be his usual abrasive self, making A'bbni seem like the meek one in comparison, to figure out what the Council was trying to achieve, since the Council did not know either of them well enough to know what parts were genuine. And Shi'chen had no doubt that he would irritate the Council quite easily with his contempt; he would not have to fake that.

Shi'chen gave his brother a gentle hug, then let go as there was a polite knock on the door. A moment later, the door opened, and Garina admitted the three Council members into the room. A'bbni stood, and Shi'chen mirrored him, knowing the etiquette was to stand to show them respect, even though he felt they deserved none.

Mii'ra smiled at them as they moved to the table where chairs waited. "Good day, Your Highness," she said, bowing her head to A'bbni.

"Good day, Your Eminence," A'bbni greeted, and Shi'chen had to admire how confident and cheerful his brother sounded. "We present our brother, Captain Shi'chen Er-Ha'sen. This is Var Mii'ra An-Sha'kri."

"Your Eminence," Shi'chen said, giving her the smallest bow polite protocol would allow.

"And Vr Jin'fen An-Gea'la," A'bbni said, nodding to the large man next to her.

"Your Eminence," Shi'chen greeted him.

"Captain," Jin'fen acknowledged.

"And Vr Ba'shea Ii-Heshar."

A'bbni had warned him of Ba'shea's ties to slave trading in the past, and Shi'chen had to suppress the urge to spit in the man's face. He wondered if he had met him before, as there seemed to be something familiar about him that was unsettling. The old goblin gave Shi'chen a smile that would not have looked out of place on a crocodile. "Your Prominence," he greeted the man, keeping his tone polite, envying A'bbni's ability to seem so calm all the time.

"Please, sit," A'bbni offered as he and Shi'chen sat down.

"How was your journey, Captain?" Mii'ra asked as the Council members sat down across from them.

"Fine, thank you," Shi'chen said with a polite smile. Even if he was inclined to talk to the Council, his experiences on the ship were not something he intended to discuss with them. "Our brother says that you are in contact with members of the rebellion against the Emperor."

"Indeed," Jin'fen said, folding his hands together on the tabletop. "We have contacts in various cities, but many are located in Er'hadin."

"Are these contacts trustworthy, considering the Emperor has placed a price on our heads?" Shi'chen asked. Next to him, A'bbni's ears turned just a bit red at his forthrightness.

Mii'ra flushed at that. "Your Highness," she started, but Shi'chen interrupted again.

"We asked a question, Var An-Sha'kri. We refuse to put ourself or our brother in further danger if our safety is not considered. Are those involved in the rebellion trustworthy or not?"

Mii'ra looked like she wanted to scold him, but he ignored it. A'bbni was the diplomatic one. He was a Captain of the palace guard, and he was not going to let them forget it.

"They are, Your Highness," Jin'fen said in his low, rumbly voice. "We can all safely agree that those involved in the rebellion support you and would not turn you in. And as the Emperor's reach grows, more people are turning away from him."

"What is the news from Er'hadin?" A'bbni asked curiously.

The Council members exchanged glances before Jin'fen said, "After the death of Commander Ahea'a An-Sher'vaat, Captain Hi'jan Hin-Ve'ssa was named Commander. Those in Honor Garrison were given the choice to swear loyalty to the Emperor or be sent to the western quarries. As far as we know, most of them swore fealty, though several did not. Unfortunately, those that did not were likely executed, as we have not been able to find them in the west. But the rest were redistributed amongst Allegiance and Courage, and Dai'chiin Hin-Ka'lla was named Captain of Courage Garrison."

Unfortunately, that answered a lot of the questions that had been burning in the back of Shi'chen's mind since his escape. Dai'chiin was from Hi'jan's Courage Garrison, nearly as vicious as Hi'jan, though not as crafty. He almost laughed at the irony of Honor Garrison being the branch that no longer existed.

He felt a lump in his throat as Jin'fen's words confirmed what he already knew, that Commander Ahea'a was dead. His hand slid into the pocket of his pants to rub his thumb over the pin he had kept on him since their escape. Without her sacrifice, he would be dead, and who knew what would be happening to his brother? He sent up a silent prayer to the gods to bless Ahea'a for what she had done for them.

"Has the Emperor signed any laws regarding the new stance on slavery?" A'bbni asked.

Everyone on the Council shifted uncomfortably, which Shi'chen assumed meant yes. Mii'ra was the first to speak up. "He has. He essentially repealed the laws the Empress Chiia'jen put in place."

Shi'chen tried to remember exactly what the laws were, but he knew A'bbni would know. No matter what, it wasn't good. "That allows for anyone convicted of a crime to be sentenced to slavery, does it not?"

The Council nodded. "Amongst other things," Jin'fen said, steepling his fingers together on the table uncomfortably. "We also have heard rumors that he is opening up negotiations with Kendarin regarding the import and export of prisoners."

Shi'chen barely kept an expletive from crossing his lips, biting his tongue hard. Next to him, A'bbni stiffened, and he could already feel the fury radiating off his twin. The elves had followed the goblin lead into abolishing slavery not long after their grandmother had outlawed it; the High King had met with the Empress personally to discuss the details of her decision, obviously not wanting to have the elves be seen as barbaric by continuing the practice. The fact that the current High King was even considering opening up talks with the Emperor about it was worrisome. "We need to do something as soon as possible, before the Emperor can do too much damage."

"We agree, Captain," Jin'fen said with a nod.

"We have plans and communications in place, Your Reverence, Captain, but before we go any further, have you discussed the line of succession?" Ba'shea asked, giving them a calculated look.

"We have," A'bbni said. But that was all he said. The Council waited for him to continue, but he did not, and Shi'chen held back a smirk.

"And?" Ba'shea asked.

Shi'chen gave the Council a cold smile in return. "Neither of us will take the throne if you intend to simply depose us once you have found a ruler you consider more suitable," he replied, narrowing his eyes dangerously. "You saved us from death at the hands of the Emperor. We will not be pawns in whatever game you are trying to play just so you can sacrifice us again."

"Are you saying you both wish to abdicate the throne?" Mii'ra asked, tipping her head curiously.

"That is not what we said, nor can we abdicate something we do not yet have," Shi'chen snapped.

"We will make no decisions now about which of us shall take the throne if this coup succeeds. Your support for both of us should be unquestioning," A'bbni said calmly, gazing back at them.

Ba'shea's eyes narrowed for just a moment at A'bbni. "Your Reverence, you do not seem to understand the—"

"No, *you* do not seem to understand," Shi'chen interrupted before the older man could berate his brother, sitting forward in his chair. "You do not create a plan without communicating it to those who need to know. And there is no reason we should not know why you are so insistent on the line of succession. One would think you have malicious intent, Your Prominence." The address came out like a curse.

Ba'shea glowered at Shi'chen as if he could set the young goblin aflame with his eyes. "You tread on dangerous ground, Captain."

"Are you threatening us, Vr Ii-Heshar?" Shi'chen asked, starting to rise out of his seat, his ears tensed back like a coiled snake about to strike.

"Your insolence is not appreciated here, Captain," Ba'shea said, his eyes narrowing in return, his ears flattening in anger. "One would think you were not grateful to us for saving your lives."

"Your insinuation that we need to follow your bidding because of that is insulting," A'bbni replied before Shi'chen could respond.

"You are nothing more than spoiled children," Ba'shea said, giving both of them a withering glare.

Shi'chen raised a brow. "Then why do you not simply leave our Cousin on the throne? He is more of a spoiled child than we."

Ba'shea let out an indignant yelp. "How dare you!"

"We are done here." Shi'chen rose to his feet, and A'bbni mirrored his movements.

"No, we are not!" Ba'shea bellowed, his voice echoing off the ceiling. "You two sit down!"

"You do not give us orders, Vr Ii-Heshar," A'bbni said.

Mii'ra held up her hands. "Your Highnesses, please," she said, giving the twins an apologetic smile, then turning to look at Ba'shea pointedly. "I know we are all concerned for the future of Hanenea'a. Let us not let petty squabbles divide us further."

Shi'chen hissed softly through his teeth, barely suppressing the urge to say that being threatened in any manner was hardly a 'petty squabble,' but A'bbni gave Shi'chen's wrist a quick squeeze to keep him quiet. "Indeed," he said. "Our apologies."

"If we may get back to the matter at hand before Captain Er-Ha'sen voiced his... objections," said Ba'shea, gazing sternly down his long nose at them as if they were misbehaving school children.

Shi'chen rolled his eyes, and A'bbni flicked his hand. "Please, proceed."

Mii'ra gave them another of her kind smiles. "We have contacts within the palace, including several members of the imperial guard who will support you if you return to challenge the Emperor. We would have you both return to Er'hadin. Once there, we have contacts in the city who will meet with you. Many people are troubled by the Emperor's stance on slavery. We believe that, with you there to lead them, the people will rise up to overthrow the Emperor."

Shi'chen gritted his teeth. "That is not much of a plan, Var An-Sha'kri."

"We understand that, Captain, but, as you said, time is of the essence if we wish to mitigate as much damage as possible before the Emperor's decrees fully spread," Jin'fen said.

A'bbni glanced over at Shi'chen, then back to the Council. "We need time to discuss this."

"Of course," Mii'ra said with a soft smile. "If you can send word tomorrow, Lord Kella knows how to reach us."

"We will send word once we have reached our decision," Shi'chen said firmly, closing off any further discussion. All he wanted to do now was escape this room and the three Council members eyeing them like they were a prize to be won at the end of a race. He stood, and A'bbni stood with him, signaling to the Council they were dismissed. He turned and strode from the room, A'bbni on his heels, until they were up the stairs and closed securely in Shi'chen's room.

The meeting had put them both in a foul mood, he already could tell as they settled onto the bed. For him, playing the strategy of court politics was exhausting and frustrating, and even more so knowing that their very lives depended on trusting in a group of aristocrat strangers. And A'bbni's empathy always made him susceptible to the emotions around him. Shi'chen could already feel his own agitation working its way into his brother, and he took a deep breath, trying to bring his roiling thoughts under control. "I don't like this plan."

"Do you have any better ideas?" A'bbni asked, raising a brow at him.

Shi'chen glared at the comforter. "No."

"I don't like it either," A'bbni said softly, hearing the front door open below and voices departing. "But I do not think we have many options."

"I could go back," Shi'chen offered, taking A'bbni's hands and giving them a gentle squeeze. "You stay here and be safe, and then I will send for you when it is done."

A'bbni glowered at him. "Absolutely not. You are not going back to Er'hadin without me!"

"I am not letting En'shea and Hi'jan get their hands on you again," Shi'chen replied firmly, giving his brother an identical glare back.

"No, you would just go alone on a suicide mission, so I do not know what happened to you," A'bbni snapped.

"You think it is a suicide mission?"

"I don't know," A'bbni said with a frustrated sigh. "I just know that I am not letting you go alone when we already have misgivings about the situation."

"I just want you to be safe."

"While you put yourself in danger."

"Yes!" Why would A'bbni not see that was his point? "I am willing to take the risk."

"As am I," A'bbni said firmly. "Do you think me such a coward?"

"You are not a coward," Shi'chen said. "I never said that. I just do not want to put you in a position where you could be harmed."

A'bbni's eyes held a fire that Shi'chen rarely saw, and it made his stomach clench uncomfortably inside him. "I would risk everything to help. You know that."

"And I cannot let you be hurt again, i-sha!"

"You do not get to make that decision for me."

"Yes, I do," Shi'chen said firmly. "After what Hi'jan did, do you think I would let you go back there?"

"I know what he did," A'bbni said, and Shi'chen had never heard so much spite in his gentle brother's voice. It sent a chill through him like an icy blast of wind. "I think about it every day. But that is my choice to make. Would you sit here if I went back to the city alone?"

"No, but I am less likely to—" Shi'chen cut himself off, realizing too late that A'bbni knew exactly what he could have said.

"You are less likely to what? Cry? Get arrested? Have someone fuck you over a table?"

Shi'chen cringed, squeezing A'bbni's hands with his own that were suddenly trembling. "It is easier for me to do something if I do not have to protect you at the same time." His words came out soft, but A'bbni's eyes still went wide with hurt, and Shi'chen instantly regretted them. "I-sha, I..."

"I did not ask you to protect me, Shi'chen." A'bbni's voice was low and flat. "I have never asked that of you. I have never asked you to defend me, or make excuses for me, or shelter me."

"No, you have not," Shi'chen admitted. He dropped to his knees, pressing the back of A'bbni's hands to his forehead. "I'm sorry. I should not have said that." He could feel A'bbni's eyes boring into him, and he pressed his forehead more firmly to his brother's hands in apology.

"You should not have, but you did," A'bbni said, pulling his hands back, and Shi'chen let them go, gazing up at his brother from the floor. "It is not your fault what happened. I do not blame you for it, and I will not. But you do not get to place your own feelings of guilt onto me."

Shi'chen cringed, his ears flat, dropping his eyes to the carpet as he nodded. A'bbni's words were true, but they still stung like a hoard of bees. He took a deep, shaky breath. He didn't know what he was going to say, he just knew he had to say something. But before he could get any sound out, A'bbni suddenly stood and brushed past him. "I need some air." Shi'chen could feel the unspoken *'do not follow me'* in his twin's words, so he just stayed where he was on his knees, feeling hot tears in his eyes that he refused to let fall until the door had shut firmly behind A'bbni.

CHAPTER SIXTEEN

A'BBNI

He wasn't even sure where his feet were carrying him as Shi'chen's words tumbled around in his mind. A'bbni made his way down the stairs and outside into the back garden without stopping. When he became aware of his surroundings, he found he was sitting on one of the cold, stone benches amongst the trimmed hedges, the stone cat eyeing him playfully from its frozen crouch. He curled his legs up under him, taking a deep breath of icy air that cleared a little of the fog in his mind. He knew his brother meant well. But just because he cried easily did not mean that he needed Shi'chen to protect him from the world. And he couldn't. Hi'jan had proved that. Thinking about that night hurt enough without having to see his pain reflected in his brother's eyes. And knowing that Shi'chen's guilt was tearing his brother apart only made it worse.

A'bbni lifted his head as the soft crunch of footsteps approached him, preparing himself to have to talk to his twin. Instead, when he turned, Lai was standing a few paces away, watching him with a concerned look in his grass-green eyes. A'bbni quickly took a deep breath and sat up, giving the blond half-elf a small smile. "Hi."

"Hey." Lai closed the distance between them. "Can I sit with you?"

A'bbni nodded, shifting a little on the bench to make room for Lai. The half-elf sat down next to him, and

A'bbni flushed just a bit at the close warmth, suddenly realizing he had walked outside without grabbing a cloak. He swallowed, finding his mouth dry as he tried to come up with something to say that did not sound completely besotted. Instead, Lai broke the silence. "Your brother sent me to find you because he was worried."

The thought that Shi'chen sent Lai to seek him out instead of coming after him himself made A'bbni's heart flutter just a bit. "Did... did you hear us fighting?"

Lai shrugged. "No. What did you fight about?"

A'bbni dropped his eyes to the ground, scuffing at the dirt with the toe of his shoe. "Shi'chen wants to go back to Er'hadin without me."

Lai raised a brow. "He spent the whole time away from you pining for you, and now he wants to leave you alone again?"

"Was he pining?" A'bbni asked with a soft laugh, lifting his head to meet Lai's eyes.

Lai gave him a grin. "Sure was."

A'bbni smiled back at him before lowering his eyes again. "We never fight. He... he said that he didn't want to have to worry about protecting me. But that is a burden he placed upon himself, not something I asked of him."

"I'm pretty sure you are capable of protecting yourself just fine," Lai offered.

A'bbni shrugged a little, scuffing his toe into the ground again. "I wasn't strong enough to... to stop what my Cousin and Captain Hin-Ve'ssa did to me, and Shi'chen blames himself for it."

Lai was silent, and A'bbni looked into his face to realize that Lai didn't know what he was talking about. Part of him felt grateful that Shi'chen had not told Lai about what happened, but then his stomach dropped like lead when he realized that meant he would have to tell Lai himself.

"En'shea was going to make me a slave," he admitted softly. "To... to a rival Captain who hates us." A'bbni couldn't meet Lai's eyes as the shame flooded back to him. Somewhere in the back of his mind, he wondered if Lai would not like him after his admission, but he couldn't stop now, and the words tumbled out in a rush. "He was going to have Shi'chen executed and let Captain Hin-Ve'ssa have me as a slave in his bed. Hi'jan has hated us for a long time, and our Cousin knew it. So, he let Hi'jan torture me, and when he was trying to get us to... to confess to treason, he..." He took a deep breath, then lifted his eyes to meet Lai's, forcing down a wave of nausea as he finished, "He raped me."

"Shit," Lai breathed, his arms moving to gently wrap around the prince, slow and light enough to let A'bbni pull away if he wanted to. A'bbni blinked at the sudden closeness of the young man, then slowly nestled into his arms, the way he would into his brother's. "I'm so sorry you had to endure that."

A'bbni shook his head, his fingers tangling lightly in the front of Lai's shirt to grip it tightly. "I'm all right."

"Are you?" Lai asked gently, and his words made tears well in A'bbni's eyes. "It's all right if you're not."

A'bbni shook his head slowly. "I have to be strong, for my brother and my people."

"You are strong," Lai said pointedly, reaching down to take A'bbni's chin gently in his hand. "You and your brother are the strongest people I know. But just because you're strong doesn't mean you can't be hurt, or that you're not allowed to feel."

A'bbni took a shuddery breath, glancing around quickly. Lai read the look and pulled him in closer, shifting to shield A'bbni from the view of anyone who might be looking out the windows. And then it all came to a head inside of him. The murder of their Father, the torture at the hands of Hi'jan and En'shea, running from their home, the weeks spent not knowing if his brother was alive or dead, the audacity of the Council, and his fight with Shi'chen all converged on him at once, and he started to sob. The next moment, Lai was gently stroking his hair as he held him. A'bbni wrapped his arms tightly around the half-elf's chest, burying his face in Lai's shoulder as he cried. Together, they sat there for he didn't know how long, Lai not saying a word, just letting the prince cry until the tears finally abated, and A'bbni went still in his arms.

In the silence that followed, all they could hear was the rustle of leaves blowing over the stone paths and A'bbni's deep breaths before he slowly pulled himself out of Lai's arms, his face and ears red as he ducked his head. "I... I apologize," he said softly.

"You have nothing to be sorry for," Lai said, shaking his head, making the sunlight catch his blond ponytail.

A'bbni shook his head, swiping at his cheeks that tingled from crying. "A member of the royal family should be better able to hold their emotions."

"Fuck that," Lai replied, rolling his eyes and pulling a handkerchief from his pocket, handing it to A'bbni. "You are a goblin first, and a prince second. You're allowed to have emotions. Especially after all the shit you and your brother have gone through."

A'bbni nodded, swiping tears off his face with the offered handkerchief. "Thank you," he said softly, and Lai gave him a smile back. Without realizing he had moved, A'bbni suddenly leaned back into Lai's arms, reaching up lightly to touch the tanned cheeks, and pressed his lips to Lai's.

Lai jumped and pulled back, standing up quickly, and A'bbni scrambled to his own feet, flushing as he backed up a step. "I... I'm sorry!" he said quickly before realizing in his haste he had said it in Hanen-sha and quickly switching back to Cserethian again. "I'm sorry. I shouldn't have..."

Lai shook his head quickly, shoving a hand through his blond hair like he didn't know what to do with it. "No, that... It's not..."

A'bbni swallowed. "I... I don't even know if you... if you like... I shouldn't have done that."

"It's all right," Lai said, his own cheeks going red. "I... Your brother didn't tell you?"

"Tell me what?" A'bbni asked.

Lai cleared his throat, glancing up at A'bbni through his lashes. "I, uh... I was married. He... he died last year."

"I'm so sorry," A'bbni said softly. "I didn't know."

Lai shook his head. "You wouldn't know if Shi'chen didn't tell you."

"Do you... want to tell me about him?" A'bbni asked.

"I will," Lai said softly. "But we should probably get back to your brother before he comes looking for you himself."

A'bbni nodded. If Shi'chen had been worried enough to send Lai to find him, he'd be even more worried if he and Lai did not come back in a reasonable time. "Yes, of course," he said, giving Lai what he hoped was an encouraging smile. "Thank you for telling me."

Lai shrugged. "I just don't want you to think that you... that I... I mean..." His face reddened again. "I just... haven't kissed anyone... since Talen died."

"I understand," A'bbni said softly. "I shouldn't have, I'm sorry."

In response, Lai stepped in and wrapped his arms around him, gently pressing his lips to A'bbni's again. The goblin melted into the embrace, letting his lips linger on Lai's as he wrapped his arms around Lai's chest, holding him close.

After a few moments, they both pulled back, and A'bbni's ember-orange eyes met Lai's beautiful green ones. "We... we should get back."

"We should," Lai agreed before their lips met again, hungrier this time, A'bbni's fingers gripping the back of

Lai's shirt while the half-elf's hands slid up to lightly tangle in A'bbni's hair. Both were breathless when they finally pulled away. Lai flushed as he gazed down into A'bbni's face. "Will Shi'chen be jealous? I will not turn brother against brother for my affections."

A'bbni warmed at that, giving Lai a shy smile. "I don't want to speak for him, but probably not," he said softly. "He has never found any sort of... affections appealing."

Lai nodded slowly, reaching down to take the handkerchief and brush it under A'bbni's eyes, clearing away the remaining traces of tear marks there. "Are you all right? Truly?"

A'bbni nodded. The last few terrible hours suddenly did not seem quite as terrible with Lai gazing into his eyes like that. "Yes," he said, squaring his shoulders and tossing his head so his ponytail hung straight down his back. "Thank you, Lai."

Lai gave him a bright grin. "I haven't done anything, Your Reverence."

"You have," A'bbni insisted, reaching up to touch his cheek lightly, then met Lai's lips once more with his own for the briefest moment. Then he pulled back, missing Lai's warmth as the wind suddenly picked up, and he realized how cold he was without him. "Let us go let my brother know we're all right before he does something stupid."

They made their way back into the house, Lai trailing half a step behind him. A'bbni made his way up the stairs, over to Shi'chen's closed door. He glanced back at Lai and shyly reached to take the half-elf's hand in his. Lai smiled and tangled their fingers together, giving them a soft squeeze. A'bbni took a deep breath and then knocked lightly on Shi'chen's door.

It took longer for Shi'chen to answer than he would have anticipated; A'bbni was expecting his brother to be waiting by the door for their return, but evidently, he had not been. When the door finally opened, his brother's eyes met his, and A'bbni was startled to see that Shi'chen's eyes were rimmed red from crying. "I-sha," he said softly, reaching up to touch his cheek.

Shi'chen just wrapped his arms around A'bbni's neck and pulled him in for a close hug. A'bbni wrapped his free hand around Shi'chen's waist, holding him close. "I'm sorry," Shi'chen whispered in his ear. "I'm an idiot."

"You're not," A'bbni insisted, pulling back to look at him, and Shi'chen's eyes drifted down to see where A'bbni's hand still clutched Lai's. He smiled just a bit, looking up at A'bbni and then at Lai, but he didn't say anything, just pressed his forehead to A'bbni's lovingly.

"I'm sorry I tried to control you. I had no right."

"I know why you did," A'bbni soothed. "I'm sorry for being angry."

Shi'chen shook his head, his forehead not leaving their connection. "You are allowed to be angry at me, i-sha, even if I don't like it. But that's my fault, not yours." He reached up to place his fingers lightly on A'bbni's cheek. "I love you."

"I love you, too." A'bbni let go of Lai's hand to wrap both arms around his twin and hug him tightly. They stood like that for several long, silent moments, before Shi'chen pulled back, clearing his throat awkwardly.

"I should... let you two..." He waved his hand vaguely.

"We are not going to have an assignation in the hallway, i-sha," A'bbni said with a laugh.

Lai raised a brow. "We're not what?"

Shi'chen rolled his eyes. "My brother is being dramatic."

"Hardly," A'bbni replied, tossing his ponytail a bit. "No, you and I have things to discuss. You can join us, Lai. We would value your opinion."

CHAPTER SEVENTEEN

SHI'CHEN

Their discussion lasted the entire afternoon, but in the end, they agreed that they had very few options available to them. Their letter of agreement was delivered to the Council the next morning, and within the hour, a note had returned to them informing them that Mii'ra would be coming by the next day.

That morning, the temperature had taken a sharp drop, and heavy, gray clouds hovered low in the sky. After lunch, the twins had been sitting in A'bbni's room together when Shi'chen glanced out the window to see large, white specks falling from the sky. "Is that... snow?" he asked, getting up and moving over to open the window.

A'bbni followed at his heels, holding his hand out the open window for a couple fat flakes to land on his charcoal gray skin and almost immediately melt into wet drops on his palm. He smiled at Shi'chen, holding out his hand again. "That is amazing!"

"It's cold," Shi'chen grumbled, wrapping his arms around himself as a breeze blew in through the window, though watching A'bbni's eyes sparkle in delight was worth it. "I'll take sandstorms over cold any day."

A'bbni rolled his eyes at his brother. "Where is your sense of adventure?"

"Left back in my room at the palace, where it's warm," Shi'chen said, moving over to the bed and wrapping A'bbni's comforter around himself.

A'bbni went quiet, his hand still held out to catch the snowflakes, but Shi'chen could see that his ears had dropped painfully. "Ah, i-sha, I'm sorry," he said, moving over to give him a hug from behind. A'bbni tensed for a moment under him, and Shi'chen quickly pulled back and moved to sit next to him instead.

"I miss our old life, too," A'bbni said softly without moving his eyes from the falling snow.

Shi'chen wrapped the comforter around both of them, resting his cheek on A'bbni's shoulder. "That life does not exist anymore."

"I know," A'bbni said softly, his fingers curling in the cool air. "It disappeared when En'shea became the heir."

He couldn't argue with that. They had not seen the writing on the wall then, but it had been there. A'bbni suddenly took his hand, and Shi'chen pulled away from him for one of the first times in his life. "Your hands are freezing!"

"Why are you so dramatic about the cold?" A'bbni asked, giving him a playful nudge as Shi'chen wrapped the comforter more firmly around himself.

"Because I can be," Shi'chen groused. A'bbni went back to staring out the window. "Do you think that Vr Ii-Heshar is still involved in the slave trade?"

"Unfortunately, it would not surprise me if he is," A'bbni said with a sigh. "Something about him does not sit well with me."

"You felt that, too?" Shi'chen asked.

A'bbni nodded slowly. "I do not know what it is."

Shi'chen leaned over and gave his twin's forehead a soft kiss. "We're together now, so I will not let anything happen to you."

A'bbni curled back against him. "I know," he said softly, and Shi'chen silently prayed that this time he would be able to keep that promise.

The snow began to fall heavier, and by the next day, the entire garden was covered in a layer of shining white. Kella sent the children off with a few of the servants to visit one of their uncles a few streets away, then offered for the twins to have some time outside. A'bbni took full advantage of it, wrapping a warm cloak around himself but otherwise not seeming to care much about the icy wind, more entranced by the falling flakes and the way they packed together. Shi'chen begrudgingly went outside with him, more than a little grateful for Lai's forethought to have him buy warmer clothing.

Lai had spent much of the last few days away from the house, not telling him where he had been going, and Shi'chen did not pry, but this afternoon Lai stayed with them. Shi'chen noticed his rapier was strapped to his hip under his cloak, even inside the confines of the garden wall. If he had one of the goblin short-swords, he might have asked Lai to spar with him. That was something he was missing terribly right now. He had not been able to do any practicing on the ship with the risk of his training giving him away, and on top of that, he was worried about his Honor Garrison. A'bbni had not been wrong when he had said that Shi'chen's guards were loyal to him, not to the Emperor, and he was sure that En'shea was vindictive enough to have retaliated against them for no reason other than that Shi'chen had been their Captain, even if they had sworn fealty to the Emperor to protect themselves.

He was so wrapped up in his own thoughts that he didn't see the snowball until it caught him in the shoulder. He whirled around to see A'bbni grinning before throwing another one at him, which he managed to duck. "That was cold," he said with a playful glower.

"Snow is cold," A'bbni pointed out, already scooping up another handful. "Get moving, Captain, the next one's coming for your head."

Shi'chen blinked, then smirked at his brother and turned to sprint across the garden, icy wind and En'shea forgotten. It was so easy for him to sometimes forget that he was still just out of adolescence when their childhood had been so regimented with studies, manners, and expectations. They both were smart and worked hard, but growing up in a palace was much different, he was sure, than growing up anywhere else.

Another handful of cold snow flew past him, and he dodged to the side, skidding on a patch of ice and having to turn it into a slide to not slip. Yes, he definitely preferred sand over snow. He could hear A'bbni laughing and saying something to Lai in Cserethian, and his brother's laugh made him feel warmer. He would do everything in his power to make sure that A'bbni never had a reason not to smile again. Except take a snowball to the face, he decided as he deftly avoided the next one his brother threw, only to get smacked directly in the chest by one thrown by Lai.

"What the fuck?" he said, giving Lai a playful glower. "That's two against one."

"You're saying that you're not as good as me?" Lai asked with a smirk, already scooping up another handful of snow.

Shi'chen laughed and dove away from the next snowball from A'bbni, only for Lai to catch him again on the arm. "How the fuck are you doing that?" he asked, brushing the snow from his cloak.

"Practice," Lai said with a grin. "There's a lot you don't know about me."

"Apparently," Shi'chen said.

A'bbni rolled his eyes. "You're being modest, i-sha," he said.

"It's slippery," Shi'chen complained.

"And sand isn't?"

"What is he being modest about?" Lai asked, packing another handful of snow together.

"I'm sure he told you that he was the youngest Captain in the palace guards, right?" Lai nodded. "He is considered something of a prodigy in spear and hand-to-hand combat."

Lai turned to look at him, and Shi'chen felt his ears redden underneath the warm hat he wore. "Really?" he asked. "I seem to recall someone getting the shit kicked out of him one of the first days on board the ship."

Shi'chen glowered. "In my defense, I had barely slept in days and had never been on the water before."

"Well, you're not on water now, Captain," Lai said with a grin.

"Technically, he is," A'bbni said, scooping up another handful of snow.

Lai laughed at that. "Fair point, Your Highness." Shi'chen watched his brother blush at that, and he quickly scooped up a ball of snow and tossed it at him, catching A'bbni on his neck, snow clinging to his brother's ponytail. A'bbni let out a yelp, giving Shi'chen a playful glare as he brushed the snow off his skin.

This time, Shi'chen was watching for Lai to throw a snowball at him, and he dove and rolled, coming up on his feet, then immediately doing a flip backward, anticipating the second one Lai threw. He gave the half-elf a grin, enjoying the way Lai was staring. "What?"

"And you had me worried for your safety on the ship," Lai said with a laugh.

Shi'chen smirked, about to retort when Garina appeared in the doorway, announcing that Var

An-Sha'kri had arrived. Shi'chen was more than a little relieved to go inside where it was much warmer. Garina took his cloak from him with a slight bat of her eyelashes that Shi'chen ignored. Lai gave the twins a smile as he pulled off his own cloak. "I will leave you to your meeting."

"No, you should come with us," A'bbni said, catching Lai's hand in his, which made the half-elf glance down in surprise at the touch.

Lai then looked over at Shi'chen, and the prince gave his friend a smile. "You should be there, Lai."

Lai nodded, and Shi'chen smoothed down his clothes and hair as best he could. A'bbni's eyes were sparkling, his cheeks and ears red from the cold, and he was smiling. That made Shi'chen feel warm inside despite his cold hands. He wanted his brother to always smile like that. Garina led them down the hall and pushed open the office door. Mii'ra was sitting in the same chair she had sat in the other day. She rose and smiled at them as they entered.

"Good day, Your Highnesses," she said, giving them an appropriate bow once the door had closed behind them.

"Good day, Your Eminence," A'bbni said with a pleasant smile, having dropped Lai's hand as the door opened.

"Good day, Var An-Sha'kri," Shi'chen said, less pleasant than his brother as they sat down across from her.

She returned to her seat, giving a quick glance over at Lai, who sat down next to A'bbni. "Your Highnesses, in anticipation of moving as quickly as we can, before the Emperor can do further damage, we are making arrangements for you to depart for Er'hadin first thing tomorrow morning. Lord Kella is providing one of the Arvay family's smaller vessels, which also means it will be faster." She folded her hands on the table in front of her.

Shi'chen felt his stomach flip-flop. More sea travel. Beneath the table, A'bbni squeezed his hand reassuringly. "But we will travel together?" he asked.

"Yes," Mii'ra assured him, giving him another smile. "Right now, the plan is for the ship to only take Your Highnesses, Lord Kella, Vr Ii-Heshar, and myself, plus a basic crew."

"And me," Lai interjected. Shi'chen glanced over at Lai curiously out of the corner of his eye. He had not expected that his friend would return with them to Er'hadin, but he certainly was not going to protest.

Mii'ra blinked in surprise, then smiled at him. "You are a sailor, is that right?" Lai nodded. "Good. As long as their Highnesses don't object."

"We do not," A'bbni replied.

"What about Vr An-Gea'la?" Shi'chen asked curiously.

Mii'ra shook her head. "He will be staying here in Csereth, as our contact."

"Lord Kella is coming back with us?" A'bbni asked, looking pleased with that revelation.

"Yes," Mii'ra said with a warm smile at him. "His contacts and knowledge of the city are helpful to us, and he did not want to leave you two alone."

Shi'chen nodded, trying to ignore the flipping of his stomach. "We shall be ready to depart tomorrow, Var An-Sha'kri."

Mii'ra rose and gave them a bow. "Thank you, Your Highnesses. We shall see you tomorrow." And then she was gone.

Once the three of them were alone, A'bbni turned to Shi'chen with worried eyes. "Do you think this plan will work?"

Shi'chen sighed and rested his elbows on the table, his forehead pressing to his conjoined hands. "I don't know. I do not like how many things can go wrong. But, as you said, what choice do we have?"

A'bbni sighed softly, turning to stare out the window again at the softly-falling snow. "I thought about reaching out to High King Fellrin and Queen Verlanon. But after what we heard about the slave trade negotiations, I do not feel that would be a wise idea."

"I agree," Shi'chen said softly. "I do not know where their machinations lie."

"Nor do I," A'bbni said, his fingers idly tracing designs on the tabletop. "And the last thing I want to do is subject Lord Kella and his family to possible danger from the elven court."

Lai was watching them curiously, and Shi'chen realized that he probably had not understood a large amount of what they had just said. "Sorry, Lai," he said. "How do you feel about this?"

Lai gave a non-committal shrug. "Like you said, it's not much of a plan, but it's better than doing nothing."

"And you will come with us?" A'bbni said, squeezing his hand.

"Yes," Lai replied, giving him and then Shi'chen a smile. "I can't sit by and let the princes of Hanenea'a get killed. People are only allowed to hate me because of my ears."

Shi'chen rose to his feet, giving Lai's shoulder a grateful squeeze. "We'll be glad to have you with us," he said.

CHAPTER EIGHTEEN

A'BBNI

The next morning was cold but not snowy. Kella took them in the Arvay family's carriage to one of the nearby docks. The ship they were sailing on was much smaller than either of the ships the twins had been on before, built for speed rather than for large transports. Both Ba'shea and Mii'ra arrived as well. Quenn had stayed behind with Cressus and Nadria, and the twins had left early in the morning before the children had woken up. A'bbni felt bad about not getting to say goodbye to them, but Kella hastily assured him that the children would be all right.

The first day on board involved a lot of Shi'chen hiding in his room away from the windows, and Lai made good on his promise to show A'bbni how to make the anti-nausea drink for him from herbs in the galley. Ba'shea and Mii'ra mostly kept to themselves, for which A'bbni was grateful. He still did not know why he felt so uncomfortable around them, but he was happy to have the time to spend with Shi'chen. Lai left them alone for the afternoon, not telling either of them where he was going or what he was doing, returning late in the evening with a meal from the crew for them all as they sat in the room that Shi'chen and A'bbni had decided to share.

The next day was slightly warmer, though whether that was because they were further south or because the third season was not quite ready to hit full-force, A'bbni was not sure. Shi'chen was feeling a little better and decided to practice on the deck, having found a few long poles that were a similar size and weight to spears. A'bbni left him to it, but being alone in their room was wreaking havoc on his nerves, and he did not feel like wandering the ship on his own either. He debated with himself for a few minutes before he screwed up his courage and headed down the hall to Lai's room. He knocked on the door but received no answer. He knocked again and waited, and finally Lai came to the door, wearing a gray silk robe draped around his shoulders and tied around his waist. His golden blond hair was loose and damp, and he was drying it with a towel. He gave A'bbni a smile. "Hey."

"I'm sorry," A'bbni said with a blush. "I didn't mean to interrupt you."

"No, it's fine, the water was getting cold anyway," Lai said, opening the door wider for A'bbni to come in. A'bbni slipped inside and moved to sit in the chair at the desk in the small room. He wasn't really sure what he was expecting right now. He and Lai had not been alone together since that time in the garden when Shi'chen had sent Lai to find him after their fight, and that had certainly not been his best moment.

"Did you need something, Your Highness?" Lai asked, tipping his head curiously.

A'bbni blushed just a bit and shook his head. "No. I just... don't want to be alone right now while Shi'chen is up on the deck."

Lai gave him a small, understanding smile. "Stay as long as you like." He sauntered over to the bed, and A'bbni tried not to watch him too closely as he sat down on it to work on drying his hair. "I'm going to have to talk to Lord Kella about getting a job on one of his ships."

Even with this ship being much smaller and not intended for luxury travel, the accommodations were still probably much better than what Lai was used to on cargo ships. "I take it your bath was enjoyable then."

"One of the best I've ever had," Lai replied, rubbing the towel over his short ears. A'bbni noticed he had undone the braids that were usually there to mask their shape, all his blond hair flowing over his shoulders. "I suppose it's nothing new for you, though."

A'bbni shook his head. "We have hot baths at the palace, as well as steam rooms."

"Are you looking forward to being home again?" Lai asked, squeezing the ends of his hair with the towel.

A'bbni was silent for a moment before looking up at him. "To be perfectly honest, no, I'm not."

"Why not?" Lai asked curiously.

A'bbni sighed and toyed with the hem of his tunic. "My Cousin killed my Father. They were the only family I had there besides my brother. And now, the rebels will want my Cousin dead. I do not know whom the guards are loyal to, or whom they will defend if it comes to a fight. I do not want to see bloodshed in the streets because of us."

Lai watched him for a long moment, then slowly said, "I don't know the Emperor, but if there are so many who don't want him on the throne because of how terrible he is, knowing that to rise up could lead to many deaths, it must be worth their lives to try to remove him."

A'bbni glanced up at Lai through his lashes. "I suppose that is true," he ventured softly.

"Shi'chen never told me what happened that made your Cousin so bad."

"He has never been seen favorably," A'bbni admitted, shifting to tuck his legs underneath him on the chair. "Even as a young child, he gave many signs of being ruthless and cruel. If it were simply foolishness, I do not think it would lead to the reaction it has. Foolishness can be culled with strong advisors. Cruelty cannot. But it is not just about slavery." He looked up into Lai's eyes. "Even before he murdered my Father and the Imperial Senate, we knew he was dangerous. He has killed before. I don't think my Father realized how quickly he would act against us, though."

"What do you mean, he's killed before?" Lai asked, running his fingers through his hair to comb it out.

"It started when he was twelve," A'bbni said slowly, staring down at his hands. "One of his attending women was found in his chambers with her throat slashed. En'shea claimed that she attacked him. There was an investigation, but no evidence of any wrongdoing was ever found about her. But with no witnesses, no one could prove it was murder, so the whole thing was swept aside."

Lai frowned. "Because he was a prince?"

A'bbni nodded. "Yes. But there were more."

"More than that one?" Lai asked in surprise.

A'bbni couldn't stop a snort of cold laughter. "Yes, more than that one. After that was one of the stable hands, a young boy not much older than En'shea. That could have been an accident; the official story was that he was struck in the head by a horse, but my Father suspected otherwise. Then there was a servant girl who was found after having fallen from a window. People were saying it was suicide, but we knew that En'shea had tried to seduce her only a few days before, and she had told him no. And her injuries were not consistent with a fall from only two stories." A'bbni rubbed at the bridge of his nose as a headache formed at the memories of all the deaths En'shea had 'not been responsible for.' "And then there was his sister."

"His what?" Lai asked, dropping the towel at the unexpected statement.

"His older sister, Prii'sha," A'bbni replied.

"Wouldn't... wouldn't an older sister of his have been the crown princess?" Lai asked with wide eyes.

"Yes," A'bbni said. "So, you can understand why what he's done is not all that surprising."

"Wait, wait, back up," Lai said, holding up his hands. "How did he get away with killing the crown princess of Hanenea'a?"

A'bbni sighed and rubbed at his forehead again. "You remember the fevers?"

"Hard to forget," Lai said softly. The fevers had decimated the populations of Hanenea'a and Kendarin for almost three years. Amongst its many victims had been A'bbni's Mother, and his Uncle, the reigning Emperor I'jjen.

"Well, just when the fevers had died down, our Cousin Prii'sha, the crown princess, suddenly became very sick. Within days, she was dead. Her symptoms were similar to the fevers, so many people blamed it on that." A'bbni met Lai's eyes. "My Father knew better. He suspected En'shea of poisoning her somehow, but he could never prove it. I... I would guess that is why he thought that it would be better to overthrow En'shea when Shi'chen and I came of age but kept it secret from us. Obviously, he did not anticipate En'shea poisoning the entire Imperial Senate to stop him."

"Fuck," Lai said breathlessly. "Your Cousin is all kinds of fucked up."

A'bbni couldn't stop a laugh. "I do not disagree with you on that." He sighed and stroked his fingers over the smooth surface of the desk. "That is why we must go back. He has never been held responsible for anything, and I can only imagine what he could do to those who oppose him now that the Senate and the Regent are gone. Reinstituting slavery is just the beginning, I am sure."

Lai flinched, tossing his damp towel aside. "Would people actually accept that?"

"I have no idea," A'bbni said softly. "I wish I could say no, but some of the nobility seem to think it is their right, and they would not stand against the Emperor."

"And what do you think?"

"I think it's barbaric," A'bbni said firmly. "No one should be treated like that." He cleared his throat, glancing down at his hands that had suddenly started to shake. He twisted his fingers into the fabric of his pants. "I... I know that I would have rather died than live as a slave to Captain Hin-Ve'ssa, but that is why En'shea did it. That's the sort of cruelty he is capable of. He had me tortured because he knew it would hurt Shi'chen. Even when he knew we didn't know anything, he still let it continue."

Hot tears burned in his eyes, and he quickly covered his face with his hand. Lai was suddenly next to him, wrapping his arms warmly around him. A'bbni leaned into his embrace, feeling the brush of Lai's soft hair over his cheek. "Lai... You know the Emperor is trying to kill my brother and I."

"I know," Lai said softly, trying to pull A'bbni closer, but the goblin pulled back.

"You... you don't have to stay."

Lai shrugged. "No, I don't."

A'bbni waited for Lai to say more, but he didn't. He swallowed hard, feeling the first tear spill down his face and over Lai's fingers. "Neither of us ever wanted the throne. I would be perfectly happy to be a physician the rest of my life."

"Then do it," Lai said, brushing away the tears with his thumb, the way he had in the garden.

"What?"

"If you or Shi'chen become the Emperor, you can do what you want, right? So, become a physician. Appoint someone else to rule. You don't have to be in charge if you don't want to."

"It's tradition for the Er-Ha'sen family to be the Emperor."

Lai shrugged. "So? Fuck tradition. If you're the Emperor, you make the traditions."

A'bbni blinked at that, then gave Lai a small smile that he knew didn't reach his eyes. "If only it were that easy."

Suddenly Lai leaned in and lightly pressed his lips to A'bbni's. The prince blinked at the sudden touch of lips against his own, but he kissed him back, his hands sliding up to stroke through the damp, blond strands of Lai's hair. Lai stood, pulling A'bbni up off the chair with him, kissing him firmer as he wrapped his arms around him. Their chests pressed together through the silk of their clothing, close enough that A'bbni could feel Lai's heart beating against his own ribs. He shifted in his arms, and then felt Lai's erection press against his hip. He slid his fingers down from Lai's hair, skimming the edge of the robe, following it down past the tie, before his fingers slipped under it, lightly wrapping his fingers around the half-elf's cock.

Lai jumped and pulled back from the kiss with a gasp, and A'bbni quickly pulled back. "I'm sorry."

Lai shook his head, his cheeks flushed, though whether from embarrassment or want, A'bbni couldn't tell. "No, it's all right, I..." He cleared his throat, gazing back at A'bbni, shifting uncomfortably to try to hide his desire with the folds of the robe. "I'm sorry."

"You don't have to apologize," A'bbni said softly. "We don't have to do anything, if you don't want to."

"I do," Lai said, gazing back at him. "I just don't want to hurt you."

"You won't," A'bbni replied, leaning up to kiss him again.

Lai pulled back to gaze down into A'bbni's eyes. "Tell me to stop if you want to stop." A'bbni nodded, and Lai pressed his lips firmly back to his, his fingers tangling in the back of A'bbni's shirt. A'bbni pressed himself close, and they both moved to the bed, sinking down onto it in a tangle of silk and limbs. A'bbni reached to undo the tie that was holding the robe over Lai, sliding it off him, leaving the half-elf naked, his blond hair tumbling around his head. A'bbni let his eyes wander over the creamy skin, noting a few scars that dotted Lai's chest, arms, and legs. He ran his fingers lightly over a few, wondering what the story behind them was, but Lai did not volunteer any information. He leaned down and pressed a soft kiss to the hollow of Lai's throat before giving it a gentle nip, followed by a light suck, all of which made Lai writhe beneath him, his fingers tangling up into A'bbni's shirt.

A'bbni reached up to pull the shirt off himself, gasping softly as Lai's fingers slid down his thighs, then back up to cup his erection through his pants, his hips giving a thrust into the touch. Lai shifted over him to catch his lips in a kiss before laying A'bbni back against the pillow, his fingers working deftly over the ties of his pants as his lips trailed down A'bbni's jawline, then down his neck and over one bare shoulder.

A'bbni gasped as Lai's hand slid into his loose waistband and stroked ever so lightly over the dark curls there, then drifted gently over his erection. His hands went up to grip the pillow under him as Lai slid his pants down off his hips and dropped them off the side of the bed, leaving both of them deliciously naked in the room's warmth.

Lai's fingers traced over the muscles of A'bbni's torso and hips before leaning down, his mouth following the path of his fingers to stroke over A'bbni's sides, kissing and licking and sucking. When he found the soft part of A'bbni's side that made the goblin jump, he sealed his mouth over it, sucking and then tickling with his tongue as A'bbni gasped and squirmed under him. When he finally pulled away from the spot, his mouth had left a small, dark bruise on the gray skin.

His tongue traced over A'bbni's hip, then up, his breath warm on A'bbni's flushed skin as the goblin writhed underneath him. He pressed kisses just below A'bbni's navel, his chin lightly brushing against A'bbni's erection, making the prince jump and grasp the pillow tighter. He gave a soft kiss to the curls at the base of A'bbni's cock, then blinked as A'bbni reached down to touch his cheek. "Wait."

Lai sat up, gazing back at him with worried eyes. "Sorry."

"No, that's not... I don't want to stop." A'bbni flushed, then said, "May I... do it to you first?"

Lai's worried expression softened into a smile. "If you'd like."

A'bbni's cheeks and ear tips were red. "I... I haven't done that before," he admitted softly. Something about the fact that he was a prince always seemed to make his partners concerned that he should not be pleasuring them in the same way that they did him, as if the prince should not be on his knees for them.

Lai reached up to touch his cheek, giving him a light kiss on the lips. "That's all right," he said, running his fingers lightly down A'bbni's neck and shoulder.

A'bbni kissed him back, then shifted to gently press him back into the mattress. Lai settled back, his blond head resting on the pillow, shifting a little to let A'bbni settle next to him. The goblin ran his hand lightly over Lai's cock, making the half-elf inhale softly. He let his fingers explore him, stroking over the tip with his thumb in a motion that made Lai squirm a little under him before he shifted to lean over, rubbing his cheek against the soft skin of Lai's thigh and hip before running his tongue lightly over the shaft.

Lai let out a soft gasp of pleasure, his fingers curling in the sheets a little. Encouraged, A'bbni ran his tongue over the tip of his erection before opening his lips to give it a gentle suck. Lai groaned softly, his eyes closing for a moment beneath him. A'bbni let his tongue explore the soft skin, enjoying the ability to take it slowly. His eyes drifted upward to watch Lai writhe against the sheets as his tongue stroked over the warm, soft flesh. He pulled back to give the head a soft kiss, and Lai's eyes opened to meet his, his chest rising and falling heavily.

"All right?" A'bbni asked softly. Lai licked his lips to wet them and nodded. A'bbni leaned down and sealed his lips lightly around the head of Lai's cock, giving it a gentle suck, then brushing his tongue teasingly up the underside. That made Lai jump and mutter something in a language A'bbni did not know, which sent a thrill through him. He repeated the motion, watching Lai go breathless under him, his thighs tensing but obviously trying not to push up into him.

He slid his hand down to stroke over the shaft that was not in his mouth as he lovingly caressed the slit with his tongue, tasting a bead of saltiness there. He continued the stroking with his tongue, his fingers playing over the half-elf's cock, listening to the hitches in Lai's breath as he moved. Lai's eyes were closed now. A'bbni gave the tip another sweet brush with his tongue before sliding his mouth down on Lai, as far as he dared with his minimal experience.

Lai jerked up with a hiss of pleasure. "Fuck," he murmured, one hand reaching up to brush through A'bbni's hair and tangle lightly in it, not pulling, just holding. A'bbni felt more than a little pleased with himself at the reaction, pulling back again to give him a firmer suck at the tip before sliding down again, a little further this time.

Lai's fingers curled tighter into his hair, his hips jerking just a bit. A'bbni let his tongue wander over the shaft as he carefully tensed his lips around the base and sucked lightly, feeling the brush of soft, blond curls against his face. Lai groaned, the hand not in A'bbni's hair moving to grip the pillow next to his head. "Gods, don't stop," he moaned, sending warmth flooding through A'bbni at the encouragement. He redoubled his efforts with his tongue, making the half-elf pant and squirm beneath him. Lai's fingers jerked just a bit at the auburn-black curls, and A'bbni pulled back in surprise as Lai suddenly came into his mouth with a soft cry, his hips thrusting up as his whole body rocked with pleasure. He swiped at his lips, swallowing what was in his mouth as Lai relaxed back against the bed, breathing heavily, his arm pressed over his eyes. Not wanting to break the spell, he swiped his damp hand over the sheets, feeling more than a little pleased with himself for making Lai come the first time he had used his mouth on anyone.

Lai's arm moved, his green eyes opening to gaze up at A'bbni as his white chest rose and fell deeply. A'bbni brushed his fingers lightly over Lai's thigh, making him jump and sit up, reaching over to pull A'bbni to him and kiss him firmly on the lips. A'bbni melted into his embrace before finding his back against the mattress, and Lai's hand sliding down his stomach to grasp between his legs. He gasped softly against Lai's mouth, his hips jerking toward the warm touch. Lai pulled back to gaze down at him, his hand continuing to move. "For not having done that before, you're very good at it."

A'bbni went crimson, ducking his head a little. "I'm glad," he said softly before Lai's lips met his again, the kiss softer this time even as Lai's hand began to move more firmly over him, his thumb stroking the underside of the head of his cock that was already slick. He slid his arms up to wrap around Lai's neck, letting the half-elf's blond hair fall over him like a curtain as he moaned against his lips.

Lai's tongue drifted over his for a moment before sweeping down his jaw, then up over his ear, pausing to nibble and tug lightly with his teeth at a gold ring he found before continuing to travel up, his hand's steady rhythm never wavering. A'bbni gasped, squirming as Lai's tongue reached his ear tip and his teeth gently caressed the rounded point there. His hips thrust up toward the hand as he pressed himself firmly against Lai, wanting to feel him against every part of him.

Lai shifted so he was curled against A'bbni, his tongue sliding down, dropping an occasional kiss in its path as he moved back down the ear, his neck, his chest, over one dark nipple. His lips closed over it, and he batted it with his tongue as his free hand slid up to the other one, brushing it with the pad of his thumb.

A'bbni made a keening sound, too overwhelmed with pleasure to be concerned about the noises he made. "Lai," he whispered, his fingers sliding over Lai's shoulders in a futile attempt to touch him all over. Lai moved to suddenly catch two of A'bbni's fingers between his lips, giving the pads a brush with his tongue before sliding them further into his mouth and sucking lightly, his tongue brushing over the tips, his hand still stroking him. A'bbni let out a whine, and Lai's hand moved faster over him, his thumb brushing the underside of the head of his cock with each stroke in a way that sent a spike of pleasure through him before he jerked up and came over Lai's hand with a gasp. Lai's hand continued to stroke him, making him writhe as he rode the waves of pleasure, twitching and squirming beneath him.

Finally, Lai's hand slowed, and he slid A'bbni's fingers out of his mouth, delivering a few soft kisses to the fingertips as his hand came to a stop. A'bbni wasn't sure when he had closed his eyes, but he opened them now to find Lai gazing back at him, looking slightly flushed and more than a little smug. He took a deep breath, sitting up, pulling Lai to him as everything still spun, pulling him down heavily on top of him as he fell back against the mattress.

Lai's lips brushed his gently before he shifted to curl up next to A'bbni, pulling the soft blanket over them both. A'bbni curled against his chest with a sigh, his fingers tracing over Lai's shoulder. "Thank you."

"For what?" Lai asked, tucking A'bbni's head under his chin.

"For... that. You didn't have to."

"I wanted to," Lai said softly, brushing a kiss over the top of his head. A'bbni squirmed a bit, feeling sticky and sweaty now but not wanting to move out of Lai's embrace.

"Would you... want to do it again?'"

"Right now?" Lai asked.

A'bbni laughed, pulling back to look into his eyes. "No. I don't think I could now. But... in the future?"

Lai slid his thumb lightly down the curve of A'bbni's ear. "If you want to."

"But do *you* want to?" A'bbni asked.

Lai smiled, leaning in and kissing his lips firmly. "I would like that," he whispered against his mouth.

A'bbni flushed, shifting to curl against Lai's chest again, his arms between their chests, one fingertip tracing nothing designs over one of the white pecs. "May I ask you something?"

"Mm-hmm."

"You told me that you have not kissed anyone since your... since Talen died. Why did you kiss me?"

Lai stroked his hands lightly over A'bbni's hair, silent for a moment before replying, "To be honest, I don't know."

A'bbni waited for him to go on, but he didn't. "You... you didn't do it just because I am a prince, did you?"

"No," Lai replied, reaching down to cup his cheek and turn A'bbni's face toward him. "I don't care what you are." He stroked his thumb over the goblin's cheek.

A'bbni blushed and turned his head to playfully catch Lai's thumb lightly with his teeth. "You would be the first to feel that way."

Lai raised a brow, leaning in to run the tip of his tongue over A'bbni's ear, making the goblin jump. "You think all your partners only wanted to be with you for your title and not because you're smart and easy on the eyes?"

A'bbni went bright red. "No! That's not... I'm not... that's not what I meant," he said, and Lai laughed, leaning in to silence him with another kiss.

"I know," Lai said, stroking his cheek lightly. "I'm just giving you shit. You overthink everything, I already know that."

A'bbni curled into his arms. "Does that bother you?"

"No," Lai said, pressing a kiss to the top of A'bbni's head. "It's probably good that you do. Your brother doesn't think enough sometimes, and neither do I."

A'bbni laughed brightly at that. "That's definitely true." Lai pulled him in, his lips meeting A'bbni's as they both went tumbling back down onto the mattress in a tangle of limbs and hair and kisses. A'bbni was so busy kissing Lai that he almost missed the knock on the door that was unmistakably his brother. He pulled back to give Lai a sheepish smile. "That's Shi'chen."

"Do you want me to go?" Lai asked, starting to sit up.

"Why would I? And this is your room anyway," A'bbni replied, pushing him back down and giving him a quick kiss, pulling the sheets over him so Lai was at least somewhat covered. He grabbed Lai's robe off the floor and tossed it on before crossing over the open the door.

Shi'chen started to say something, then grinned and leaned against the frame as he saw A'bbni's appearance. "I was looking for Lai, but from that smile, I am guessing I know where he is."

A'bbni stepped aside so Shi'chen could see Lai curled up in the bed. Shi'chen flushed and ducked his head.

"Did you need me, Your Highness?" Lai asked, giving him a lazy smirk.

"Lord Kella wanted to speak with you," Shi'chen said, deliberately avoiding looking at either Lai or his brother. "Just when you two are... done."

Lai nodded. "I'll be there shortly."

Shi'chen flushed. "I'll let him know," he said, then gave A'bbni a small smile. "I'll leave you two alone."

A'bbni hesitated, then softly asked, "Are you... are you all right with this, i-sha?"

"With what?" Shi'chen said, tipping his head to one side.

"With Lai and I, sleeping together."

Shi'chen gave him a soft smile. "If he makes you happy, that is all I care about."

A'bbni dropped his voice to a whisper, switching to their usual mix of Hanen-sha and Hanen-vir. "I do have to ask, Shi'chen. Do you love him? If you do, I would not keep him from you."

Shi'chen gave him a small smile. "You are the romantic, not I."

"That does not mean you do not feel love."

Shi'chen glanced over his shoulder at Lai on the bed, who was pointedly making himself comfortable in the sheets, doing his best to ignore what was obviously meant to be a private conversation. "I... do not know," he said softly. "I have never been in love before, or even felt the desire for it. I would consider him my friend, and if he treats you well, that is enough for me. I would not take him away from you."

"Thank you, i-sha," A'bbni said softly.

"But, so you both know," Shi'chen said, switching to Hanen-shii and raising his voice again so Lai could hear it. "If he breaks your heart, I will have to kick his ass."

A'bbni laughed at that. "I am sure you would, too."

"I would probably let you," Lai replied. "I promise, Your Highness, my intentions with your brother are entirely honorable," he said in very affected Hanen-sha.

Shi'chen rolled his eyes. "Gods, I hope not," he said with a grin before giving A'bbni's shoulder a light squeeze. "My brother has entirely too much honor for both of us." He stepped back, giving his twin a playful bow. "Good afternoon, Your Highness."

A'bbni laughed, then closed the door as Shi'chen headed off down the hall.

Lai reached up to pull him back down next to him in the bed. "I hope you know that I did mean that. I don't ever want to hurt you."

"Nor I you," A'bbni said, curling against him and kissing him warmly. "You know that he will kill you if you do, though."

"I know. He loves you more than anything."

A'bbni flushed a little at that, tangling his fingers into the sheets. It was one thing to know it; it was another to hear it said out loud, especially by Lai. "I know."

"I've been meaning to ask you," Lai said, shifting to rest against the pillow again, his fingers playing over the curve of A'bbni's shoulder. "What is that word you and your brother use?"

"What word?" A'bbni asked, nestling closer into Lai's arms.

"I think it's, i-sha?" Lai said, his tongue stumbling over the word just a bit. "I've never heard it before, though my Hanen-sha is not great, and I know shit of Hanen-vir."

"Ah." A'bbni let out a soft chuckle. "It's not actually a word. My Father," he swallowed at the sudden lump in his throat, pushing it back. "My Father used to call my Mother 'i'jaa,' which means 'beloved' in Hanen-vir. Shi'chen couldn't pronounce that when he was little, so he would call me 'i-sha.' As we got older, it just became our nickname for each other."

Lai smiled into A'bbni's hair at that. "That is sort of disgustingly cute."

A'bbni laughed at that, rolling over to look into Lai's green eyes. "I suppose it is."

And then Lai leaned in and tackled him down into the mattress, kissing him firmly all over, making the prince squeal in a very undignified manner.

CHAPTER NINETEEN

SHI'CHEN

When he was not practicing on the ship, Shi'chen spent too much time worrying. He didn't like that A'bbni was going back with him to Er'hadin where En'shea and Hi'jan were looking for them. But, as A'bbni had pointed out, he did not get to control what his brother did, and the thought of being separated from him again was terrifying. So, he spent the majority of the return trip trying to keep himself occupied.

He was not surprised to have found A'bbni in Lai's bed, nor could he really blame his brother. Whether it was just a fling or something more, he was not sure, but as long as A'bbni was happy, that was enough.

Lai had passed him to go into Kella's cabin later that afternoon and had been inside for a long time. Occasionally Shi'chen could hear a few words being exchanged, but whatever language it was, he had never heard it before. It was not Cserethian or any variation of Hanen. When Lai came back out, Shi'chen noted that his smile was fixed perfectly in place in a way that made him suspect something was wrong. "Hey," he said, giving the pole he held a twirl. "Everything all right?"

"Yeah," Lai said, leaning against the railing to watch him. Shi'chen sensed there was something more, but his friend just tossed his hair that was still flowing loose instead of up in its usual high ponytail and didn't say anything.

"I didn't understand any of it, but what language was that you were speaking?"

Lai blinked, then smiled. "Jilbrechtian."

Shi'chen paused in his movements. "You know Jilbrechtian?" Not even A'bbni knew the language of the elves on the continent that lay so far across the sea and so far north that it was nearly impossible to get to.

"Yeah," Lai said, shrugging like it was no big deal.

"How many languages do you know?"

Lai was silent as he thought about it. "Seven," he finally said.

"Gods… Between you and my brother, I feel so dumb," Shi'chen said with a shake of his head that sent his curls tumbling into his eyes.

Lai laughed and gave him a playful punch in the shoulder. "Your brother got the brains; you got the brawn. Nothing wrong with that. You two are like two sides of a coin."

"The dull side and the shiny side," Shi'chen said with a grin, making Lai roll his eyes. "What did Lord Kella want?"

Lai shrugged. "I'll tell you later."

Shi'chen raised a brow. "Are you sure everything is all right?"

"Please stop asking me that," Lai said before suddenly turning and walking away from him without another word. Shi'chen stared after him in surprise. Lai didn't sound angry, but he definitely did not want to talk about whatever it was. Combining that with Lai disappearing for hours on end when he and A'bbni were together, his friend was starting to worry him.

The ship they were on was much smaller and sleeker than the passenger or cargo vessels, and Kella told them that because of that, they could get much closer to Er'hadin than Kandrea'a because the smaller ship could navigate the tributary waterways that led further inland from the sea. They would be able to dock only a few hours' ride from Er'hadin, at a port on the Hela'nna River, where the aqueducts were built that supplied water to all of Er'hadin, including the palace. He had been to the aqueducts before, though it had been several years, but Shi'chen was glad to have a more familiar landmark to reference.

Ba'shea and Mii'ra had mostly left them alone during the days at sea, but as they neared land, Mii'ra told them that the twins, Lai, and Ba'shea would take a longboat to shore to avoid any soldiers that might search the ship, while she and Kella would stay on board to deal with the paperwork and port authorities. Then, Mii'ra would go to the city and send one of their contacts to fetch them.

Lai and Shi'chen rowed the longboat ashore that night, Ba'shea and A'bbni with them, and then Ba'shea led them through a wooded area near the water to a small fishing cabin. Lai had the twins go to sleep on one of the mattresses there, promising to stay awake and keep an eye on them. Shi'chen was too happy to be back on land again to protest, curling protectively around his brother. But he found sleep was hard to come by; every sound outside, every rustle of leaves, snap of twigs, or gust of wind caught his attention. Now that they were back in an area where they might be more easily found or recognized, every muscle in his body felt a hundred times more tense than it had in Csereth. He ended up sitting by Lai in the darkness, trying to relax both his body and his racing mind. How did A'bbni deal with his mind constantly imagining worst-case scenarios all the time?

Shi'chen was happy when the sun came up, and he sent Lai to get a few hours of sleep. Once they had all risen again, they ate a simple meal from the supplies they had brought from the ship, and then there was nothing to do but wait until Mii'ra sent someone for them. Ba'shea mostly ignored them, and Lai stuck nearby where he could see the twins at all times, which Shi'chen appreciated but wished that he felt less apprehensive about Lai's protectiveness.

It was early afternoon when a cart came rumbling down the road, and an older goblin in a cloak stepped down from it. Lai had been watching it carefully, but Ba'shea stepped out and greeted the goblin man. Shi'chen felt himself relax as he recognized Nen, the older man who had taken the twins to Kandrea'a. Nen clasped their hands in greeting, giving them a small smile. "Your Highnesses," he said. "It is good to see you both again."

"You as well," Shi'chen said, giving his hand a squeeze in return. "Is Var Rell all right?"

"Yes. You will see her shortly," Nen said. "Come."

Shi'chen took A'bbni's hand to guide him over to the cart. "I suppose we must hide again," A'bbni said with a sigh.

"I am afraid so, Your Reverence," Nen said. "It will only be for a few hours, at least."

A'bbni nodded, spending a few moments talking to Nen and Ba'shea as Lai pulled Shi'chen aside and suddenly pulled one of his daggers from the small of his back, handing it to him. "Keep this with you, just in case."

Shi'chen looked up into his friend's eyes. "Are you concerned about something?"

"Not yet," Lai replied.

Shi'chen slipped the dagger into his boot. "Be careful."

"You be careful," Lai replied with a bright smile.

Shi'chen moved back over toward the cart. A'bbni held out his hand, and Shi'chen could see a slight tremble in it. "I-sha?" he asked softly, taking his hand and pulling him in close. "Are you all right?"

A'bbni nodded slowly, but his ears had dropped as he wrapped his arms around Shi'chen. Shi'chen held him tightly, stroking the back of his hair gently with his fingers. "I will be right by your side the whole time. Nothing will happen to you, I promise. And Lai will be nearby, too."

A'bbni cast his eyes up at the half-elf standing nearby, watching them with concern. Shi'chen gave his brother a nudge toward Lai and watched the sailor wrap his arms lovingly around A'bbni to hold him close. It hurt a little that he was having to share his twin with Lai and that Lai could provide comfort when Shi'chen couldn't. But, he realized, it was unfair of him to be jealous. A'bbni was hurting, and Lai was able to help him through that. And while A'bbni's words not so long ago had stung, he was right in that he had never asked Shi'chen to defend him or protect him.

He watched Lai drop a soft kiss on A'bbni's lips and his brother almost melt into the half-elf's arms, and he forced himself to look away. That was just the way it was going to be, and he would have to accept that.

A'bbni moved back over to Shi'chen, taking his hand and giving it a squeeze, and Shi'chen gave him an encouraging smile. "Come on, i-sha," he said, giving him a light tug up into the cart. A'bbni followed him up and stepped down into the hidden compartment. Shi'chen took a deep breath of fresh air before sliding in next to A'bbni and curling against him. The top closed over them, followed by something that blocked out the light, and once again, they were alone in the muffled darkness that smelled of hay and horse. At least this time he could not smell dried blood on his brother's skin, and for that he was profoundly grateful.

He heard some words exchanged between Lai, Nen, and Ba'shea, then heard a creak as Nen stepped onto the front of the cart to drive the horses. Ba'shea said something to Lai that Shi'chen could not make out, and

Lai responded with a cheerful-sounding reply. Then there was the familiar sound of Lai's worn, leather boots on the wood above them, and Ba'shea's tread as well. Next to him, A'bbni curled close and pressed his cheek to Shi'chen's shoulder.

The cart began to move, and Shi'chen felt a sudden jolt of anxiety go through him at how familiar that felt. He groaned and draped his arm over his eyes. "I-sha?" A'bbni whispered softly in his ear.

"I'm all right," he said softly back. "Just... I do not like this."

A'bbni's fingers brushed gently over his cheek, and Shi'chen moved his arm to look at his twin in the darkness. A'bbni gave him a soft smile. "Close your eyes. I am here."

Shi'chen blinked, then gave his brother a small nod. He closed his eyes, and A'bbni's fingers tangled with his, holding his hand close so he could feel the beat of A'bbni's heart against his palm, and that reassured him until the sounds and smells of the imperial city once again reached them.

The wagon bumped and clattered along the cobblestone paths, and Shi'chen was very, very glad when the wagon finally came to a stop and the trap door of the cart was pulled open. They were in a stable of some kind, with multiple horses in the stalls. Everything was clean and well cared for, and they had ridden for some time within the confines of the city. He assumed they were likely at the home of a noble family, though he did not see anything familiar enough to place whom it might be.

He stretched as he climbed down from the wagon, then helped A'bbni down. Nen had them put up the hoods of their cloaks for the short cross from the stables to the back door of the long, single-story house. It was definitely a noble family's home, with bright stained-glass windows in colorful patterns and a maintained exterior and roof.

The back door opened, and Nen ushered them all quickly inside. Once the door closed behind them, Shi'chen turned to see another familiar face. He gave her a bright smile and grasped her hand. "Var Rell," he greeted. "It is nice to see you again." He was actually quite relieved to see her. That meant En'shea had not gotten his hands on her.

The woman smiled softly at them. "Your Highnesses," she greeted. "I am so glad to see you are both well."

"As we are to see you," A'bbni said, giving her a grateful smile.

Rell motioned for them to hang up their cloaks and then pointed to a nearby room with a long dining table. "Please, sit, you must be starving. I will have the servants bring some food."

"Servants?" Shi'chen asked curiously.

The woman laughed at the implied question, her ears flicking, the gold rings in them making a tinkling sound. "Ah, yes, I forgot to actually introduce myself. My name is Zea'dda. Zea'dda An-Hila'ra."

Shi'chen gave a small start at that. "As in, Captain Ra'shii An-Hila'ra of Allegiance Garrison?"

"Captain Ra'shii is my sibling," Zea'dda said. "I am their older sister." That explained why she had seemed familiar to him. He suspected that "Nen" might be Zea'dda and Ra'shii's father; they all had the same shape to their face and eyes, and that would explain a lot.

"Is Captain An-Hila'ra all right?" Shi'chen asked, remembering the ominous rumors about Honor Garrison.

Zea'dda nodded. "Yes. Let us sit, there is much to say about it."

Mii'ra and Lord Kella were already seated at the low table in the dining room, and Kella gave them a small smile as they entered. "I am glad to see you arrived safely, Your Highnesses."

"Thank you, Lord Kella, Var An-Sha'kri," A'bbni said as he sat down on one of the cushions, pulling Shi'chen down next to him.

Ba'shea moved over to sit further down, and Nen followed him, pulling out a long pipe as he sat. Lai hovered uncertainly nearby until Zea'dda gave him a smile. "No need for formality, ma'iir," she said, giving him a bob of her head. "You are most welcome."

Lai gave her a smile and sat down next to A'bbni. Shi'chen could see Zea'dda giving Lai's ears a curious glance as the half-elf moved past her, but she did not say anything, only motioned further down the table at Nen. "As you probably already guessed, this is my Father, Gii'han An-Hila'ra."

Shi'chen gave the older goblin a nod. "It is an honor to meet Captain An-Hila'ra's family."

"And again, we are eternally grateful to all of you for your sacrifices and risks in saving us," A'bbni added.

Zea'dda nodded as the servants set down dishes of food. "It is the least we could do after what happened to the Regent and the Imperial Senate. We are only sorry we did not act sooner. Perhaps the Regent and the Senators would still be alive. And for that, we beg Your Highnesses' forgiveness."

"Please," Shi'chen said, holding up a hand. "We do not blame you, or anyone, for the actions of our Cousin."

Zea'dda gave him a soft smile. "You are too kind, Captain."

"I wish to ask," A'bbni said, glancing around the table at the assembled group. "If this attempt is successful to remove the Emperor from power, what do the people want?"

"What do you mean, Your Reverence?" Zea'dda asked.

"I mean, if the current Emperor is no longer on the throne, there is no reason that a new Emperor has to be installed," A'bbni replied. "If the people do not want to be ruled by such."

Zea'dda was quiet for a moment. "I understand your point, Your Reverence, and I think I understand your trepidation. If the line of succession holds, and you or your brother assume the throne, you would be concerned that you also could be overthrown by the people."

A'bbni nodded solemnly. "Seeing as it would be our risk to assume, I believe we deserve to know if the people will accept a new Emperor crowned, or if another option should be sought."

"Is this really the time to worry about that?" Shi'chen asked with a slight frown, squeezing A'bbni's hand lightly.

A'bbni shrugged a shoulder. "As good a time as any. If our heads are on the chopping block next, I would prefer to know."

Zea'dda nodded. "I understand, Your Reverence. I do not believe any of us would force you to assume the throne if you did not wish to, nor if we intended to simply depose you at our whim."

"Of course, that depends on whether or not the Emperor deserves to be on the throne," growled Gii'han from the other end of the table, giving an angry puff of his pipe that sent a waft of black smoke into the air.

"I believe there is a difference between a ruler who does not deserve to be on the throne, and a leader who will do their best," A'bbni said slowly. "I believe my brother or I would be the latter, but that is a very large assumption on my part of how the people feel."

"If I may, Your Reverence," said Kella suddenly from across the table. "I do not presume to know how everyone in Hanenea'a feels, nor is my own opinion relevant, but I believe the fact that you are willing to ask such a question means that you would be a ruler worthy of the role."

A'bbni's ear tips went scarlet in the firelight, his fingers unconsciously grasping Lai's hand to hold. "Thank you, Lord Kella. If our goal is to eliminate slavery and free all goblins, and others," he gave Lai's hand a gentle squeeze, "then we need to ensure our system of governing is fair."

Zea'dda's violet eyes scanned the table. "Change takes time, but time is something that many of our fellows do not have. For now, I recommend we move forward as planned, in the hopes of moving toward a more equitable future."

"I believe that would be prudent," Mii'ra said from down the table, swirling the wine in her glass. "Var An-Hila'ra, you mentioned to me that we can convene a meeting tomorrow that is representative of the city and decide on a plan?"

Zea'dda nodded. "I believe so."

Shi'chen opened his mouth to say something, but A'bbni suddenly squeezed his hand, and he shut it again, squeezing back. There was something in the intensity of A'bbni's grip that kept him quiet the rest of the meal.

After they had eaten and everyone seemed to mostly be talking amongst themselves, Lai rose, pulling A'bbni up with him and whispering something into his ear in a language that Shi'chen did not know. A'bbni nodded, turning to him. "Will you walk with us, i-sha?" he asked, holding out his hand to his brother with his usual sweet smile in place.

It may have sounded like a question, but Shi'chen knew it wasn't. "Of course," he said, taking A'bbni's hand and rising to his feet. He bowed his head at Zea'dda and Gii'han. "Thank you for the meal."

They both followed Lai down the hallway toward the guest rooms, but Lai suddenly turned the way they had come in and took them out the back door and toward the stable. Shi'chen frowned, watching Lai's steps pick up once they were outside. "Lai, what—"

Lai shook his head, keeping silent until they were back in the stable. He did a quick circuit of the space to make sure they were alone, apart from the horses, before he came back to them. "Lord Kella is sure that Vr Ii-Heshar is going to betray you both to the Emperor."

"What?" Shi'chen demanded, and Lai gave him a pointed look to lower his voice.

"That's what you heard Kella and I discussing in Jilbrechtian the other day."

"You know Jilbrechtian?" A'bbni asked in surprise.

"That's what you got out of that statement?" Shi'chen asked, raising a brow at his twin, and A'bbni blushed.

"I did some investigating while we were in Csereth, too," Lai said. "I don't know a lot of details, but Vr Ii-Heshar is definitely still involved in the slave trade."

"Of course, he is," Shi'chen grumbled, giving a furious kick to a bundle of hay. "What about Var An-Sha'kri or Vr An-Gea'la?"

Lai shook his head. "I did not find out much about them, but I think we need to assume that they cannot be trusted either. They haven't done anything, but Kella says they have made demands of him before."

A'bbni frowned darkly. "Then our first priority should be to protect Lord Kella."

"No, the first priority is to protect you two," Lai replied firmly. "Kella can handle himself, and frankly, he's worth a lot more to both the goblins and the elves alive than dead. You two are not."

Shi'chen glowered at the ground, knowing Lai had a point. "There is no good way for us to make a plan without Vr Ii-Heshar and Var An-Sha'kri being involved. So, they will know every move we're going to make."

"They may know every move, but they may not know when we're going to make it," Lai said, a glint in his green eyes that Shi'chen hadn't seen before. "I've never overthrown a kingdom before, but I would assume in order to remove the Emperor, we only need the Emperor, right?"

"Right," A'bbni said slowly, and Shi'chen squeezed his brother's hand lightly.

Lai grinned. "I have an idea, if you know how you can get to your Cousin."

Shi'chen thought for a moment, then nodded. "The Keep is the easiest place to find him, and I know how to get into it."

"Shi'chen!" A'bbni protested, and Shi'chen winced as A'bbni's hand clenched around his fingers. "The Keep is literally a fortress!"

"Yes, and one we escaped from," Shi'chen reminded him.

"Only with Commander Ahea'a's help," A'bbni said firmly. "And she is not here to help us this time."

"No one else knows about the entrance she showed us," Shi'chen said, gently brushing A'bbni's fingers with his own to get him to loosen his grip.

"That you know of!" A'bbni pointed out. "You have no idea what she or anyone else might have said if En'shea tortured them."

"It's still my best option to get in without being spotted."

"I do not want you to go by yourself," A'bbni said softly. "I will go with you."

"No," Shi'chen said firmly. He remembered the argument that had ensued the last time he told A'bbni 'no,' but this time it was more serious, and he would rather upset A'bbni again than put him in danger.

A'bbni raised a brow at him. "You are not going by yourself, Shi'chen."

"I will not let you go in there with me, i-sha," Shi'chen said, reaching up to gently touch A'bbni's cheek. "I will not let En'shea or Hi'jan get their hands on you again." A'bbni leaned into his touch, his ears drooping at the thought.

"I'll go with you," Lai said, making both of the twins jump.

Shi'chen turned to him, shaking his head. "I could not ask you to do that, Lai."

"You're not. I'm volunteering."

"It's too dangerous for you," Shi'chen replied.

Lai shrugged. "Then it's too dangerous for you, Your Highness. You shouldn't go in there alone."

"You should be protecting A'bbni."

"I am safer here than anywhere else," A'bbni retorted. "Is that not why you wanted me to stay here instead of going with you?"

Shi'chen narrowed his eyes at his brother. "I hate it when you use that kind of logic."

"I know." A'bbni actually looked a little smug at that, and Shi'chen couldn't help but smile.

"Would you rather I take Lai with me, i-sha?"

A'bbni glanced over at Lai, who gazed back at him, the expression in his green eyes unreadable. Shi'chen was sure that the anxiety of the two people he cared about most in the world leaving on a dangerous mission would be overwhelming, but Shi'chen knew he also trusted both of them more than anyone to protect each other. Lai had protected Shi'chen on the ship before ever knowing who he was. "Yes," A'bbni said softly, curling against Shi'chen's chest and tucking his head beneath his brother's chin in a warm hug.

"Then I will," Shi'chen said softly, glancing at Lai over A'bbni's head. Lai gave him a small smile. "Let's hear your plan."

CHAPTER TWENTY

A'BBNI

That night, A'bbni curled up in the bedroom that he had requested from Zea'dda for him and Lai to share. He had tried to fall asleep, but his mind was racing in circles. There were so many things that could go wrong, so many people who could be hurt. And he had to think about every single one of them, even if he didn't want to. It was just the nature of how his mind worked; plan for everything.

After a while, Lai's lips pressed lightly to the tip of his ear. "I know you're awake. Do you need to talk?"

A'bbni sighed and rolled over to face him in the dark, the light from beyond the door catching the beautiful green of Lai's eyes. "I don't know," he said softly. "I don't like any of this."

Lai slid his hand up to gently stroke A'bbni's curls away from his forehead. "Do you think something will happen?"

"No..." A'bbni leaned into the touch. "I don't know what I'm feeling."

Lai leaned down and gently pressed his lips to A'bbni's, his thumb stroking lightly up the back of A'bbni's ear. "You don't have to know everything," he said softly.

A'bbni tipped his head so Lai's hand moved to his cheek, reaching his own hand up to hold it there. "I... I'm afraid," he finally said, his breath catching at the admission he had never said out loud, even to his brother.

"What are you afraid of?" Lai asked gently, pulling him back into his arms. A'bbni leaned his head against Lai's chest, his ear flicking a bit as he caught the beat of Lai's heart beneath it.

"All of it," A'bbni said softly, wrapping his hands around one of the arms that held him. "Losing Shi'chen. Losing you. Being hurt again. Failing the people who are relying on us."

Lai pressed a soft kiss to A'bbni's forehead. "But if you don't try, you won't succeed, right? Isn't that what courage is?"

A'bbni sighed and closed his eyes. "Yes. But foolishness often masquerades as courage."

Lai let out a soft snort of laughter that made A'bbni open his eyes and smile at him, his hand sliding up to caress Lai's cheek lovingly. "It's all right to be afraid," Lai said gently, his hand catching A'bbni's and holding it against his face.

A'bbni leaned up to kiss his lips softly. "Make me forget?"

Lai blinked at him in the dim light before smiling and leaning in to nibble lightly on the tip of A'bbni's right ear, which he had found was a spot that made A'bbni squirm and whimper with pleasure. His tongue tickled the rounded point there as he shifted to rest lightly on top of him, his hands sliding down to hold A'bbni's waist. A'bbni made a soft keening sound that he obviously was trying to muffle, considering they were not alone in the house, his hands sliding up to clutch at Lai's shoulders.

Lai trailed his tongue lightly down the edge of A'bbni's ear, then dropped several kisses on his jaw before their lips met again, a little firmer this time. His fingers slid down to tangle in the hem of A'bbni's tunic and slowly pull it up. He dipped his head down and trailed kisses over A'bbni's stomach, and A'bbni clapped a hand to his mouth to keep his noises quiet. Lai laughed softly and looked up at him. "You know you don't have to be silent."

A'bbni opened his mouth to respond, then caught his lower lip with his teeth to stifle a whimper as Lai's teeth grazed over the soft skin of his chest, then drifted over to one dark nipple, giving it a loving caress with his tongue. "We aren't exactly alone," he said once he was not making unintended noises.

"I have a feeling we'll never actually be alone," Lai pointed out, his fingers moving to the ties of A'bbni's pants, deftly undoing them with practiced fingers.

A'bbni supposed he had a point. It had never concerned him before when he had been in the palace. There were always servants and guards around. He wondered if their weeks of anonymity and privacy had made him wish for it more. It wasn't exactly like goblins were prudish most of the time either, but something about being alone with Lai, just the two of them, not having to worry about being seen or overheard, was so much more appealing. He leaned up and pressed his lips to Lai's as he slid the shirt off him, Lai's smooth skin beautiful in the dim light. He lifted his hips as Lai slid his pants down and off his legs, pressing kisses to his thighs as he went.

Lai's hand slid down over the crease of his inner leg, and A'bbni felt himself suddenly tense just a bit. He let out a breath, his fingers curling into Lai's hair, closing his eyes. The touch was so gentle, so soft, it made him shiver. Lai's fingers skimmed over his hips, teasing lightly at his shaft, then drifting lower to fondle his balls, making A'bbni writhe under the touch. Until Lai's fingers slid between his cheeks to lightly skim against him. A'bbni froze, his breath catching in his throat as the scent of blood and death suddenly filled his nose, feeling the gape of a slack mouth and cloudy eyes watching him. Lai looked up with a frown as he suddenly went rigid under him. "A'bbni?" he asked softly. "Are you all right?"

He knew he was being ridiculous. It was Lai, someone who had never hurt him before. He squeezed his eyes shut, hearing the hammering of his heart in his ears, his hands curling into fists in the sheets below him. He struggled to take in a breath, shifting to curl his legs against his chest.

"Hey, A'bbni, breathe," Lai said softly but firmly, his hands moving to rest on the sheets by his knees, keeping them away from the prince.

A'bbni forced his eyes open to meet Lai's, his breath leaving him in a gasp of air. "I... I'm sorry..."

"Don't apologize!" Lai said. "Gods, it's not your fault. Did I hurt you?"

A'bbni shook his head slowly. "N... No... No, you didn't hurt me..."

Lai slowly moved his hand over to grab his pillow, holding it out to A'bbni. The prince took it, hugging it to his chest and pulling his legs back up again. "Do you want me to go get Shi'chen?"

"No!" A'bbni said, much too quickly and a little too loudly, making Lai jump. "No," he said, dropping his voice down and clutching the pillow tighter. "I... I'll be all right."

"You don't look all right," Lai said softly, grabbing the sheets and gently pulling them over him to cover him up.

A'bbni shook his head, aware his ears had dropped back. He felt like a child being afraid of the dark. There was nothing to be afraid of, nothing that would hurt him, but his heart still raced in his chest much too quickly.

"You... you haven't done that since... since that Captain...?" Lai ventured.

A'bbni shook his head. "No..."

"Fuck, I'm sorry," Lai said again. "I shouldn't have..."

"You couldn't have known. I didn't know," A'bbni replied, feeling guilt tug at his heart. "I'm sorry."

"Don't apologize," Lai said again. "Just breathe, please?"

A'bbni took a deep breath in and let it out, forcing his body to release some of the tension he didn't realize he had been holding. He uncurled his legs and stretched them out just a bit. "Hold me?" he asked softly.

Lai nodded and laid down next to him, wrapping his arms around him. A'bbni curled into them, still clutching the pillow to his chest. He tucked his head under Lai's chin as strong fingers stroked over the skin on his arms and shoulders lightly. "I... You didn't hurt me," A'bbni said softly against Lai's neck. "I promise."

"Good," Lai said softly, cuddling him close and just holding still.

A'bbni closed his eyes, letting the warmth and the scent that was Lai wash over him. "I... I didn't think that I... I would panic..."

"You're allowed to panic," Lai said, pressing a kiss to his head. "He hurt you. Your body remembers that, even if you know I wouldn't."

A'bbni pressed closer to him. "I... It's not like I haven't done that before."

"You don't have to justify it," Lai said softly, stroking his fingers up A'bbni's ear lightly. "I'm not mad, I'm just worried."

"I'm sorry to make you worry."

"A'bbni, stop apologizing," Lai said, shifting so he could look down into the goblin's face. "You don't ever have to apologize to me. Especially not for how you feel."

A'bbni leaned up and pressed his lips to Lai's. Lai held him close and let him control the kiss, stroking his thumb over his ear gently. A'bbni finally pulled away from the kiss as tears began to glide silently down his cheeks. "I hate him," he said softly. "I hate that he did this to me and that you have to be a part of it." Lai was silent, wiping away the tears before they could fall off his jaw. A'bbni curled against him again. "I... I don't want to think about him when I'm with you. I don't want to be afraid." Lai's heart was steady under his ear, a reassuring sound that seemed to thrum in his head. "I don't... want any of this. I want to just be with you, and Shi'chen. Just the three of us."

Lai pressed another kiss to A'bbni's hair. "It will always be us," he soothed gently. "You, and me, and Shi'chen together."

"And the entire country," A'bbni said, hearing the bitterness in his tone.

"Fuck the country, they don't matter right now. You and Shi'chen are the only things that matter to me," Lai replied, stroking A'bbni's hair. "The rest can wait."

A'bbni reached up to run his fingertips lightly over the point of one of Lai's short ears, and Lai held still for him. "I would go away. With you, and Shi'chen. The three of us could run away, together."

"No, you wouldn't," Lai said softly, reaching to stroke A'bbni's cheek. "You have honor, and compassion, and a good heart. You came back here to challenge your Cousin because it's the right thing to do, for your people."

A'bbni curled tighter into his arms. "I... I want to... to be able to be with you, Lai. I want to be able to give all of myself to you."

"Hey." Lai shifted so he could look down into A'bbni's eyes, and A'bbni felt his heart quiver at the softness in the gorgeous, green depths. "We take it at your pace. You're the one in control. And if you never want to do it, we don't have to. It's not about sex. I want you for you."

A'bbni slid his arms around Lai's neck, sitting up on his knees so he could kiss the blond firmly. Lai held him close, kissing him back. A'bbni tangled his fingers into Lai's hair to hold him tighter before pulling back to look at him. "I'm in control?"

"Yes," Lai said firmly.

A'bbni hesitated for a moment. Lai frowned, catching his eye. "What is it?"

A'bbni flushed a little, his ears dipping. "Nothing."

Lai raised a brow. "You know you can say anything to me."

A'bbni leaned in to plant a soft kiss on Lai's throat. He wasn't usually this shy when it came to asking things of his partners. Maybe it was harder because he didn't have the reputation of a prince behind it? He licked his lips and tried again. "Could... we try me fucking you?"

Lai's cheeks went pink, and A'bbni flushed and pulled back, not meeting his eyes. "I'm sorry, that was too blunt of me."

"No," Lai said, sounding like he was trying not to laugh. "Just startled me, is all." He leaned down to press a kiss to the sensitive spot on the tip of A'bbni's right ear. "If you want to."

A'bbni shifted to look up into his face again. "I've done both, and I prefer to be on the bottom, but my partners tended to be more interested in me on top."

Lai leaned down and kissed him lightly. "I understand. I've done both, too, and I like being on top, but... Talen didn't like being on the bottom very much, so it was usually me."

A'bbni flushed, not sure if it was from Lai's words or the mention of Talen. "If you don't want to, we don't have to. I wouldn't want you to not like it."

"No," Lai said quickly, giving him another kiss. "I have no objections, especially if it might help you."

"I'm sorry, I'm not usually this shy when it comes to talking to my partners," A'bbni said softly.

"Stop apologizing," Lai scolded him gently again. He gave the prince a bright grin. "I guess that means that you really like me, if I leave you speechless."

A'bbni laughed and pushed himself to his knees so he and Lai were face to face. "So, you are all right with it?"

Lai nodded. "Yes. But only if you're feeling up to it."

A'bbni slid his hands up to hold Lai's face, pressing a firm kiss to his lips, which Lai returned, sliding his arms around A'bbni's waist to hold him close. A'bbni hesitated just for a moment before letting his tongue press past Lai's lips into his mouth, and Lai let out a moan against him that went straight to his cock. He let his tongue explore, shivering a bit when Lai's tongue met his and then teased over his lips. He nipped lightly at Lai's lower lip, causing the half-elf to gasp against his mouth. A'bbni shifted to lay them both down on the bed, nestling himself between Lai's legs, their chests pressed together as he deepened the kiss again. His racing heart had slowed a little, and now the speed of it was because of Lai's lips on his and the way the half-elf's body curved against him, all soft skin and firm muscle. He pulled back to look down into Lai's eyes, reaching his hand up to stroke Lai's cheek. "Gods, you are so gorgeous."

Lai flushed, ducking his head a bit, and looking up at A'bbni through his lashes. "So are you."

A'bbni gave him another soft kiss, gazing into Lai's eyes. The most beautiful green, his favorite color. He could stare into those eyes for hours, get lost in them. He pressed a kiss to the flat expanse of Lai's stomach, then started to slide his pants off, pressing kisses to each bit of skin that he bared as he went. Lai sat up to help pull them off and toss them to the floor, kissing A'bbni firmly, his hands going up to hold his jaw as their lips met. A'bbni tangled his hands into Lai's blond hair, his hips pressed to Lai's eagerly. After another moment, he pulled back, taking a deep breath. "You're really okay with this?"

Lai nodded, stroking his cheek gently. "Yes, I promise."

A'bbni smiled and kissed the palm on his cheek gently. "I'll be right back then," he said, sliding off the bed and heading over to the washroom to grab one of the bath oils from beside the tub. When he came back, he had to stop and just stare at Lai stretched out on the bed, so beautiful that it took his breath away again. He slid back onto the bed next to him. "You're so perfect," he said, kissing him firmly again.

Lai pulled him down on top of him to kiss him again. "I'm nothing special."

"You are," A'bbni insisted, giving Lai's lower lip a soft nip. "You're mine."

Lai flushed at that, pulling A'bbni close against him. "Yours, huh?"

A'bbni smiled softly down at him. "Is that all right?"

Lai smirked slightly. "Doesn't everyone dream of being kept by a prince?"

"I don't own you," A'bbni said softly.

"Not yet," Lai said, thrusting his hips up against him, making A'bbni groan out loud in pleasure. "But I want to be yours, Your Highness."

A'bbni grinned and slid down to plant kisses at the tip of Lai's cock before opening his mouth and starting to tease him with his tongue. Lai moaned softly, his hips shifting a little as he pushed up toward the wet heat. A'bbni slid his mouth down further as he opened the bottle and dipped his fingers into the oil. He wrapped his fingers around the base of Lai's cock that he couldn't swallow, letting his tongue and fingers stroke over him. Lai moaned softly, his hands gripping the pillow. A'bbni swirled his tongue around the head lovingly, making Lai let out another moan, before sliding his slicked fingers between his legs to stroke gently at Lai's entrance. The half-elf jumped just a bit, his hands moving to stroke over A'bbni's hair, tangling in the soft curls of his ponytail.

A'bbni gave him a long, leisurely stroke with his tongue, followed by his hand, as he pushed his first finger just inside the tight entrance, making the half-elf moan louder and arch his back. He let his tongue explore his lover's skin as he slid his finger in deeper, going slowly as he watched Lai writhe under him. He gave his finger a little curl, and Lai gave a gasp of pleasure. "Fuck..." he murmured, leaning in to pull A'bbni up to kiss him firmly. A'bbni laughed softly and twisted his finger before drawing it back and then sinking into Lai's heat again. Lai moaned and laid back again, pulling A'bbni on top of him. "Gods, don't stop," he said softly.

A'bbni gave him another kiss as he slid a second finger in, and Lai jerked, giving him a firm kiss in return. His hips moved up against A'bbni's hand. "Fuck, I need you," he groaned, his hands sliding up to grip A'bbni's shoulders lightly.

"I thought I was the one in control," A'bbni teased, and Lai's green eyes flew open in surprise to look at him. A'bbni curled his fingers lightly again, making the half-elf stifle a yelp of pleasure.

"You... you are," Lai said, his breath hitching. "I just want you."

A'bbni leaned down to trail his tongue up the edge of Lai's pointed ear, making the half-elf writhe under him. "You want me?" he purred before giving the tip of the short ear a light nip.

"Yes," Lai groaned. "Please, A'bbni."

Lai's words went straight to his groin, and A'bbni gave his ear another loving nip. "Make me slick for you."

Lai sat up, fumbling for the jar of oil, his lips meeting A'bbni's in a firm mesh of lips and tongue as he dumped the oil over his hand and reached between them to stroke A'bbni's cock with his hand. A'bbni moaned against his mouth, his hips thrusting against Lai's touch, giving Lai's lower lip a suckle as the hand worked over him eagerly. He gave his fingers a sudden thrust, and Lai gave a soft whine, his hand working faster over A'bbni's cock.

A'bbni groaned and pushed Lai's shoulders down, adjusting himself between Lai's spread legs. Lai lifted his hips eagerly, and A'bbni slid forward, Lai's heat taking him in and stealing his breath from him. Lai gasped and murmured something in a language A'bbni did not know, which sent another thrill through him, and he gave his hips a thrust to fully seat himself, making Lai cry out softly.

Lai wrapped his legs around A'bbni's waist, opening his eyes to look into A'bbni's face. "All right, i'jaa?"

Lai's unexpected use of the Hanen-vir word for 'beloved' sent a spark of heat down A'bbni's back, and he growled softly in pleasure, his hands capturing Lai's in his to hold them. "Yes. You?"

Lai nodded, squeezing his hands. "Yes. Gods, you feel so fucking good."

A'bbni grinned and pressed his lips to Lai's eagerly. "So do you," he said softly, giving his hips a roll that made the half-elf moan and sent waves of pleasure through him.

This was what he wanted, to have Lai in his bed, their bodies pressed together, making him forget the rest of the world, to forget Hi'jan and En'shea, forget Hanenea'a, forget the risk to their lives. Just him and Lai together like this.

He began to move his hips, watching Lai's handsome face as the half-elf gasped and moaned, his hands holding tightly to A'bbni's. A'bbni leaned down to give him a hard kiss, and Lai shifted beneath him to wrap his legs around A'bbni's waist.

As he thrust against his lover, A'bbni leaned down to stroke Lai's hair, and Lai leaned up to bury his face in A'bbni's shoulder, his arms going around A'bbni's neck to hold him. His fingertips brushed over the rounded points of A'bbni's ears, making the goblin growl eagerly and jerk against him, which in turn made Lai gasp and wrap his legs tighter. A'bbni leaned down to nip and suck at the hollow of Lai's throat, leaving a red mark on Lai's paler skin. Lai caught A'bbni's lips with his own, and A'bbni paused in his thrusts to kiss him deeply, resting on top of him. "You're amazing," he purred against Lai's lips.

Lai flushed and brushed a tendril of hair out of A'bbni's eyes. "So are you," he moaned softly, then gasped when A'bbni rolled his hips against his, his hand sliding down to stroke over Lai's cock between them. Lai arched up, his body tensing around A'bbni, making the goblin gasp and move his hips and hand faster. Lai wrapped his arms around A'bbni's neck, burying his face in A'bbni's shoulder before he let out a loud gasp, spilling himself over A'bbni's hand with a sharp thrust of his hips that sent A'bbni's mind reeling. Lai tensing around him made him almost dizzy with pleasure, and a few thrusts later, he lost himself inside of him, collapsing on top of him as he rode out the pleasure of Lai's tight heat. Lai's fingers dug into his shoulders to hold him as he came down from the little jolts that thrummed through his body from every movement of Lai's hips under him.

He gazed down into Lai's eyes, his own half-lidded as he came back to himself. Lai leaned up and pressed their lips together in a tender kiss, and A'bbni curled against him, kissing him sweetly in return. He shifted to pull back from Lai and rolled onto his side next to him. Lai turned to him, his long, blond hair scattering everywhere as he leaned in for another kiss.

A'bbni shifted to tuck his head under Lai's chin like an oversized cat, and Lai's arms went around him to hold him close. "Are you all right?" Lai murmured in his ear.

"Mm-hmm. You?" A'bbni asked softly.

"Yeah," Lai said, giving his ear tip a gentle kiss. "We should probably clean up."

"We should," A'bbni agreed, stifling a yawn.

"Stay here," Lai said, giving his cheek a kiss before he got up and headed to the washroom, returning after a minute with a damp cloth. A'bbni was already half-asleep and barely moved when Lai wrapped an arm around him to hold him as he worked the cloth over him. "Lai?" he whispered sleepily.

"Hmm?"

"Love you."

Lai's hands suddenly stopped moving, and A'bbni blinked, forcing himself back to wakefulness. He rolled over and sat up to face the half-elf. Lai gazed back at him for a long moment, silent, his green eyes unreadable in the dim light. A'bbni flushed, realizing what he had said, even if he had still meant it in his sleepy state. "I'm sorry. That was very presumptuous of me."

"No, it wasn't," Lai said softly, his eyes dropping to the bedding beneath them.

A'bbni hesitated a moment before reaching up to lightly run his fingertips down Lai's arm. "If this plan succeeds... would you stay?"

Lai blinked, gazing down at him. "Would I stay where?"

"With me. At the palace."

"Do you want me to stay?"

A'bbni nodded slowly. "Yes."

Lai swallowed, shifting to sit on the bed, facing him. "I... I don't know," he said softly.

A'bbni felt his heart twinge in his chest, but he nodded slowly. "I... I understand if you cannot. It is not a little thing I ask."

Lai lifted his head, a smile on his face that still didn't quite reach his eyes. He stroked a hand down A'bbni's cheek before leaning in and touching his forehead to A'bbni's, reminiscent of the way Shi'chen and A'bbni would. "I only want the best for you. Please don't ever let me come between you and Shi'chen. You are his everything. I am the intruder here."

"You're not an intruder," A'bbni replied firmly, a bit surprised at the sudden shift of focus, but Lai pulled back so he could meet his eyes.

"A'bbni, please. However much you care for me, please don't let me take you away from him."

Lai's voice was so sincere, it was actually startling. A'bbni let out a soft breath. "I won't."

"Promise?" Lai sat up and held up his hand in a fist.

A'bbni blinked in surprise, but he mirrored the action, touching his wrist to Lai's. "I swear it," he said, opening his fingers and bringing his palm to his chest.

Lai gave him a weak smile. "Thank you." He reached to lightly stroke A'bbni's curls with his fingers before they drifted over the length of his ear. "You know I don't want to hurt you."

A'bbni leaned into his touch, his eyes half-closing. "Nor I you. Nor do I seek to replace Talen in your heart." Lai's fingers stilled for just a moment at that before he shifted to sit and hug his knees to his chest as he stared across the room, seemingly at nothing. A'bbni swallowed hard. "If your life is elsewhere, Lai, I understand."

He stayed quiet, just watching Lai breathe for a long time before Lai finally said, without turning to him, "A'bbni, I... I've only known you a few days. And... I already know I want to love you. But I have lost everyone in my life that I ever loved. That makes it very hard, knowing that they could suddenly be gone, and I'd be alone again."

A'bbni could feel tears gathering in his eyes. "I... I have never been in a long relationship like you were, and nothing I have ever felt for anyone compares to what you have lost. I would never want to be the cause of that pain for you."

Lai swallowed hard, and A'bbni waited, his heart beating a little too rapidly in his chest. "I never had a brother," Lai finally said. "At least, not one that I ever knew. But I imagine the connection you have with Shi'chen is similar to what I lost when Talen died. I have never felt pain like that in my life, and it has never gone away."

A'bbni felt his breath catch as he remembered when he had to leave the stable for the docks, wondering if he would ever see his brother again. He could only imagine what it would have felt like if he had not been reunited with Shi'chen, had suddenly been completely alone in the world, with no one he knew to turn to for help or comfort as he grieved. He wrapped his arms around Lai's chest, resting his cheek on the half-elf's smooth, muscular back. "You do not have to love me, Lai. It would be enough for you to be my friend."

"Would that really be enough?" Lai still wasn't looking at him.

A'bbni felt tears prickle his lashes, but he forced them back. "If that is what you want."

Lai lowered his head down to press his forehead against his knees. "It's not."

A'bbni gave him a gentle hug and stroked his fingers through Lai's hair. "You don't have to say it if you don't want to," he said softly, pressing a kiss to Lai's bare shoulder. "Not ever. I know you don't want to hurt me, and I don't ever want to hurt you. But I think neither of us would want the other to be unhappy."

Lai was silent again, and A'bbni just rested his cheek against his shoulder, listening to Lai's breathing until the half-elf shifted around to pull him into his arms. Their lips met in a soft, chaste kiss before A'bbni pulled back. "You... you should get some sleep," he said, hoping his voice didn't sound as wavery as it felt. "Tomorrow is going to be busy."

Lai nodded and shifted to lie down, pulling A'bbni down next to him. A'bbni curled against his chest, a few tears gliding silently down his jawline as he wondered if this would be the last night he ever spent in Lai's arms.

The next morning, Lai was up and taking a bath by the time A'bbni woke. Zea'dda had breakfast delivered to their rooms to give them a chance to rest longer before the meeting later that afternoon, and Shi'chen joined him. They sat on the floor cushions, though neither of them really felt much like eating.

A'bbni glanced up at his brother over a cup of tea that he had barely touched. "I have to ask while we're alone, i-sha. Do you want to assume the throne?"

Shi'chen blinked. "What?"

"You are the heir presumptive after En'shea. Following the line of succession, it would be you who would become Emperor."

Shi'chen sighed and rubbed the bridge of his nose. "I know..."

"But?" A'bbni prompted.

"You know I do not want it, i-sha. I'm a guard. But..." Shi'chen reached out and took A'bbni's hand in his own, giving it a gentle squeeze. "I know you want to be a physician. If you want to pursue that, I will take the throne."

A'bbni glanced down at their joined hands. The thought of not continuing his studies was a painful stab in his heart, and he found that, for a moment, he could not breathe. He felt Shi'chen squeeze his hand when he did not respond, and he took a deep breath, setting down the teacup with as much poise as he could. "I want to help people and alleviate suffering. I can do that as an Emperor just as well as I could as a physician."

Shi'chen gazed back into his ember eyes. "Are you sure that is what you want, i-sha?"

A'bbni gave him a small smile and squeezed his hand back. "Yes," he said, hoping the falsehood was not obvious in his voice. He had never deliberately lied to his brother in his life, and it felt bitter on his tongue. If that was what the people wanted, he was not going to let them down. There was too much turmoil for that right now. Hanenea'a needed competent leadership, and without someone at the helm to guide it, and especially without the Imperial Senate in place, their entire way of life could come crashing down. And while Shi'chen was a brilliant fighter, he was not good at court politics, and his desire to not rule would be obvious to everyone. A'bbni's heart ached in his chest as he felt his future plans blow away like sand scattered on a breeze, and he had to take a deep breath to steady his nerves. "I will do it. But if I am the Emperor, I want you to be my Commander of the palace guard."

Shi'chen's eyes widened in surprise. "I-sha... I... I am way too young to be the Commander."

"No, you are not," A'bbni replied. "And the job of the Commander is to be someone the Emperor can trust. And who do I trust more than you?"

Shi'chen shook his head again, taking A'bbni's hand. "I know that, but... I have not earned it. I am your brother."

"How have you not earned it?" A'bbni asked, raising a brow. "You withstood capture and torture, you traveled across the continent, you're preparing a plan to capture a dangerous criminal. That sounds like someone I would want to have by my side, and it is my choice whom I want to trust with my life." He did not bother to add that in no way would Hi'jan continue to be Commander under him; he was sure Shi'chen already understood that part of it.

Shi'chen looked like he was trying to protest but was coming up with nothing to say. "I would be honored to be your Commander."

A'bbni let go of his hand to hold up his fist. "Swear it to me."

Shi'chen did not hesitate, his right wrist touching A'bbni's. "I swear, Sovereignty, I will be your Commander."

A'bbni felt warmth flood through him as their fingers uncurled and palms pressed to their chests. Shi'chen smiled at him, and A'bbni couldn't stop himself from throwing his arms around his neck in a warm hug. "I never want to be without you by my side, i-sha."

"You never will," Shi'chen replied. "Except when I go to The Keep."

"I still do not like this plan," A'bbni said softly.

"I know," Shi'chen said, pulling back to look into his brother's eyes. "But getting our hands on En'shea is the only way we will be able to accomplish anything." He did not say it out loud, but A'bbni could see in his eyes the unspoken, *It's the only way I can keep you safe.*

CHAPTER TWENTY-ONE

SHI'CHEN

That afternoon, Lai and A'bbni went to specifically offer their assistance to Ba'shea to keep an eye on him while Shi'chen found Mii'ra, Zea'dda, and Kella in quiet discussion in one of the sitting rooms. All three looked up at him and smiled as he entered. "Captain," Kella greeted.

"My apologies for interrupting you," Shi'chen said, coming inside and closing the door behind him.

"Not at all, Your Highness," Zea'dda said. "What may we do for you?"

Shi'chen moved over to kneel on one of the cushions by them, wishing Mii'ra would leave, but he could not ask her to do so without arousing suspicion. "Before we move any further with a plan, I must know. Is Captain Ra'shii with us? Or will they protect the Emperor?"

Zea'dda shook her head. "They hate the Emperor. They will do everything they can to get him out of power, as much as they can influence Commander Hin-Ve'ssa, at least."

Kella stared down at his cup of tea, but Shi'chen could see him listening closely to Zea'dda's words and watching Mii'ra's reaction out of the corner of his eye. Mii'ra's smile did not change. Shi'chen felt bad for potentially putting Captain Ra'shii in danger, but Ra'shii could handle themself, and hopefully in only a day or two, it would not be a concern.

"If we are able to capture the Emperor, would Captain Ra'shii stand down?" he asked.

"Yes," Zea'dda said confidently.

Shi'chen nodded slowly. That was something. "I have an idea, but it will rely on the people of the city to rise up, and it may put them in danger."

"I believe that if there is a plan in place and someone to lead it, they will," Zea'dda replied firmly.

Shi'chen nodded, then took a deep breath. "My plan should work. But I need you to trust me." He glanced over at Kella, who met his gaze coolly over his teacup and nodded in agreement.

"Of course, Your Highness," Mii'ra said, seemingly just a little too cheerfully. "We will trust your expertise in this matter."

"Thank you, Var An-Sha'kri," Shi'chen said, giving her a polite bow of his head. At least they would not have long to wait.

There were several dozen individuals squeezed into Zea'dda's large dining room later that evening, the table and cushions having been pushed against the wall to make more room. Shi'chen was impressed with the number of people Zea'dda, Kella, and the Council had been able to assemble in only a day. He recognized a number of faces in the crowd, from some of the merchant nobles to a few of the local leaders, as well as many faces he did not know, seemingly from all levels of the economy. He wondered if this had happened before as they plotted against the Emperor, or if this was entirely unique to their situation.

Zea'dda clapped her hands, and the room eventually quieted. "Thank you for joining us, ma'iir," she said, addressing the group in a mix of Hanen-shii and

Hanen-sha, which Shi'chen realized was probably because most of the common people he saw in the room would not know Hanen-vir. "I will get directly to the point. The Regent's sons have returned safely to us after Commander An-Sher'vaat's most noble sacrifice, may she rest in the tranquility of the gods." Several goblins made blessing gestures at that while a few mumbled words in response, and Shi'chen tried very hard not to let any emotion cross his face. Next to him, A'bbni squeezed his hand gently. "Captain?" Zea'dda said, turning to him. "You said you have a plan?"

Shi'chen nodded, glancing over at A'bbni, who looked a little drawn in the firelight, but his brother just gave him the barest nod, and Shi'chen stood up and crossed over to stand by Zea'dda. "The palace itself is not easy to protect. The walls can be breached with relative ease if a large enough army attacks. The easiest place to protect the Emperor and anyone of importance is The Keep. If the walls and courtyard are threatened, the palace guards will escort the Emperor to The Keep and make their stand there. Due to the cliff against its north edge, it is nearly impossible to get in from that side, and a frontal assault would be repelled. But," Shi'chen paused to glance around the crowd, forcing himself to not let his eyes linger on Ba'shea and Mii'ra. "We know the way in."

The crowd rustled. "What do we do once we're in?" someone called.

Shi'chen held up a hand. "We are not sending in an army of people," he replied. "In order to depose the Emperor, we only need the Emperor, correct?" There was another murmur through the crowd as people thought about this for a moment, then seemed to agree with his assessment. "It is much easier to sneak in one than it is a whole group. We need all of you, the city, to rise up and keep the focus on you. Then a few of us slip in, capture the Emperor, and slip back out. Once the guards realize we have the Emperor, most of them should lay down their weapons."

"And the ones who do not?"

"I suspect, not enough to be a danger to us," Shi'chen replied, with another quick glance over at Zea'dda. "We can overpower and arrest those who do not surrender."

"When would we do this?" Zea'dda asked.

"The guards change every four hours," Shi'chen said. "If we catch them during a switch over, it will cause a disruption. I would recommend the later afternoon watch, before the evening meal. It will be hot; the guards will be distracted." Another wave of chatter went through the crowd.

A'bbni stood up and crossed over to stand next to his twin. "I also think we should do it sooner rather than later," he said, and Shi'chen was surprised by the confidence in his brother's voice. "The Emperor very likely already knows that we are nearby."

"Tomorrow?" Zea'dda asked.

Shi'chen nodded. "Yes, I think that makes sense."

"Who will get into The Keep to find the Emperor?" Gii'han asked with a fragrant puff of smoke from his pipe.

"Me," Shi'chen replied firmly. "I know the likely movement of the guards."

Gii'han nodded in agreement, and the crowd began to mumble amongst itself. A'bbni gave Shi'chen's hand a quick squeeze before raising his voice over the crowd again. "Tomorrow afternoon, we ask for your help in assembling as many of the citizens of Er'hadin as you can to rise up in protest of the Emperor. There must be a significant show of strength."

"We are not seeking bloodshed," Shi'chen added firmly. "Our desire is that no lives are lost. But we cannot deny that there is not risk involved. If you choose not to do this, we understand and accept your decision. But without your support, our ability to strike against the Emperor is limited and will likely result in failure, and the execution of my brother and myself."

Another buzz ran through the crowd, and Shi'chen held his breath without realizing it. And then one of the merchant nobles was on her feet, her arm bent and hand fisted in promise. She was quickly joined by several others around her, and then the entire room was on its feet, arms held out to swear their intentions. Next to him, A'bbni let out a soft gasp of relief, and Shi'chen felt his heart race in his chest as he and A'bbni lifted their own arms. Fists opened and touched chests in allegiance, and Shi'chen did not know when he had ever felt prouder.

After the crowd had begun to dissipate, Shi'chen found himself growing more and more nervous. He kept his eye on Ba'shea and Mii'ra, who were talking to different people around the room. As long as they did not leave, Lai's plan would hold. The half-elf had been hovering in the background for most of the meeting, keeping an eye on the assembly and not wanting to bring attention to himself at A'bbni's side. But now, as the last of the goblins left Zea'dda's house, Lai suddenly appeared by the twins with a bright smile. "I think it will work," he said brightly, wrapping his arm around A'bbni, who nestled into his embrace.

Shi'chen gave him a grin in return. "I do, too."

Lai held up a bottle of some sort of dark liquor he had had Kella get for him, giving Shi'chen a grin. "Join us for a drink, Captain?"

Shi'chen glanced over at Ba'shea and Mii'ra, who were standing near Gii'han and Kella, making idle conversation. "Sure," he agreed, keeping his answer short, as A'bbni had suggested. Lai leaned down and caught A'bbni in his arms, giving him a soft, sweet kiss that Shi'chen tried very hard to ignore. "All right, enough," he groaned, starting toward the guest rooms. A'bbni laughed and followed after him, pulling Lai by the hand until they reached the room he and the half-elf shared. All three of them slipped inside and closed the door tightly.

Lai moved over and grabbed Shi'chen's cloak and the short sword Zea'dda had given him, holding them out to the older twin. Shi'chen slid the cloak on, checking that the dagger Lai had given him earlier was still safely tucked in his boot, then turned to A'bbni, a sudden lump forming in his throat. "I-sha…"

A'bbni wrapped his arms around him and squeezed him tightly. "We will see each other again soon, i-sha." He pulled back to give Shi'chen a brave smile, though he could see the tears glittering in A'bbni's eyes. "May the gods grant you wisdom and safety."

Shi'chen pressed his forehead to A'bbni's for a moment. "I love you."

"I love you," A'bbni replied, giving him another firm hug before pulling back. "Go."

Shi'chen nodded, moving over to the room's window. He pushed open the casement windows and hopped up onto the sill. He glanced over his shoulder, feeling a small spark of jealousy flare as A'bbni hugged Lai tightly and pressed their lips together, but he forced it down. Then Lai was by his side, and Shi'chen jumped down into the soft dirt under the window. Lai followed him down, holding his rapier silently in his hand as he landed. Shi'chen turned to see A'bbni standing at the window, watching them. He pressed his hand to his heart, and A'bbni did the same. And then Shi'chen turned, Lai on his heels, and raced into the darkness of the city.

"So, this is how you two got out before?" Lai asked, his voice echoing oddly against the stone around them.

"Yes," Shi'chen said softly. The tunnel seemed much less foreboding now that he had some light to see, the flickering torch sending their shadows scattering over the uneven walls.

Lai let out a soft whistle. "Brave."

Shi'chen snorted softly. "Desperate, is more like it," he said. "It was this or death."

"Both shitty choices," Lai said.

"Yeah, well, shitty situation," Shi'chen replied with a sigh.

"That seems to happen to you a lot," Lai said with just the hint of a smile in his words.

"It does," Shi'chen agreed. "I'd love for that to stop. But I am sure it won't until we have taken care of En'shea."

"I hope you're right about this plan working," Lai said.

"I hope I am, too," Shi'chen said. "If it does, I have you to thank for it."

Lai shrugged a little. "Just assisting my friends by helping overthrow an Emperor. All in a day's work for me."

Shi'chen laughed at that, then nodded as the light from the torch caught the stone stairs that had just become visible in the darkness. "And now we climb."

Going up the stairs, even with light, took longer than going down them, and both Shi'chen and Lai were silent most of the way up, concentrating on not falling down. When they finally reached the top, Shi'chen was relieved to see that the wall panel was still firmly in place where he and A'bbni had pushed it closed all those weeks ago.

The only problem he was now seeing was that the panel was meant to swing inwards toward them from inside The Keep, not the other way around, so there was no ring or handle to grab to open it. This was easily solved by using his short sword as a lever to get the stone away from the wall. Lai doused the torch they held, and then he and Shi'chen were able to pull it open just enough for them to slip into the deserted hallway, lit only by a few beams of moonlight from windows far down the hallway.

They dragged the door as closed as they were able to without a handle on the hallway side, and then Shi'chen motioned for Lai to follow him down the short corridor. Both had their swords out and ready, but this area of The Keep seemed to be deserted. For now, at least, he told himself.

They made their way down the hall, passing the wooden door of the room he and A'bbni had been held in. That felt like a lifetime ago. Shi'chen felt sick to his stomach even thinking about it, so he just hurried past it and headed up the stairs, Lai following after him, silent as a shadow.

Shi'chen silently thanked the gods and Commander Ahea'a for the knowledge that he had of the layout of the interior of The Keep. The entire royal family did, which meant that En'shea and Hi'jan would as well. The room they had been tortured in was on the second level. The third held several prison cells, and the fifth level was where Traitor's Ledge and the open courtroom was. But it was the fourth level they wanted. Because that, Shi'chen knew, was where the Emperor would be taken. There was a set of rooms on this level intended for the royal family to stay in the event of an attack, and while it was not lavish, it was comfortable enough that a few days would not be spent sleeping on the floor. There were no windows on the interior rooms either, so no lucky arrows or other projectiles could make their way in, which meant the rooms would be dark until someone bought oil and flame to light the lanterns.

They rounded the corner to the fourth level, and Shi'chen pulled up short when he saw that a singular guard stood watch at the door that led to the interior rooms. En'shea would not be inside yet; if he had been, there would have been several more guards stationed in front of the door. The guard looked very bored and tired, at least, not expecting any issues this late at night.

Shi'chen motioned to Lai, who slipped past him, pulling a couple coins from his pocket. He suddenly tossed two of them down the hall, and the rattling of the coins hitting the stone sounded unnaturally loud in the stillness of The Keep. The guard jumped, grabbing his spear and turning toward where the coins had hit. Lai tossed another one, further this time so it came from further down the hall. After a quick glance around, the guard moved down the hall to investigate. As soon as he had vanished, Shi'chen and Lai sprinted for the door. Shi'chen pulled it open, and they ducked inside the darkened room, shutting the door behind them. And then they held still in the darkness, silent as the grave, as the guard's footsteps returned and settled back just on the other side, a door and a stone wall the only thing between him and them.

Shi'chen's heart hammered in his chest, so loud he wondered how it couldn't be heard through the wooden door, and he forced himself to calm it, feeling Lai's warmth next to him. They stood there for a very long time, waiting, no sounds coming from them or the guard on the other side. Every once in a while, he would hear some sound from somewhere in The Keep, the sound of voices talking, footsteps on floors below them or on the stairs, but not in the hallway by the guard for another long while.

Shi'chen was just starting to question whether Hi'jan had changed the guard rotation schedule when he heard sandaled footsteps approaching, and the guard by the door straightened and called out a greeting.

He reached out a hand to touch Lai's arm and felt him touch his hand in return. As the two guards stood talking, they carefully made their way across the room in the darkness, the vague outline of a few furniture pieces barely visible from the bit of light under the door, even after what had been several hours of staring into the blackness. They managed to cross the room in almost complete silence, reaching the doorway of the inner bedroom with the luxurious poster bed. They slipped inside, and then Shi'chen finally sparked one of the matches he had to give them the barest bit of light to see.

There was a bed against one wall, taking up most of the space in the room. A desk and chair were against the far wall, but otherwise the room was free of furniture. Shi'chen motioned his head at Lai to the bed, and they both ducked down and slid under it. Shi'chen sent up another grateful prayer that he and Lai were both fairly short and thin, so they were able to get under it, though with not a lot of room to spare. The match went out, plunging the room back into solid, suffocating darkness. And now all they could do was wait.

CHAPTER TWENTY-TWO

A'BBNI

A'bbni groaned softly, feeling the heaviness of his head as he dragged himself back to consciousness. He was lying on something cold and hard, that much he could tell. He forced his eyes open, the rough stone beneath his shoulder and against his back being the first thing he could focus on. He closed his eyes again for a moment, trying to collect his jumbled thoughts.

When he had woken up at Zea'dda's house the morning after the meeting with the crowd, the house had been quiet, only a few of the servants up getting things ready for the day. He had sat down at the dining table to work on writing several documents, and then... He thought hard, vaguely remembering an arm going around him, and the world had gone black.

He swallowed and felt the sides of his throat pinch. Someone had choked off his air until he had passed out. He took a deep breath, his heart racing in his chest like a company of charging horses. He opened his eyes again, pushing himself up to sitting from the floor on arms that were not quite sturdy, trying to discern where he was. The floor was stone, as were the walls, and as his eyes landed on the singular slit window, he felt panic gather in the pit of his stomach. He was in The Keep, in the same room where he and Shi'chen had been held weeks earlier when En'shea had them arrested. Even the stale, smoky smell of the air and the lingering scent of old blood was hauntingly familiar. His stomach surged into his throat, and he had to force himself not to vomit, taking several deep breaths to try to settle his stomach and calm his racing heart.

He was alone, the door closed. The only piece of furniture in the room was the same scarred wooden table that had been there last time, though now four plain wooden chairs were around it as well. The table where his Father's head had sat, and where Hi'jan had forced himself on him while En'shea made his brother watch. He took another deep breath as the corners of his vision started to go black, and he leaned against the wall, closing his eyes and resting his forehead on his knees as the world swam. This had to be a dream, he told himself. Just a nightmare that he would wake up from...

The creak of the door opening forced him to lift his head, and he scrambled to his feet much too quickly as Ba'shea and Mii'ra stepped into the room, the lines of their faces cast into sharp eeriness by the flickering torches on the wall. "Vr Ii-Heshar, Var An-Sha'kri," he said, aware that his voice was shaking. "What is going on?"

"Our apologies for bringing you here this way, Your Highness," Mii'ra said, giving him a smile that might have been friendly anywhere else as Ba'shea closed the door behind them. A'bbni did not hear the lock click, and he wondered if he would be able to circle around both of them to reach the door. "Please, sit." Mii'ra gestured to one of the wooden chairs around the table.

"I prefer to stand," A'bbni replied, eyeing her closely.

"That was not a request, Your Reverence," Ba'shea said, his voice much lower than he usually addressed the prince. "We have much to discuss."

"What must we discuss that could not have been discussed at the house?" A'bbni asked.

"I am sure you would be more comfortable sitting in a chair than chained to the wall, Your Reverence. But it is your choice." Ba'shea's voice held a coldness that set A'bbni's teeth on edge.

"Your Highness, please." Mii'ra's voice was sticky-sweet. A'bbni hesitated a moment before slowly moving over to sit in the indicated chair, the one facing the door, trying to calm his racing heart. He sat down in it with as much dignity as he could muster, which was not much right now.

Ba'shea took a seat on his left, Mii'ra on his right, meaning he would have to run past one of them to get out. The fourth chair facing him was empty. In front of it, he could still see a discolored stain on the tabletop where his Father's head had rested all those weeks ago, and he swallowed down another wave of nausea. "Whom else are we expecting?" he asked, trying to keep his voice from shaking.

Neither of them answered, just watched him like two hidden snakes watching a mouse approach. He took a deep breath, though he heard it tremble and knew Ba'shea and Mii'ra did too. "Why have you brought me here? Is Lord Kella all right?"

"Lord Kella is fine, Your Highness," Mii'ra said with a soft smile. "A simple sleeping draught in the tea this morning to ensure there was no interference from him or anyone else in the house. We do apologize for having to render you unconscious in the way we did, but you are much more likely to recognize additives."

A'bbni swallowed hard. "What of the An-Hila'ras?"

"Also fine for now," Ba'shea said. "And before you ask, no, we have not done anything to Captain Ra'shii An-Hila'ra, either. However, what happens to any of them going forward depends on you."

A'bbni took another deep breath and let it out, realizing his hands had started to shake in his lap, and he gripped the hem of his tunic to still them. "What is it you are asking for in return for their safety?"

"We have a proposition for you, Your Highness," Mii'ra said, tossing her blond hair back. "Your Cousin is hardly fit to rule Hanenea'a, wouldn't you agree?"

A'bbni raised a brow at that. "Please come to the point, Var An-Sha'kri," he said, wishing he sounded more confident.

"We present an opportunity to you, Your Reverence," Ba'shea said, and his tone made A'bbni's skin break out in a cold chill despite the heat of the room. "An opportunity to remove your Cousin from the throne. We can continue forward with this coup attempt that will fail. Your brother and your half-breed whore will be killed, and you will end up in the Commander's bed at the behest of the Emperor." Ba'shea's eyes glittered, and A'bbni forced back a shudder. "Or we allow your brother to kill the Emperor, he will abdicate the throne to you, and you will take Commander Hi'jan as your spouse to rule by your side."

Whatever A'bbni had been expecting to hear, that was not it. He jerked in his chair, almost upending it before unclenching his fingers from his shirt and letting out a sharp breath. "What?" he managed to force out.

"Come now, Your Highness, surely you can see the logic of it," Mii'ra said. "The people will rally behind you to depose your Cousin."

"And what of my brother and Lai?" A'bbni asked through gritted teeth.

"Obviously the half-breed will be executed," Ba'shea said, waving his hand airily. "After all, someone must take the fall for the Emperor's death. But as for your brother." He gave him a cold smile. "He will be allowed to live. His level of comfort beyond that would be entirely up to you."

They would keep Shi'chen alive to ensure that A'bbni was always under their thumb. He narrowed his eyes at Ba'shea. "You would hold us both hostage to your whims."

"Your Highness." Mii'ra's voice held the motherly tone that she had used multiple times with him. "Think of all the good you could do for your people. You would still be in a position of power."

"As your pawn, with no choices of my own," A'bbni said stiffly.

"Your choice is now," Ba'shea replied, folding his hands on the table. "You decide whose blood is shed today, Your Reverence. It can be the Emperor's, or it can be your brother's."

"Either way, you kill Lai," A'bbni said.

"We could perhaps be persuaded otherwise," Ba'shea said with a calculated smile. "If you are willing to cooperate with us and the Commander."

"And how long would I have to cooperate?" A'bbni asked bitterly. "Until enough people support you for you to be able to kill me without repercussions? Until you have enslaved enough of your opponents in my name to not stand against you?"

"This is not about enslaving anyone, Your Highness," Mii'ra said, her voice low and soothing.

"How is it not, Var An-Sha'kri?" A'bbni demanded, aware his voice was rising. "Because you cannot control my Cousin, you will use my brother to control me instead?"

The look in Mii'ra's eyes was all the answer he needed to that. They would hold him under their thumbs with the constant threat to his brother and his fear of Hi'jan, whether the Commander laid hands on him or not. "Why are you doing this?" A'bbni asked her softly.

On his other side, Ba'shea laughed, a mirthless sound that sounded like dry wood scraping over sand. The sound made A'bbni's pulse race further, and he swallowed hard as Ba'shea said, "Frankly, I am surprised you of all people did not figure it out. I had thought you smarter than that, Your Reverence."

"What are you talking about?" A'bbni asked.

Ba'shea's mouth curved into a cold smile. "No reason to keep it a secret any longer. Commander Hi'jan Hin-Ve'ssa is my grandson."

And now he could see it. The same thin lips, the same yellow hawk-like eyes. A'bbni realized why looking at Ba'shea had turned his stomach, and it wasn't only because of his previous ties to the slave trade. His fingers clenched around the edge of the table. "How?"

"Born to my son's mistress, but obviously not sharing the same family name made it much easier for him to become a soldier, and then a Captaincy in the palace guard."

"Just think about it, Your Highness," Mii'ra said gently. "With the An-Heshars on the throne, you could be free to continue your studies. That is what you want, is it not?"

A'bbni had a feeling the word 'free' was used very loosely here, and Mii'ra's use of the new honorific for the Heshar family did not escape his notice. "Was it planned for him to try to seduce us when he came to the palace?"

"Of course," Ba'shea said with a throaty chuckle. "Our exact plans would be determined by whom he was able to get closer to. Just think, Your Reverence, all this unpleasantness and all those deaths could have been avoided if you had just spread your legs for him."

A'bbni jolted out of his chair, knocking it to the floor with a clatter. He darted around Mii'ra and lunged for the door handle. But suddenly Ba'shea had leapt up and grabbed him by his ponytail with surprising speed and strength for his age, and jerked him back with enough force that he stumbled backward into the table. "Sit down, boy."

He shoved A'bbni to his knees next to his chair, still holding his hair as tears stung A'bbni's eyes from the tension.

"You think I would submit to your beast of a grandson after what he did to me?" A'bbni demanded, his hands coming up to claw at Ba'shea's grip on his hair. "I would rather die than let him touch me again!"

"What is he talking about, Vr Ii-Heshar?" Mii'ra asked. A'bbni turned his eyes toward her.

"Did he not tell you, Var An-Sha'kri?" he asked, deciding to let the tears of pain spill down his cheeks. "Did he not tell you that his grandson tortured me and raped me in this very room? In front of my brother and the Emperor?"

Mii'ra's gold eyes went wide, and she looked up at Ba'shea. "Is... is that true, Vr Ii-Heshar?"

Ba'shea's yellow eyes narrowed down at A'bbni. "Be quiet, boy."

A'bbni's fingers scratched at the hold on his hair, but he kept his eyes on Mii'ra. "Lord Kella knows, you can ask him if you do not believe me," he said. "Did Vr Ii-Heshar make you think that I would be all right with taking the Commander as my husband? That I would quietly submit to him, out of fear for myself or my brother?"

"Vr Ii-Heshar," Mii'ra said quietly, staring at the prince on his knees on the floor.

Ba'shea's fingers pulled his head back painfully. A'bbni swallowed hard but forced himself to continue. "Tell me, Vr Ii-Heshar, how long has your family been defying the imperial law against slavery?"

"Ah, your half-breed told you about that, did he?" Ba'shea asked. A'bbni gritted his teeth at that. "We never stopped. It was hard to keep it secret sometimes, but there are so many quarries and mines, it's easy to find buyers. Some were even sent out of the country."

"To Kendarin? Does the High King know? How long have you been lying to Var An-Sha'kri and Vr An-Gea'la about your intentions?" That last comment was a guess on A'bbni's part, but the stunned look on Mii'ra's face told him that he judged correctly.

"Vr Ii-Heshar," Mii'ra said, her voice suddenly becoming stronger. "Slavery is illegal! It is the reason we are so concerned about the crown prince. Have you been defying the liberation edict all this time?"

Ba'shea's grip suddenly loosened, and A'bbni fell forward onto his hands, his hair pulling loose from its tie, and he took a deep breath.

"Var An-Sha'kri, are you really so foolish that you did not see it?" Ba'shea asked.

Mii'ra straightened up, though her height was nowhere near comparable to Ba'shea's. "That was not the plan, Vr Ii-Heshar. Our goal was to remove En'shea Er-Ha'sen."

Ba'shea laughed, and A'bbni shuddered at the sound, so much like Hi'jan's laughter. "Really now, Mii'ra, you think that your family does not benefit from the slave trade? Where do all those gemstones your family receive come from, do you think?"

"You said nothing about your grandson abusing the princes," Mii'ra said, her voice full of undisguised fury. "That is despicable!"

The room suddenly rang with the sound of Ba'shea's palm connecting with Mii'ra's cheek. A'bbni gasped and scrambled to his feet, staring at Mii'ra, who clutched her face, a trickle of blood coursing from a cut on her cheek where one of Ba'shea's rings had caught her. "Leave her alone," he said, trying to bring some authority he did not feel into his voice.

"Now why would he take orders from a fugitive slave?" came a cold voice from the doorway that flooded A'bbni's mind like a burst dam and made his heart skip a beat painfully in his chest. He turned his eyes toward the door and met familiar golden eyes. "Dear Cousin," En'shea greeted, his smile predatory. "We have missed you."

A'bbni forced himself to take a deep breath, despite his pounding heart. "We wish we could say the same about you, Cousin," he said, keeping his voice light and pleasant like En'shea did.

"We must say, your disappearing act was quite impressive," En'shea said, tucking his hands into the long sleeves of his yellow and gold robe. "But we will ensure it does not happen again." En'shea stepped into the room, but he was not alone.

"Hello, little mouse." Hi'jan's voice sent ice through his veins, and A'bbni backed up with an involuntary gasp, the edge of the table hitting his lower back and preventing him from going further. "You are not going to greet your master after you've been away for so long?" Hi'jan's eyes sparked with cold amusement. He came in and closed the door behind them. He was wearing the scarlet cape of a Commander; the gold Commander pin he wore on one shoulder was new. It gleamed under the flicker of the torches against the wall.

A'bbni felt his ears drop back in fear. There was no way he was going to get past all four of them to the door, and even if he did, he was sure Hi'jan had guards stationed nearby with the Emperor in The Keep now. The best he could hope for was to keep them all talking long enough that they would leave. He forced his eyes away from Hi'jan and back to the teenager in front of him.

"Did you know, Cousin, that Commander Hin-Ve'ssa and the Council offered the throne to me in exchange for your life?" he asked.

En'shea's eyes glittered, his gold-painted lips pulling up into a cold smirk. "Did they? Is that supposed to surprise us, Dear Cousin?"

"No," A'bbni said lightly. "We just assumed you would wish to know."

"Your concern for our well-being is touching," En'shea said dryly. "And what did you say to that, Dear Cousin? Did you accept their offer?" A'bbni said nothing, though his eyes flicked unconsciously back over to Hi'jan, whose glare made his skin crawl. En'shea's gold lips curved into an icy smirk. "Ah, we see. Perhaps you should have. We are certain their offer would have spared you significant amounts of suffering."

A'bbni thought that unlikely, but he just said, as lightly as he could manage, "I will take my chances."

En'shea quirked a dark brow and said, "Do you wish to know what we did to Commander An-Sher'vaat when we found out it was she who helped you escape?"

A'bbni bit his tongue. He would not give En'shea the satisfaction of an answer that he was going to ignore anyway.

"It took five days for her to die. Can you imagine the suffering?"

Unfortunately, he could. A'bbni forced himself to evoke his physician's composure and again said nothing, keeping his features carefully schooled into neutrality. A flicker of disappointment seemed to cross En'shea's face that he had not gotten a reaction from him, but just as suddenly, it was gone. "We will look forward to sharing the details with you when we do the same to your brother," he said. "We may even take you to see for yourself. Her head is on the wall next to your perfidious Father."

The words stung like En'shea had slapped him with them, and A'bbni felt his fingers clench into fists, but he forced himself to give En'shea a smile. "You always did have a knack for decorating," he said, keeping his tone pleasant, the same way he had with the Council when he knew they were trying to provoke him.

En'shea stared at him, and A'bbni felt a slight thrill that he had rendered his ruthless cousin speechless, even if only for a moment.

"The time for games is done, Your Reverence," Ba'shea sneered, breaking the tense silence. "When your brother and your blond bitch come, you can have the satisfaction of knowing that you killed them by refusing to cooperate with us."

'When your brother and your blond bitch come.' The words bounced around in A'bbni's mind, a swell of relief coursing through him. Ba'shea did not know that Shi'chen and Lai had snuck out of the house late last night and should already be in The Keep. Ba'shea and Mii'ra had not seen Shi'chen or Lai leave his bedroom after Lai's offer of a drink the night before, and they had not checked his room before grabbing him from the dining room this morning. A'bbni forced his eyes to fill with tears, as if Ba'shea's words distressed him. "Please, don't do this," he said softly.

Ba'shea only gave him that cruel smile. "Perhaps His Sovereignty will not execute your brother right away. I would relish the chance to crush his spirit." Ba'shea reached up to slide one bony finger down A'bbni's cheek. "After all, children are easily broken, and we know what his greatest weakness is, don't we?"

A'bbni shuddered, trying to turn away from the touch on his face. Ba'shea's gnarled fingers suddenly grasped his chin and jerked his face toward him. "I asked you a question, boy, and you will answer me."

A'bbni swallowed hard, his hands starting to come up to push Ba'shea's fingers away from him before he saw movement out of the corner of his eye. Mii'ra had pulled a blade from her sleeve and suddenly flung herself at En'shea, arm raised to strike. En'shea did not move, but Hi'jan did. Quicker than A'bbni could see, the Commander had unsheathed his short sword and swung. Mii'ra stopped in her tracks, a line of red suddenly opening across her throat. Blood began to pour from the wound as her head tipped back at an unnatural angle, barely still connected by her spine, and her body collapsed to the floor. Blood poured from the stump that had been her neck.

A'bbni opened his mouth to scream, but Ba'shea's hand on his chin slid up to clamp over his mouth and shove him back against the table, cutting off the sound. A'bbni's back hit the tabletop, knocking the air from his lungs as he struggled against the hold. He felt a wave of dizziness hit him as the smell of fresh blood reached his nose, and he squeezed his eyes shut for a moment as his stomach surged into his throat, the feeling of the scarred wood beneath him sending a tidal wave of panic over him. Ba'shea was suddenly leaning over him, his thigh pressed painfully between A'bbni's legs, holding him in place, so close that A'bbni could feel the other man's heat against him.

He couldn't stop a soft whimper that escaped his throat as he stared into Ba'shea's yellow eyes, so close to his that he could see the striations in his irises. Eyes exactly like Hi'jan's. He wanted to scream, to strike him, to do anything to get away, but all strength seemed to have fled his body, and his mind was a terrifying mess of blankness except for the dark gape of his Father's mouth, the stench of death, the single drop of blood on the ruby stone, and the pain as Hi'jan took him from behind. He saw that same cruelty in Ba'shea's face, knowing that the man could see every whisp of weakness in him that he could exploit, knowing that Ba'shea could see in his eyes exactly what Hi'jan and En'shea had done to him. His hands flew up to desperately try to pry the hand off his mouth, but Ba'shea only squeezed tighter, his fingers digging viciously into the soft parts of his cheeks.

A'bbni closed his eyes for a moment, trying to get his racing heart and mind to calm. The last thing he wanted to do was pass out again in this room. He knew if Shi'chen were at his side, his brother would stroke his hair and tell him to breathe. Ba'shea held his mouth, so he forced himself to inhale through his nose, his fingers curling slightly against Ba'shea's hand. The first one was a struggle, but he let it out and slowly drew in another one, and then a third. His mind strained to focus on something, anything, that would keep the smell of Mii'ra's blood from sending him into a panic he couldn't get out of.

He knew what Ba'shea wanted, what all of them wanted from him. Submission. Compliance. To play the meek little scholar they thought he was and follow their commands. If he did what they wanted and did not fight back, the fun would go out of it for them. Keeping his eyes closed, he slowly pulled his hands away from Ba'shea's grip, opening his fingers in submission and letting them rest on the table by his head, trying hard to relax the tension in his body.

Laughter from all three of the goblins echoed hollowly against the stones, but once his hands went still, Ba'shea's grip on his face shifted down, pulling A'bbni up by the front of his shirt until he was on his feet again, the small of his back still pressed to the table's edge.

En'shea had not moved from where he had first stopped before Mii'ra leaped at him. He was watching them all move around him like they were no more than shadows. His eyes met A'bbni's, and A'bbni felt a shiver go down his spine as those unfeeling, golden eyes bored into his, reading something in him, though he didn't know what.

"Sovereignty, we should get you to safety before Captain Er-Ha'sen has the crowd assembled," Hi'jan said, bending down to scoop up the blade that had fallen from Mii'ra's limp hand. A'bbni leaned back against the tabletop, bracing his hands on it as his body felt too heavy to stay upright, focusing all of his effort into not screaming or crying. En'shea was still watching him with that unnerving stare, as if he were looking for something.

"Commander." En'shea addressed the tall goblin over his shoulder without moving his eyes from A'bbni's. "You said that the half-elf that returned with them is our Dear Cousin's lover, is that correct?"

"Yes, Your Sovereignty," Hi'jan said, casting his eyes over at A'bbni as well, and the prince felt heat rush to his cheeks and ears as he stared back at En'shea.

"Capture him alive, and then bring him to us," En'shea said, giving A'bbni another of his icy smiles. "We want to ensure our Dear Cousin gets the chance to say goodbye to him. He will have a very. Long. Time."

The air left A'bbni's lungs like he had been punched in the stomach, an unbidden sob wrenching itself from his throat before he could stop it.

"Of course, Your Sovereignty," Hi'jan said with a smirk at A'bbni. "It would be my pleasure."

And with that, the three goblins turned and left, leaving him in the room with Mii'ra's corpse and the flicker of firelight over the widening puddle of blood. The door closed and locked as A'bbni dropped to his knees and vomited.

CHAPTER TWENTY-THREE

SHI'CHEN

The problem with having to wait for so long was that his mind wandered to all the things that could go wrong. Of which there were many right now. What if the people of the city did not assemble? What if Hi'jan did not bring En'shea to The Keep for protection? What if Ba'shea had found out they left the night before and had Hi'jan search The Keep? If he and Lai were discovered and captured, no one would know. All these thoughts were circling in his head in a whirlpool of frustration that threatened to drown him like the ocean.

Shi'chen thought he might have dozed off, because there was a sudden clatter outside the door, and he heard En'shea's sharp, nasal voice. "We do not care about them; we want our Cousin arrested!" The hallway door the guards stood at opened, and a faint flicker of light could be seen from the hallway as several servants entered and began lighting the lamps around the rooms. Next to him, Lai stiffened and went completely still, and Shi'chen followed suit.

"I know, Your Sovereignty. I have guards at every entrance." That voice was unmistakably Hi'jan's.

"We grow tired of your incompetence, Commander," En'shea said, stalking into the first room and knocking aside what must have been a goblet with a sharp, tinny crash as it hit the stone floor. "If you allow our Cousin to breech The Keep, it will be your head on the wall next."

"Yes, Sovereignty," Hi'jan said smoothly, as if he had heard this threat many times before. "He would not dare to make a move against us while we have his brother. You are well protected here, and we will not let him get to you or the prince."

The impact of the words hit him like a physical blow. Shi'chen had to clap his hand to his own nose and mouth to keep from screaming, turning with wide eyes to Lai next to him, who looked just as shocked. His heart began to thunder in his chest, so loud he thought it might be heard in the next room. Hi'jan had A'bbni, and he was holding him prisoner somewhere in this tower. Unfortunately, enough time had passed between them leaving the night before until now that he doubted it was a bluff on Hi'jan's part; the Commander was too confident.

He felt his muscles tense, ready to spring from under the bed and grab Hi'jan by the throat. Lai shifted almost imperceptibly next to him, laying a hand on his arm, though whether as reassurance or warning, he didn't know. He forced himself to relax one muscle at a time, though his heart continued its drumbeat in his ears.

"We hope we have made ourselves clear that you do not get our Dear Cousin until his brother is dead," En'shea said, suddenly coming into the bedroom. Shi'chen could barely see his slippered feet under the edge of the comforter, coming closer.

"Yes, Sovereignty." Hi'jan sounded like he had heard that before, too. Several servants entered and began to light the lamps around the bedroom, and Shi'chen and Lai didn't even breathe.

"We are considering not even letting you have him," En'shea said coldly. "Your grandfather's willingness to betray us to placate the Council does not reflect well on you, Commander. If we have reason to question your loyalty again, we will simply have our Dear Cousin executed as well, and you will join him."

"I understand, Sovereignty." Hi'jan sounded like he was speaking through clenched teeth.

"We want this rebellion crushed once and for all, whatever the cost," En'shea said, sitting down primly on the edge of the bed. "Do we make ourselves clear?"

"As glass, Your Sovereignty," Hi'jan said. "My guards will be at the door. Do you require anything more from me?"

"No. Leave." En'shea's tone was brusque, and Hi'jan bowed quickly and left. Shi'chen held his breath, listening for any other sounds, but it sounded as though the servants had all departed after Hi'jan as well. It was just them and En'shea, who got up from the bed and paced nervously around the room for several minutes before lying down on the bed again. Shi'chen was more than a little tempted to just stab his sword up through the mattress and be done with it.

He had made a mistake, a terrible one, thinking that A'bbni would be safe with Kella and Zea'dda and Gii'han. For all he knew, they were dead now, too. And that miscalculation had once again put his brother in danger, despite everything he had done to try and protect him. All he wanted to do was scream, but he couldn't. Lai's hand resting reassuringly on his arm was the only thing keeping his mind on the task at hand.

He listened to the sounds around them. Every now and then there would be a shuffle of feet outside the main door or a brief conversation exchanged, but otherwise, everything seemed fairly calm. He suspected most of the preparations for the impending riot were happening on the lower levels. His fingers twitched in agony as he wondered what was happening to A'bbni. He was grateful in that moment to have Lai next to him, because if he had been by himself, he would already have given himself away when Hi'jan had first mentioned his brother. He knew that Lai probably was feeling just as frantic about it as he was, but the fact that the half-elf was holding it together and trying to help him do the same was at least a minimal comfort.

En'shea's breathing seemed more rhythmic now, possibly asleep. Every now and then, the door would open as a guard or servant would check on him, but otherwise, there was no movement in the closed-off room. Shi'chen knew it had to be mid-afternoon by this point, though it felt like they had been lying in wait for a thousand years. The city would be assembling and coming toward the palace; at least, he hoped they would be. If something had gone wrong, they were not going to make it out of The Keep alive.

He could tell when the crowd had actually been spotted, as the commotion outside the door suddenly increased for a short period, and he could hear more movement in the hallways before it quieted down again. It was time, while the guards were distracted by the protest.

He glanced over at Lai, catching the half-elf's eyes in the dimness. Lai gave him the smallest nod. Shi'chen held up three fingers and took a deep breath, counting them down. Simultaneously they rolled out from under the bed and were on their feet, Lai's dagger in his hand, Shi'chen drawing his short sword.

En'shea was sleeping on his stomach on the bed, his head on the pillow, his face toward Shi'chen. For just a moment, he looked so young, but that thought vanished as quickly in Shi'chen's mind as it had come. Lai snatched En'shea up from the bed, wrapping his arm around En'shea's upper arms to pin them, his dagger pressing to En'shea's throat. En'shea's golden eyes flew open, his hands coming up to try to grab Lai's arm around him as he gasped, and then his eyes met Shi'chen in front of him. He relaxed just a bit in Lai's grip, a cool smile spreading across his features. "Hello, Cousin."

Shi'chen glowered at him. "What have you done with my brother?"

En'shea laughed, despite the blade at his throat. "What makes you think we had anything to do with it?"

Shi'chen pressed the point of his short sword to the soft spot under En'shea's ribcage. "Do not fuck with me, En'shea. I am just looking for an excuse to gut you like a fish."

En'shea laughed again, seeming unperturbed by Shi'chen's threat. "You know if you do, your brother dies."

"That is the only reason you are still breathing," Shi'chen growled, pushing the point a little harder, enough that he felt it prick En'shea's skin through his thick robes.

En'shea did not move, just gazed back at him with unblinking, golden eyes. "It is such a shame that you betrayed us, Cousin. You would have made a much better Commander than Captain Hin-Ve'ssa."

"As if I would serve under a contemptible monster like you," Shi'chen growled, unable to stop himself from rising to En'shea's jibe.

"What do you want from us, Cousin?" En'shea asked, suddenly sounding bored.

"You are going to abdicate," Shi'chen replied.

"Mm, no, we do not think we will," En'shea said thoughtfully, as if he had given the matter some consideration.

"That was not a suggestion," Shi'chen snarled.

"What are you going to do, Cousin? Kill us? Have your half-breed whore do it for you? How many pieces do you think Commander Hin-Ve'ssa will cut your brother into if you do?" En'shea's smile was chilling.

Shi'chen wondered how much of anything En'shea had said in Hanen-vir Lai could understand, but he couldn't worry about that right now. With a growl, he set down his sword so he could grab a thick piece of silk to wrap around En'shea's mouth, tying it much tighter than he needed to, then used another piece to bind En'shea's hands behind him; all the while En'shea stared him down with his unfeeling, reptile eyes.

Shi'chen turned to Lai, who still held his dagger at the ready. If it had just been them and En'shea, there were several options for them to get out of The Keep with the Emperor as a hostage, but as soon as they were no longer in The Keep where A'bbni was, they would lose their leverage against Hi'jan. Lai's green eyes met Shi'chen's own, and Shi'chen could see the worry swirling in them, just like in his. But they had a job to do. As long as En'shea was alive, they had a bargaining chip, and he was going to have to rely on Hi'jan feeling the same way about A'bbni. "If we can get out the way we came in, you take him and go. I'm not leaving without my brother."

Lai glared at him. "You are not going anywhere on your own. Only when he," he gave En'shea's throat a tap with the flat of his blade, "is with you do you have anything to negotiate with."

Even though Lai was right, Shi'chen decided now was not the time to argue about it; they had to find a passage out of there first. It was possible that Ba'shea may have discovered the route that he and Lai took to get in, or that he had known about it to begin with as a trusted member of the Council. If they could get to it, he suspected that would still be the easiest way to get out, as it opened into the city, not within the palace grounds. There were other secret passages out of The Keep if needed, but all the ones he knew about would also be ones Hi'jan would be aware of and would have guards at the exit points, likely assuming he and Lai would be trying to get in one of those passages during the protest. "Either way, we need to go. Ready?"

Lai nodded, his hand moving to hold En'shea's arm to steer him. "Ready."

Shi'chen swallowed hard. The last thing he wanted to do was harm any of the palace guards, most of whom he knew by name. Maybe that would work to their advantage. He hurried across the room, Lai following and pulling En'shea along with his dagger still at the Emperor's throat. En'shea seemed inclined to move, at least, which Shi'chen supposed he should be grateful for, as carrying his unconscious cousin would not make escape any easier or faster. With a last glance back at Lai, he pulled open the door to the hallway.

Three guards stood, seemingly bored at their post, but their faces when they saw the former Captain with the bound Emperor in tow made it clear that they had not been expecting it at all. Shi'chen glowered at them. "Stand down," he said, sword held up to engage if any of them came at him. They all held spears, so they had the advantage of distance, but he could react quicker than they could.

"Captain Er-Ha'sen?" one of the guards asked in surprise, her gold eyes wide as she took in the prince and the half-elf with a dagger pointed at the Emperor.

"I said, stand down, Lieutenant Hin-De'rra," Shi'chen said.

The woman glanced between the other two guards. One was young, maybe Lai's age, that he knew was An-Kaa-rai'a, and the other was a large, older half-goblin that he recognized as Hin-Ni'rae. Both Hin-Ni'rae and Hin-De'rra had been members of Courage Garrison under Hi'jan when he was a Captain. Hin-Ni'rae turned to Shi'chen. "Captain Er-Ha'sen, you are under arrest. Release the Emperor, and we will be merciful."

"I do not want to fight you, Hin-Ni'rae," Shi'chen said, hoping the warning in his voice was enough.

It was not. Hin-Ni'rae thrust his spear at him, and Shi'chen deflected it with his short sword, the sound of the blade against the wood sounding much too loud in the stone corridor for them not to be heard. Hin-De'rra turned to the young guard. "Go alert the Commander!"

An-Kaa-rai'a turned to run, but Lai suddenly threw the dagger he had had at En'shea's throat, catching the young man in the back of his calf, the blade embedding deep in the muscle. An-Kaa-rai'a hit the ground with a cry of pain, and Shi'chen glanced over to see that Lai already had another dagger in his hand, poised to throw if needed.

Hin-De'rra moved to block both the injured guard and the stairs downward, her spear angled to be more of an obstacle than a weapon. Shi'chen cursed silently to himself as he heard several pairs of feet approaching on the stone steps from below. Hin-Ni'rae suddenly stabbed at him with his spear, and Shi'chen narrowly avoided it. "Go!" he said to Lai, pointing upward. Lai took off for the stairs, dragging En'shea along with him. Shi'chen ducked another swing of Hin-Ni'rae's, darting forward to slash at the man's mid-section with his blade. He did not intend to hit him, but his movement had the desired effect of throwing Hin-Ni'rae off balance to stumble into Hin-De'rra's path, which distracted them both long enough that he could turn and bolt up the stairs after Lai to the top level. He realized with dread in his stomach that while there was an escape from the former courtroom, it would take time to open it, and they did not necessarily have that as the pounding feet came closer.

They reached the fifth level, the entire room wide open, with the gaping view and the precarious slanted stone of Traitor's Ledge at the far end. Shi'chen glanced around, spotting the hidden wall panel to the left side. "If we can get that open, it leads down to the cellars."

Lai sprinted over and planted his shoulder against the panel. It did not move. Shi'chen tossed En'shea to the floor and moved to help him. The panel still did not move, and he felt a stab of panic in his stomach. The panel was heavy, but both he and Lai should have been able to move it easily together. "It must be blocked," Lai said, turning to Shi'chen with wide eyes.

Shi'chen swore under his breath, giving one last futile shove at the panel that remained as solid as ever. His eyes met Lai's. "I'm sorry," he said, his voice barely above a gasp.

Lai gave him a small smile and placed a hand on his shoulder. "We're not dead yet, Your Highness. I guess you'll get to show me what you can do."

Shi'chen blinked, then gave him a small smile in return. "Don't worry about me."

Lai smirked and drew his rapier from his side, the blade catching the sun that streamed in through the open wall at their backs. "I don't."

And then the guards were in the room. Hin-Ni'rae and Hin-De'rra were at the front, and three more guards that Shi'chen recognized from Courage Garrison were behind them. They immediately fanned out, and Shi'chen realized they were going to try to flank them and push them back toward the open wall. He was not about to let that happen. He rushed forward, ducking a slash from one of the spears and swiped at the back of an unprotected calf of one of the guards, causing him to stumble.

Quick as a flash, Shi'chen leaped behind him to stab him in the back, making a conscious decision at the last moment to angle the sword away from any vital organs, the blade sinking downward into the man's shoulder. He jerked the blade back up, realizing somewhere in the back of his mind that he had never actually stabbed another living thing before and that it was harder than he expected.

A short sword was coming at him from the guard next to him, and he pushed off the other guard's back into a flip out of the way, landing just as the ring of blade against wood signaled that Lai had met with an opponent. For just a moment he was grateful that Lai was a trained fighter; he could not worry about him right now. He dodged another swing of the short sword, then moved over to kick up the spear the guard he had stabbed in the back had dropped. He sheathed his sword, then spun the spear in a fierce attack, knocking the guard's sword from his hands with a sharp clatter. He swung the spear around, catching the guard across the face with the handle, knocking him down. He swung the spear again and stabbed downward in rapid succession, into the guard's torso, opening up several wounds in multiple places. He wanted to feel guilty about it, but he couldn't right now.

Lai was up against Hin-De'rra and Hin-Ni'rae. Shi'chen looked around for the fifth guard, seeing him crouched over by En'shea, removing the gag from the Emperor's mouth. Before the guard could untie En'shea's hands, he threw the spear, catching the guard in the back, and the man slumped forward with a grunt. Shi'chen grabbed his sword again from his belt, rushing Hin-De'rra who was attacking Lai, dodging around her spear attack to deliver an elbow strike to her solar plexus, causing her to stumble back, choking for breath. He was vaguely aware that several more guards had rushed into the upper room, and a sword met his with a clash that made his teeth clack together.

He was starting to recognize that while he was trying very hard not to actually kill the attacking guards, many of whom he had known all his life, most of them were not taking the same precautions with him. And they would have no qualms about Lai, whom they did not know, nor did they know what his skill level was, as they had not watched him fight. He realized that would make Lai a much more appealing target than the former prodigy Captain of Honor Garrison.

Shi'chen delivered a sharp kick to the ribs of the guard coming at him, then turned to find Lai in the midst of three guards, including Hin-Ni'rae. He started toward his friend, but two other guards swooped in, and he had to duck into a slide under their swords coming at him, catching one of them across the back of the ankles with his blade, and then stabbing backward into the back of the knee of the other, sending them both to the stone floor with severe, but non-life-threatening, injuries.

Lai had managed to drive back two of the three guards enough to give him room to at least face off with Hin-Ni'rae, but the older half-goblin was taller and had a longer reach both with his arms and his spear and was doing quite an impressive job of keeping Lai from being able to reach him with an attack, even with his rapier. He started toward Lai again, but the two guards Lai had pushed back suddenly turned to him, and Shi'chen was forced to contend with them.

The next moments happened almost like he could see them suspended in time. Hin-Ni'rae lunged forward, turning his spear to hook it around the guard of Lai's rapier, and suddenly the rapier was out of Lai's hand, the force of the pull sending Lai to one knee. Shi'chen thought that Hin-Ni'rae would either strike down with his spear, or drop it and pull his short sword, but instead, the half-goblin tossed aside the spear and sprinted forward, catching Lai around the throat with both hands and lifting him off the ground. Lai grabbed for Hin-Ni'rae's hands around his throat, but the bigger guard had a firm grip, and he suddenly took a few steps to the side so Lai's feet dangled at the edge of the slanted stone ramp of Traitor's Ledge.

"No!" Shi'chen yelled, suddenly aware that all the fighting had stopped, and everyone was looking at Hin-Ni'rae or En'shea, who was on his feet, his hands still tied behind him.

"Throw your weapons down, Captain." En'shea's voice was deadly calm, the echo of it bouncing off the stone walls around them.

Shi'chen's eyes tried to catch Lai's, but the half-elf was struggling against Hin-Ni'rae's hands. En'shea glanced at the guard and inclined his head toward the opening. Hin-Ni'rae suddenly thrust Lai out into the air, only his hold on the young man's throat holding him in place. Lai gasped around the hold, his boots scrabbling on the slick stone, trying to find purchase.

"No!" Shi'chen gasped again, taking a step forward, but stopped when Hin-Ni'rae gave Lai a warning shake.

"This is your only chance, Cousin. Throw down your weapons, or he flies like a bird," En'shea repeated.

"Don't do it," Lai rasped around the hold on his throat.

Shi'chen ignored Lai's words, bending his knee and placing the short sword on the ground. He gave it a slight shove, so it slid out of his reach across the stone floor.

En'shea watched with dispassionate eyes, his lips quirked into a small half-smile as he looked at Shi'chen. "You surrender?"

"I do," Shi'chen said, holding his hands out, palms up, from his sides. "Let him go."

En'shea raised a brow. He turned to Hin-Ni'rae. "You heard him. Let him go."

The guard glanced at En'shea, then at the half-elf still gripped in his hands, his toes straining to grip the slanted stone ledge, his hands simultaneously holding onto him to not fall while also trying to pry them off his throat. "Yes, Sovereignty." The next moment, he released his hands so Lai's toes hit the incline. Shi'chen barely had time to register Lai's boots skid on the sloped stone before he disappeared into the blue beyond the stone window.

He might have yelled, he wasn't sure, but Shi'chen surged forward in a desperate attempt to reach the ledge. The guard behind him slammed the butt of his spear into his back, causing him to sprawl forward. He landed hard on his hands, scraping them on the stone, but he didn't feel it as he stared at the empty space where Lai had just been.

En'shea seemed entirely unperturbed by the half-elf's disappearance over the ledge, nodding to the guards. "Bind him."

The guards reached for him, but despite the shock that seemed to have flooded his entire body, without having to think, Shi'chen had already grabbed the dagger from his boot and swung it, catching one of the guard's hands across the palm. The man stumbled back with a yell of pain, clutching his hand. The other guard was Lieutenant Hin-De'rra, who rushed forward with her blade unsheathed, and he caught her swing with the dagger, sweeping his leg under her to knock her to the ground. Hin-Ni'rae suddenly surged at him, and Shi'chen threw the dagger, catching the half-goblin in the arm. It was not enough to stop him, but it distracted him just long enough for Shi'chen to kick the spear one of the guards had dropped up into his hand and spin it to catch Hin-Ni'rae across the throat with the point of the blade. Blood flew as the man fell, but Shi'chen barely had any time to think about the fact that he had just killed him before Hin-De'rra was on her feet and lunging at him with her sword again.

Shi'chen knocked the blade away with the spear, his feet quickly moving over the stone floor, carefully avoiding the slanted ledge. He could tell she was driving him backward toward the remaining cluster of guards still standing. He let her push him back another step before he launched at her, catching her off guard, shooting his spear forward to catch her in the chest just below her throat with a sickening, wet sound. He jerked the spear back to catch it close to the metal end, the blunt wooden handle flying back to catch a guard behind him in the face as he lunged for Shi'chen.

He pivoted, swinging the spear around in a slash that caused the guard to stumble and lose his balance, which gave Shi'chen an opening to strike the guard in the side, just above his hip. The guard went down with a crash, and Shi'chen pulled the spear free just in time to knock aside a blade before the guard who had thrown it turned tail and sprinted out of the room and down the stairs.

The only palace guard still upright was the one he had caught across the hand with his dagger, who was on his knees, cradling the hand to his chest. Shi'chen moved toward him, spear poised to strike downwards, but the man held up his wounded hand pleadingly. "Mercy, Captain, please!"

Shi'chen froze, feeling blood rushing in his ears. He had fought other guards many times, but it was always just sparring and training, not killing. He realized with a start that the guard on his knees was not much older than he was, and that made his stomach lurch into his throat. He forced the feeling down, taking a step back and turning the point of the spear away from the young man as he struggled to breathe, not from exertion, but because his heart was beating too fast in his chest to allow him to take a bigger breath.

He suddenly heard the slap of slippered feet on stone, and he turned to see En'shea dashing toward the doorway. He threw himself after him, slamming into En'shea from behind. En'shea stumbled on the stone landing and almost pitched down the stone steps, but Shi'chen caught him by his bound wrists to stop him. He debated just throwing En'shea down the entire flight of stairs, damn the consequences, but if he was dead, Shi'chen had no leverage against Hi'jan. So, he hauled En'shea back, tossing him to the floor again. He grabbed the gag from where it dangled around En'shea's throat and pulled it up to tie it over the Emperor's eyes.

"Are you going to kill us, Cousin?" En'shea asked, but the question was more curious than anything. Shi'chen didn't answer, giving him a shove back against the wall. He moved over to retrieve his dagger from where

Hin-Ni'rae lay in a pool of blood from his slashed neck, slipping it into his boot. Hin-Ni'rae's spear lay discarded to the side, Lai's rapier still attached to the point where it had been hooked. Without realizing it, he dropped to one knee, starting to shake, his breath catching in a gasp that turned into a single sob. How was it possible that Lai was gone, just like that? And it was his fucking fault. He should never have let Lai come with him; he should have been the only one putting himself at risk. His heart ached, and then shattered into a million tiny shards in his chest when he realized he was going to have to tell A'bbni once he found him. That was going to hurt more than anything, breaking his brother's heart.

All he wanted to do was scream and cry until the entire Keep echoed with his voice, but the thought that Hi'jan still had his brother somewhere forced him to his feet again. He took a deep, shaky breath to stop any more sobs, closing his eyes for just a moment until he was sure the tears inside him would not fall. He untangled Lai's rapier from the spear and attached it to his own belt, then picked up one of the dropped spears as he started back across the room. Two of the fallen guards were not moving, a few more laid where they fell but were still alive, moaning or crying out in pain, but he could not bring himself to care. All he felt was numbness that was creeping outward from his chest into his limbs.

The young man with the wounded hand had crawled over to Lieutenant Hin-De'rra, who was lying on the ground, bleeding heavily from the wound in her chest. Her breath was coming in gurgling gasps, each one pumping a gush of blood out of the injury. There would be no saving her. He picked up a short sword, moving over to hold it, handle-first, to the young guard. "She is dying. Show her mercy," he said, his voice low and flat.

The young man looked up into his face, almost without seeing him, slowly taking the sword from him.

Shi'chen crossed to grab En'shea off the floor, hauling him to his feet by the back of his collar. He did not look back as he dragged his cousin out the door and started down the stone steps. Behind him, Hin-De'rra's agonized breathing suddenly ceased.

"Do you wish to know what we did to your traitorous Commander?" En'shea asked as Shi'chen shoved him down the steps, not letting him fall but not doing much to stop him from slipping either. "Do you want to know how your Commander screamed, Captain? She screamed for days until she was begging us for death."

Shi'chen gritted his teeth. Whether or not it was true, it wouldn't change what happened. Commander Ahea'a was dead, and his memories of her would not be swayed. En'shea laughed, the sound echoing off the stone walls, eerily reminiscent of his laughter when the twins had been tortured only a few levels below them. Each inhale felt like he was in a windstorm, trying to breathe in a pressure that threatened to crush him.

After a few seconds of silence and several more steps, En'shea's prim, nasal tone broke into his mind again. "Was it worth the loss of your brother's fuck toy? We hope we get to see when you tell him, Cousin. We think that will hurt more than anything Commander Hin-Ve'ssa can do to him. But we could always be proven wrong."

Shi'chen was glad they had reached the bottom of the stairs because he could not stop himself from slamming En'shea face-first into the wall, pressing the shaft of the spear across En'shea's shoulders to hold him there. The breath left the Emperor with a gasp, a trickle of blood running down En'shea's cheek to drip onto his yellow and gold silk robe. But still, he laughed, the sound strangled as Shi'chen pressed him against the wall.

CHAPTER TWENTY-FOUR

A'BBNI

A'bbni did not want to admit how much his cousin and Ba'shea had rattled him, but there was no way for him to ignore it. The thought of Commander Ahea'a's suffering was bad enough, but then to imagine such a fate inflicted on Lai or Shi'chen was enough to send him into a panic that he was not sure he'd be able to get out of. So instead, he made himself sit against the wall and focus on each breath and the sounds around him. His mind kept wanting to drift, but he would force himself to concentrate, staring at the cracks in the stone under him or at the lines on his palms until he was sure he would not start screaming.

Eventually, he was able to calm himself enough to retie his hair and give a cursory search to Mii'ra's body to see if there were any other potential weapons on her. He found nothing, and while he was angry over what she had done, he took a moment to ask the gods to bless her for her final attempt to stop En'shea's reign. The smell of blood and death was nauseatingly familiar, and he could not bring himself to move her body from where it had fallen. Instead, he curled in the corner closest to the door where he could not be seen by anyone looking in.

He heard Hi'jan pass by the locked door several times, giving orders to his guards, though he did not hear Ba'shea's voice again, which worried him. The Emperor had ordered the uprising to be contained and ended, no matter the cost, and A'bbni buried his face in his knees, knowing that Hi'jan would have no qualms about killing the civilians who dared to defy his commands.

Then everything went somewhat quiet again. The shadows through the slitted window were starting to lengthen. It had to be later in the afternoon, he thought, wondering how much longer it would be before the citizens would protest in the streets. *If,* he reminded himself. It was certainly possible they could change their minds and decide not to risk it, and that would be it. Shi'chen and Lai would fail in their attempt to capture En'shea, and he would lose them both forever. He had to trust in everyone else, and that thought by itself was terrifying.

A'bbni jumped when he heard the door lock click. Hi'jan stepped inside, closing the door behind him, and glancing around until he found A'bbni curled in the corner. He was alone this time.

"You think you're so clever, don't you?" he asked, and A'bbni glared back at him. "Trying to turn your Cousin against me."

"No more than your grandfather trying to use my brother against me," A'bbni said, getting to his feet as anger surged in his chest. "You are nothing but a coward."

Hi'jan laughed and took a few steps toward him. A'bbni forced himself to stand his ground, glowering at the taller man. "You have a little more spark in you now, little mouse. I'm feeling generous, so I will give you one chance to save your brother. Name me to rule by your side, and I won't kill your brother today. As long as you submit to me, I will let him live. And if you ask me nicely, on your knees, I'll even give your little half-elf whore a quick death."

"Go fuck yourself," A'bbni hissed.

Hi'jan laughed. "I see your brother has had an influence on you after all. Of course, you do not have as much fight in you as he does."

Suddenly he was in front of him, his hand wrapping around A'bbni's throat to push him back against the wall. A'bbni gasped, trying to bring his hands up to push Hi'jan away, but Hi'jan's hand slid from his throat to grip the back of his neck in a touch that froze A'bbni in place as Hi'jan's fingers dug into the base of his skull under his hair. "Tell me, what do you think your brother would do to get you back?"

His fingers tightened on A'bbni's neck, making him wince. "He will not give up the Emperor to you," he hissed, aware that his heart was beating loud enough in his chest that he could hear it in his ears.

Hi'jan stroked his hand down the back of A'bbni's head like a dog. "You may act brave, Your Highness, but we both know your brother. He will not leave you in my hands."

A'bbni knew Hi'jan was right, but he just squared his shoulders and lifted his chin as best he could. "My life is not important when it comes to stopping En'shea's cruelty."

"Of course, it's not," Hi'jan said, his fingers sliding down A'bbni's cheek, then suddenly grasping his chin tight in his fingers, not unlike his grandfather had done earlier that day. "But your brother won't see it that way. And, of course, your life not being important to anyone else won't stop you from suffering."

A'bbni forced himself to swallow the fear that wanted to escape his throat, instead glaring at Hi'jan with all the fire he could muster. "If I have nothing left to lose, I will spend the rest of my life trying to take yours."

For just a moment, Hi'jan looked surprised at the words. But he recovered quickly and ran his thumb down A'bbni's cheek. "We'll see, little mouse. Perhaps me killing your brother won't crumble you to dust like I thought."

A'bbni's eyes narrowed, but he didn't respond. Hi'jan's thumb slid lower down A'bbni's cheek, brushing over his lower lip, and A'bbni snapped his teeth together on the thumb. Hi'jan let out a yell, kneeing A'bbni in the stomach; that sent the prince to his knees, releasing the thumb with a streak of blood down his chin and Hi'jan's hand. He sucked in a breath, then heard the slap before he felt it, suddenly finding himself on the floor, his cheek on fire, his ears ringing. He winced and tried pushing himself up on trembling arms, not quite managing to get himself off the floor.

"You will regret that, boy," Hi'jan hissed, clutching his bleeding hand to his chest.

A'bbni glowered up at him, spitting out a mouthful of blood, though whether it was his or Hi'jan's, he didn't know. "I only regret I did not bite it off. I will have to try again the next time you put something in my mouth."

Hi'jan's eyes flickered, but he only smiled that cold smile again. "Such big words from the little mouse. I bet that bravery makes your brother's cock even harder for you."

A'bbni ignored the jibe, glad Shi'chen wasn't there to hear it and fly into a rage at Hi'jan's goading. His cheek and jaw throbbed painfully, and his ears were ringing enough that he did not dare to try to get to his feet. He instead pushed himself into a sitting position and leaned back against the wall so he would not lose his balance. Somewhere in the recesses of his mind, he thought to himself that it was good he never pursued military training. How did Shi'chen deal with getting tossed around in sparring all the time?

Hi'jan's eyes glittered as he cradled his hand. A'bbni felt a momentary surge of pleasure that Hi'jan was right-handed, and that was the hand he had bitten. It wasn't much, but hopefully it would help if it came down to a fight, which he suspected was exactly what Hi'jan intended. "Don't worry, Your Highness, I'll make sure you have a chance to say goodbye to your brother. I want you to hear every scream I draw out of him before I kill him."

He strode out of the room and slammed the door, making A'bbni's ears flatten from the echo. Then he became aware of a noise that was gradually growing louder. Eventually he was able to discern that it was outside the palace walls. It had to be the insurgency, which he knew would be the moment that his brother and Lai would grab En'shea, if their plan was still in place. He felt a surge of pride in his chest that the city had actually risen up in protest of En'shea.

The movement of guards in the hallways increased, growing louder and then softer, and he would catch occasional bits of conversation. From what he could discern, no one had seen Shi'chen anywhere in the crowd or at any of the entrances into The Keep, and that gave him hope. In his role as a Captain of the palace guard, Shi'chen had often strategized with their Father or the Commander about scenarios both real and figurative, and while inexperienced, his ideas were well thought-out. And Lai's plan to move immediately instead of waiting might have just been the idea that saved their lives.

There was a sudden disruption in the orderliness of the guards nearby as a muffled shout came from somewhere above them, and then several guards were running past his cell toward the stairs leading upward. A'bbni felt his heart pick up as he listened, trying to hear what might be happening, but all was suddenly quiet again for a time before he heard someone coming down the stairs nearby and calling out, "Commander!"

He heard Hi'jan's feet in the corridor, and A'bbni instinctively shrank back, but Hi'jan did not come in. Instead, he passed by the closed door, and then he heard him speaking to the goblin on the stairs. A'bbni strained to hear. The first part was muffled, but he made out 'Emperor,' and then his heart did a flip in his chest when he distinctly heard, "Captain Er-Ha'sen."

"What?" Hi'jan's voice demanded, rising up enough that A'bbni could hear him clearly.

Whomever he was speaking to said something A'bbni could not catch, but then he heard Hi'jan say, "Are you serious?"

The other voice said something, and then came the distinct sound of Hi'jan's hand striking whomever he was speaking to. A'bbni flinched at that, knowing it had to be one of the palace guards at the receiving end of that strike, and he felt a small surge of fury that Hi'jan would raise his hand against one of the guards under his command, even though it did not surprise him. Someone stumbled past the door, and then sounded like they fell or were tossed down several of the stairs. Hi'jan stood outside the door. "Bandage up his injury, and do not let anyone leave The Keep, alive or dead. Is that fucking understood?"

A'bbni heard several voices respond affirmatively from what must have been the first level of The Keep by the door, and then suddenly the room's lock clicked, and the door was shoved open. Hi'jan stormed into the room in a black cloud of fury that A'bbni had never seen from him before, and he wished he could disappear into the wall as Hi'jan's yellow eyes turned on him, burning with rage. Any courage A'bbni might have been able to summon fled, his ears flattening back in terror as he scrambled back away from the murderous gaze. He hit the wall much too soon, curling defensively against it, expecting Hi'jan to strike him.

Instead, Hi'jan stalked over to him and grabbed him by his ponytail, wrapping his right hand, now bound with a blood-soaked bandage, around it to jerk A'bbni up and back against him, making the prince cry out, tears stinging his eyes at the grip that felt like it would tear his hair from his skin. "Let's say hello to your brother, shall we?" Hi'jan's voice was no more than a ferocious hiss, and A'bbni was sure he had met desert snakes with less venom than Hi'jan had in him now.

Hi'jan jerked him toward the door, and A'bbni's vision blurred both from the agony of the twisted fingers in his hair and the tears that pain caused. His hands flew up, clawing at the grip on his hair, but Hi'jan seemed beyond feeling the scratches, yanking him out the door, and A'bbni hurried to keep pace with him so as not to be dragged.

When they reached the steps leading up, Hi'jan let go of his hair, and A'bbni had barely a moment of relief before Hi'jan wrapped his hand around his mouth, and he felt the prick of a cold steel blade against his throat. He could not stop a soft whimper of fear around the hand crushing his mouth, but Hi'jan ignored it, pulling him up the stairs to the third level, down the corridor, and then up the stairs to the fourth level.

At the top of the fourth level stairs, there was a small pool of blood that had not yet dried, and A'bbni wondered if that was from the injury the guard Hi'jan had struck had received. He did not have much time to consider this as they stepped into the corridor, and he saw two familiar shapes at the other end by the stairs. Shi'chen had En'shea pinned face-first against the wall with the shaft of a spear. Despite the fact that they were all the way down the corridor, A'bbni could hear En'shea laughing in his eerie way, and the sound sent chills down his spine. Lai was nowhere in sight. He felt his breath catch around Hi'jan's blade at his throat.

And then, suddenly, Shi'chen's eyes met his down the corridor, and A'bbni couldn't help but give a struggle against Hi'jan's hold on him. Shi'chen grabbed En'shea by the back of the neck and shoved him to his knees, and A'bbni could see his cousin was blindfolded and had his hands tied behind him.

"I applaud your ingenuity, Er-Ha'sen. Too bad it was all for nothing." Hi'jan's voice echoed in the stone hallway.

"Release my brother," Shi'chen hissed, the point of his spear angling down to En'shea's throat the same way Hi'jan held him.

Hi'jan laughed. "You really think I would just give him up to you?"

Shi'chen's eyes narrowed. "You know I will kill him," he said, the blade pressing harder against En'shea's skin, but the teenage Emperor only smirked.

"Of course, I do," Hi'jan said, and A'bbni could hear the roll of his eyes in his voice even if he couldn't see it. "You certainly have the upper hand in this negotiation. But I know how to level the playing field."

A'bbni suddenly found himself tossed to the ground, and before he was able to even consider moving, Hi'jan's booted foot slammed down on his knee.

CHAPTER TWENTY-FIVE

SHI'CHEN

The snap of bone and shriek of pain that came from A'bbni's throat made Shi'chen's heart skip a beat in his chest, knowing that sound would haunt his nightmares. He dove at Hi'jan, his spear whistling through the air, but Hi'jan dodged away and laughed, his sword coming up to meet the spear with a sharp ring of steel on steel.

Shi'chen planted his feet as Hi'jan's strike connected, shoving him back with all his strength. Hi'jan stumbled back only a step, but it was enough for Shi'chen to get his spear around to strike at him, catching the Commander across his arm. Hi'jan snarled and dashed at him, but Shi'chen dove aside and spun the spear to catch Hi'jan in the back of the head with the shaft, causing the man to stumble.

Shi'chen planted himself in front of A'bbni. "Are you all right, i-sha?" he asked over his shoulder without turning his eyes away from the Commander in front of him, who had turned toward him, a trickle of blood running down from his temple.

"I... I will be," A'bbni said, though Shi'chen could hear the sob of pain that he was forcing back.

That was all he could ask before Hi'jan rushed him again, and Shi'chen struck swiftly multiple times, driving the Commander back. Now that he was between Hi'jan and A'bbni, he was not going to let Hi'jan get any closer to him.

Hi'jan swung his sword in an arc that was much too wide, and Shi'chen let go of his spear and leaped. As much as his guards may have good-naturedly teased him for being short, he was undeniably quick. His legs went around Hi'jan's neck, and he used his momentum to pull him over. Hi'jan hit the ground hard as Shi'chen whirled to his feet, grabbing his spear up in one smooth motion. Hi'jan scrambled backward for his dropped sword as Shi'chen came at him, and Hi'jan managed barely deflect his strike with his blade.

He went in to try to knock Shi'chen's legs out from under him, but Shi'chen easily turned it into a flip and landed on his feet again. Hi'jan backpedaled, but his foot caught one of the stones on the floor, and Shi'chen took his moment. He threw his spear with deadly accuracy, catching Hi'jan in the side of his chest, right in the gap where his chest plate met his arm. Hi'jan stumbled back with a grunt, turning his eyes to see Shi'chen flying at him, the smaller goblin's foot catching him across his face as Shi'chen grabbed the spear and yanked it the opposite direction of Hi'jan's momentum, ripping it free of the man's body in a shower of blood and bone.

Hi'jan was bleeding profusely down his side from a gaping wound under his arm. Blood loss would kill him shortly, but that was not enough for Shi'chen. Hi'jan let out a harsh, forced laugh as blood trickled out of the corner of his mouth. "It looks like you... you won, Captain," he said, stumbling a bit as his blood hit the stone like raindrops. "But I will die kn... knowing that I have taken what was m... most precious to you."

Shi'chen started to lunge at him, but he recalled A'bbni's words, all those weeks ago. *You know he tries to provoke you to get you in trouble.* Shi'chen pulled himself up short and backed up a step, leaning back just as Hi'jan's hand that had been holding his injury swung forward, a blade slicing the air where Shi'chen's throat had been a fraction of a moment ago. He swung the spear, ducking low and shoving it straight up with all his strength into the spot between Hi'jan's ribs. The point of the spear went under the chest plate and came out the back of Hi'jan's neck. The next moment, the Commander had slid down onto the spear's shaft as his body went limp.

Shi'chen dropped the weapon, not even bothering to watch Hi'jan fall. He turned and sprinted back to A'bbni's side, skidding to a stop and kneeling down next to him. A'bbni's face had drained of blood, giving his charcoal skin a ghastly pallor, heavy sweat having broken out on his face and neck, his breathing hard and fast, each exhale an effort not to scream.

Shi'chen leaned down, sliding his arm under A'bbni's shoulders. A'bbni curled into him, his fingers tangling into Shi'chen's shirt and gripping it like he would never let go. "Breathe," he prompted, stroking A'bbni's damp hair out of his eyes. "He's dead, i-sha. I'm here."

"E... En'shea," A'bbni said softly.

"I do not care about him; I care about you. We need to get you to a physician."

A'bbni's damp eyes turned up to look at him. "Wh... where is Lai?"

Shi'chen swallowed hard, his ears dropping as he gazed down into his twin's pale face. "I... I'm so sorry, i-sha. He—"

"Was chasing down the Emperor that you lost," came a voice behind him, and Shi'chen nearly dropped A'bbni as he whirled around to see two figures coming down the stone steps from the fifth level. One was En'shea, wrists still bound, though his blindfold was no longer in place, being prodded along by a second person whose golden blond hair caught the torchlight.

"Lai?" he asked, feeling A'bbni shift in his arms, too.

Lai gave Shi'chen a bright grin. "Hey. Sorry I wasn't here to help you." He gave En'shea a prod with the tip of his dagger, and the goblin stumbled forward another step, glowering at the twins. "Luckily, he didn't get too far."

"How the—" Shi'chen started to ask and then realized that telling his injured brother that Lai was somehow alive after being thrown off the top of The Keep was not what A'bbni needed to hear right now. He exhaled a sharp breath, his heart racing in his chest. He had so many questions, and he wanted to run over and throw his arms around his friend, but A'bbni's ragged breathing next to him brought him back. "Are you all right?" he asked, trying to keep his tone lighter.

"Better than him," Lai commented, gazing at Hi'jan's fallen, impaled form. He then grabbed En'shea by the neck and hauled him over to the twins, dropping him a few steps away before kneeling down next to A'bbni. "Hey. I'm sorry, i'jaa." He brushed his gloved fingers gently over A'bbni's cheek, and A'bbni leaned into his touch, letting go of Shi'chen's shirt to wrap his arms around Lai. Lai held him close, rubbing his back gently, though he gave Shi'chen an apologetic look over A'bbni's shoulder. Shi'chen gave him a small shake of his head. He was exhausted, and Lai was not dead. That was the most important thing.

He stood up, crossing over to the battered body of Hi'jan. He grabbed the Commander pin from the man's shoulder, ripping it free of the scarlet cape that had turned a deeper red with blood. He stuck the pin in his pocket, then turned back to haul En'shea to his feet. "We need to get him to Reverence Sa'ben," he said, motioning to A'bbni.

"I can take him," Lai offered, inclining his head at En'shea, but Shi'chen shook his head firmly.

"No. The last thing I want right now is for the city to see you holding a knife to the Emperor's throat. Let me be the bad guy here. You just take care of my brother."

Shi'chen pulled Lai's rapier off his hip and handed it to him.

Lai took it with his gloved hands, giving him a grateful smile. "Thanks for watching it for me."

"Looks better on you anyway," Shi'chen replied with a grin. He reached over and retied the gag on En'shea, who glowered murder at him, before giving him a shove in the back. "Let's go." He headed down the stone stairs, steering En'shea in front of him, glancing back every few steps to make sure his brother and Lai were all right.

His mind whirled, trying to figure out how Lai had managed not only to survive the drop off Traitor's Ledge, but then to reappear there seemingly unscathed. He was sure Lai would tell him later, but hopefully not in front of A'bbni. His brother was anxious enough already, and Shi'chen was more than a little worried what Reverence Sa'ben would say about A'bbni's injuries.

They reached the second floor, and Shi'chen could see the open door to the room he and A'bbni had been imprisoned in. A flood of anger rushed through him, and he gave En'shea an extra hard shove toward the stairwell. He could hear a contingent of guards at the bottom, and he steeled himself for another potential fight. He placed his dagger at En'shea's throat and started down the stairs.

As soon as they saw him, the seven guards below all drew their swords, eyeing him and the bound Emperor warily. Shi'chen glowered at them. "Commander Hin-Ve'ssa is dead. We wish to speak to Captain An-Hila'ra."

The guards exchanged nervous glances. Shi'chen found one of his former Honor Garrison guards amongst them and pegged him with a stern look. "Second Lieutenant Hin-Schaa'ven, go find Captain An-Hila'ra and bring them to us. Go."

The young palace guard bowed hesitantly. "Yes, Captain," he said before backing to The Keep door that was barred. Two guards opened it for him, and the young goblin disappeared outside into the late afternoon sunlight. The guards all shuffled nervously, watching him and the half-elf behind him, but Shi'chen held his ground for the time it took the young guard to find Captain An-Hila'ra. When they appeared, the guards all snapped to attention.

Captain Ra'shii stepped inside The Keep, eyeing En'shea and Shi'chen warily. Shi'chen sheathed his dagger and pulled the Commander pin from his pocket, tossing it to them. Ra'shii caught it and examined it. "Commander Hi'jan Hin-Ve'ssa is dead, and the former Emperor is under our control," Shi'chen said. En'shea gave a jerk in his arms, but Shi'chen yanked him back. "As the eldest son of the Regent Bel'kir Er-Ha'sen, we assume the temporary role of Regent of Hanenea'a." A rustle went through the guards, but a look from Captain Ra'shii silenced them again. "Captain An-Hila'ra, we must know where your loyalties lie."

Ra'shii knelt and placed a hand on their chest, bowing their head. "Our loyalty lies with the realm, Your Highness. As you are acting Regent, we are your servant."

Shi'chen nodded, letting out a breath he didn't realize he had been holding. "For now, we want all of Commander Hin-Ve'ssa's former Courage Garrison placed in custody and guarded at all times. But there shall not be any bloodshed or mistreatment without just cause."

"Yes, Your Highness. And the... former Emperor?" Ra'shii asked, casting an uncertain glance at En'shea.

"Stays with me," Shi'chen replied.

Ra'shii stood and bowed their head. "Yes, Your Highness. Do you wish to speak to the crowd?"

"We do," Shi'chen replied. "But first we must see to our brother's injuries."

A'bbni shook his head. "I will be all right, i-sha. Please reassure the crowd so no one gets hurt."

Shi'chen turned to Lai, who was cradling A'bbni against his chest. His twin was a color he had never seen a goblin turn before, and his heart ached knowing A'bbni must be in absolute agony. "Are you sure?"

"Yes." The word came out through gritted teeth, but Shi'chen could see the determination in his brother's eyes.

"Come," he said, dragging En'shea as he went, and Lai followed at his heels. Shi'chen strode across the courtyard, hauling En'shea along with him by the collar, Captain Ra'shii a step behind him. The guards that spanned the walls and clustered at the bolted gates turned to watch him, and he recognized a large number of them from Honor and Allegiance. "Stand down," Captain Ra'shii said. "Commander Hin-Ve'ssa is dead, and Captain Er-Ha'sen is the acting Regent. Any guard who does not stand down immediately will be arrested for insubordination and treason."

Looks were exchanged amongst the guards, but they all quickly lowered or dropped their weapons, many of them pressing their hands to their hearts as they gazed back at Shi'chen, a few of them hiding relieved smiles. He felt a surge of pride at his former troops as he surveyed them all obeying him so readily. "Open the gates," he ordered. The guards scrambled to follow his command. Shi'chen expected the crowd to come flooding in when the gates opened, but surprisingly, it did not. Those gathered there were standing back and watching anxiously, and Shi'chen felt another moment of pride as he realized that Captain Ra'shii must have been coordinating with and controlling the crowd to keep the situation from becoming violent.

As he moved over to the gates, he saw Zea'dda, Gii'han, and Kella break through the front of the assembly, and he let out a silent sigh of relief to see his friends unharmed. He glanced over at Lai and A'bbni, who still looked absolutely miserable but was holding himself together with much more dignity than Shi'chen was sure he could have mustered in the same circumstances.

Shi'chen grabbed En'shea by the back of his neck and shoved him to his knees on the cobbled courtyard, keeping his dagger to the Emperor's throat. A roar went up from the crowd, dozens becoming hundreds becoming several thousand voices, cheering and yelling. Shi'chen glanced over at Kella, who gave him a small, encouraging nod. Shi'chen raised his free hand, and the crowd slowly quieted again. "The former Emperor, En'shea Er-Ha'sen is under our control. By the laws of succession, we claim the right to the throne and assume the role of temporary Regent of Hanenea'a. We ask you to please return to your homes. Select your witnesses and have them come to the palace at mid-day tomorrow. Until then, please, let us not shed any more blood this night," he said firmly, directing the words both to the crowd and to the guards behind him.

Another cheer went up from the crowd, but Shi'chen did not care. He saw Zea'dda, Gii'han, and Captain Ra'shii step forward to direct and disperse the crowd, and Kella moved to his side. Shi'chen gave the dark-haired elf a small smile. "I am glad to see you are all right, Lord Kella."

"The same to you, Your Highness," Kella said. "I will beg your forgiveness later. Let us see your brother's injuries tended to first."

Shi'chen nodded, hauling En'shea up again. He glanced around at the guards, finding two of his former Honor Garrison members. "Lieutenant Hin-Re'nna, Second Lieutenant An-Fer'haaj, with me," he ordered, shoving En'shea in between them. And he was suddenly so exhausted he could barely stand. The next moment, Kella had slid his arm under his shoulders to help support him, and Shi'chen could not even lift his head to thank him, just letting the nobleman and the two guards lead the way into the palace.

"Please drink this, Your Highness," Reverence Sa'ben said, holding out a cup of steaming liquid to A'bbni who was sitting on the examination table in the physician's rooms.

"What is it?" Shi'chen asked, eyeing the cup suspiciously from where he sat in a nearby chair.

"Hargren root tea. It will help with the pain and put him to sleep," the physician said. "I will test it first if you wish it, Your Highness."

A'bbni shook his head before Shi'chen could answer. "That... will not be n... necessary," he said, his breathing still uneven and shaky. He took the cup in trembling hands. Lai reached up to gently help him steady it. A'bbni drank the entire cup of tea in a few swallows. Then his fingers tangled into Lai's shirt to hold onto him. Lai pressed a kiss to the top of his head before helping him lie down.

"Once you are asleep, Your Highness, I will examine your leg," Sa'ben said, setting the cup aside. "I will likely have to immobilize it for it to heal."

"Will it heal?" Shi'chen asked softly.

"I am afraid I do not know that yet," the physician said.

A'bbni groaned and buried his face in Lai's shoulder. "I trust your expertise, Your Reverence," he said softly.

"Thank you, Your Highness, I will do my best. It should not take long for the root to help with the pain.

The dose is enough that you should sleep through the night."

Lai helped ease A'bbni down on the table. A'bbni gripped his hand, and Shi'chen noted the wince that briefly crossed Lai's face. "You won't leave me, will you?"

"Never," Lai replied, pressing a kiss to the back of A'bbni's fingers.

Shi'chen frowned and scuffed a toe into the floor. Lai glanced over at him, then back at A'bbni. "Your brother and I will both stay with you."

A'bbni smiled at that, his eyes already half-closing. He reached out his hand past Lai for Shi'chen, who took it and gave it a squeeze. "Rest, i-sha. We will both be here when you wake up."

A'bbni nodded, seeming like he wanted to say something more, but his eyes closed, his body relaxing as the tension from the pain seemed to drain out of him. Shi'chen felt his own tension release too as he watched A'bbni relax. He pressed a soft kiss to the back of his brother's hand and felt A'bbni's fingers curl tighter against his. He watched until he was sure that A'bbni was asleep, then carefully extricated his hand from his twin's as the physician moved over to examine A'bbni's right leg with his fingers. "Please, Your Highness, do not hover," Sa'ben said, giving him a pleading smile. "I know you are worried, but I do need room to work."

Shi'chen sighed and brushed a few strands of auburn-black hair off A'bbni's damp forehead before taking a reluctant step back. Lai suddenly caught his arm and gave him a gentle tug. "Can I talk to you?" he asked, motioning to the corner of the room. Shi'chen blinked but followed him over where they could still keep an eye on everything, knowing that the half-elf was trying to distract him but allowing himself to be led.

Once they were out of the way, Shi'chen turned to Lai. "How in the name of the gods are you alive?" he demanded in a whisper so no one else would hear them.

Lai pulled off the leather gloves he had been wearing since reappearing on the stairs with En'shea. Shi'chen couldn't stop a gasp. Lai's hands were covered in scrapes and cuts, several of which were deep enough that they were still bleeding. Several of his nails had broken, and his palms and fingertips were a shredded mess. "I told you, knowing how to catch yourself when you fall is a big part of rigging, and I got lucky that the guard just let go and didn't fling me. Destroyed my knife and my hands in the process, but I'll be fine."

"That is not fucking fine!" Shi'chen replied, taking Lai's hands in his own.

Lai winced but let him examine them. "Shi'chen, I'll be all right. But I have to apologize to you."

"Apologize for what?"

"I promised I would never break your brother's heart, and I intend to keep that promise. But I'm sorry I was not there to protect him from that bastard soldier."

"That was not your fault. He wanted you to go with me."

"I know, but I should have made sure he was safe. That's my job as his lover."

Shi'chen felt a pang of something in his chest at that word, and he cleared his throat to give himself time to formulate a response. "You... you love him?"

Lai nodded, his face more solemn than Shi'chen had ever seen it. "I do."

"Have you told him yet?" Lai shook his head, and Shi'chen imagined his ears would be drooping in shame if Lai's ears could move. "Then you should tell him when he wakes up."

Lai gave a slow nod, and then his leaf-green eyes focused on Shi'chen's flame ones. "I never asked you. How do you feel about it?"

"A... about what?" Shi'chen asked, aware his voice caught in his throat.

"About your brother and me. Is... is it all right with you?"

Shi'chen scuffed his toe into the floor, not meeting Lai's eyes. "It is not my place to say what my brother can or cannot do."

"That's not what I asked," Lai said with a frown.

"No, it's not," Shi'chen agreed. He lifted his eyes to Lai's. "You're a good friend to me, Lai. And he loves you. I can see it every time he looks at you. I would never want him to be unhappy."

"Shi'chen," Lai said, letting out a frustrated sigh. "You're not answering my question. If it's not all right, I'd like to know."

"And if I said I wasn't all right with it, what then?" Shi'chen said, his voice dropping but his eyes staying on Lai. "You would leave him?"

"No, I..." Lai frowned, crossing his arms loosely over his chest. "You are very frustrating."

"I know," Shi'chen said. He smiled softly and suddenly wrapped his arms around Lai, which made the half-elf jump. He rested his temple against Lai's shoulder, feeling the beat of his heart under his cheek. "You are a good friend to me, and... I do love you, Lai." Shi'chen shifted so he could look into the half-elf's face. "But not the same way A'bbni does. I don't... I don't *want* you the way that he does. I want to be your friend, and I want A'bbni to be happy. And you make him happy. And that is enough for me. So, yes, I am all right with it, even if I'm a little jealous once in a while."

Lai looked a little uncertain, but he slowly wrapped his arms around Shi'chen and embraced him in return. "I made him promise I would not take him away from you."

Shi'chen blinked up at him, then smiled softly. "You won't. And he's going to need both of us once he becomes Emperor."

"You sure you don't want it?" Lai asked.

Shi'chen shook his head firmly. "Gods, no. Absolutely fucking not!" He pulled back from Lai's arms to give him a grin. "Besides, we both know he'll be a much better Emperor than I would be anyway."

Lai shrugged and gave his shoulder a squeeze. "I think you'd be pretty good. But yes, he will be better than you."

Shi'chen laughed softly, then sobered again. "If the people wish to have an Emperor. It could be decided in time that they do not want someone to rule over them."

"What will you do if they decide they don't?" Lai asked.

Shi'chen shrugged. "No idea. I guess we'll find out."

Sa'ben glanced up at them from where he and his assistant were working. "Your Highness." Shi'chen hurried over to him, drawing Lai along with him. Sa'ben's face was calm as he said, "The kneecap is fractured in multiple places. We can immobilize it and try to let it heal, though, I am afraid..."

"What?" Shi'chen demanded, a little louder than he meant to, making everyone in the room jump.

"Afraid he may not regain full mobility of it," Sa'ben said quickly.

In his head, Shi'chen cursed Hi'jan with every fiber of his being, but he just responded, "But you can do something."

"Yes, Your Highness. We will have to see how it heals over time, and we may be able to do more in the future. Until then, we can bring down the swelling and treat the pain."

"See it done," Shi'chen replied before resting his fingers gently against A'bbni's cheek. He did not know what the afterlife held, if it held anything at all, but he hoped that for Hi'jan it was endless torture until whatever fragment of a spirit he had was ripped apart.

Lai looked confused, and Shi'chen repeated back to him in Hanen-shii what Sa'ben had said. Lai nodded slowly. "I've seen this injury before. It's not going to be easy."

"Well, as you said, he has both of us," Shi'chen replied. "After he has taken care of my brother, we need to have your hands looked at, too."

"I told you, I'll be fine," Lai replied.

Sa'ben glanced over at Lai's hands, and his calm expression did not change as he replied, "They should at least be cleaned and bandaged, ma'iir."

Lai started to protest, but Shi'chen shot him a look. "I know you are used to being on your own, but you are not anymore. So let us help you."

Lai gave him a small smile. "This is going to take some getting used to."

"You picked the wrong partner if you don't want someone to fuss over you," Shi'chen pointed out, brushing his fingers over A'bbni's forehead lightly.

Lai laughed at that. "You're right. But now he has two of us to fuss over."

"And the rest of the nation," Shi'chen muttered under his breath, though he knew Lai would hear it.

Lai sighed at that. "Yes... We're just going to have to support him."

"We will," Shi'chen said, resting his hand on Lai's shoulder. "We will."

CHAPTER TWENTY-SIX

A'BBNI

Everything hurt when he woke up. A'bbni was sure he was dying as he shifted, feeling something soft under him. He opened his eyes to find a familiar green comforter over him, in a familiar room. His room, in the palace, in the apartments he shared with his brother. He sat up slowly, every muscle and bone protesting the movement.

"You're awake," said a voice nearby, and A'bbni turned to see Lai sprawled in a chair, as if he had slept there all night. A'bbni smiled, then winced as even that hurt his jaw where Hi'jan had hit him. In the next moment, Lai was by his side, taking his hand gently, his fingers reaching up to lightly touch A'bbni's swollen cheek.

"Wh... where is my brother?" A'bbni asked softly.

"In the next room, with your bitch of a Cousin," Lai replied, which made A'bbni laugh despite himself. "He wanted you to rest."

"Did he get any sleep?" A'bbni asked, shifting to curl into Lai's arms.

"Yes, I made him get some sleep," Lai replied, tucking A'bbni's head beneath his chin. "How are you feeling?"

"Terrible," A'bbni admitted.

"I don't blame you," Lai replied, stroking his hair gently. "The physician delivered a bottle of hargren root this morning for you."

A'bbni sighed. "That will make me tired."

"I don't care, you're in pain," Lai replied, pulling back to give him a pointed look. "You can sleep until the end of time if it makes you feel better."

"I will be all right. I promise." A'bbni smiled and gave Lai's hand a squeeze. Lai winced, and A'bbni looked down to see that Lai was wearing the pair of leather gloves he wore for rigging work, which he never wore when he was on land. He reached down and pulled one of the gloves gently off, then blanched when he saw Lai's entire hand and fingers wrapped in bandages to the elbow. "Lai!"

Lai gave him a sheepish smile. "It's fine."

"That is not fucking fine!" The urge to grab his medical bag and examine Lai's hands closer was only tempered by the fact that A'bbni was pretty sure he would collapse if he tried to walk across the room.

"Your brother said that exact same thing," Lai said with a roll of his eyes.

"What happened to your hand?" A'bbni demanded, turning it back and forth, carefully moving the bandaged fingers to look at the mobility.

"Your Cousin had me thrown out of the tower," Lai replied, fiddling with one of the finger wrappings with his other still-gloved hand.

A'bbni's eyes went wide. "You... you mean, Traitor's Ledge?"

"Yeah, that was what Shi'chen called it," Lai replied, pulling off his other glove to reveal his other hand that was just as wrapped up.

"How... how are you alive?" A'bbni asked, taking Lai's hands gently in his own and tracing his fingers carefully over them, feeling the rough skin under the bandages.

Lai shrugged his shoulders, letting A'bbni hold his hands. "A lot of luck and a big-ass knife."

A'bbni gritted his teeth. He wanted to find whoever was responsible for Lai's drop and rip them apart with his bare hands. "I'm sorry," he said softly, bringing Lai's hands up to place gentle kisses on the bandaged palms.

Lai smiled and brushed the back of his fingers over A'bbni's cheek. "I'm fine, stop fussing over me."

"I'm always going to fuss over you!" A'bbni protested, as if it were the most obvious thing in the world.

"I know." Lai suddenly leaned down and pressed his lips gently to A'bbni's. The prince's eyes closed, and he slid his hands up to lightly grip Lai's shoulders. "I'm just glad you're all right," Lai said after pulling back. "Or... as all right as you can be, considering what happened."

A'bbni reached up to hold Lai's face with his hands. "I was afraid I had lost you both."

"I'm sorry," Lai said as A'bbni's fingers brushed over the curve of his jaw. "A'bbni, I... I wanted to tell you before we left, and I'm sorry that I didn't..." A'bbni tipped his head, waiting for him to continue. Lai hesitated for just a moment, then slowly leaned in so his lips brushed A'bbni's ear. "I love you," he whispered.

Tears flooded A'bbni's eyes, and he leaned into Lai's chest, hearing the rapid thump of the half-elf's heart under his head, his ear flicking a bit against it. "I love you, too," he said softly, closing his eyes, wishing he never had to move from that spot.

Lai leaned down and pressed his lips lightly to A'bbni's. A'bbni kissed him firmly back, sitting up on his knees to wrap his arms around Lai's neck to hold him close. When they finally pulled apart, A'bbni said softly, "Lai, if you ever don't want to be with me, no matter why, will you please tell me?"

"You're about to be Emperor, i'jaa," Lai said. "You could order me to be by your side always, and I would have to do it."

"No, you wouldn't!" A'bbni protested. "And I would not do that to you. You are not a slave, or even my servant. I would not hold you back if your heart was elsewhere."

Lai raised a brow at him, his green eyes catching the light from the nearby lamp. "I hope it's not a bad omen that our relationship only just started, and you're already thinking about it ending." A'bbni blushed and started to protest, but Lai gently laid one bandaged finger against his lips. "I know you're just overthinking, but I've made my choice. If I regret it one day, that's on me, not on you. If you ever wish to send me away, do it, but I won't leave without your word. I will do my damnedest not to ever hurt you or break your heart."

A'bbni swallowed hard and held up his fist. "Promise?"

"Promise," Lai said, leaning in to press a soft kiss to the inside of A'bbni's wrist.

Shi'chen suddenly appeared in the doorway, looking more than a little battered and bruised and like he had not slept much, but A'bbni had never been so glad to see him. "Good morning, i-sha," he greeted his brother as he pulled back from Lai, and Shi'chen almost dove onto the bed to wrap his arms around him and hug him tight. It hurt, but A'bbni didn't care, wrapping his arms around Shi'chen's waist and burying his face in his twin's neck.

"Do not ever fucking scare me like that again!" Shi'chen said, stroking his fingers through A'bbni's hair, and A'bbni was surprised to feel tears fall onto his skin that were not his own. He pulled back to look into his brother's eyes that were wet with tears of... anger, sorrow, joy, he couldn't tell.

"I'm so sorry, i-sha," he said softly, reaching up to brush a line of tears off Shi'chen's cheek with his thumb.

"To be fair, it wasn't his fault," Lai chimed in.

"I know, it was that fucking bastard, Hi'jan." Shi'chen shifted to sit on the bed so A'bbni could lean against him.

A'bbni felt his stomach clench. "I... I do not... remember... Where is he?"

"He's dead," Shi'chen replied firmly. "I killed him myself, and he will never hurt you again, i-sha, I promise you that."

A'bbni let out a breath and closed his eyes, feeling his own tears, these ones of relief, sting his eyes. "Thank you," he said softly.

Shi'chen shook his head, wrapping A'bbni in his arms again. "It was the least he deserved. If I could, I would resurrect him just to be able to kill him again, over and over."

A'bbni laughed at that, giving his brother's hand a squeeze. "Once is good enough for me."

Shi'chen held his hand for a moment, then stood up. "Are you feeling up to dealing with the court today?"

A'bbni sighed. "No, but I will."

"If you want to, I can—"

"No," A'bbni cut him off firmly. "I know you have no desire to rule. I am not going to make you do it any longer than you have to."

Shi'chen gave him a gentle shoulder squeeze. "Everything is going to be a mess."

"When is it not with En'shea?" A'bbni replied.

Dressing and eating took longer than he would have liked, every part of him protesting in pain at even the littlest movement, but A'bbni just gritted his teeth and forced his way through it. He put copious amounts of hargren root in his tea, knowing it would make him drowsy, and opted for strong, black coffee to try to combat it, despite the fact that he hated the taste of it. Several servants helped him bathe and dress, and he was grateful to see that many of his personal attendants were still alive and looking as well as could be expected under the circumstances. He was going to have to do a comprehensive sweep of all the servants and guards in the palace to determine who was still alive and where they had ended up. He added that to his mental checklist of things to do that was growing longer by the second.

After eating, which at least made him feel slightly more awake and alert, Reverence Sa'ben arrived to examine his injured leg. He wrapped it tightly with bandages to immobilize it, and A'bbni sighed in frustration as that basically made his right leg useless. The pants and long formal robe he put on at least hid the wrappings, which he was grateful for.

Lai sat next to him and let Sa'ben unbandage his hands to put more medicine on them before wrapping them up again. A'bbni went pale at seeing the deep gashes and scrapes that marred his lover's strong hands, but Sa'ben assured him that the wounds would all heal with time. Hands were very resilient when it came to surface injuries. Lai pulled his gloves on again, and A'bbni made yet another mental note to have better gloves made for him that were not weather-worn and dirty from his work on the sea.

And then it was time to face the court. Lai stayed at his side, letting A'bbni lean on him as much as he needed for support on his injured leg. The half-elf had bathed and tied his hair up in his usual high ponytail, and A'bbni had to admit that the dark green tunic the servants had provided for him suited him quite well, bringing out the gold of his hair and the brightness of his green eyes.

Shi'chen appeared next to him to walk with him to the throne room, where much of the nobility had gathered in the seats to the sides. Two long tables had been put in the center of the room. At one sat five individuals that appeared to be representing the outer city inhabitants, their "best" clothes still looking out of place against the fine fabrics of the various nobles and courtiers. Nine members of the noble houses sat at the other table, Zea'dda amongst them. The whole room was packed with people, almost entirely goblins. Kella was off to the side, looking none the worse for wear, which A'bbni was grateful for.

He felt his heart thundering in his chest as they entered and crossed up to the two chairs on the dais, the seats normally occupied by the Emperor and their spouse when court was in session. Every step he took hurt, and he felt hundreds of pairs of eyes on him as he walked, Shi'chen supporting him with his arm, Lai on his other side. He heard whispers sweep through the crowd as they noticed Lai, and he realized his lover had not braided his hair to camouflage his short ears. Lai seemed to be ignoring the whispers, at least. And he was grateful to see that someone had placed a third chair off to the side for Lai to sit next to them.

Shi'chen helped lower him into one of the chairs, going to one knee in front of him. "All right, i-sha?" he whispered.

"Yes," A'bbni replied, giving his brother's hand a squeeze.

Shi'chen nodded, then rose and turned to the assembled crowd. He held up his hands, and the room went mostly quiet. "Our nation has been dealt a serious blow these last few months," he said, trying very hard to keep his voice level and calm and not let the anger he was feeling show. "The Er-Ha'sen family has been on the throne of Hanenea'a for seventeen generations, and while the opportunity to re-examine our way of governing has come with the murder of the Regent and the Imperial Senate by the former Emperor, we also acknowledge that in this time, a competent leader is needed to guide our country through whatever transition may occur." He turned to glance over at A'bbni, and A'bbni felt his stomach clench. No going back now. This was going to happen.

"We are the elder brother, and thus the role falls to us," Shi'chen said, turning back to the assembly. "However, we have decided to formally abdicate the throne and instead continue the line of succession to our brother, A'bbni Er-Ha'sen. If he will agree," Shi'chen added.

A'bbni swallowed hard. Shi'chen was giving him an out if he wanted it. And he wanted it. All he wanted to do was go back to his studies and spend time with Lai and his brother and pretend that the entire country was not fucked up. But he couldn't do that, no matter how much he wanted it. Someone had to lead the country right now, and until they were able to figure out how deep En'shea's treachery had festered, there were very few people that could be trusted.

He pushed himself to his feet, having to rely much more on the arms of the chair than he would have liked to and hoping that it was not as obvious to the entire court as it was to him. He gave a solemn nod to his brother. "Thank you, brother. We allow your abdication and will accept the position of Emperor as the next in succession."

Shi'chen smiled at him, reaching out to grasp his hand and stepped in close. He gave him an embrace but asked in his ear, "Are you all right?"

"Yes," A'bbni said back. He pulled back, giving his brother a small smile. "Do you have Commander Ahea'a's pin?"

Shi'chen nodded, pulling the pin from his pocket and handing it to him. A'bbni took it, running his thumb over the gold etched design there. Honor, Courage, and Allegiance. All of which Commander Ahea'a had had and sacrificed to save them. He lifted the pin up, touching it to his forehead respectfully to thank Commander Ahea'a, then shifted just a little to address the court. "The role of Commander of the Imperial Guard is currently unfilled with the death of Commander Hi'jan Hin-Ve'ssa." The words felt satisfying on his tongue, at least, and A'bbni hoped he would never have to say the man's name again. "It falls to us to appoint a new Commander, and we wish to bestow the honor upon our brother, Shi'chen Er-Ha'sen, for his years of service to the throne and his loyalty and bravery in the face of danger. Do you accept?" he asked, looking at his twin.

Shi'chen looked like he wanted to smile but just touched his fingers to his forehead and then his heart. "We do, Your Sovereignty. We swear to serve you with wisdom and fealty for as long as Your Sovereignty wishes it of us."

A'bbni smiled softly, taking a careful step forward. Shi'chen gave him a quick glance and moved closer to him so his brother would not have to put weight on his injured leg. A'bbni gave him a grateful look as he placed the pin on Shi'chen's left shoulder, just above his heart. He wished he could feel proud at this moment, but between everything that had happened in the last day and the pain that was lancing through his whole body like lightning, all he wanted to do was curl up and go to sleep again. But that would not happen. There was too much that needed to be done already.

He moved back to his chair, and Shi'chen gave him a light hand in support until he was settled again. He did not like all the eyes on him, everyone in the court knowing that he was injured so severely he could barely stand. That was not a great start to his reign either, and he was sure many of the nobles could read the weariness on his face.

Captain Ra'shii suddenly stepped forward, bowing their head at A'bbni. "Sovereignty, there is an urgent matter that we feel must be resolved with due haste."

"Yes, Captain," A'bbni said. It wasn't like he had a choice.

Ra'shii motioned, and two guards dragged En'shea forward. Their cousin looked in complete disarray, which was very unlike En'shea's normal fastidious appearance. His black hair was pulling loose from its elaborate braid, the gold paint around his eyes was smudged and streaked down one dark cheek, his tunic and pants were wrinkled. A'bbni realized that somewhere after his capture, someone had stripped En'shea of his royal robes and jewelry. He had never seen En'shea looking less than perfect except the few rare times he lashed out at a servant or someone around him, and the effect was startling. His hands were manacled in front of him with two heavy-looking iron cuffs on his slender wrists. He stared at the twins on the dais with a look that A'bbni had never seen on his cousin's face before, and he wasn't quite sure how to read it.

The two guards pushed En'shea to his knees on the stairs, then used the butts of their spears to push his shoulders down until his forehead touched the floor in forced obeisance.

"Your Sovereignty," Ra'shii said, bowing their head. "As you know, the law is that any criminal found guilty of a capital crime must be sentenced to death by the Emperor."

A'bbni had a sick feeling in his stomach that he knew where this was going. "Yes, Captain, we are aware of the law."

"The former Emperor is guilty of murder and treason against the crown, both of which are crimes of the most heinous nature," Ra'shii continued. "As such, it is up to Your Sovereignty to impose the sentence upon him."

A'bbni tightened his fingers ever so slightly on the arm of his chair. How in the name of the gods was he supposed to do that? He looked down at his cousin who bowed only a few feet away. En'shea looked so small all of a sudden. He was only seventeen, A'bbni had to remind himself. Still a child. He had done monstrous things, many of them to the twins over the course of many years. En'shea was the reason their Father was dead. En'shea was the reason Hi'jan had assaulted him. En'shea was the reason that every single fiber of him hurt. En'shea was the reason that A'bbni was on the throne right now instead of pursuing his dream. En'shea had killed before, many times over, and no one would mourn his death.

He could see En'shea's very slight trembling where his forehead rested on the ground, though he wasn't sure if anyone else could see it besides him. He did not want to have to sentence En'shea to death in front of the crowd. Or ever. His mind was too all over the place; he needed time to think it through, figure out what he could do. The last thing he wanted to do was act out of vengeance in his first ruling as Emperor. He was exhausted and in pain and barely holding his emotions together in front of the court, none of which was conducive to being a fair and just ruler. He took a deep breath and tried to calm his nerves, turning his eyes toward his brother in silent pleading. "We must take time to reflect upon his actions and a sentence appropriate to the crimes."

Shi'chen caught the look in his brother's eyes and held it for just a moment before dropping his eyes down to the goblin on the ground. "En'shea Er-Ha'sen," he said in a voice that carried across the room. "In the name of the Emperor, we place you under arrest for the murder of Regent Bel'kir Er-Ha'sen and the six members of the Imperial Senate, to be held in confinement until sentence is passed upon you by the Emperor."

The guards stepped forward and pulled En'shea to his feet as the crowd began to cheer. En'shea watched A'bbni through narrowed eyes as the guards began to pull him away. He suddenly spat at A'bbni's feet, and one of the guards punched him squarely across the face.

A'bbni held up a hand. "It is all right, Lieutenant," he said as En'shea's eyes turned back to him in shock. He realized that probably was the first time En'shea had ever been struck in his life. "Take him away."

En'shea eyes were golden daggers directed at A'bbni, but A'bbni ignored it, shifting his weight as subtly as he could as a lance of pain spiked up through his leg. He turned his eyes toward Shi'chen, silently pleading for this to be over. Shi'chen gave him a small nod, and A'bbni turned his eyes to the representatives at the tables. "We beg the court's indulgence, as the last few days have been trying. We will appoint a secretary to whom business may be addressed for the rest of the day, and we shall handle it in private."

A soft murmur ran through the court, but A'bbni didn't care. He pushed himself up, and Shi'chen immediately moved to slide an arm casually under his arm as if to embrace him, but A'bbni could feel his brother taking most of his weight so he was not on his injured leg. A silent conversation passed between their orange eyes in just a few moments, and Shi'chen turned to Lai, who rose to his feet nervously, looking uncertain if he should jump in to help or not. A'bbni gave him a small shake of his head. Now was not the time that he wanted the court to cast aspersions about the curious, short-eared blond. So, Lai just trailed after them as Shi'chen helped his brother down the dais and out of the court.

One of the clerks guided them to a nearby receiving room for them to sit. Shi'chen ordered food to be brought and Reverence Sa'ben summoned, and then it was just him, A'bbni, Lai, a single servant in waiting, and the clerk in the room to take notes. A'bbni couldn't bring himself to care anymore if the servants saw his pain or his indecision. "I do not know what to do with En'shea," he said softly, propping his elbows on the table in a very undignified manner, resting his forehead on his interlocked fingers.

"I have plenty of ideas," Shi'chen said darkly.

"I know you do, Commander, but I will not pass down a sentence out of vengeance, nor do I want to start my reign with more bloodshed."

Lai reached out and gave A'bbni's forearm a gentle squeeze with his gloved hand, and A'bbni gave him a tired nod.

"I'm happy to arrange an accident," Shi'chen replied darkly.

A'bbni sighed. "I appreciate you trying to help, Shi'chen, but please don't."

"I won't," Shi'chen said, not looking thrilled about it. "But if you need me to, I will."

A thought occurred to A'bbni, and he was ashamed of himself for not thinking about it earlier. "Has Vr Ba'shea Ii-Heshar been found?"

"No," Shi'chen said with a dark glower. "No one has seen him since the crowd assembled at The Keep. I suspect he has fled."

A'bbni sighed again and rubbed the bridge of his nose. "We should prioritize finding him, before he can do any more damage."

"The guards are already on it, Your Sovereignty." Shi'chen's face was impassive, but his voice held a reassuring smile just for his twin.

A'bbni glanced over at Lai. "How much of what happened in there did you understand?"

Lai shrugged. "Enough." His green eyes gazed back into A'bbni's, holding something he couldn't read.

The door opened, and Reverence Sa'ben and one of his assistants entered with a bow. "Your Sovereignty, Commander, Ma'iir Ablewood." He crossed over to kneel by A'bbni. "May we, Sovereignty?"

"Yes," A'bbni said with a wave of his hand, too tired to care what anyone was asking at this point. Sa'ben bent down and ran his practiced fingers over A'bbni's bound leg. A'bbni hissed softly, and Sa'ben apologetically placed a bottle of hargren root extract on the table as Lai gave A'bbni's shoulder a light touch of reassurance.

"We are afraid the pain will take some time to abate, Sovereignty. We are sure you know what our advice to you would be."

That made A'bbni warm just a bit at his mentor. When would he ever get the chance to use his medical knowledge again? "We do. Stay off it, lots of rest, hargren root as needed."

Sa'ben nodded, then motioned to his assistant, who crossed over to him and held out a beautifully carved rosewood walking stick with a place to rest his forearm. "We had this made to help support your weight, Sovereignty. We hope that you will find it acceptable."

A'bbni gave him a gracious nod. "Thank you, Your Reverence. We are most grateful."

Sa'ben bowed again and left as a servant returned with tea, to which A'bbni added several drops of the hargren root extract. He was going to have to talk to the physician to work on finding something that could help with pain without causing drowsiness. There was too much work to be done for him to be tired all the time.

And the work came. Documents, missives, letters, requests for an audience that A'bbni refused to grant today. He had the rest of his life to deal with these requests; he could take one day to get his feet literally and figuratively underneath him.

The only person he allowed an in-person audience with was Kella. The dark-haired elf entered the room and dropped to one knee, bowing his head at the twins. "Sovereignty, Commander," he said.

A'bbni forced himself to sit upright in spite of his exhaustion. "Please, rise, Lord Kella."

Kella did not rise. "Sovereignty, I wish to beg your forgiveness for the danger you were put in with Vr

Ii-Heshar and Var An-Sha'kri. I should have done more to protect you."

A'bbni bit back a sigh, rubbing at his eyes with his hand. "Lord Kella," he said, his voice a little firmer than he meant it to be. "You have done a great service to us and to Hanenea'a. Without your help, none of this would have been possible, and as we have said before, you have our eternal appreciation for the assistance you have rendered us. You have nothing to be forgiven for, but if you seek it, we offer you our forgiveness, in addition to our friendship and our gratitude."

"Thank you, Sovereignty," Kella said, finally lifting his head and giving A'bbni a small smile. "We are forever in your service and look forward to speaking with you again." He rose gracefully to his feet, bowing his head at first him, then at Shi'chen, and then at Lai, his hand gently resting on the underside of the growing bump at his waist before turning and leaving the room.

It finally came time for the evening meal, and A'bbni gratefully pushed himself out of his chair, Shi'chen giving him a little assistance as he steadied himself. The rosewood crutch was the perfect height to rest his forearm on and support his weight, so he did not put so much on his injured right leg. But he immediately realized how much he was going to be hampered, since he was right-handed. "I already know this is going to be extremely frustrating," he grumbled, shifting the support in his hand as he leaned a little more into his brother.

Lai moved to his other side to give him a gentle side-squeeze. "I guess Shi'chen and I will both have to be your right hand for now."

A'bbni blinked at that, then nodded. "Yes," he said, resting his head on Lai's shoulder as he gave his brother the first smile he had been able to manage since he had been handed the empire only a few long hours ago. "I would like that. I would like that very much."

The twins and Lai will return in the sequel,
The Right Hands of the Emperor.
Thank you for reading!

Acknowledgments

I have been writing for myself since I was old enough to hold a pencil. When I decided early in 2022 to finally write something to publish, little did I know that my initial novella would turn into a full-blown political epic and create a whole new fantasy world for me to explore. I had no idea what I was getting into, but once the story solidified in my mind, I knew that I wanted the best of everything. If there was going to be a weak link in the publication chain, it would start and end with me; no half-assing was allowed!

A big thank you to my alpha and beta readers: Jae Dixon, Kirsty Dunn, Janet Hunt, Julie Mannino, Erica Montrose, Grenevic Sharladanel Stremski, and Jennifer Oestreich-Garner, who gave me reassurance and feedback, and who helped shape the plot and dig me out of many holes along the way.

An especially big thank you to Jae Dixon, whose insight as a trauma therapist was invaluable in creating believable and accurate portrayals of PTSD and trauma response, and Erica Montrose who dealt with me sending her multiple questions and revisions at a time.

A huge shout-out to my editor, Sierra McLean for all of her work and feedback, and my cover artist Elyon for making my ramblings into the most gorgeous cover I could have imagined!

Thank you to all the writers and readers of the MM community, who have been so kind and supportive through this whole process. No author is an island, and no new writer could ask for a more encouraging, helpful group of people!

And of course, no acknowledgements would be complete without a thank you to my wonderful, understanding husband, who talked me through many plot issues, kept our household running and our food goblins fed, and encouraged my creativity even when I holed up in our office for hours at a time.

My motto throughout this whole process has been, "Go big or go home," and I hope that I have come out of the gate with a bang. I don't know what the future holds, but for now I am so glad to be able to share with you a little piece of my fantastical imagination. I hope that you have enjoyed it!

Love and Laughter Always!
Kit

About the Author

Kit Barrie (she/her) was raised by pirates in a traveling carnival where she learned how to fly and to weave fantasy into reality. She identifies as chaotic bisexual, with good intentions and questionable methods. She lives in an utterly unfantastical state in the Midwestern United States with her very supportive spouse (VSS) and at least 4 food goblins who might just be cats gobblin' food.

Please visit www.kitbarrie.com or scan the QR code below for more information on Kit and her other available titles.